Pavel Kornev

The Dead Rogue

thank you for being
my reader!
Without you Books
ARE nothing!
PAVEL KORNEV

An NPC's Path

Book One

Magic Dome Books

The Dead Rogue
An NPC's Path, Book One
Copyright © Pavel Kornev 2018
Cover Art © Vladimir Manyukhin 2018
English Translation Copyright ©
Petr Burov 2018
Editors: Neil P. Mayhew, Irene Woodhead
Published by Magic Dome Books, 2018
All Rights Reserved
ISBN: 978-80-88295-40-2

Also by Pavel Kornev:

An NPC's Path LitRPG series:

The Dead Rogue
Kingdom of the Dead
Deadman's Retinue
The Guardian of the Dead
The Nemesis of the Living

The Sublime Electricity steampunk series:

The Illustrious
The Heartless
The Fallen
The Dormant

Table of Contents:

Chapter One
A Plague-Ridden Corpse

1.

THE BRACELET WAS COVERED with hypoallergenic plastic but the skin underneath still itched like hell. I pulled the tracking device away from my ankle as far as it would go so I could scratch it. The bracelet vibrated and buzzed in reply.

"Relax, Comrade Major," I quickly said. "All quiet on the western front!"

The tracking device that traced offenders under house arrest was full of various electronic modules such as GPS, GLONASS, Wi-Fi, GSM and even an altimeter, so I was in no doubt that they would have added a simple microphone to it. It didn't matter what the actual rank of the controller assigned to me was — a little sympathy goes a long way. At least it was someone to talk to...

It was already my second month of being under house arrest and I already managed to really start missing normal human contact. I wasn't even a hardened criminal or a sociopath — I was just in the wrong place at the wrong time.

I got a job at the wrong place, to be more exact.

It had all started so well! My salary wasn't bad, there was a great package of perks and excellent career prospects, but it all went down the drain when the bank's senior management ended up behind bars accused of money laundering! I was never made part of the illegal scheme, but most of the payments had gone through my department, so the most that my defense attorney could do for me was a concession to get me placed under house arrest. At least it was better than jail.

Ah, here comes my attorney...

I picked up my buzzing smartphone which could only accept incoming calls from a single number and put it to my ear.

"Good evening, Jan!" I was greeted with a clear baritone voice.

"Hello, Boris!"

"Jan, I have good news for you!"

"Are you serious?"

Life hadn't been treating me to good news lately. It was becoming increasingly similar to being repeatedly hit around the head with a hammer.

"Why would I be messing with you? There's been some sort of malfunction in the data center tonight and there is talk that they lost the records of a number of your most dubious transactions. It's unknown whether that's true or not, but the prosecution has finally decided to make a deal. Evidence against Kogan in exchange for becoming a witness instead of one of the accused and complete immunity to prosecution."

"I agree!" I replied without the smallest hesitation as I had no intention to cover for the bank's former chairman of the board.

"I had no doubt!" Boris laughed. "The deal

is in our pocket but it's really important not to do anything stupid now. Relax. Listen to music, watch some TV, get into your gaming box..."

"I thought I wasn't allowed to use the Internet?" I asked with surprise, looking over at the virtual reality capsule.

"The way it works is completely different. I'm telling you as a lawyer — it won't be considered a breach of your conditions. Tomorrow won't be easy, so I would definitely recommend and even insist that you relax and rest. This is only the beginning of this nerve-wracking mess and we have to stay strong until the last."

The attorney disconnected, so I threw the smartphone on the sofa and approached the capsule, which the bank had given me as a bonus for one of my deals.

I chronically lacked the time to have a full virtual reality experience and only managed to walk around the starting location which experienced players contemptuously called the "Playpen". I'd still managed to get my rogue up to level 9 already.

One more level and I could move into the open world.

✟ The Dead Rogue ✟

So why not?

I would at least have a distraction and relax a bit...

THE MAIN MENU of Towers of Power met me with the gloom and silence of a palace hall. My rogue appeared a couple of feet above the stone floor and skillfully landed on it in complete silence. It was me that stood up straight.

John Shadow, Rogue. Level 9
Strength: 9
Agility: 14
Constitution: 11
Intelligence: 10
Perception: 11

Health: 99
Stamina: 103
Energy: 94
Damage: 6-10
Stealth: +9

Critical damage when attacking in stealth mode, backstabbing or attacking a paralyzed target.

✝ An NPC's Path: Book One ✝

Some stats could have been increased at the expense of others during character formation, but I didn't go for that. Ten points were considered to be the baseline and lower stats would carry penalties. If you decreased Perception, you turned into a half-blind mole with minimal accuracy and no chance of getting a critical hit and if you decreased Intelligence you wouldn't be able to open even the simplest of locks. The purpose of a rogue isn't just stealth attacks, it's a universal character. Just what someone needs that has no friends among the players and no clan.

A pentagram glowed red upon the floor. I stepped inside it and fell through the stones, appearing on the uneven paving of the square, with the graceful Tower of Power reaching to the skies in the middle.

It was late evening in the game. Old Gardens was a small town for newbie players and it sank into the dusk as the sky quickly darkened. However, this was good, as there was nothing better than the darkness for a rogue like myself who was focused on stealth.

I adjusted my weapon belt, which was weighed down by a shortsword and dagger and

---

strode away from the square down one of the narrow side streets. The starting location was not particularly big — the only things interesting for newbies were the city park with its pair of dungeons, the swampy riverside and the catacombs under the monastery. You could get some tasks from the characters populating the town, but they held no interest for me right now. I just wanted to relax.

After pulling a bright green leaf from a tree, I rubbed it between my fingers as I walked. When I smelled it, my nose was filled with a sophisticated and pleasant aroma. Everything in the game seemed to be completely real, but that didn't particularly surprise me — I was used to it. Unlike the equipment of their competitors like Swords and Fire or Distant Space, the patented technology of Towers of Power allowed the player to get information about the virtual world and fill in some of the small details themselves. What this basically meant was that the brain became a dedicated server which increased the processing power of the gaming hardware.

So was this smell programmed by the creators of the game or did I think of it myself?

Who knows?

Anyway, it didn't matter...

THE SQUARE in front of the monastery was unusually full of people and a monk with a scrap of parchment stepped out of a back alley.

"Could the noble sir clear the city park of the undead?" he asked me, offering me a map.

Do you want to accept the Malicious Corpse quest?
[Yes/No]

I agreed, took the map and carefully looked through the objectives. They turned out to be as easy as they could be — I just had to kill the slow-moving walking corpse that I'd already got to hack into pieces a couple of times without being on any quests.

A green dot appeared on the map to mark the cave that I needed and I went off towards the park. The monk didn't ask other players for help but returned to the alleyway, to my great relief.

A personal quest? That was absolutely great!

I only had to earn a little more XP to reach level 10. Kill the zombie and immediately get out of the city, where I'd get to relax.

THE PARK WAS LARGE and neglected. It was surrounded by a decrepit fence that had magical crystals shining with yellow light upon it. Apart from the cave with a lonely walker, there was a descent into a much larger dungeon somewhere among the trees, but the Skeleton Lord that lived on its bottom level could only be defeated by a large group of players. I never went there and I was satisfied with hunting foxes, wolves and random undead.

After I'd crossed a stone bridge over the quiet little river and its swampy banks I activated stealth mode and dissolved into the shadows. My Energy bar immediately started to crawl downwards and I was happy that I hadn't reduced Intelligence and Perception which would have affected this stat.

I never had to wander around through the darkened avenues as the mark on the map led me directly to my destination. I only turned from my path once, when I noticed a rabbit under a tree.

Stealth allowed me to get right up to the creature. My sword cut through its spine and I killed the animal with my first attack.

Critical hit! Damage: 20
The Rabbit has been killed!
Experience: +5 [1658 / 1730]

It was a shame that it was far from every time that this worked with wolves — the predators often had a sense of smell and hearing that was too acute and they noticed me in advance.

I waited a little and then entered the shadows again and moved on straight towards the cave through the bushes that grew thick down the hillside. I carefully stepped into the empty mouth of the dungeon and set off on my search for the corpse in the faint glow of the mold that covered the walls.

It smelled... quite bad there. I could sense the smell of dead flesh and decomposition.

I felt an unpleasant feeling in my throat but I easily dealt with the nausea and continued to carefully step over the human bones that were strewn here and there. I couldn't make any noise.

The walking corpse was found in a far corner of the dungeon. Fat and swollen, it stood by a sealed chest, its dead rags unable to hide its pustule ridden skin.

A wave of the foul smell came over me again. I held my breath and circled around the back of the corpse with bared blades in both hands. The shining slime on the walls didn't give enough light, but my senses were sharp enough to make out the whiteness of the bones in the darkness and avoid stepping on them.

The corpse didn't notice my approach and I attacked it in the back. I slashed it with my sword and immediately followed up with my dagger.

The Walking Corpse has been killed!
The Malicious Corpse quest is complete!
Experience: +350 [2008/2070]

You've gained a level!

I decided against making up anything new and raised my Agility as well as improving my Stealth skill.

Then I opened the wooden lid and the shadows of the dungeon suddenly laced together into steel snares.

Shadow Snares: you are paralyzed!
Damage taken: 37 [73/ 110]

I tried to jerk away but my body refused to obey me.

"Greetings from Kogan!" someone whispered from behind.

Damage taken: 37 [36/ 110]

"You should have kept your mouth shut!"

Damage taken: 37 [0/ 110]
You have died!

2.

00:01:00... 00:00:59... 00:00:58..

THE TIMER SLOWLY COUNTED the time until I would return to the game, but I felt completely bewildered inside, as my thoughts flew around inside my head like terrified sparrows.

"What the hell?" I shouted into the emptiness.

† The Dead Rogue †

Did Kogan decide that he can scare me by telling someone to kill a game character in a virtual world? What was this madness?

Or was this just a warning? A hint at what awaited in real space?

I had to call my attorney immediately!

However, I couldn't exit to the main menu as I was thrown into the game again.

IT WAS DARK and cramped and something was crushing my chest.

I flexed my muscles, trying to push the weight away and my hand went through the crumbling obstacle. I tried to get up and... found myself standing up from a shallow grave in that already familiar cave, bathed in the light of the slime covering the wall.

What was going on? Resurrection in the start location was only possible by the side of the Tower of Power!

Something appeared to be clenched in my hand. I took a closer look and threw away what turned out to be a human skull, skillfully carved from some sort of bright stone. After throwing away the skull, I stared at my hand with amazement and disgust. My fat and clumsy sausage fingers were covered in pustules and purplish cadaveric spots.

No! This simply could not be!

No one died inside a game!

I lowered my gaze and discovered that I had been trapped in the body of a walking corpse through some quirk of the game. I recoiled in fear, tripped over a bone under my foot and clumsily fell to the floor. What the hell?

I opened the menu, staring at the grayed-out and inactive tabs until I noticed that there was no quit button either! Was it an error? Had I been hacked? Were the game servers being restarted? I had to contact the game admins!

There was no more in-game chat or personal message service in the menu anymore.

I was overcome by a terrible panic, so I had to lock my swollen fingers together and force myself to calm down. This was nothing! It was a total non-issue! All I needed to do was ask one of the players for help and they would get in touch with the admins to resolve this situation.

Elementary!

I somehow got up from my hands and knees and strode off through the cave with the shambling gait of a living corpse. I was simply brilliant at finding my way in the darkness but my sight started to swim more and more from the bright light the closer I got to the exit from the dungeon.

Was it day already? Hmm... That was strange.

Shading my eyes with my hand, I stepped forth under the open sky and my skin immediately started to smoke!

Bright sunlight! Perception penalty: 75%
Damage taken: 1 [22/23]
Stamina: -3 [17/20]

An insufferable radiance cut through everything around me. I blindly took another step, hoping to hide in the shadow of the trees, but the sun struck me again immediately. Damn it! I would never reach it!

I started to panic again so I had to return to the cave. I calmed down a little once I got inside.

It would be all right! There was nothing to be afraid of. Someone would come here sooner or later. That's when we would talk.

The sunlight streaming in from outside

suddenly blinked — I started to turn around and this was the only reason why the level 3 Rogue appeared to my side, rather than behind my back. A falchion darted towards me, as I protected myself from the attack with my left hand and shouted, "Stop!"

An incomprehensible growl came out of my throat instead of words and the blade slashed into my wrist a moment later, cutting my hand clean off. My arm immediately hung limp by my side.

Damage taken: 5 [16/23]
Left arm injured!

"Just wait a minute!" I howled, but it seemed like the rogue didn't hear me.

He slashed at me once again. I let an attack on my chest through, swayed and swatted at him with my right hand, but I was unable to get even close to the agile rogue. In an instant, the blade flashed down and cut through my skull. The shadows of the dungeon merged into an impenetrable darkness.

You have been killed!

✟ The Dead Rogue ✟

DARKNESS. WEIGHT. The whisper of falling soil.

I got out of the grave and threw the skull that appeared in my hand away again in disgust, shouting, "You scum!"

All that came out of my mouth was a throaty growl, so I angrily punched the wall so hard with my swollen fist that the pus burst out of my boils.

What the hell? How could I have forgotten how to speak?

A horrifying realization flashed through my mind. I opened up the menu, selected the Character Attributes and went stone dead with terror as I suddenly realized that everything that happened to me was not a random error but the work of a hacker!

Walking Corpse, Undead. Level 1.
Strength: 18
Agility: 3
Constitution: 23
Intelligence: 1
Perception: 5

Health: 23
Stamina: 20

✝ An NPC's Path: Book One ✝

Energy: 3
Damage: 1-4

Damn it! The hacker that sent Kogan's greetings had thrown me into the body of one of the walking dead who had an Intelligence of only one! This zombie isn't just on the dim side, he's just an animal! The developers strongly recommended never making your Intelligence lower than five, because the character won't even be capable of understandable speech, so I wouldn't understand whoever I'm speaking to if I had one point!

Bloody hell. It wasn't enough for the hacker to just trap me inside the game, but he also made any interaction with other players impossible! How long can a body lie in a virtual reality capsule without food and water before it dies of hunger?

Two days? Three days?

A timer would have switched it off in a normal situation, but I was sure that my attacker took care of this as well.

The malfunction in the data center was no accident, was it?

Everything had been thought through in

advance! They destroyed the evidence and got rid of the key witness...

I growled and shambled off towards the exit from the dungeon, stumbling and shaking. The low Agility was making itself known, while the rather good Strength and Constitution stats could not compensate for the terrible clumsiness of the undead.

I gathered my determination and stepped from the cave into the clearing, and the light only cut into my eyes but didn't burn my blistered skin.

Dim sunlight! Perception penalty: 50%
Stamina: -2 [18/20]

The world was becoming blurry and getting lost in the whitish haze, but I stubbornly shambled on through the clearing towards the trees.

One step and then another, as the Stamina bar inexorably crept down to the left. One step, one more and yet another one...

I finally found shelter in the shadow of the trees, but a new surprise awaited there. It was an unpleasant one as always.

Diffused sunlight! Perception penalty: 25%
Stamina: -1 [3/20]

My attempt to move under the broad canopy of an oak was not a success. The sun had already burned away the last of my Stamina when I'd only gotten halfway there so I froze in the middle of the cluster of trees like a clockwork toy that had come unwound. My Stamina restored itself with time, but the rays of the sun brought it back down to zero before I'd even had the chance to take a step. Would I really have to wait for darkness to fall?

Time was passing! How long had my body already been in the capsule?

I suddenly heard a rustle — I lowered my eyes and saw a rabbit which had fearlessly come near to the immobilized undead. As soon as I got a single unit of Stamina I immediately grabbed the creature, squeezed it to my chest and twisted its neck with my clumsy but powerful fingers. The rabbit started to shake and shrink before I heard the crack of bone. All that was left in my hands was a skin full of bones.

Deathgrip!

✟ The Dead Rogue ✟

Energy: -3 [0/ 3]
Stamina: +3 [3/ 20]

The Rabbit has been killed!
Experience: +5 [5/ 100]

Without wasting any more time, I shambled towards the oak, tripped on a root fell down and continued at a crawl, without even trying to rise to my feet. Stamina no longer burned away in the thick shadows, so I crouched under the tree, trying to make sense of what had happened.

Had I earned some experience? Was that even possible for NPCs?

The stats tab confirmed that this was possible. I just needed to earn another ninety five points of XP to reach the next level. This would be an additional point that I could add to Intelligence!

So, another nineteen rabbits? Well, at least I could do that. I had no choice anyway.

I started to rise off the ground and nearly fell back down when an arrow hammered into my shoulder.

Damage taken: 6 [17/ 23]

I turned to face a level 5 Ranger in a green jacket, tight leggings and a tall pair of boots, got another arrow in my chest and tried to protect myself with my arms.

"Don't shoot!"

My incomprehensible wail had no effect on the player as he drew his bow again. It was impossible to run away so I bent down low and ambled towards the shooter. I reached him, swung and tried to hit him with my empty hand, missed and raised my arm again. Another miss. The ranger put away his bow and drew his dagger, took a punch in the face and didn't even notice the pathetic single point of damage I caused as he confidently drove his blade into my pus-ridden eye.

Critical hit!
You have been killed!

Darkness, the weight of loose earth and the stench of the dungeon. The skull that I was already sick of in my hand. I hurled it at the wall with all my strength and growled in disappointment and shame.

My wounded eye was still pulsating and

reminding me of my recent demise, while my whole body ached as if it had been broken into pieces and clumsily reassembled.

It was very unpleasant to be dead. Even though the blades that pierced my body caused no pain, each death took away valuable time, so I had no intention of dying again. Nobody would pepper me with arrows, chop me into pieces or crush my skull with a hammer anymore.

I would hunt the players now!

I opened up the description of my undead character, but I found only one positive feature which was neutral relations with other undead and immunity to death magic, poisons, curses, bleeding and for some odd reason, spells of banishment. However, this was more than compensated by being unaffected by blessings and healing. My Deathgrip would be of no help in fighting players either as it didn't cause physical damage and only drained the target of Stamina.

Weapons! I needed weapons more than life itself! Only rabbits could be fought bare handed.

With hope, I opened the lid of the chest, but all I could find inside was a handful of coppers. I searched around the cave, but there was no result again. But then, some bones crunched beneath my feet, so I picked up one of the pieces and couldn't believe my eyes.

Sharpened bone
Damage: 1-2
Additional corpse poison damage: 1 per second for 3 seconds
Durability: 2

Now this was already something. While my swollen fingers refused to hold the piece of bone tight, I still managed to arm myself in the end and I moved towards the exit, where the players would spend a while getting used to the meager light in the dungeon. I squeezed myself into a small niche and stood still, awaiting my first victim. It was unexpectedly easy to stand there unmoving, even though my emotions welled up inside me.

What was happening to my real body? How much time did I have left? Would I manage to get out of this accursed game or had the hacker completely cut off this option? And where were the other players, damn them all!

A shadow quickly appeared as if in answer to my silent curse as an incredibly tall Priest in a long sleeveless chainmail hauberk appeared, with a mace upon his belt.

Level 6! Damn it!

However, I didn't retreat but stumbled out of my niche and hit him in his scrawny neck as hard as I could with my bone. It was a great hit, so good that a powerful stream of blood gushed out of the wound.

Critical hit! Damage: 32

The priest swayed, turned around and let through another attack — the bone cut into his temple, taking away another eight points of Health. It's a shame I didn't poke out his eye!

The player's figure started to be surrounded by a blinding light, but the corpse poison made itself known before the priest could cast his spell. The healing magic dissipated without trace!

I stabbed at the eye of my opponent with the bone but missed, while the astounded player tried to use priestly magic again to be met with failure for the second time. The poison interfered with concentration as well as causing damage.

The priest back-pedaled so I grabbed him

with my free hand and actually hammered the bone into him, aiming just above the edge of the chainmail. I surprised myself by hitting yet again — my opponent didn't have a particularly high Dodge skill. He'd obviously never bothered to raise his Agility either...

The next stab was met by the iron chainmail rings and the bone shattered, while the priest finally snapped out of his daze and swung his mace. He took away a quarter of my life with his first hit and then we traded strikes, but fists are not the best choice against a mace. My Health instantly went into the red.

Thankfully, the corpse poison continued to damage my opponent so he panicked. The priest stopped swinging at me and grabbed a flask with the elixir of life out of his bag. I caught his hand, trying to stop him from restoring his Health. After a short struggle, I managed to bite into his wrist but his leather sleeve proved too tough as my fangs simply fell out of my rotten gums.

That didn't matter. The priest was shaken by a short seizure and he fell to the ground, dead from the poison.

Player Faroukh the Bright has been killed!

✟ The Dead Rogue ✟

Experience: +120 [125/200]
You have gained a level!

I was overcome with the sense of euphoria that I always felt when I reached another level and I hurriedly opened the character's Attributes menu.

Yes! I had a free point and the menu was working!

I put my hard-earned point into Intelligence, but I didn't have to modify any of my skills. Deathgrip got automatically improved. It would now suck twice as much Stamina from its victims.

Walking Corpse, Undead. Level 2.
Strength: 18
Agility: 3
Constitution: 23
Intelligence: 2
Perception: 5

Health: 46
Stamina: 41
Energy: 7
Damage: 1-4

I was no killing machine of course, but I was no longer a punch bag. I had a rather decent amount of Health for the Playpen. I also simply wanted to get some sort of normal weapon.

However, to my great disappointment, I could only take that flask with the healing potion from the body of the player. Without much hope, I poured it into my crusty mouth but nothing happened, just as I expected.

Interesting. How do you heal the dead?

After I threw the empty flask away, I returned to the deep cave and spent a long time digging through the pile of bones, but I couldn't find a single poisoned one. I had to make do with a simple sharpened shard, but at least it caused 1-3 damage.

BY THE TIME that I'd gotten out of the dungeon, it was already getting dark in the park so I didn't suffer a Perception penalty. Dark shadows coalesced between the trees as I tore through the bushes into one of the alleyways and trudged towards the gate. My revenant clumsily put one foot in front of the other as he swayed from side to side, but I soon got used to the way that the grotesque character moved and quickly reached the iron fence.

I don't know what I was expecting when I got out of the park. Did I think that I could quit the game, move into my own body, talk to someone, even an NPC if not a player?

None of this actually happened. I never even managed to come up to the gate. As soon as I approached, the magical crystals on the fence shone with bright blinding light and furiously shot out zigzagging electrical charges.

An instant later, I was toast...

DARKNESS AND A SHALLOW GRAVE, with earth carelessly thrown over it. The annoying skull was in my hand as usual.

Raging, I shambled to the exit from the cave and threw the stone skull with its bared teeth into the bushes.

I was fed up with it!

The bone that I'd picked up the last time turned out to still be in my inventory and I didn't have to come back to the cave for a weapon, so I set off into the forest. It was completely dark by this time and the Perception bonus that the undead got at night kicked in.

I didn't have to get that much experience to

get to level 3, so I decided to avoid players and hunt animals instead. One of the walking dead could easily take care of a fox and should be able to bring down a wolf. I had a decent amount of Health and it was a shame that everything was spoiled by issues with accuracy.

This time, I went in the opposite direction from the park fence and soon got out onto the swampy bank of the river. A twisting path led me to a log which was laid across a stream and I recklessly tried to use it to cross to the other side. My lack of Agility showed itself and my second step already resulted in me falling in.

The stream turned out to be unusually deep and the surface of the water was above my head. I prepared for yet another death and suddenly realized that I didn't feel any discomfort whatsoever. Ah, yes. The dead didn't have to breathe!

I had to struggle for a while to get out onto dry land, but there were no injuries or wounds in the end. I fell down, but so what, it was no matter. I just needed to keep it in mind for the future. What if I had to run away from other players? Well, if I managed to level up higher than level 10, it would be the local noobs who would be running away from me.

I just wanted to know how much time I had left before I would die in real life. How long had I already spent in the virtual reality capsule?

My mood was hopelessly ruined, even though it didn't seem like it could get any worse. Things can always get worse though...

WHEN A HILL APPEARED by the riverside ahead, I turned away from it, crossing a swampy meadow full of darting snakes and flowers that glimmered in the night, finding myself by a ring of stone menhirs that had been dug into the ground.

Suddenly, a bolt of lightning arced nearby and I froze in place, completely still. My feet started to slowly sink into the unsteady swampy ground, but I kept standing there and cursing my rather low Perception.

What was going on over there? Damn it, I couldn't make it out!

Another flash, then a howl and a roar!

As soon as the noise abated and the soft light of a healing spell emanated from the stone circle, I dragged my head out of the sticky mire and went around it, giving it a wide berth. The

---

swamp was soon behind me and a fence with bent and sometimes completely torn bars appeared in front of me.

An abandoned cemetery!

The darkness of the night was split by a battle spell yet again as an armored paladin entered the gate with a shield in one hand and a longsword in the other. Level 10, I automatically noted, as the warrior kicked down one of the gravestones, turned around and ran from the cemetery. Clumps of earth exploded and flew everywhere as a ghoul that had been disturbed by the noise rose up out of the grave.

The humanoid creature with its tooth filled maw and sharp claws chased after the one that had disturbed its peace, but the paladin didn't keep running, he just lured the beast out of the graveyard. By the time I got near the gate, the knight was easily resisting the ghoul's attack as he defended against it with his shield, while two level 9 elven archers were turning the undead creature into a pincushion. The creature was tearing into things and jumping around, sometimes reaching the player with its clawed hands, so the healer mage in a gray cloak and pointed hat had to restore the warrior's Health.

✟ The Dead Rogue ✟

That was a great idea, but I had an even better plan.

I climbed into the graveyard through a hole in the fence and started to shake and push over one gravestone after another. The ghouls that came out to face the light angrily snapped their terrible fangs and wandered between the graves looking for prey in confusion, while paying no attention to my walking corpse whatsoever.

Undead neutrality!

I had already managed to push over ten or eleven gravestones before the paladin returned. The player tried to run away but it was too late — the furious pack noticed the human and ran after him. I couldn't catch up with them so there was a real battle going on by the time I managed to shamble back to the circle of menhirs.

Without the armor, the archers were torn to pieces in an instant, while the paladin was skillfully swinging his sword and causing an amazing amount of damage for his level. The healer mage was casting one healing spell after another on his companion.

The well-coordinated pair had quite a good chance of winning the battle, but a ghoul that had broken away from the pack suddenly rushed towards the spellcaster. One strike from a clawed hand took away half of the Health of the puny mage so he immediately forgot about providing support to the paladin who was surrounded by the undead.

A ball of lightning from the healer's staff hit a ghoul, immediately frying it, while I threw myself into the attack, not wanting to miss such an opportune moment.

One step, two steps, stab!

The sharpened bone went through the spellcaster's cloak without meeting any resistance and sank deep into his human flesh. The healer turned around and tried to shout a spell, so I poked the bone into his open mouth.

Critical hit! Damage: 28
Enemy stunned!
Weapon destroyed!

The mage fell to the ground, choking on his own blood. I bent down over him meaning to finish him off, but then the paladin showed his extraordinary capabilities. He threw his shield to the side, gripped his sword with both hands, raising it over his head and a blinding bolt of lightning fell from the skies. The ghouls were thrown in every direction and I was paralyzed.

Sky Sword: defenses failed!
Stamina: 0/41

I lay curled up on the ground, unable to move my hands or feet as the paladin ignored the ghouls and headed straight towards me. The player had suffered much in his battle with the undead as his armor was dented and splattered with blood, so the paladin walked slowly and heavily. The slot in his helmet shone with a dark fire. The warrior gathered his strength for a moment, gripped the longsword with both hands again and had already started to raise it above his head when the Deathgrip ability icon appeared in front of my eyes.

The unconscious spellcaster was easy prey and it was no problem to suck the Stamina out of him. The paralysis set me free, so I got up and punched through the throat of the spellcaster with my fist.

An instant later the sword fell from up above and the long blade took off my head with a single strike. Everything spun in front of my eyes as it rolled along the ground!

The usual darkness engulfed me immediately.

7.

DARKNESS, LOOSE EARTH and tree roots. Tree roots?

I crawled out of the shallow grave and was surprised to find myself in the bushes at the edge of the meadow where I had thrown that irritating skull instead of the cave.

The stone skull had appeared in my hand again too. Was it really responsible for the location where I was resurrected? I didn't waste time thinking about this mystery because the sun was already rising and my skin started to smoke under its bright light. I had to hide in the thick shadow under the canopy of the oak. Once I was there I opened the game log and couldn't help growling happily.

You've gained a level!

The game mechanics didn't just give me XP

for killing the healer; it also gave me the XP for the archers that had been torn apart by ghouls as if I was the master of the pack, so my level immediately jumped from two to five! I quickly invested the three free attribute points in Intelligence and admired the results.

> *Plague-ridden Corpse, Undead. Level 5*
> *Strength: 18*
> *Agility: 3*
> *Constitution: 23*
> *Intelligence: 5*
> *Perception: 5*
>
> *Health: 115*
> *Stamina: 102*
> *Energy: 25*
> *Damage: 1-4*

Wow! I was no longer a Walking Corpse, I was a Plague-ridden Corpse and my Deathgrip now sucked the life out of the victims along with the Stamina! A new skill called "Aura of Fear" appeared as well. However, the greatest changes were to my appearance. The bloating had disappeared, the leaking pustules had dried out and were partially replaced with cadaveric spots. The Perception penalty from sunlight was reduced by five percent but the main thing was that my fingers were no longer like sausages that had been boiled too long and they could now bend properly.

The change from the Walking Corpse category to the ranks of the Plague-ridden Corpses really made me happy, but I also started to feel hunger. It was not in-game — I had the impression that this was the way that my brain was letting me know that my real body needed food.

Alas, there was nothing I could do about it now. Or could I? My Intelligence was sufficient to speak now. So what was I waiting for?

After hiding the mysterious skull among the roots of the oak I went towards the nearest alleyway, but I still lost several points of Health and a third of my Stamina no matter how much I tried to keep to the shadows because of the rays of sunlight burning my skin.

I even thought of getting a cloak, but I didn't take the idea seriously. If I managed to talk to some player I wouldn't need it anymore.

However, I didn't come across any players

for some reason. I only came across a lovely looking elf in green clothing that hugged her shapely body like a second skin by the gates of the park.

Eladriel Emeraldvine, elf. Druid, Level 8

I spread my hands in front of me and quickly stammered, "I'm not going to hurt you! I'm a player too and I need help!"

There was no more howling and incomprehensible moaning. I said exactly what I meant to say. The problem was that I said it in some unknown language!

Throaty sounds, short phrases and unfamiliar intonations. If I wasn't dead already, my hair would have stood on end.

The elf reacted immediately. She threw a green sphere at me and gripped her battle staff with both hands.

Growing Thorns: defenses failed!
Damage taken: 2... 4... 8...

A rough-looking warrior jumped out from somewhere to the side, raised his club and shouted, "Leave it to me!" to the elf.

"Go away!"

I decided against getting into a hopeless battle and jumped into the bushes, but I fell and started to convulse after taking two steps. There was no pain, but something alien was growing inside me. My swollen skin burst and the spiky shoots of a thorn bush started to rupture outwards.

Damage taken: 64
You have been killed!

Earth, tough oak roots and the whisper of leaves above my head.

I was reborn in the forest this time, right in the place where I had hidden the skull. When I got out of the grave I shuddered as I remembered the thorns piercing my insides and decided to find a more reliable shelter. Thankfully, the wind had brought clouds from somewhere and it was overcast. The first place that came to mind was the abandoned cemetery, so that was where I went, taking the skull along. The question that kept coming to my mind along the way was, "What went wrong?"

✝ The Dead Rogue ✝

Why did I speak gibberish instead of normal words? What was that language? Why did I start speaking it? A lack of Intelligence was definitely not the issue.

I WAS DISTRACTED from my uneasy thoughts by loud shouts and the ring of steel. I carefully moved out onto the edge of the forest and immediately understood that I shouldn't look for shelter in the abandoned graveyard. Half a dozen players were methodically clearing it of ghouls, checking one grave after another. The undead couldn't put up a worthy fight against humans in the light of the sun. Their cries kept ringing out.

"This one's mine!"

"Don't touch it!"

"Leave it to me!"

"Get lost, noob!"

The newbies were trying to beat each other, shouting and swearing. None of them noticed the lone undead creature in the bushes. I retreated, but then a red dot suddenly appeared on the map. One of the players had managed to get a pet and the little cur ran straight towards me, barking furiously.

There was no point in counting on hiding

from a dog in the forest so I had to run to the swamp. The bark soon quietened down, but I had suddenly reached the river, surprising even myself. I was forced to walk along the bank.

The sun that shone through the cloud was burning away Stamina at a fearsome pace. Even though I could have gone under the water and waited for the coming of darkness, I didn't want to waste time for nothing. When a riverside hill appeared ahead with some sort of ruins on its bald top I immediately headed there to find shelter from the burning rays.

I barely managed to walk up it. I thought that I'd just remain lying there on the slope, but no, I managed to curl up in the shadow of a ruined wall. I sat there awhile, waiting for my Stamina to be restored and set off to examine the ruins.

There was a broken gate in the wall on the side of the river, but as soon as I stepped through it, a stone slab sank under my foot and an unpleasant metallic creak rank out. "A trap!" rushed through my head, as a log hanging on chains swung towards me, hammered into my chest and threw me off the hill. After immediately losing half of my Health, I fell into the water with a great splash and went to the bottom like a stone.

I spent a while struggling around in the silt, but then I calmed down, gathered my strength and crawled out onto the shore, covered in weed and ooze. I couldn't believe my eyes — the river had washed away the slope, the earth had fallen off and revealed a rough stone of laid walls. To add to it, there was even a black hole in the wall.

Knee deep in the mud, I burst through the cattails and entered the comfortable dimness and gloom of the dungeon. It turned out to be spacious and empty inside, apart from a steel-bound chest with a great padlock hanging on it. A stairway was nearby, but the way up was blocked by collapsed walls while the lower level had been flooded by the river, with the slimy steps descending into the dark water.

A small and dark niche was by the side of the stairway with a smaller wooden chest inside. It turned out to be unlocked, so I immediately opened it, becoming the owner of a dozen gold coins, an unidentified magic bracelet, a worn-out chainmail hauberk and a rusty knife which caused 1-2 points of damage.

There were many holes in the hauberk and it was not too good at protecting from stabbing or blunt weapons, but I put it on without hesitation. At least it was armor of some sort!

Next, I hid the enchanted skull in a pile of stones and tried to use the knife to pick the lock on the large chest with no success. I walked around the dungeon again but I couldn't find any hidden passages so I returned to the hole in the wall. It was starting to rain outside, so I decided to use the bad weather to get out into the forest.

I didn't need much more experience to reach the next level, and the more I would level up my Plague-ridden Corpse the more chances I'd have to survive... Survive a conversation with yet another player.

There was a sandbank overgrown with cattails by the slope and I used it to reach the already familiar swamp to gather fifty points of experience slicing up the snakes that lived there with my knife. The map soon burned with numerous red dots, so I had to get away from the poisonous creatures which were infuriated by my intrusion. Snake venom had no effect on me, but every bite took away one or two points of Health, which didn't restore by itself, unlike Stamina.

✟ The Dead Rogue ✟

So how could I heal? To hell with it, anyway.

Maintaining some distance from the graveyard, I went deeper into the forest and came across a rabid fox almost immediately. The predator jumped to the attack and fiercely bit into my leg.

I bared my teeth, grabbed the fox by the scruff of its neck and activated the Deathgrip.

Energy: -11 [14/25]
Health: +11 [34/115]
Stamina: +11 [102/102]

Now I was healed.

After spending another eleven units of energy I killed the fox and kept going. The XP I received for killing the animal was not enough to get to level 6, but I came across no more minor forest creatures and I gave the bear I saw a wide berth. It could have easily torn one of the undead to pieces.

It started to rain harder and darkness started to fall. The Perception penalty went away but the distance I could see still decreased to one and a half dozen paces. I got out of the thick forest into one of the alleyways and literally walked into a sorcerer.

The tall, thin and pale Necromancer immediately cast a battle spell at me, but the stone ball powerlessly burst into ghostly shards without causing me any harm.

Command Undead: Immunity

"Stop!" I shouted when the level 9 necromancer raised his staff with a menacing steel hook on the end. "Wait!"

"A talking undead?" the necromancer asked with surprise, but didn't lower his weapon. "What do you want, creature?"

The necromancer and I were speaking the strange throaty language but still understood each other perfectly. He understood me and I understood him!

What could I say which wouldn't scare away the player and provoke him to attack? Everything got mixed up inside my head and I blurted out the first thing that came into my mind.

"A quest!"

The quest generation menu immediately

opened. The necromancer put the staff behind his back and graciously agreed to hear me out.

"Speak, creature!"

I wasted no time and put up the maximum reward of ten gold that I could afford and asked him to bring a hooded cloak, footwear, trousers, gloves and a morning star. I could have also transferred ten percent of the experience I had collected but I didn't think that it was a good idea.

Ten gold was a more than generous reward for this junk.

The necromancer didn't seem to think so, however. He frowned and hesitated until I quickly moved one of the sliders changing the single quest into a series of three tasks.

The necromancer surrendered and waved his hand dismissively.

"You've persuaded me, dead one. Wait here."

Garth Deathblade has accepted your quest!

The sorcerer left and I closed the system message and hid in the bushes. Waiting for the necromancer in the alleyway would have put me in danger of coming across other players and I had no desire to die and fail to find Garth.

I wasn't sure that anyone else could understand me, as necromancers were not a popular class among the players at all. When would I end up meeting another necromancer?

This was why I didn't tell him my sad story immediately. People visit virtual worlds to relax and they don't need anyone else's problems. Garth may have believed the dead man and wouldn't have refused help, but he could also tell me to go somewhere very far away.

A quest was something else entirely. Quests were sacred.

THE NECROMANCER RETURNED when the rain had calmed and the wind started to gradually blow the clouds away from the city. After giving him his reward, I immediately dressed in a black robe of rough black cloth and put the hood over my head.

My Perception penalty decreased to ten percent.

"What next?" Garth asked hurriedly, staring at me intently with the red eyes of an albino.

✟ The Dead Rogue ✟

The necromancer's white hair flew in the wind and he looked rather unfriendly.

I decided that I shouldn't test the sorcerer's patience and set up the objectives of the second task.

Quest: Deliver a message.
Reward: Help in the game.

"Help?" Garth sneered. "What could you help me with?"

"Command Undead," I replied and clarified, "How many ghouls are you able to take control of at a time, necromancer?"

The sorcerer thought for a moment.

"Four or five. If I do them all at the same time. So what?"

"I'll collect five ghouls in one place. You'll be able to clear any dungeon around here with that sort of support."

The necromancer looked doubtful. He would usually be barely able to rely on taking control of more than one of the undead, so my offer did interest him in some ways.

"What sort of message?" Garth asked at last. "And who do I need to deliver it to?"

"It won't take much time. Do you agree?"

Garth Deathblade has accepted your task!
Garth Deathblade is your temporary ally.

That was right — the marker that showed the position of the necromancer on the map glowed green.

"So what is the message?" the necromancer repeated impatiently. "Get a move on! Time is money!"

Time really was valued as much as money in virtual reality, so I immediately wrote my message with a knife on the wet earth. I first wrote down the email address of my attorney and then added in English, "I have got stuck in the game. I can't get out. Tell the admins that the program has been hacked."

"What the hell?" Garth swore as he watched my actions.

"Take a screenshot," I demanded, "and send it to this email address."

"I don't like it," the white-haired necromancer shook his head. "It's some sort of setup!"

"Just send the letter!"

"I'll have to quit the game!"

"You don't have to do it right now," I replied, feeling like I had to agree to this inconvenient concession.

"Well, if it's like that... All right, I'll do it..." Garth decided reluctantly. "Now take me to the ghouls!"

"Let's go, necromancer..."

TO MY GREAT RELIEF, there was no one by the abandoned graveyard apart from the crickets singing in the grass and the larks circling in the clear sky. Steam rose from the wet earth and it became hot, but I didn't lower my hood — the thick fabric offered great protection from sunburn. Even my Stamina didn't get depleted any longer and the penalty was limited to the loss of sixty percent of my Perception.

"Wait for me behind the gate, necromancer," I demanded, as I entered the graveyard and started to lure the ghouls by hammering the gravestones with my morning star.

The denizens of the graveyard hadn't yet completely regenerated from the previous clearance so I had to go through a couple of

---

dozen graves until I'd gathered the required number of undead.

"Everything's ready, necromancer!" I shouted.

As soon as the necromancer appeared in the gates, the fanged monstrosities went on the attack, with a bone sphere sent to meet them. When it hit the first ghoul the spell exploded and burst into half a dozen pieces. One of them hit me, making my eyes go blurred for a moment, but my eyesight was instantly restored.

Command Undead: Immunity

The ghouls had no such protection from enslavement so all of them fell under the control of the sorcerer.

Wait. The necromancer captured all but one of them! The beast with its blue-black hide roared fiercely and jumped upon Garth. He only managed to use his staff to block the attack aimed at his head at the last moment.

A second later I was by his side, slamming the ghoul with my morning star. The spiky ball smashed into its back with the power of a cannonball and immediately took away fifty points of Health. My Stamina only slightly decreased and I immediately changed to a two-handed grip and bashed the creature on the head as it turned around.

A miss!

The ghoul swatted at me with its fearsome claws but didn't manage to penetrate the chainmail. I struck again but there was no result. It was even worse than that — the claws of my opponent sliced through my arm and cut it to the bone. Thankfully, the damage was not high and I was protected from the corpse poison by my immunity.

A moment later, Garth stabbed the hook on his staff into the ghoul and literally tore it in half.

Garth Deathblade has killed the Old Ghoul.
Experience received: +55 [844/1000]
You have gained a level!

Level 6! I used the stat point I'd received to raise my Agility and caught the thoughtful eye of the necromancer.

"The experience is split between the two of us?" he frowned, but then waved his hand and strode out of the graveyard. Four ghouls ambled along after him, whining quietly because of the bright sunlight.

"The ghouls won't last long!" I warned as I caught up with the sorcerer.

"I won't be able to hold onto them long myself!" Garth replied angrily and drunk an Elixir of Mana to restore the Energy he'd spent on the spell. "It'll be fine. They won't have time to rot. The skeleton dungeon is nearby."

A skeleton dungeon? Well, if the experience keeps trickling in, why not?

We met several other players on the road to the cave. Some looked at Garth with respect and others with apprehension. No one paid any attention to me. Just another of the undead under the control of a necromancer and that was all.

There was no one by the entrance to the dungeon — the players would usually descend there in groups of ten to fifteen people, as there was no other way to get to the lower levels afterwards.

"You're going first!" Garth ordered.

I remembered about the neutrality of the undead towards me so I made no argument. The ghouls had also been quite severely burned by the sun, so they needed to be preserved.

"If one of us dies, we'll meet by the graveyard!" the sorcerer warned.

"All right, necromancer," I replied as I went ahead of him to go down the stairs.

The darkness was kept at bay by the burning torches on the walls and the floor was flagged with cracked stone slabs. A Skeleton Spearman stood at the far end of the corridor by the entrance to the hall. I fearlessly walked right up to it and tried to hit it with the morning star on the top of its skull but missed unexpectedly. The skeleton stepped back and stabbed out with its spear.

Damned creature!

I caught hold of the shaft to prevent my opponent from using its weapon and started to smash it over the head. Most of the attacks missed, but I eventually managed to knock off its helmet as a ghoul appeared by my side and broke the skeleton's spine with a swing of its clawed hand.

Screwing up my face from the unpleasant feeling in my chest as it had been pierced by the spearhead, I stepped over the pile of bones and got completely shocked by the surprise. Ten Skeleton Crossbowmen awaited their uninvited guests among the stone pillars. I retreated, but my plague-ridden corpse moved slowly. Way too slowly...

Whoosh! Whoosh! Whoosh!

Three or four crossbow bolts immediately sent me to be regenerated.

DARKNESS, ROCKS and the nearby splash of water.

I got out of the pile of rocks and curled up in the niche, unable to rise to my feet. The pain in my chest soon went away, but the durability of the chainmail hauberk which had been pierced by many bolts obviously didn't come back. One or two hits and I would have no armor anymore.

When I scrolled the game log back a little I discovered a notification that Garth Deathblade had left the game. Suddenly, I heard the ringing sound of chains and a loud thud. A moment later, the body of yet another simpleton that had visited the ruins on the hill splashed into the river, but it turned out that the one that got caught by the trap was a truly lucky devil. Judging by his loud cursing, the player had enough Health to survive the attack without their heavy armor dragging them down to the bottom.

There was a series of squelching sounds as the dim light became even darker and the lithe figure of a dark elf appeared in the opening.

Iss El-Morten, Drow. Rogue, Level 10.

"Unbelievable!" the dark elf exclaimed and rushed straight towards the chest.

Without looking around the dungeon, he immediately fell to his knees in front of the lock and started to dig around inside it using his picks. As soon the click of an open mechanism rang out, I stepped out of the niche and moved towards the thief. He strained to open the massive lid of the chest and only noticed my presence when we were but a couple of paces away from each other. I decided against attacking with the morning star as I was not at all sure of my own accuracy, grabbing the drow instead and dragging him down the dark flooded stairway instead of the floor. We fell into the water and rolled down the stairs into the depths.

The rogue twisted around and stabbed me in the hip with a curved dagger, while I activated my Deathgrip. The dark elf jerked around but didn't manage to get free, so he started to feverishly stab me with his blade. He only managed to take away half of my Health before his own Health bar shook and started to rapidly decrease.

Air. His lungs had run out of air!

The thief let go of his dagger and started to convulse, but I only gripped him tighter, preventing him from rising to the surface.

Player Iss El-Morten has been killed!
Experience: +259 [1103 / 1200]
You have gained a level!

Wow, I was already at level 7! It was far quicker to level on players than the puny local monsters.

I didn't spend long choosing the stat to increase and raised Agility to five points. I took fifty silver coins and a pair of unidentified boots off the body, picked up the dagger that the rogue dropped and started to climb back up the flooded stairway.

I needed to get out of here as soon as possible. If I was the drow, I would hurry back immediately after regeneration to pay back my assailant and take the items I lost. The dungeon could no longer serve as a safe harbor.

The first thing I did was find the skull hidden among the ruins and then took the gold which had appeared in the wooden chest again. I was already heading for the exit, when I remembered about the opened chest. Its lid was wide open, I looked inside and took out a strange looking dagger — it was white and very light, carved out of the shard of a gigantic bone.

Bone Dagger
Damage against Skeletons: 500
Durability: single use

A quest item to use against the Skeleton Lord? Whatever, I would work it out later. Right now, I had to head to the graveyard. The necromancer could already be waiting for me there. That's what I really wanted to believe.

4.

GARTH WAS NOT at our meeting place. I

wandered around the forest for a while, looking at the cemetery gates and then went deeper into the forest, planning to hide the skull in a hole of some kind.

It was shady among the elm trees, so being resurrected there wouldn't put me on the fringe of destruction even if I lost my cloak.

Annoyingly, a pair of boars decided to pick on me almost immediately and only the Aura of Fear helped me to avoid a battle with the grizzled beasts. I only managed to get away from them when my Energy had almost run out, so I decided to return to the graveyard.

The necromancer and I noticed each other at the same time. We received a system message.

You have met Garth Deathblade!
Continue with your quest? [Yes/No]

I confirmed that I was ready to carry out my obligations and then a new message appeared.

Garth Deathblade has chosen to continue your quest!
Garth Deathblade is your temporary ally.

✝ The Dead Rogue ✝

"Has the message been sent, necromancer?" I demanded, encouraged by his decision.

Garth swept the hood back from his head, ran his fingers through his white hair and then suddenly asked, "Are you really stuck in the game or is this a joke from a bored admin?"

"What?" I was taken aback.

"I put the message through an online translator," the necromancer replied. "Then I checked out the email address online. I worked out the country and city, dug around in the news..."

"Have you sent the message, necromancer?" I interrupted him "Yes or no?"

"I sent it, calm down," Garth reassured me. "Immediately after I quit the game. There's been no reply so far."

"When was that?"

"Five hours ago."

Damn! I cursed to myself, but also felt an immense sense of relief. My attorney knew that I was trapped in this game. They would get me out of here soon.

"Now then," Garth continued, "I dug around in the local news and came across a story about a man that fell into a coma while playing. The Towers of Power tech support department stated that the user isn't online and the issue was deliberate damage to the gaming equipment for which they are not liable. They left the victim in the capsule and transported him to a hospital. A military hospital, for some reason. Is that what they do where you come from?"

A military hospital? Did they really put him under guard? Or was there a mistake in the translation and they just put him into a normal prison hospital?

"In any case, if that person is you, there's nothing to worry about. As long as the medical insurance is in place, they won't take you off life support," Garth told me in a casual tone of voice, as if we weren't talking about me being in a life and death situation.

"They'll get me out of here!"

The necromancer chuckled strangely and offered, "I'm prepared to listen to your story and give you some advice if you gather the ghouls. I have a quest to destroy a pack of wolves."

"And what about the skeleton dungeon?" I asked, noticing that Garth was still at level 9.

"It's too difficult to solo," the mage

grimaced. "So are you in, or are we parting ways? I can't waste my time!"

"I'm in, necromancer," I decided against refusing the offer. "I have three magic items, can you find out their properties?"

"What will I get out of it?" Garth chuckled.

"You can choose one and take it for yourself."

"Let's have a look, then."

I gave the mage access to part of my inventory. The necromancer had no problem with the boots and the bracelet, but had to use a spell to identify the dagger.

Bracelet of Agility (part of a set: 1 of 2)
Agility: +1

Boots of Stealth
Stealth: +10%
Movement speed in stealth mode: +5%
Durability: 20

Shadow Dagger
Damage: 1-3
Critical damage: x3
Chance of causing critical damage: +10%

"The dagger is mine," Garth chose the most valuable item, as expected.

I didn't argue. I put the bracelet on my wrist, put on the boots and set off to the graveyard. Luring the ghouls from the graves presented no problems — I knocked over the headstones as usual and then called the mage over. He did his job well, managing to control all five monsters at the same time.

"The wolf pack's lair is nearby," Garth told me and asked, "So what is it you're saying happened to you? How did you manage to get stuck here?"

I told him what happened.

"Wait," Garth replied with surprise. "So it wasn't a bug? This was done by a hacker?"

"Exactly."

"That's really shit, my friend. Now I understand why the Enslave Undead spell didn't work. You're basically a player in the body of an NPC!" Garth laughed, as if he had found the solution for a riddle that had eluded him. "What's your name?"

"John," I introduced myself using the English version of my name.

"John, do you have access to the log at the

time of your murder?"

I could only spread my hands.

"Where from?"

"Just check. Have a look through the tabs."

A young wolf jumped out of the bushes to be immediately torn apart by the ghouls.

"Keep looking for it, John, keep looking. We'll manage by ourselves here."

I opened the system window and started to check through all of the tabs available. Amazingly, Garth turned out to be right — the stats of my rogue showed up on one of the screens. It was just inactive.

"I see the stats of my old character," I told the necromancer.

"Look through the game logs!" the mage demanded as he started the ritual to raise a zombie wolf. "They must have remained somewhere."

"Oh! I just found them. What will that give me?"

"Send me the time of the murder in our group chat."

"I can't. The chat is read-only."

Garth thought for a moment, ran his hand through his white hair and offered, "Open the

Settings and tick the Special Options box and select "text to voice" and "voice to text". You'll be able to send messages to authorized players within your line of sight."

I did it.

"Yep, it works!"

Shadow Snares: You are paralyzed!
Damage taken: 37 [73/ 110]
Damage taken: 37 [36/ 110]
Damage taken: 37 [0/ 110]
You have been killed by Player Someone Someone

The necromancer froze, as if he was some consulting some in-game resource and then whistled.

"Wow! Level ninety nine! Well, we're going to spoil his cornflakes now!"

"What're you doing?"

Garth laughed.

"I wrote a complaint. The PvP mode really does become available when a noob reaches level 10, but high level characters can't enter the playpen. It's a direct violation of the rules."

"Won't they ask why I didn't make the

complaint myself?"

The necromancer only laughed.

"I wrote that because of the emotional distress you suffered you still can't make yourself log into the game. You'll see — it'll work. It always works."

"And what will I get out of it?"

"Don't you get it?" Garth sighed. "The game itself cannot be hacked, so there must have been some sort of hardware added to the capsule or some way of tapping into the connection. The hacker had to find your character here to shove you into the body of a dead man, so he'll be unable to do anything for the duration of the ban. Stop! The lair is nearby!"

That was right — red lights started to appear on the map one after another.

"Damn!" the necromancer cursed. "There are more wolves than I thought!"

I armed myself with the morning star in the nick of time. The pack that rushed to the attack immediately tore one of the zombies raised by the necromancer apart and bit through the paws of two ghouls. The battle was on. I crushed the head of one wolf, smashed into the spine of another and then struck again — it was the effect of my increased Agility.

The necromancer was busy with his staff, trying to keep a huge she-wolf at bay, so the ghouls rushed to help him. They easily brought the animal which was the size of a small calf to the ground while I was left alone fighting four powerful wolves. I swung the spiked ball of my morning star into the ravening maw of the first wolf and immediately felt a bite on my hip and wrist. My Health bar immediately went yellow, but then there was a loud crack behind my back and bone shards flew all around, cutting down the predators like sorcerous shrapnel.

The ghouls quickly finished off the wounded wolves and Garth looked around in confusion.

"The quest isn't complete!" he declared and suddenly looked alert. "Oh! There's been a response to the complaint! Your hacker has been banned for three months!"

"Write about me! Write that I'm stuck in the game!"

"Have you lost your mind?" the necromancer was taken aback. "They're just going to delete you! Erase your undead and say that this is the way it was!"

"But why?"

"The admins have already answered that you're not in-game, that's why! Just think about how much the share price of the company will crash if this story surfaces. A person trapped in a game is a developer's nightmare!"

"But maybe that is a solution? They'll delete my undead and I'll wake up?"

Garth took out a mana potion and shook his head.

"I don't think so. You just won't pass the verification. You entered the game as a rogue and now you are undead. Who knows where you'll be stuck. At least you can play like this."

"Damn it!" I swore. "How could something like this even happen?"

The necromancer drew a line around the ravaged body of the she-wolf with his staff and suggested, "If you can see your old stats, the hacker probably used unimplemented code for the introduction of dual classes. They were planning this immediately after the game was launched. In the end, they decided to limit themselves to specializations and professions.

"How do you know?"

"I'm here since more or less the first few

days!"

"And you're still level nine?" I asked with disbelief.

"Oh! That?" Garth laughed. "I sell characters. I level them up to 24 and sell them. There are different options."

Players got their specialization on level 25 but I didn't ask how one was connected to the other and asked a question instead.

"Then why can't I use my Rogue skills?"

"It will be like that until the level of your new class reaches the level of the old one. This will never happen to you. You're an NPC."

"I'm rising in level!"

"Seriously?" the necromancer sounded surprised as he added power to his Raise Undead spell. "Ah, yes! The difficulty of almost every quest depends on player level! The levels of the monsters rise as well..."

The magic that spread around Garth was scaldingly cold, there was the smell of an upturned grave and then the ravaged she-wolf rose from the ground, jerkily and awkwardly. Bloody drool sank to the ground from her open maw, as the black fire of darkness burned in her eyes.

✝ The Dead Rogue ✝

"Excellent! Just excellent!" the necromancer breathed a sigh of relief. "We can now check out the lair of the wolf pack!"

We broke our way through the bushes and stopped at the entrance of the cave. The ghouls moved into the dungeon and one of them immediately exploded into chunks of rotten meat. A huge black werewolf tore his victim apart in a split second and immediately jumped on the second undead monster. Its terrible jaws clacked as its fangs crunched through the ghoul's clawed hand and the beast jerked its head, tearing it from the ghoul's body. An instant later it had already gutted the ghoul and crouched, preparing to leap to the attack again.

Garth threw an Orb of Cold and the paws of the werewolf got frozen to the ground. The beast twitched and tore one of its limbs away from the icy covering and then started to free another...

This was the moment that the zombie she-wolf struck. Her fangs pierced the neck of the werewolf, but it stood fast. I also rushed into the fray, using my impetus to smash the ribs of the beast, taking away 45 points of Health and raised my weapon again, but then missed and almost sent the morning star flying out of my hand.

THE ICE MELTED, so the blood-soaked werewolf threw the zombie she-wolf off himself and then bit me on my side. Thankfully, my chainmail blocked the damage. The zombie bounded up from the ground and sank its teeth into the werewolf's back foot. As the beast turned, I smashed it in the back of the head, while Garth took a run-up to stab the terrible hook of his staff into its side.

Blood sprayed out of the wound.

Player Garth Deathblade has killed a werewolf!
The Wolf Pack quest is complete!
Experience: +205 [1403/ 1440]
You have gained a level!

So, here was level eight. I put the point into increasing Agility again. I was sick of being so clumsy.

It turned out that the experience we received was enough to raise both my level and that of the necromancer.

"Level 10!" he announced, unable to hide

his satisfaction. "All right, John, it was nice to play with you, but it's time to move on!"

A system notification about the completion of the task was displayed and Garth disappeared from the list of Allies. However, a new notification about a third quest which was the last in the chain immediately came up.

"Oh no!" the necromancer groaned. "I don't have time for this!"

"I'll turn it off right away," I promised, as I opened the quest generation menu. "By the way, can every necromancer talk to me? It's just that no one understands me apart from you."

"Yes, any of them," Garth confirmed. "They are going to launch a global update adding the Kingdom of the Dead in a week, so necromancers will be worth their weight in gold. Wait!"

"What?" I glanced back at him.

"One of the artifacts announced for the Kingdom of the Dead is the single use Scroll of Rebirth. It can bring any creature back to life. If your character is resurrected you might be able to quit the game."

"Wow!" I burst out.

"However..." the necromancer paused. "No, it's not an option. Resurrecting some sort of epic creature bears a heavy price and there is no way you will get into the Tower of Decay before the others."

"But can this help?" I asked hopefully.

"It doesn't matter," Garth parried, as he wiped the blood off the staff. "What's going on with that quest?"

"I can't cancel it," I lied. "Why don't we do something else — take this skull outside the city and throw it into some deep hole."

"What is this skull?" Garth asked with interest.

"I don't know," I lied again, "but it is somehow connected to the quest to kill me. If it no longer exists, the other players might leave me alone. I am so sick of dying."

"What's the reward?" the necromancer asked.

I put all of my gold in the quest generation menu, but the amount didn't impress the necromancer.

"Add the boots and the Bracelet of Agility," he demanded. "You must also let the reward be collected once the quest is completed, as I'm not planning to come back here."

I did everything as he asked, remembering

to set a minimum distance for the skull to be carried to get the reward.

Garth Deathblade has accepted your quest!

"See you, John!" the necromancer waved his hand and strode off towards the park gates. "It was nice to meet you!"

"Same to you," I answered with complete honesty.

Now I had a goal. A goal in life and in the game.

My situation didn't seem hopeless any more. Even if my attorney wouldn't be able to get me out of the game, I could escape from this place into the real world. I would just have to get the Scroll of Rebirth by beating the highest level players in Towers of Power to it. Even if Garth would help me get out of the annoying park, I wouldn't have a good time in the future. There was nothing much to do outside the playpen at a pathetic level 8.

I opened my Inventory, checked my Bone Dagger and resolutely set off towards the skeleton dungeon.

Why miss my chance to earn a bit of

experience?

5.

THE GOLD, Bracelet of Agility and the Boots of Stealth disappeared from the Inventory when I had already reached entrance to the lair of the Skeleton Lord and hidden myself under a fallen tree to avoid attention from players.

Garth Deathblade has completed your quest!

I read the system notification again and climbed out of the bushes into the clearing.

The Skeleton Dungeon was considered to be one of the most difficult locations in the playpen. The players had to get together in large teams to storm it and it was sparsely populated the rest of the time. The owner of a bone dagger didn't have any advantages compared to anyone else — no newbie would be able to get to the bottom level by themselves. But a plague-ridden corpse wouldn't need to use strength to get through! I just hoped that the skeletons wouldn't remember my last visit here...

I was quite reticent as I approached my old friend the skeleton spearman, who stood frozen in the doorway, but I gathered my courage and squeezed past him into the underground hall full of crossbowmen.

Undead: Neutral

None of the skeletons made a move when I appeared. Encouraged by this, I set off to look for the descent to the next level, but then heard the sound of running feet and the excited shouts of players by the entrance.

As soon as I'd hidden behind one of the stone pillars, the skeleton gatekeeper fell with its head crushed and three half-naked barbarians burst into the hall. The pyromancer that appeared in the doorway threw a fireball at the crossbowmen, but only three skeletons were destroyed by the flames because of the many pillars.

There was the whistle of flying crossbow bolts and one of the barbarians fell. The guards dropped their empty weapons and met the players in hand to hand combat. They were armed with bucklers and hand axes as well as their crossbows.

I took advantage of the commotion to slip towards the stairway, descended a floor and immediately sprung a trap — the rusty spike that protruded out of the wall was just a handbreadth away from my belly, otherwise it would have pierced right through me.

The sound of battle continued above so I threw caution to the wind and carried on moving along the corridor, managing to somehow reach the next stairway without getting caught in yet another trap. It was way more dark and gloomy below. There were shackles hanging down from the walls everywhere, while the floor was littered with bones and the gray wisps of cobwebs peered out from every corner. Three skeleton guardians passed by, their chainmail clinking, with halberds resting upon their shoulders and the shape of a ghost floating alongside.

The rag-clad shape of a conjurer stood still and waited at the descent to the last level, with orange flames burning inside its skull. It seemed that its empty eye sockets were watching my approach with a malign interest. He even almost made a move towards me, and I could immediately make out that there were no legs under the torn cloak — the skeleton floated in the air.

As I passed by, I felt a gust of hot air, with the dead conjurer turning his head and clacking his teeth, as if he suspected some sort of deceit, but he didn't do anything else.

And then I fell and rapidly rolled down the steps into the lair of the Skeleton Lord!

The hall turned out to be small, with burning torches on its stone walls. The Lord sat upon a high throne, with an immense two-handed flamberge that had an undulating blade resting on his knees. Even though the blade had been eaten by rust, it looked impressive and fearsome, as did its owner. An open helmet was on the Lord's skull, his body was covered by intricately woven chainmail and his shinbones were hidden in a tall pair of boots with iron toecaps.

Four skeleton bodyguards with normal two-handed longswords stood at attention in the corners of the hall, but they made no move at my appearance, unlike the conjurer up above. The Lord also sat there unmoving, yet I still didn't risk approaching him, choosing to go around the throne and crouch by a dusty chest that stood there instead. To my great regret, it turned out to be locked.

There was nothing else I could do other than step up to the Lord and stab him with the Bone Dagger. The skeleton shuddered and dissolved into a cloud of gray dust. The helmet that fell off the skull bounced off the armrest, flew through the air and then rolled towards the wall. Only the chainmail and the sword remained on the throne. A heavy money pouch also fell on the floor by the empty boots.

The Skeleton Lord has been killed!
Experience: +250 [1653/ 1730]

You have gained a level!

Without spending time to improve my stats, I threw the two-handed flamberge, chainmail hauberk and boots into my inventory and rushed to the chest behind the throne. I never even managed to get the key out of the looted money pouch. A skeleton bodyguard stopped me by slicing into my legs, with the heavy blade of the two-handed longsword crunching through my bones under the knees. I collapsed to the floor and never managed to rise again. The skeleton raised his two-handed longsword above its head and slashed downwards, nailing me to the stone-flagged floor.

You have been killed!

Darkness, the viscous weight of refuse and the unbearable stench of the gutter.

Garth hadn't bothered overmuch and immediately threw the skull away as soon as he'd left the confines of Old Gardens.

Covered in filth from head to foot, I climbed out of the gutter, swore angrily and looked around. The city walls could be seen nearby, but the sun had already set and the guards couldn't see me properly, while newbies would usually never risk going out for nocturnal walks. There were no more favors for those of a low level in the open world anymore, so it was easy as anything to get into serious trouble.

That also applied to me.

The first thing I did was leave the road towards some mysterious ruins, cleaned the skull with the edge of my cloak and stuffed it into a hole in the partially crumbled masonry. Next, I added the stat point I earned by reaching level 9 to Agility and started to look through my loot.

I discovered a hundred gold coins in the Skeleton Lord's pouch, as well as an emerald and the key to the treasure chest which was of no value to me anymore. The rusty long chainmail hauberk turned out to lack any magical abilities and I put it on instead of the one ruined by the strike of the skeleton bodyguard. However, the boots and the double-handed flamberge made me whistle in surprise.

> *Boots of Silence (Deadman's Set: 2 out of 13)*
> *Armor: 2*
> *Damage: 2*
> *Noise in stealth mode: -10%*
> *Restrictions: Undead, Necromancers*

> *Bloody Flamberge (Deadman's Set: 2 out of 13)*
> *Damage: 6-12*
> *Accuracy: +10%*
> *Chance of causing critical damage: +10%*
> *Chance of causing bleeding damage: 4% for each wave of the blade used in the strike*

✝ The Dead Rogue ✝

Bleeding damage: 2 points of Health per second over 2 seconds
Status: Very Rare
Restrictions: Undead, Necromancers

I respectfully tested the weight of the flamberge in my hands, admiring its undulating blade, which would be an unpleasant surprise for any opponent at the early stages of the game and then put on my boots. I paused to admire my character's stats.

Health: 207
Stamina: 184
Energy: 45
Damage: 48-96

Wow, that damage wasn't bad! A level 9 player would usually only have around a hundred points of Health, unless they concentrated on their physical stats. I sliced through the air with the flamberge a few times, but then immediately got distracted by a strange ball of light that cut through the darkness by the city gates. The light stayed still for a moment and then set off to rapidly approach the ruins, or, to be more precise, approach was the gutter where I was resurrected this time around.

I went cold inside from an unpleasant premonition, but I didn't run away, hiding behind the crumbling wall and adjusting my grip to be more comfortable on the hilt of the flamberge.

The magical light approach and I could then make out that the shining ball hung in the air above a man who was running along the road. My low perception didn't let me work out who the player was and a hint with their name never appeared.

The stranger spent a while standing by the gutter and then jumped down inside, digging around enthusiastically. I immediately took the enchanted skull out of the hole in the masonry and put it away in my inventory. Whoever it was scrabbling around in the filth had to have come here especially to get hold of it.

I was already carefully falling back around the ruins, when the player that climbed out of the gutter waved his hand. Bright energy flowed in waves in all directions from the dark figure, making the trees shine with a pearly light as the waves reached them and the darkness of the night receding to make it clear as day.

I could no longer make a run for it, but I couldn't be seen in the ruins.

That was what I thought, until I lowered my eyes and discovered that I shone like a burning brand.

"Come out, Johnny!" I heard from outside. "Come out, we need to talk."

The mage swept his hood back from his head and ran his fingers through the white hair of an albino.

Garth Deathblade. A level 11 necromancer.

Eleven already! That was quick...

It was stupid to keep hiding. I rested the wavy blade of the flamberge upon my right shoulder and walked out of the ruins to stand before the necromancer.

"Long time no see, Garth."

"Where's the skull, Johnny?"

"What business is that of yours?"

"Just answer me. You've got it on you, right?"

I shook my head and cracked my back.

"So what?" I asked again.

"You lied to me!" Garth shouted. "You never

told me that your resurrection point was tied to this artifact!"

"I told you that it's a quest item. Isn't it?"

"I need it!"

"What for?"

"None of your business!"

"Oh yes, it is."

"Give it back, or I'll take it by force!" the necromancer threatened.

"Tell me what's changed, and I'll think about it."

Garth looked at me as if he was aiming to strike, but then held back and told me reluctantly, "I was offered fifty thousand for it. Euros, not game gold! Fifty thousand euros! I'd have to work for that money for two years. I'll haggle with them for it, too!"

I was taken aback.

"How did someone find out that you had the skull?"

The necromancer sneered.

"The offer came from the address you gave me. You know what that means?"

That meant that I was in trouble.

My very own attorney had offered money for the skull. It was him that advised me to relax and have fun playing for a while. Damn it! He must have been working for Kogan! The technical support complaint meant that the hacker was banned from the game for three months, so there was only one way left to shut my mouth — throw my resurrection point into the desert or the mouth of a volcano. Somewhere where I could not talk to anyone and where I'd die again and again until my real body was taken off life support.

"And you, Garth. Do you understand what this means?" I answered his question with one of my own. "They want to kill me, and you are asking for me to give you the skull!"

"You're a dead man already anyway! You won't get out of the game in any case. You're more likely to see the back of your own head than a Scroll of Rebirth! So why don't I earn myself 50 K?"

The necromancer had managed to convince himself that he was doing nothing wrong and maybe he just didn't give a damn, so I shook my head and retreated from the circle of light.

"Just leave me alone, and no one gets hurt."

The necromancer threw a cloud of bone spears at me and charged into the attack.

Death Magic: Immunity

Garth had no idea about my protection from death magic and bet on the wrong card. The bone spears didn't pierce me, paralyze me, or drain my will. They just broke on my chest in streams of gray dust.

However, the hooked staff was a dangerous weapon even in the hands of a necromancer, which was why I stepped forward to meet my opponent and hacked down from my shoulder with the flamberge.

The undulating blade sliced downwards, cutting through the flesh and throwing the necromancer to his knees.

Damage: 65

I hesitated for a moment, unsure about finishing off my opponent, but Garth didn't even think of trying to stop killing me.

A milky white shining ball of energy started to burn between the hands of the necromancer as hoarfrost spread over the ground, but just before he managed to use his Sphere of Cold, I turned around and took his white-haired head off his neck with a single, powerful strike.

His blood gushed out.

Player Garth Deathblade has been killed!
Experience: +311 [1964/2070]
You've have gained a level!

I added another point to Agility and suddenly my vision blurred. I had to prop myself up by leaning heavily on my sword so I wouldn't fall down, but the feeling of sickness refused to let go.

My thoughts were a jumble and I was unable to comprehend what was happening. I couldn't even understand who I was!

And then a system message suddenly appeared and started flashing:

Main Class available!

Main Class available!

Main Class available!

I came back to my senses, opened the menu and couldn't believe my eyes.

† An NPC's Path: Book One †

[…]

Undead, Flesh Eater. Level 10 / Human, Rogue. Level 10

Experience: [1964/2070] [2008/2070]

Strength: 20

Agility: 13

Constitution: 24

Intelligence: 5

Perception: 6

Health: 480

Stamina: 440

Energy: 110

Damage: 60-120

Stealth: +10

Critical damage when attacking in stealth mode, backstabbing or attacking a paralyzed target.

Creature of the Dark: night sight, penalty for being in sunlight, Deathgrip, Aura of Fear, Fearsome Bite.

Neutrality: undead

Immunity: death magic, poisons, curses, bleeding, sickness, cures and blessings.

✝ The Dead Rogue ✝

Both of my characters had merged and my stats were equal to player at level 20! Rogue skills and human speech were available again, but I didn't stop being undead — there was still skin covered with livid spots underneath. However, there were almost no welts and pustules anymore and my mouth had also become much wider for some reason, with suspiciously sharp teeth, as if they had been deliberately filed into shape.

Stop! I wasn't thinking right!

I looked for the button to quit the game, but it hadn't appeared. The technical support hotline also remained unavailable.

Damn it! I was still locked inside the game!

I swore and tried to close the menu. A request demanding that I enter a character name appeared. The old one turned out to have been deleted when the classes were merged.

I smiled wryly and typed: "John Doe". I stepped back from the pool of blood forming around the necromancer and refrained from looting. I wasn't afraid of getting my boots dirty, but I wanted to believe that I was above this. That I'd manage to remain human even in the dead body of a flesh eater.

I rested my flamberge on my shoulder and

strode down the road away from the city. I had no idea where it would lead me, but I was sure of what awaited me at the end.

Scroll of Rebirth, I am coming to you!

Chapter Two
Village Of The Dead

1.

RAIN, DIRT AND PLAGUE.
This was exactly the way the new global event in the world of Towers of Power began, without fanfare or colorful writing in the sky. The Kingdom of the Dead expansion was being added to the game slowly but surely and somehow too realistically. Epicenters of plague appeared here and there as the epidemic struck down whole villages. Unusually, the villagers left their homes en masse and carried the disease

further and further afield. Roadblocks appeared on the roads. Depending on the dark or light alignment of the Lord of the local Tower, the paladins of the Order of the Fiery Hand or the black knights of the Night League tirelessly cut down the diseased, but were unable to affect the situation as a whole.

To add to this, the plague started to infect players as well as NPCs and everyone was trying to decide whether this was an error or the desire of the developers. However, the second option seemed more realistic, considering the fact that the disease would recede immediately after death and resurrection.

I found out the latest news from the game chatrooms, which I'd gotten access to but unfortunately only in read-only mode. There was enough to think about even without chatrooms anyway...

I WALKED THROUGHOUT the night. I was in no hurry to get anywhere; I just wanted to get as far away as possible until Garth returned to the game. I didn't believe that the stubborn necromancer would leave me be for a moment. The price they'd offered him for my skull was just too great.

I would have walked along during the day, as the sky was thankfully covered by heavy clouds and a cold drizzle began to fall, but I was suddenly overcome by a strange apathy. I became afraid. A small, dead man in an open world was like a grain of sand in the universe. Anyone could grind me into dust without breaking a sweat. But I lived! I was alive!

My mind was probably overcome with recent events and it needed a rest. I found some rather thick bushes, crawled inside and froze, as if in a strange trance. I didn't go to sleep, but switched off from the realities of the game. That was when I looked through the chatrooms. When it was closer to evening and I'd continued along the forest road, I came across a dead horse that had had its belly eaten out almost immediately. It smelled absolutely terrible. Even though the sense of smell of a flesh eater was not too great, I started to feel sick.

Or was I feeling sick from hunger?

I shuddered and picked up the pace. The road turned and a cart abandoned in the middle of the forest appeared up ahead.

Abandoned? I had some doubts...

✝ An NPC's Path: Book One ✝

It looked like the owners were lying around somewhere nearby. The sound of muffled growling and the crunching of bones came from the bushes and I froze in midstep, taking my flamberge off my shoulder and clutching its long grip with both hands.

There was a flash of gray among the greenery and I carefully started to retreat.

An encounter with a wolf pack could certainly send me off to be resurrected, so I wasted no time in activating stealth mode and dashed under the wide canopy of a pine tree.

Stealth mode: On
Energy: -1 [109/ 110]

I don't know whether I managed to deceive the wolves or if they just didn't want to leave their terrifying meal, but the predators didn't pursue me. I walked around the cart and returned to the road, noticing a deer that was peacefully munching on a bush. I quietly approached it and slashed it with my flamberge with full force, killing it with my first strike.

Critical hit! Damage: 180

✟ The Dead Rogue ✟

The Spotted Deer has been killed!
Experience: +5 [1964/2070] +5 [2008/2070]

Ah-ha! Experience was divided equally between both classes!

Was that good or bad?

Deep in thought, I wiped the wavy blade of the flamberge on a clump of grass, put it upon my shoulder as usual and returned to the road.

Good or bad? It was probably good, actually. I'd probably have to get almost twice the experience that other players need to rise in level, but I'd rise two steps at the same time. Further along, I'd develop quicker than the others. As far as I could remember, twenty five thousand XP would be needed to get to level 25. Multiplied by two, it would be fifty thousand. I'd also have to honestly earn fifteen times more points to get to level fifty fairly.

Was there a difference? There was. And what a difference!

However, the maximum level of 100 was still there and a character that was at level 50 twice was definitely weaker than a player that reached the top using traditional leveling Due to my lack of access to high level skills, dual classing promised me serious problems down the line, but I decided not to think that far ahead. I would find the Scroll of Rebirth and immediately leave the game. That very moment. Without pause. As if they had barely seen me!

The issue was to find that scroll before the other players. Well, no, I had a great plan which I'd already tested in the skeleton dungeon: while the others would storm the Tower of Decay, I would carefully make my way into the Treasury and steal the scroll. NPCs wouldn't react to me and players had no business being among the dead. It was just that no one knew where the Kingdom of the Dead was and how to get there...

THE RAIN BECAME more intense by the evening, and mud started to squelch under my boots. I stopped trying to go around the puddles — catching a cold was no threat to a dead man, while my clothes were filthy beyond measure anyway. The road twisted between the trees until it entered a field, where I spent a long while in the bushes, observing a village which was built beyond the forest edge. No people could be seen, while the gates were wide open. It was completely silent. No dogs barking and no cows mooing. And a bloated corpse floating in the gutter by the roadside.

A plague village?

I carefully set off down the road, having decided to look through the houses and search through the possessions of the villagers. Money was no use for the dead, but it was to me.

Everything was quiet and peaceful, so I didn't spend any Energy to activate stealth. I was just ready to become invisible at the first sign of danger. I stepped up to the gates and immediately saw a diagonal red cross, the symbol of a plague quarantine.

A dead man shouldn't fear the plague...

As soon as I stepped inside the boundary of the village I immediately felt the cloying smell of rotting flesh. A dead body gnawed down to the very bones lay at the entrance to the village, with a crossbow bolt protruding from its back. Another body lay nearby — this villager hadn't been shot, but cut in half with a heavy sword.

This place had probably been visited by a quarantine unit of the Order of the Fiery Hand and it was only bad weather that had stopped them from burning the village down to the group. They did make attempts to do this — there were fresh burn marks running up the walls...

I nodded, agreeing with my own conclusion and then froze as I noticed a dog with a ragged piece of rope on its neck which had suddenly appeared from somewhere. The dog bared its teeth and growled, with other dogs immediately starting to come out of the doors of the huts.

I immediately dissolved into the shadows, but it was to no avail — the feral curs surrounded me in a circle. The smell! I was betrayed by the smell of my dead body. A smell that had become very much to their taste over the last few days.

Eleven, twelve, thirteen. A devil's dozen dogs!

The first to bound forwards was a rangy looking bitch and I met her with a kick. The steel toecap of the boot broke her spine, as I immediately followed up with the flamberge to interrupt the leap of the pack leader, spraying blood everywhere.

Critical hit! Damage: 168
Bleeding wound! Additional damage: 2

The dog whined and quickly jumped aside.

† The Dead Rogue †

Inspired by my success, I resolutely attached the pack. My long blade sliced downwards to cut a growling dog in half and hacked into the ground.

The ring of dogs scattered and I quickly swung to cut through the legs of a red haired mongrel as it tried to run. The mongrel rolled along the ground, but a huge hound attacked me from behind and sank its teeth into my leg.

I changed my hold on the flamberge to take the grip in one hand and the ricasso, the unsharpened part of the blade above the cross-guard in the other. I raised the sword above my head and drove it violently downwards, pinning the disgusting beast to the ground, killing it instantly. I freed my weapon and stepped towards the gate, but I was too late — I heard the growl of the leader and the whole pack rushed into the attack.

This was when my inexperience in using two-handed weapons made itself known. A normal swordsman could hit several opponents with one swing, strike accurately at vulnerable spots, parry, disarm and even sweep enemies off their feet. I looked like I was swinging around a long steel bar — one attack, one hit. I was slow. Too slow...

A wide swing sliced through the side of a flea-ridden cur, with my blade going to the side, and while I restored my balance two dogs bit and hung on to me at once. One had sunk its teeth into my already bitten leg, while the teeth of the other glanced off the chainmail so it tore at my cloak.

I swayed, barely staying on my feet and then cut through the bitch which had recovered from my first attack. Some other beast then grabbed my left wrist. I didn't manage to fight back against the leader with one hand, so its terrible fangs tore into my throat, immediately sending my Health into the red.

The dog used its weight to bring me to the ground and I didn't even have time to flinch. I was torn apart in an instant.

2.

NIGHT. RAIN. DIRT.

I was resurrected in a ditch, so I forcefully got up from the foul-smelling goo and put the enchanted skull back into my inventory first. Then, I hesitantly checked my stats, but no — I didn't get penalized for death and my experience was still the same.

Anyway, I had something else to worry about — a pair eyes suddenly shone red in the darkness of the night, and then another one!

The eyes of dogs don't shine at night — I had this thought for a moment and then it immediately disappeared. At the end of the day, the walking dead didn't exist in real life either. I got out of the ditch and swung my sword, making a huge hound keep its distance. It jumped away and barked, causing a cacophony of barks to answer from all around.

I had no time to run to the nearest house so I retreated to the gates and used my Aura of Fear ability when the dogs set upon me. The shadows swirled around me and hoarfrost crawled out along the ground. The dogs moved away, but they didn't go far — they just stood around about fifteen feet away. They stopped barking and started to growl, as the wet fur on the backs of their neck rose.

What the hell? Run away!

I looked at the description of the ability I was using and quickly retreated from the pack. Aura of Fear reduced the accuracy and the willingness of an opponent to attack, as well as scaring them away, but the chances of making them panic were slim.

Damn it, my Energy was literally slipping through my fingers!

I backed away through the gates and continued my retreat towards the forest, with the dogs padding along after me. I wanted to turn around and run as fast as I could, but the Aura of Fear perceptibly weighed me down. If I ran, I'd lose concentration and that would be the end of me.

I was walking along and swaying. Swaying and walking along. Understanding fully that I'd never make it to the forest in time. It was too far to the edge and my Energy level was falling too fast.

The dogs kept coming after me. Running, baring their teeth and growling. They were preparing to jump on me and tear me to pieces and that was exactly what they'd do after I stopped scaring them away.

I didn't want to die. I especially didn't want to die several times in a row, but...

I suddenly realized something when the last drops of energy were disappearing. I took the skull out of my inventory, took a swing and threw it towards the forest with all my strength. The skull didn't quite reach the trees, but it bounced and rolled into the bushes.

This was when the dogs attacked!

I kicked the first mongrel away with my heavy boot, caved in the skull of a rabid bitch with the hilt of my sword and sliced into the side of another dog that leaped towards me.

The Maneater Dog has been killed! The Grizzled Maneater Dog has been killed!

Experience: +35   [2029/2070]   +35 [2073/2500]

Rogue: You've have gained a level!

I never even had the time to be happy about my latest level. The dogs jumped on me as if they were huskies attacking a bear, hanging off my arms and legs and then dragged me to the ground, not letting me use my flamberge. Some agile beast managed to reach my throat and sent me off for resurrection.

NIGHT, MUDDY GROUND and the roots of trees.

I got out of a shallow grave, buried the

skull in the fallen leaves and looked around. It was quiet in the forest and no one was following me. My clever trick had made the dogs lose track of me. I spent a while longer lying on the wet grass and then finally calmed down and opened the character stat menu. I increased Agility again, but I didn't improve my Stealth any further, choosing to improve my Dodge skill instead. My Agility was already at level 14, so quite a few hits would miss me now when it was combined with Dodge.

I'd have rather learned the Two-handed Weapon Fighting skill, but that option turned out to be closed. A Rogue used shortswords and daggers, there wasn't much you could do with that... I got off the ground and swore. I no longer had my chainmail on me.

Damned dogs!

The loss made me change my initial plans and return to the edge of the forest. Once I got there, I hid in the bushes and listened. I soon heard a strange chewing sound even though there was no one in the field. Strange.

I entered stealth mode and moved along the trees with my flamberge raised, ready to strike. One step, two steps, hide behind a thick tree trunk. I moved along to the next pine tree and could already see a small clearing by the roadside. That was where the sounds were coming from.

WHEN I LOOKED OUT of the bushes, I saw a huge hound that was tearing into the bloated belly of a corpse. The leader was not accompanied by his pack this time, so it was gnawing the rotting body on its own.

The hound seemed to be completely taken up with its meal of dead flesh, so I decided to take a risk and approached the leader in the hope of finishing the fight with one resolute strike. A critical hit is guaranteed from stealth mode...

Then the hound moved its ears and jumped back from the corpse. He had smelled me!

A charge, a swing and a hit!

The wavy blade of the flamberge flew through the air and cut into the side of the hound, but didn't manage to cause critical damage.

Damage: 115
Bleeding wound! Additional damage: 2... 2...

The hound whined loudly and quickly bounded aside. One of its paws was damaged, but then it still easily dodged my next strike and flew through the air in a high leap. I had no time to parry, so I protected my neck with a raised shoulder.

Its terrible fangs bit into my flesh and the beast hung upon me, pulling me down to the ground. There was no chance to use a two-handed sword in this situation, so I let go of the hilt and smashed my fist into its side, but to no avail.

The hound began to shake its head, worrying at my wounds, and then I surprised myself by biting into its neck. It turned out to be surprisingly easy to bite through its coarse and thick coat of fur and my mouth was full of hot blood in an instant.

Fearsome Bite! Damage: 30
Bleeding wound! Additional damage: 5
Poisoning! Additional damage: 5
Health: +30 [494/504]
Stamina: +30 [462/462]

The hound's jaws went slack and the

hound let go of me and leapt away. Plenty of blood was pouring from its lacerated side and pumping out of the deep wound on its neck. I spat out the chunk of flesh that I had torn from the beast and picked up my sword. The leader jumped, but the undulating blade caught it in its flight and brought it down to the ground.

The Dog Pack Leader has been killed!
Experience: +50   [2079/2500]   +50 [2123/2500]
Undead: You have gained a level!

I exhaled loudly and went over to the roadside, sitting down in the high grass, completely out of strength.

When the level rose, the Fearsome Bite skill got automatically upgraded and I spent a while thinking before I spent the free stat point to raise my Perception. This attribute wasn't just used to find traps and secret places but also affected the accuracy of attacks and the probability of causing critical damage.

The holes that the fangs left in my shoulder were still there, so I set off towards the village without much hesitation, deciding that I wanted to get the chainmail hauberk back no matter what.

I found the armor at the location of my previous battle and heard the barking of dogs by the gates as soon as I put it on.

I flinched with surprise and stepped towards the forest, but then I immediately stopped. Only two dogs ran out of the open gates — a constantly barking bitch and a hound that was just a little bigger than her.

Would I manage? It would be easy!

The barking bitch came out ahead and ran onto the point of the blade by herself. The hound tried to attack my legs, but my Dodge skill saved me. I moved aside just in time and then sliced across its spine with all my strength, cutting it in half.

Both down!

I stepped towards the forest, but then I stopped and looked at the village thoughtfully.

Why don't I clear it out? The experience will definitely come in handy and I can look through the possessions of the dead. If they tear me apart it's no problem. The skull is hidden in the forest. I set off towards the open gates with determination.

⚔ The Dead Rogue ⚔

THANKFULLY, the pack had scattered and the dogs were separated, so they attacked when they could instead of as a group. I only had some bother with a shaggy wolfdog, while the others were no problem to dispatch. I even earned the Dog Slayer Grade 3 achievement by the end of the massacre. It didn't give me any particular advantages, only allowing me to find the most vulnerable parts of four-legged victims. However, something that was a trifle for high level players could be quite a bit of help for my dead rogue...

7.

IT WAS NEARLY MORNING by the time I left the village. I looked through all of the houses first, but I didn't have much loot to show for it. I only found a couple of gold coins and five silver coins as well as a handful of small change. I also took a threatening looking kitchen knife. The damage it caused was not that impressive, but if one of my hands was disabled and I couldn't use the flamberge the knife would be easy to handle.

The rain had already stopped at night and the low clouds started to disperse. I crossed the field in the twilight, dug out the buried skull and went deep into the forest. I walked fast, wanting to make the time I'd lost with the dogs back, so my Stamina soon started to fall. This forced me to lower my pace.

When I reached a crossroads I came across a figure in a dark cloak, so I took the flamberge off my shoulder and slid into stealth mode, but my worries turned out to be unfounded. A blind preacher stood amidst the forest with a clay cup for donations. This was a strange place to collect alms, but this was just a game, wasn't it?

However, that was also the difference, as a lot of things in a game are not what they seem to be at first glance...

I carefully approached so the preacher hadn't noticed the presence of another in some amazing way.

"The times of strife are coming!" he announced hoarsely. "Death has spread her black wings over the world! The prophecy of the return of the Kingdom of the Dead is coming true and none can escape the wrath of the Master of the Tower of Decay!"

I slowed down and asked the preacher, "What do you know of the Kingdom of the Dead?"

✝ The Dead Rogue ✝

Now that my main class was opened again, the skill of human speech had returned to me and I doubted that the blind man could determine that I was a dead man by ear.

"The Kingdom of the Dead is born of love and hate! Once upon a time, the Lord of the tallest Tower of Power lost his wife and firstborn in childbirth and neither Dark nor Light could help him in his plight. For Light and Dark are parts of one whole, which is called Order and death is an essential part of the universe. Only Chaos answered the call of the Lord, but the gifts of that force always have a double bottom. The Scroll of Rebirth could only bring one to life, either the wife or the son. That is when the Lord declared that he'd banished Death from his lands! But where there is no death, there is no life either. His subjects became undead!"

I wasn't interested in a lecture about the history made up by the game plot writers, so I interrupted the preacher and immediately changed to the main thing that interested me.

"Where is the Kingdom of the Dead?"

The blind man seemed not to hear the question.

"The Lord wanted to free the whole world

from death," he continued, carefully going through the plot line, "and then the Gods of Light and Dark had to unite to banish the forces he had called forth. The Kingdom of the Dead was drowned, but the spire of the Tower of Decay has already broken the surface of the Lake of Glory, which has become shallow."

"The Lake of Glory? Where can I find it?"

Instead of answering, the preacher rattled the coins at the bottom of the cup. There was nothing I could do but throw a copper coin there.

Blessing: Immunity

"Where can I find the Lake of Glory?" I repeated my question.

"The days of strife are nigh!" the blind man started again. "Death has spread her gray wings above the world! The prophecy of the return of the Kingdom of the Dead is coming true!"

I didn't listen to his tale for a second time, cursed and strode away. The road twisted between the high trees and sunk in the heavy shadows. As soon as I reached an open space, the rays of the sun expanding above the horizon found their way under my hood and slashed at my eyes. My Perception immediately dropped. The world shrunk to a few hundred feet as my burnt skin started to smoke.

My flesh eater's Health didn't suffer from the sunlight, but my Stamina immediately started to decrease. I covered my face with my hand and returned to the shade of the trees.

Until the sun rises properly and the sunlight stops reaching under my hood, I'd never cross the cornfield. I was lucky that the dogs hadn't torn my cloak to shreds! Only two points of Durability remained...

I didn't waste time at the edge of the forest and trudged back the way I'd come along the road. I reached the crossroads with the preacher and turned in the other direction, but the sun had risen above the trees and started to get to me there as well. Even though its rays didn't get under the hood and burn away my Stamina, the substantial Perception penalty made a dead rogue as blind as a mole. I had to leave the road for a narrow path which went to and fro under the thick crowns of the trees. That's when I got some relief.

The path led me to a sun-drenched clearing as it got closer to midday, so I decided to have a rest and let my Stamina restore itself as it had firmly established itself in the yellow zone by that time. A grassy mound at the edge of the clearing attracted my attention. I walked around it and saw that it was a dark and damp pit-house.

I pulled my head into my shoulders so that I'd not hit the logs of the roof and climbed into the underground shelter. I looked around its bare contents — a table, a bench and a bed hammered together out of thick planks and that was it. There was also a fireplace made from rocks in the corner and a small chest by the table, which was unfortunately empty.

It didn't look anything like a forest bandit hideout and looked more like the home of a hermit. Perhaps it was that blind preacher's?

The bed was covered in some sort of suspicious rags, which was why I decided against lying down on it and spread myself along the wide bench. I felt no need to do so, but it just seemed that my Stamina would be restored a little faster for some reason that way.

I decided to use the time wisely and opened a window with the game forums to study the news about the coming expansion, but didn't find out anything new about the location of the

⸸ The Dead Rogue ⸸

Kingdom of the Dead. However, there were constant mentions of the Lake of Glory. That would've been good, but this body of water was nowhere to be seen on the map. Those on both the side of light and dark were lost in their theories on that account.

Was that bad? Well, it wasn't good, that's for sure.

Still, I had time to level my character. According to the open statistics, the overwhelming majority of active players was between levels thirty and seventy. They could put paid to my dead rogue easy as pie. It would be good to find an appropriate place and carry out a little genocide of the local fauna.

I GOT UP off the bench when the sun started to set towards the horizon. The light coming from outside dimmed and deep shadows extended from the trees. I stopped in the entryway for a moment and carefully looked at the nearby bushes and then stepped aside. As soon as I did that, I heard an unpleasant chuckle from the top of the mound.

I flinched in surprise and spun around, taking the flamberge off my shoulder. The figure of a man seemed to be cut out of a piece of darkness with the bright sky as the background, but that didn't stop me from recognizing him.

Garth Deathblade! He was already at level 17!

When had he had the time to level up?

"Thought you'd run away?" the white-haired necromancer asked mockingly, the air around him sparkling with the blessing he had recently received. "No one has ever escaped me yet! Especially an undead scumbag!"

"Get lost!" I retorted.

Garth just laughed and waved his hand. Through bitter experience, he didn't try to attack me with death magic this time around and used the Summon Undead spell. The earth started to pucker and move, as skeletons climbed out, tearing through the turf with their clawed hands. One, two, three...

Eight! There'd be eight of them, one creature for each of the necromancer's levels!

Even though any remotely accurate hit would easily turn any skeleton into a pile of bones, a gang of the things under the control of a necromancer could easily turn me into a piece of battered meat.

✝ The Dead Rogue ✝

I retreated towards the forest, but Garth predicted this move and immediately cast a Quickening spell on his minions, immediately cutting off any hope of escape. They would catch up with me!

So I didn't run. Instead, I slashed the wavy blade into the skull of the nearest skeleton and broke it in half, smashed another to the side with the hilt and jumped into the bushes. The game log exploded with messages about the damage I received and my health fell almost by half, but I managed to escape being surrounded — all that the skeletons got was some torn pieces of my cloak.

The minions of the necromancer quickly followed, but I'd already activated stealth mode. The skeletons had no supernatural power of detection, so they immediately lost sight of me and started to run through the bushes.

Garth was still there. I couldn't maintain stealth mode for that long because that skill took my Energy too quickly and the necromancer would never give up looking for me. That was the problem...

A confused Garth ran down the hill and broke into the thicket. The necromancer had probably focused on raising his Intelligence, but he could also have raised his perception, so I hid behind a hazelnut tree.

Garth didn't notice me. He looked around and angrily shouted, "I'll still find you, you bastard! You won't get away! You will die, you scum! Die!"

The furious necromancer turned around and walked back to the clearing, angrily breaking off the branches that were getting in his way. I silently went behind him and followed him. My hands itched to use the flamberge, but there was still a risk of catching the long blade on a random branch when swinging it, so I had to choose an opportune moment. It was only when Garth entered the clearing that I sped and up slashed down with my double handed sword at the necromancer with full force. The wavy blade went into his body unexpectedly easily, slicing through his collarbone and several ribs, getting stuck fast in his chest.

Garth's clothing turned the color of blood, as he made choking sounds, trembled and fell on the grass. The skeletons that were following their master fell apart in a rain of bones.

He was done!

I did gather loot this time, so I was soon trying on a nearly new necromancer's robe instead of my cloak and it wasn't even too soaked with blood. It didn't provide any armor and I didn't need the death magic damage bonus, but it had a deep hood which seemed like it was especially made for protecting my face from the burning rays of the sun.

I also took the money. Garth was now definitely a mortal enemy and anything goes when fighting such foes.

He was so cheap that he'd only been promised fifty thousand...

4.

I DIDN'T SPEND too long by the pit-house. The sun didn't shine so strongly now and the necromancer could return. He'd probably been taken to the closest Tower of Power for resurrection, but what if Garth had spent money on a portable altar? It's something he would do.

Having decided to make my tracks harder to follow I didn't follow the path, but instead returned to the road and followed it wherever it would take me. I walked for two or three hours, getting to the middle of nowhere and even started to feel a bit sorry for my choice. However, I didn't have the right character to go into the cities and villages. They'd cut me to pieces.

This was when I really thought of what to do next. Ideally, I should base myself somewhere in the forest and level myself by killing some local animals, but then the stubborn necromancer would be sure to find me. I didn't know what Garth would think of next time, but I was sure he wouldn't give up on his attempts to get my skull.

Understanding this fact made me no less worried than the impossibility of quitting the game. At the end of the day, I had a vague but real chance of getting out using the Scroll of Rebirth, while I could never get rid of the necromancer no matter how much I wanted to. We were all immortal here!

The forest became full of twilight and the evening cool came to replace the heat of the day. Animals got out of the way of a deadman before I reached them, while I hurried to get as far away from the location of my fight with the necromancer and didn't waste time on tracking them. I earned fifty points of experience only once, when I cut down a rabid wolf.

The flamberge showed itself from the best side again — I managed to attack the beast just before it struck, so the animal didn't even have the time to bite me.

I only had to have a little more experience to increase the level of the Rogue, so I started to think about which of the skills to increase — Dodge or Stealth. There was no point in developing anything else.

What sort of burglar could I be with my level of Intelligence and Perception? And what sort of pickpocket? Who would I steal from, the dead? I also had no intention of choosing a one handed weapon as my main yet. Even though my Agility had risen, the focus of rogues was on short blades and critical hits, and the chance to notice a vulnerable area depended exclusively on the level of Perception.

Everything was rather sad with Perception. I did intend to get it up to at least 10, but gradually as a result of my dead side, while planning to increase Agility and Strength when the rogue achieved new levels. I had great Constitution anyway, while Intelligence would have to be left at the current level. That wouldn't be that good in terms of Energy, but there was nothing that could be done here — it was unrealistic to raise all of the stats.

While I was deep in thought, I almost entered a crossroads between two forest roads, but I noticed green smoke floating over the ground just in time and went into the thickness of the forest. I sat down beneath a wide-crowned pine tree and started to think about what to do. Should I go around the crossroads or should I investigate what was going on?

Energy did get restored by itself, unlike Stamina, so I really didn't want to spend it, but it felt too risky to just thoughtlessly plough on ahead. I hid the enchanted skull in a tree hollow inside a dried out oak, activated stealth mode and moved towards the crossroads, but immediately retreated as soon as I glanced out of the bushes at the roadside.

I was lucky enough to have come across an Order of the Fiery Hand roadblock.

I really was lucky, as the fire at the crossroads was being tended by standard warriors and they didn't have any player paladins or high-level NPCs with them. Otherwise they were bound to have felt the presence of an undead...

I quickly returned to the oak, took the skull and strode away. I canceled stealth when I'd gone a few hundred feet through the forest, but then a young bear suddenly appeared from somewhere.

I continued on my way, limping with a lacerated leg. It was good that the flamberge easily pierced the thick fur and I managed to cut the bear down before it could tear me to pieces. I still lost a third of my Health! Of course, I could have used my Deathgrip and heal at the expense of some forest creature, but then I'd lose even more Energy, while I had no chance without stealth!

What a predicament!

It was getting darker, but that caused me no inconvenience as I had a night vision bonus. My dead rogue was great at finding his way at dusk, but I still had to soon get out of the forest onto the road. It just became too annoying to keep avoiding the branches and twigs that kept trying to scratch at my face and poke my eyes out. There were a lot more predators by evening and I'd have to fight my way through soon. That wouldn't be leveling my character, it would be a real battle for survival.

THE ROAD LED ME to a swamp. It ended at a fast flowing river with a swampy field beyond, which was completely overgrown with reeds. The little wooden bridge was burnt and all that remained of it were the tops of the supporting logs which had been dug into the ground.

I could have gotten on to the other side easier without any kind of bridge, but I decided against risking it as I didn't know what sorts of beasts could be lurking in the water. I walked upstream to try and find a crossing but the river narrowed the further I went and it gradually turned into a normal stream. However, there seemed to be no end to the swamp that stretched out ahead. When I saw a log that had been put across the water, I stopped to think.

A path went into the reeds, which would lead me somewhere. Should I risk it? I carefully looked over the reeds and noticed a dark tree looming in the night. A hint immediately went up: Dead Oak.

This was the decider. If a dry tree stuck in the middle of a swamp was given a name, it was probably connected to some sort of quest or important location. It was worth checking out.

I ran across the log to the other side of the

forest and went along the path, with oozing mud immediately starting to squelch under my boots. However, the level of the water didn't rise and I got to the Dead Oak without even getting my feet wet. The tree turned out to be huge, with a moss covered trunk that would have taken several men to embrace. Its dry branches spread out over a large clearing, with no reeds or grass growing in its dark shadow, only dead black earth.

I stood at the edge of the clearing for a little while, and then the shout of a child came from somewhere up above, all of a sudden.

"Help! Help me!"

I didn't get the chance to decide whether to help the child. Three squat silhouettes charged at me over the clearing, bow-legged, covered in wild hair and very, very quick.

Swamp Goblins, came the hint.

In an instant, poisoned needles were flying at me, accompanied by the soft pops of blowguns.

Swamp viper venom: Immunity

I charged into the attack and swept my flamberge down at the nearest ugly greenskin so the blade cut it in half. The tip of the sword got stuck in the ground and while I was freeing it I got two additional poisoned needles in my side. With a wide sweep, I took off the head of the second goblin, but the last of the three, which was a shaman's apprentice, suddenly sprinted towards the Dead Oak. He stopped there, took out a little pipe and started to play a simple melody. Immediately, swamp vipers came from all sides. The snakes couldn't bite through my tough boots, but started to spit venom at me instead of attacking me.

My immunity to poisoning worked again, but my clothing started to quickly lose Durability.

Damn it! This way, I'd soon be left wearing only boots!

I started to stamp on the vipers and hack at them with the flamberge, but more and more of the serpents crawled out of the swamps to replace them. What upset me the most was that I got no experience at all for them!

I decided to ignore the snakes and rushed towards the shaman's apprentice, but the cunning creature decided against facing me and hid behind the oak. I ran after him and ran around the oak several times until I understood that I'd never catch the small and quick creature.

✝ The Dead Rogue ✝

I stopped abruptly and threw myself in the opposite direction, raising my sword to strike in advance.

When the goblin understood his mistake it was already too late, so he literally ran onto my blade.

A moment and he was done!

The vipers immediately stopped spitting venom and slithered back into the reeds, while I raised my head and shouted, "Come down!"

A rope uncoiled as it fell downwards and a scrawny boy skillfully slid down it.

Oh... A scrawny dead boy.

"Will you walk me home?" he asked, as if nothing had happened.

[Escort the dead boy / Attack]

I chose the first option and asked, "Do you know the way?

"It's not far! I 'd get there myself, but there are goblins around here."

The "dead boy" behaved just like he was alive. At least, he didn't have the sluggishness associated with zombies.

"Lead on, then."

✝ An NPC's Path: Book One ✝

The boy coiled the rope, took a huge branch which looked like it must have been cut from the oak and pointed at one of the paths leading from the clearing.

"We need to go there!"

We set off along the swamp and I soon understood that I had no idea at all where I was. The map I called up didn't help me orient myself as the paths were not marked on it. The question was, where could a dead child take me?

Seriously! Perhaps the Kingdom of the Dead? Or...

But no, the strange boy took me to a completely normal village, surrounded by a tall fence. Even though the hour was late, the gates were wide open, with guards crowding around them.

If I was a normal player, I'd think twice before going on ahead, but because I was dead myself, in a way, I had no fear as I approached the gates. The boy slipped inside and then ran as fast as a lightning bolt. The village guards paid him no heed, but targeted me with their crossbows, but looked very unsure doing it and then completely lowered their weapons. The chief guard kept trying to say something and got stuck with his mouth open every time.

The conditions for the quest probably didn't suppose that the boy's escort could be dead or there was an issue with the guards themselves. They were just as dead as I was.

A whole village of zombies? Very interesting. Unfortunately, it wasn't the Kingdom of the Dead at all...

And then another message appeared:

The Escort the Dead Boy quest is complete.
You have received a new quest: Speak to the Elder
Experience: +100
Rogue: You've have gained a level!

I improved my Agility and my Dodge skill, checked my stats and snorted with disappointment. I was missing only a point to get my undead to level 12.

Anyway, it was nothing! There was probably a reason that the Elder wanted to speak to me.

THE ELDER TURNED OUT to be a wrinkled old man with a scraggly beard. He was dead, of course. His dark skin was covered with livid spots, but that didn't surprise me anymore.

"Who are you?" the elder asked as he came outside the gates.

"A traveler," I answered tersely, without hurrying to take my hood off to reveal my face.

"Thank you for your help!" the old man declared. "You can spend the night in our village and no one will harm you.

Village of the Dead: Neutral

I could only just hold back from grimacing unhappily. Neutrality from undead was something I had from the beginning.

Anyway, that wasn't all.

"You could help us, traveler," the Elder continued, "and we would give you all the money we have in our village for your labors"

The offer of the old man made me suspicious, but I graciously nodded.

"Continue."

"The vile goblins of the swamps stole a relic from us and hid it in their caves. They only bring it out under the sun exactly at midday, during the day, when we are powerless. Can you help us?"

"What is the relic?"

"A crystal skull."

I chuckled with interest.

"And what does it do?"

"I will tell you, but later. Do you agree?"

"How will I find it? I don't know these swamps."

The old man took out a scroll with a map.

Do you want to accept the Bring the Crystal Skull quest?

[Yes/No]

"I will help you."

The old man gave me the map and reminded, "Exactly at midday. Have a rest for now."

He turned around as he was about to leave, but I stepped after him and asked, "What happened here?"

"The plague," the old man answered simply.

"People die from the plague."

The old man shrugged.

"Something is changing in this world. Bring

the skull and we'll talk about everything."

The dead old man set off down the street and I looked around. The houses in the village were single floored, with roofs covered with reeds. There were boats by the walls and nets hung upon pillars, but considering their bedraggled state, no one had used them for a long time now. There were no people in the streets and only the sound of a blacksmith's hammer broke the silence from somewhere nearby.

I opened the map and discovered that some new marks had appeared inside the fence: the home of the Elder, the guesthouse, the blacksmith, the tailor, the healer and a shop. Various marks had appeared in the swamp as well. They mainly showed the locations of various monster lairs and they immediately put paid to any desire I had to go beyond the gates at night. It looked like the boy had taken me here using the only safe path.

That didn't matter though. What was the skull the Elder talked about, I wondered? What sort of artifact was it, and how was it connected to what was happening here?

I decided to use my time well and ask the local denizens, but it was as if they had been struck dumb. I almost had to use sign language to communicate with them. Still, I did walk around the village and did a lot of good for myself. The healer sewed up my rib as it was damaged by the bear and restored my Health. I also bought an Energy Restoration Potion that worked on the undead from him. It was incredibly expensive, so all of my savings were only enough for three vials, but there was no point in holding money back — if I successful completed the Elder's quest, all of the money would be returned to me anyway.

I didn't find anything interesting at the blacksmith's. He used to specialize on harpoons and tridents, but made strange looking armor now. His apprentices hammered out arrow bold heads. There were a couple of rather decent daggers on sale, but I didn't waste my last money on them. I was right to do that, as I'd found a baldric for a double handed sword.

I could finally wear the flamberge behind my back!

Next, I walked around the shop, which was lit by the dim light of a candle and looked at the goods. I turned to the trader, who was a pale and thin middle-aged man. A fly crawled across his bald pate, but he didn't notice it.

"Have you been in this state for long?"

"No," he answered curtly.

He still answered though!

I came back to the counter.

"What's the story with the crystal skull?"

The trader just shook his head.

"I know nothing about that."

"And who might know?"

The dead man shrugged his shoulders.

"I would have advised you to talk to master Frederick, but he's disappeared. Talk about this to the Elder."

"Who is Frederick?" I asked with interest.

"A mage who stopped over here a few days before the plague came," the trader answered, and it was impossible to get a single word out of him after that.

5.

I SPENT THE NIGHT at the guesthouse and moved out into the swamp in the morning before it was even fully light. The night monsters had already hidden in their holes by that time and the goblins hadn't yet appeared, either.

The possible appearance of Garth worried me a little, but it was doubtful that he would dare to go into the swamp without a map and I didn't plan to spend a long time in the village. I'd complete the Elder's quest, as him about the Kingdom of the Dead and be on my way.

The path gradually led me to the hills that were surrounded by impenetrable bogs on all sides. I had to go from one landmark to another, and every wrong step threatened me with drowning in black and noisome goo. If I had to run away, it wouldn't be particularly easy.

There were dark holes on the hillsides which led to the underground dwellings of the goblins, but I decided against going in there. The small creatures could provide me with many unpleasant surprises in the low and narrow passages. I climbed on top of one of them instead, lay down in the yellowing grass and stared at the clearing at the foot of the hill. Not a single blade of grass grew there and a charred pillar was dug into its middle.

The map stated that this was the place that the goblins would bring the crystal skull, but they would only bring it at midday.

The sun rose higher and higher and started to gradually push its heat upon me, thankfully the necromancer's robe was great at protecting from its fiery rays and my Stamina didn't burn away. However, my level of Perception noticeably lowered and everything around became fuzzy and lost in the white shining light. This is why I heard the goblins instead of seeing them.

I first heard the distant, ululating sounds of singing and only after that could I see the movement of the high reeds. The swamp goblin shaman that appeared in the clearing was quite short and covered in blue and orange paint from head to toe. He held a spitting torch in his hand and started to use it to burn away any young shoots in the clearing.

The shaman worked slowly and precisely — I got very exasperated and even thought of finding a better position, but decided against hurrying things. I ended up being right — the reeds started to move again and half a dozen goblin spearmen entered the clearing. They made a circle and it was only then that the high shaman with the crystal skull appeared. He was accompanied by two acolytes who were surprisingly strong and wide shouldered for representatives of this swamp people.

The young goblins raised the shaman and he placed the skull at the top of the pillar dug into the middle of the clearing. He then started to move clockwise, without stopping his ululating song for a single moment.

I quietly descended down the hill, slipped into the thick clumps of reeds and changed into stealth mode. Midday was not the best time for stealth, but the swamp goblins were creatures of the night, so they didn't see particularly well during the day. Definitely no better than the undead...

I left my flamberge in the baldric on my back and armed myself with the knife I'd found at the village, smearing its blade in swamp mud so that the blade wouldn't glitter in the sun so much.

The crystal skull shone so much that it was blinding, but the guarding goblins never took their eyes off the holy relic. This is what I took advantage of. I came up to the nearest short creature from behind, clamped one hand over its mouth and stabbed my blade into its solar plexus with the other, immediately dragging its limp body into the thick reeds.

Critical hit! The Goblin Warrior has been killed!

Experience: +25   [2524/3000]   +25 [2658/3000]

Undead: You have gained a level!

As before, my skills were distributed automatically when I reached a new level. I just raised my Perception to 8.

Then I sneaked up on the next guard, but it turned out to be tougher, so I had to stab it with the knife twice.

At least my hand had been clamped hard over its maw, so the ugly greenskin couldn't alert the others with its death screams.

I decided not to take any more risks, went into stealth mode and moved towards the skull at the top of the pillar.

My plan was as audacious as it was simple. I called it my "grab and run" plan, which was why I needed to clear my path of retreat in advance.

The idea of coming up to the pillar, grabbing the skull and losing myself in the reeds without getting into a fight with the goblins was good, but went to the dogs as soon as I came near the entranced high shaman.

✟ The Dead Rogue ✟

He never saw me, as his eyes remained closed, but used some sort of supernatural sense to feel the presence of an outsider and waved his ritual staff. A gust of hot and humid air stripped away the fog of stealth and the shaman's apprentices immediately threw themselves into the attack.

I kicked one away and slashed the other in the face with the knife. I didn't kill either of them, but the time I won was enough to grab the skull and put it into my inventory. Then I was immediately hit in the back by a caustic green blob!

Swamp viper venom: Immunity

The high shaman howled and waved his staff around, conjuring up new enchantments. His wounded acolyte skillfully dived at my legs, grabbed them and sank his teeth into my shin. I stuck my knife into the back of his neck, drew my sword from the baldric and cut down the second acolyte.

The guards immediately charged into the attack.

My chainmail withstood the attack of three

bone points, but the last goblin managed to pierce my left arm with his spear so the flamberge immediately became unbearably heavy and simply impossible to lift.

Crippling hit! Left elbow damaged!

I growled with fury and used my Aura of Fear.

The goblins immediately stepped back and even the high shaman shuddered. However, he didn't stop chanting his spell.

To hell with him! I rushed towards the tall reeds, planning to lose myself in them, but the earth suddenly exploded in damp clumps as a gigantic snake which was as big as an ancient oak burst forth.

A head the size of a small hut flashed above me and a maw full of sharp teeth immediately opened up.

I raised my flamberge, trying to protect myself in vain.

Oh damn...

You have been killed by a Giant Infernal Serpent!

6.

WATER, DIRT, REEDS.

I didn't want to get stuck in the domain of the swamp goblins at all, so I hid my skull as soon as I went beyond them and climbed out of a shallow puddle. I wiped the thick mud from my face and put my enchanted skull away in my inventory. I also checked whether its crystal twin had fallen out, but thankfully it was still in place, just like all of my other items. Only the necromancer's robe had a hole where the blob of poison conjured up by the shaman had hit.

I got to my feet and got out of the clearing which was surrounded by the clumps of reeds and strode off to the village of the dead.

It was getting closer to evening, so the gates of the village were wide open, while the guardsmen hid from the setting sun in the shadows of a canopy. They paid no attention to me whatsoever.

I had no idea what would be the result of returning the crystal skull to the Elder, so I visited the tailor first to repair my robe that had been burnt through by the poison. The dead woman took only two minutes to sew up the hole on the back and restored the Durability of my clothing, even though there was a ten percent penalty compared to its maximum value.

It was cheap and quick, but I was starting to like indestructible items more and more. Nothing ever happened to those deadman's boots I was wearing!

I found the Elder at home. The old man sat at his table and listlessly looked out of the window. His eyes were empty and dead. Nothing unusual for a dead man...

However, when I appeared the old man jumped to his feet and flung up his hands.

"You brought it! You brought it!"

The Bring the Crystal Skull quest is complete.
Experience: +150

I confirmed the obvious.

"Yes, I brought it."

"Praise be to the Lord of the Dead!" the Elder happily declared. "I have a new quest for you!"

"What about the reward?" I reminded.

"I will collect the money, I really will! Don't worry, I will keep my word. You can leave the skull for yourself for now. Yes, you can leave it for now..."

The old man stroked his beard and fell silent, so I broke the silence.

"What happened to those that lived in the village?"

"The plague," the Elder frowned. "We all became ill on the same day and we would have been dead with no return, but the conjurer that arrived managed to hold us at the edge of death. As you see, we died, but not completely. The conjurer gave us a chance."

"And where is he now?"

The Elder shook his head.

"I don't know. Frederick went to the neighboring village to find some sort of artifact, but he disappeared. Then we found out that the goblins got his crystal skull. You must find Frederick and return the skull to him!"

"What for?"

The Elder looked hesitant, but then continued.

"Only Frederick can open a portal into the Kingdom of the Dead. We can't remain here as

---

the paladins of the Order of the Fiery Hand will find a way through the swamps sooner or later and burn the village together with us. We must leave! Can you help us? You're one of us!"

Do you want to accept the Find the Village Conjurer quest?
[Yes/No]

I accepted, of course! I didn't even ask about the reward for completing the quest. Damn it, a portal to the Kingdom of the Dead! This really was something to celebrate!

"Where should I look for your conjurer?"

The old man unfurled the map and drew his finger from the swamps to the forests, tapping a crossroads with a yellowed nail.

"This is where he went, to Pine Log. We used to trade with this village, but we don't anymore."

I opened my own map and made sure that new marks had appeared on it and then asked, "Should I just give the skull back to him?"

"Give the skull back and help him to return."

"What if he is dead?"

✟ The Dead Rogue ✟

The Elder nodded.

"He is dead," he calmly confirmed. "Like all of us. But the skull is the concentration of Frederick's power, it will make him reborn and bring him back to life!"

I chuckled. My undead side had a skull that was nearly the same, but it was not made of crystal, so maybe this was some early work by the developers for some long and complex quest? This was really interesting.

"Will you help us?" the dead old man asked again.

"I'll help you."

I didn't want to waste time before I did the quest so I left the village without waiting for darkness to fall. The last thing I wanted was to have to fight through the restless denizens of the swamp that went on the hunt at dusk. My relations with the local goblin tribe had also been ruined beyond the point of no return.

I felt a little ill when I remembered the beast that had been summoned by the high shaman. Five hundred units of Health in one hit was no joke!

THANKS TO THE MAP, I didn't get lost in the

swamp and reached the edge of the forest when the sun was only just touching the tops of the trees. I didn't dare to go on the road due to the roadblock at the crossroads so I went straight through the forest.

There was no choice here — it would be better to slowly find my way among the trees and risk coming across a bear or a pack of wolves than going to battle with the guards of the Order of the Fiery Hand. Even if I managed to fight back against the normal warriors, the paladins were sure to burn with desire to annihilate the undead creature that insulted them.

No way, no way.

It was still light in the forest, so there were no unexpected meetings. The smaller animals saw me coming in advance and hid among the trees, while I avoided the larger predators myself. This was no time to fight them for experience — I didn't want to die and randomly lose the crystal skull.

I wasn't afraid of getting lost in the forest in the slightest — the Pine Log marker on the map didn't go anywhere. That was the issue though.

It was a village! It was unlikely for them to be happy to see a flesh eater. They were likely to take me for a plague bearer and try to burn me. I didn't want that to happen. However, didn't the fact that the conjurer's artifact had somehow gotten into the hands of the swamp goblins say that the unfortunate Frederick never reached Pine Log? He'd either come across a band of the little greenskins or got stopped by the guards of the Order of the Fiery Hand. He could also have been killed by the villagers, with his body thrown outside the fence where it was looted by goblins. That was also an option.

Whatever had happened, I wanted to first take a walk in the surrounding territories and only try to get myself into the village afterwards.

Once the crossroads with the crossroads with the roadblock was behind me, I went back towards the road and soon came to the roadside. I went on my way, looking at the map of my surroundings as I went and looked for a place where the goblins could have come across the conjurer or his body. The mired river interested me the most, as it began in the swamps. It flowed directly from there, so the ugly greenskins could well have traveled through the domains of men along its banks.

It was a shame I'd never thought to ask the

Elder about this...

The forest soon ended and I found myself at the edge of a cornfield — the one that I'd turned back from before because of the rays of sunlight shining in my face. The sun was now descending beyond the forest, sending long shadows stretching out from the trees. I moved along the edge of the forest under their cover, gradually distancing myself from the road as I'd only get into trouble further along it.

I could come across some men from the village or some paladins. I would then have to somehow try and hide from them in the open field. It would be better to have a look around by the river first. Even if I wasted my time, it would already be dark by then. It is easier to sneak around in the dark.

After drawing my flamberge from the baldric behind my back and laying it upon my right shoulder, I strode through the high grass and carefully looked around, until a narrow path suddenly appeared under my feet. It twisted and turned among the bushes in the right direction, so I followed it.

Could the conjurer have decided to give the field a wide berth as well? He could have... This

---

thought made me feel uneasy. I took the enchanted skull with me this time, as I would be resurrected in this field if I died.

Why didn't I hide the artifact by the village of the dead? I was just afraid — if the goblins found the skull, the little scumbags were sure to drag it away to their bogs. One thing I definitely wanted to avoid was a meeting with their high shaman. Garth could also be looking for me somewhere nearby.

Danger was only a stone's throw away wherever I'd go...

God! How would I get out of here? I hoped I could get out somehow...

The answer to my hopes and fears were the mocking calls of crows.

I tilted my head back and saw black dots circling above the field. They didn't circle over the whole field, but only at its very center. They were landing, taking back off, crowing and going back down again.

Was it carrion that attracted them?

I left the path and walked straight across the field. The tall stalks of corn immediately surrounded me, but the loud calls of the birds helped me walk in the right direction. When I saw fluttering black wings right above my head, I gripped the flamberge more comfortably and went into stealth mode.

After a few strides the corn parted and I found myself in a clearing with a scarecrow standing right in the middle.

A scarecrow? Damn it, it wasn't! It was a crucified man that was attracting the crows here! I knew who the feathered predators were feeding on in advance, so I went to the post that had been dug in the ground.

I saw that my guess was right — it was really the missing Frederick who was hanging there. The flesh on his head had been pecked clean down to the skull and the crows were now cleaning the flesh from his arms.

As soon as I left stealth mode, the black birds immediately rose into the sky and started to circle the clearing, waiting for the man that disturbed them to leave. I was in no hurry to do that though. Neither was I in a hurry to get the crystal skull out.

My attention was attracted by an amulet on the chest of the dead man. I rose on my toes and roughly tore it away, breaking the chain.

What did we have here?

Silver Deadman's Amulet

I immediately received two system notifications:

Deadman's Set: Altered
Deadman's Set: Saved

What was this all about? I opened up the stats of the silver object I had in the palm of my hand and couldn't believe my eyes.

Silver Medallion (Deadman's Set: 3 of 13)
Regeneration of Health, Stamina and Energy: 3% per 10 minutes
Durability: Indestructible
Status: Rare
Restrictions: Undead, Necromancers

Great! Just brilliant!

Energy and Health regeneration was just what I was missing! My Stamina would regenerate faster as well. Killer!

Why did I receive a message about the set being saved though?

I checked the stats of the other items and

saw that the armor and damage dealt by the deadman's boots had grown by one, while the stats of the flamberge had improved even more.

Bloody Flamberge (Deadman's Set: 3 out of 13)

Damage: 8-14

Accuracy: +11%

Chance of causing critical damage: +11%

Chance of causing bleeding damage: 6% for each wave of the blade used in the strike

Bleeding damage: 3 points of Health per second over 2 seconds

Status: Very Rare

Restrictions: Undead, Necromancers

Wow! My maximum damage from a single attack had grown to 130!

The only thing was... When I tried to take the medallion off my neck I couldn't. I could only take it off together with the boots and the flamberge.

Was it an inseparable set? Damn, I needed to be careful with its potential component parts. There were probably more than thirteen. I didn't want to put on some useless rubbish. However...

✟ The Dead Rogue ✟

It was difficult to imagine a situation where I wouldn't take something from the Deadman's Set and just let the artifact lie around on the ground. Normal players could be picky, but not me. For me, it was a question of survival.

Once I realized that I had spent way too long in the inventory, I took the crystal skull out of the bag and came up to the conjurer with it. The artifact noticeably glowed in the dusk.

So what did I have to do with it? Just apply it, or...

"Don't do that..." I heard a soft voice behind my back.

I turned quickly and was absolutely dumbstruck by the sight of a knight in full battle gear. Lamellar armor, bracers, steel knee and elbow guard and chainmail gloves. His head was covered with a closed helm with narrow eye slits and he held a bastard sword in his hands. The long blade glowed slightly orange in the dark. The black-hemmed cloak was also yellow and red. I wished I could sink beneath the ground! This was a paladin of the Order of the Fiery Hand! He wasn't alone either — four crossbowmen stepped into the clearing after him. Argh...

I did still have a chance of survival — the

paladin and the guards were NPCs and the game balance never put players into completely hopeless situations. I was just unsure that this would work in my case...

"Give me the skull!" the knight demanded.

Judging by his calm tone of voice, he hadn't recognized that I was undead yet. He would, though. I only had a few seconds left. And if I couldn't face this battle alone...

I made a sharp turn and raised the hand with the skull to the crucified conjurer and this was the moment I heard the snap of the crossbows of the guards. Two bolts missed, another slid off my chainmail, but the last sank into my hand and knocked the artifact out of my fingers.

The crystal skull rolled along the ground and the warriors bared their shortswords and charged into the attack.

Should I fight them?

I didn't hesitate for a moment, entered stealth mode and ran with it towards the thick rows of corn.

But I had no such luck.

The paladin uttered a word and light shone from the sky, so bright that the whole world was only filled with its limitless radiance. My stealth was ripped to shreds and I was suspended in the air by the dead conjurer, mimicking his pose.

Word of Power: Save Failed
Paralyzed: 2:59... 2:58... 2:57...

On no! Three minutes of immobility!

This was definitely the end of me! More than that, I would be resurrected in this very clearing and it was doubtful that I could do anything against the paladin next time as well. He would kill me over and over again!

The guards of the order surrounded me on all sides, but the paladin didn't hurry with the execution. He returned his sword to its scabbard, took off his helmet and rested it in the crook of his left arm. The knight turned out to be young, with a short, fair haired beard, but there was no hint of softness in his face, while his blue eyes looked at me with genuine scorn. That scorn could also be heard in his voice.

"What manner of beast are you?" asked the paladin.

I kept my silence and the knight didn't need an answer anyway. He drew the silver blade of a dagger from the sheath on his belt, but a new character appeared in the clearing before he had the chance to raise his hand to strike.

"Leave him be!" demanded a female elf with ash-gray skin and a bunch of black hair, fixed in place with stiletto pins.

As I said, the game never put a player into a hopeless situation.

"My capture is just a part of the plot that the NPCs are playing through," I thought for a moment, but the female elf turned out to be a player!

Isabella Ash-Rizt, Drow. Priestess, level 53.

Amazing!

The knight returned his dagger to its sheath, put his hand on the hilt of his sword and told her threateningly, "None of your business, witch! Begone!"

The priestess shook her head and moved towards the paladin. The cloak draped over her shoulders didn't hide her slim waist, while her short iron breastplate and short lamellar skirt could barely serve as reliable protection, but they were great at showing off the lines of her seductive figure. Not very practical, but very, very sexy.

The elf held a staff which was styled after a backbone in her hands, which was slightly bent at the top. An iron skull crowned it.

"None of my business? We'll see about that..." the priestess said and turned to me. "Hey, Kitten, want me to help you get down?"

A system notification immediately appeared:

Player Isabella Ash-Rizt is offering her help Accept*? [Yes/No]

A lot of small print text followed which said that an affirmative answer would lead to taking part in a quest which belonged to another player that was called "The High Priestess of the Mistress of the Crimson Moon" but I had no time to read through it carefully, so I agreed.

"You vermin!" the paladin growled and pulled out his sword. The guards immediately repositioned in a semicircle around Isabella.

Strange transformations suddenly started to happen to the witch. The short breastplate suddenly extended and fused with the lamellar skirt into a single piece of armor, the lace gloves turned into chainmail sleeves and her high boots fully covered her legs. One moment and the elf was covered in armor which only left the head open.

"Die!" the paladin shouted as he charged.

Something demonic showed itself in the pretty face of the priestess. She laughed, and her dark eyes shone with the crimson fires of the underworld.

A Fury!

The elf hit the knight with her staff and the carved bones cracked as they bent and the staff turned into a flail. The priestess' weapon went around the blade of the bastard sword that was raised to parry and the skull hit the paladin in the face, knocking him to the ground. It didn't just knock him down! The steel jaws also tore out a chunk of flesh, sending blood cascading down to the ground.

The power that had crucified me in the air disappeared and I fell, rolling to the side and entering stealth mode. I didn't run away though — I stood up straight and slashed down at the nearest guardsman with my flamberge. His cuirass was cut through and the undulating blade went into his body down to the middle of his chest.

I tore the blade free, but there was no one to fight anymore. The priestess had dealt with the others by herself.

Level 53 and a fury to boot...

The Furies were the battle priestesses of certain gods. When they entered a battle rage they became stronger and faster, but there were few that chose this specialization, because healing skills became unavailable automatically. All types of cleric were mainly valued for their healing abilities.

Isabella's magical armor returned to its sexually aggressive form and the staff straightened out, but the skull remained covered in blood.

"Now then," the drow priestess looked at me with interest, "half the job is done, shall we continue, Kitten?"

"What do you mean?" I didn't understand and I was suddenly happy that I hadn't returned the flamberge to the baldric behind my back.

Isabella screwed her face up in disappointment.

"You accepted my help without reading the

conditions?"

"Um..." I hesitated and then nodded. "Well, yeah."

The elf sighed.

"Kitten, you were really lucky! I am the servant of the Mistress of the Crimson Moon, the goddess of death and rebirth, fury and passion. Your rescue from the claws of the Order must finish with a tantric ritual. Are you happy?"

"Tantric?" I was taken aback.

"Yep," Isabella confirmed, as she had already thrown her cloak to the ground and was working at the clasps on her breastplate. "We'll screw and part ways. Nothing personal."

Sex was not something forbidden in Towers of Power — more the opposite, as only adults were allowed access to the game. I would have happily had some exercise with the sexy priestess in any other situation, but her demand put me into a rather unusual situation now.

"I'm afraid there might be some issues with that," I admitted, pulling back my hood.

When Isabella saw my face and the spots of lividity that covered it, Isabella screwed up her face and said unhappily, "Urgh, an undead"

"It just turned out that way..."

The priestess waved her hand.

"All right, it could be worse. I'll bear it somehow."

"You don't understand. The dead do not have any blood pressure."

This statement of mine seriously worried Isabella.

"Erection problems?"

"No erection at all."

"What about the terminal erection?"

"Not in my case."

The priestess frowned.

"Kitten, are you trying to say that I have spent one and a half years on completing a horribly complicated quest only to come across a useless deadman? Is that what you are trying to say?"

"Try it with someone else," I shrugged.

"I obviously can't wait!" the woman growled and then hit me in the face with the skull on her staff with all her strength.

I also noticed how the skull was getting covered with spikes and then my head just exploded. That is no exaggeration — my brains flew everywhere, sprinkling the corn stalks with red and gray

Sudden attack: Save Failed
You have been killed by player Isabella Ash-Rizt!

7.

DAMP EARTH, DARKNESS and the roots of corn.

I had to spend a while to get out of the shallow grave and then I fell on my back completely drained and swore. Damn it! Why was there some trend to kill me with one hit? I had over half a thousand Health now, after all.

Insane bitch!

I raised myself up on my elbow and then saw a torch light up nearby. A torch? No, it was the skull on the staff of the elven priestess burning with a crimson flame. Isabella stepped up to my grave and hissed at me in a hateful voice, "You piece of carrion..."

I rapidly rolled aside and dove into stealth mode, but it didn't help me get out of the clearing. The priestess waved her staff and the stalks of corn suddenly turned into iron rods, with their leaves turning into razor-sharp blades.

Damn it! The Fence of Steel spell was

supposed to be defensive, but it became a deathtrap in my case!

"I will never retreat!" Isabella declared. "Was one death not enough? No problem! You will die sooner or later, and I'll get the chance to take this task again!"

I shuddered. The stubborn priestess was not joking at all and even if she wouldn't be able to stay in-game forever, I really didn't want to get another mortal enemy. I also simply didn't want to die yet another time!

"Stop hiding!" the elf demanded. "Come on out!"

My Energy was drifting away, but not too fast, so I opened the system menu and glanced through the conditions for my acceptance of help from the priestess. It said that I definitely had to take part in the tantric ritual — there was no getting out of it.

Damn it! What sort of lover could a dead rogue be?

However...

I moved further away from the berserk priestess and left stealth mode.

"Isabella, wait!" I shouted at the priestess as she charged towards me. "I'm a player, I'm on a quest as well!"

My Dodge skill helped me to avoid the attack with the staff, I leapt into the darkness, entered stealth mode and ran to the other side of the clearing.

"I can become alive again!" I told the priestess once I got there. "This is just a temporary state!"

Isabella stopped and stuck her staff into the earth, freeing her hands.

"What're you talking about? What sort of quest can you have?" she asked, putting aside her desire to turn me into a pile of battered flesh for a moment.

"A portal to the Kingdom of the Dead! Can you imagine how much money the first player to get there can make?"

"You're full of it, Kitten!" Isabella curtly replied.

"Want me to invite you? You can read the conditions yourself!"

The priestess hesitated. Her own quest was far more important to her, but getting access to the Kingdom of the Dead before other players was the same as hitting the jackpot!

"When will you become alive?" the elf

✝ The Dead Rogue ✝

asked.

"Is that so important?"

"Damn you to hell!" Isabella said furiously. "You barged into my quest and I can't move along it until the ritual is complete! I want to become the high priestess! I threw away one and a half years for that!"

"I need to get into the Kingdom of the Dead to become alive again," I answered, actually telling her the honest truth.

"Are you definitely a player?"

"Yes!"

"Open your profile!" the priestess demanded. "No, not like that! We'll make a group!"

The request came up — I hesitated a little, but didn't want to make the situation any worse and accepted. Isabella was completely still for a while as she studied my stats and then asked, "John Doe, how did you manage to take a second class?"

"It was an individual quest which I got with my VR capsule."

"A rich Kitten?" Isabella chuckled. "All right, send me an invite. But take note that if you lied about the portal, I will destroy you!"

✝ An NPC's Path: Book One ✝

I wasted no time and sent the elf an invitation to join the "Find the Village Conjurer" quest, and Isabella started to look through all of the logs connected to it.

"I can't believe it!" she said with surprise. "The Kitten didn't lie to me! A portal to the Kingdom of the Dead, how cool!"

Her condescending tone annoyed me, but it was difficult to expect anything else from a player who had a level twice as high as yours.

"What do you need to do with the glass skull?" Isabella asked.

"I think I need to give it to the dead man," I supposed.

"Well, go for it, Kitten! What're you waiting for?"

Player Isabella Ash-Rizt has joined the Find the Village Conjurer quest
Group created. Members: 2

Crystal skull in hand, I approached the dead man who was turned into a scarecrow and the priestess followed. As I approached the dead conjurer, the clear stone in my hands shone brighter and brighter, with its ghostly light soon spreading through the whole clearing, but there was no heat coming from the artifact. My fingers started to get perceptibly colder instead.

I hesitated for a second and then pressed the skull to the chest of the village conjurer and he suddenly started to twitch and thrash around on his cross. Flesh started to grow back onto his head, his eyes lit up with a dark light and then the ropes tying him up started to smoke and he collapsed to the ground like a sack.

"Is he alive?" Isabella frowned and poked Frederick in the ribs with the tip of her boot.

The Find the Village Conjurer quest is complete!
Experience: 80

The crystal skull shone even brighter than before and then slowly melted, leaving only hoarfrost upon my gloves. Frederick groaned as he got to his feet and turned out to be a gaunt middle-aged man with a short black beard and deep-set eyes. He was dead, of course.

"Oh..." he said hoarsely. "I'm back, praise be to the Tower of Decay!"

"A Portal to the Kingdom of the Dead!"

Isabella immediately interrupted him. "Can you open it?"

"Portal!" Frederick looked up and then nodded slowly. "Yes, I can!"

"So go for it!" the priestess demanded. "We're waiting!"

The conjurer shook his head.

"To do this, I need the ritual silver sickle which is stored in Pine Log. I couldn't get it!"

"What was it that stopped you?" Isabella chuckled.

"It is guarded by paladins! Will you help me? But we must act before the sickle is taken to the Citadel of the Order!"

A system notification about a new quest to "Steal the Silver Sickle" appeared and the priestess accepted it for both of us, without even asking my opinion. I had no intention of protesting anyway.

"Kitten, you're a thief, aren't you?" Isabella stared at me. "Will you steal this knick-knack for us?"

"I will, but only if you deal with the paladins."

The elf then turned to Frederick.

"Are you with us, conjurer?"

The dead man made a small bow.

"I will help how I can."

OUR PLAN WAS NOT particularly cunning. Isabella and Frederick had to distract the guards by storming the gates so when the paladins of the Order counter-attacked and left the sickle unattended I'd have a great opportunity to freely enter the elder's house and steal the ritual blade.

It would all have been fine, but I had to take the enchanted skull with me.

I couldn't give it to my random acquaintance to look after!

Could I hide it? Unfortunately, that wasn't an option either.

"I can take down the gates," Frederick announced when we got to the village, after thinking for a little while. "But I can't help you with anything else. We'll meet on the cornfield."

Me and Isabella glanced at each other and the priestess nodded.

"Do it!"

The dead conjurer walked ahead and used a piece of a simple branch to start drawing a summoning circle in the dirt of the road. At first, Isabella just watched his actions with an obvious skepticism and then suddenly rapidly retreated. It was no wonder, as even I felt the energy spreading through the air even though I had no magical abilities whatsoever.

The complicated diagram lit up with ghostly fire as the mud swelled and started to grow into the giant figure of a bloated and slimy earth golem. Frederick shouted a hoarse order and the terrible creation moved out towards the village.

Huge pieces of mud and damp earth fell off it on the way, but the golem still made it to the gates. The magical creature used its whole body to smash into them, sending one door crashing down and making the other hang askew before it shuddered and collapsed into a formless pile of clay. This immediately caused a great commotion in the village — the dogs started barking, the guards started shouting and the distant sounds of tolling bells could be heard through the din.

"The rest is up to you," the dead conjurer declared and disappeared into the night.

Isabella raised her staff and a blindingly bright flame burst forth over her head. I quickly ran aside and hid myself in the bushes.

The first to run out was around a dozen

guardsmen, but the villagers were no serious opposition for the elf. She threw a fireball at them and the explosion threw them to and fro. It didn't kill anyone, it only scared them and forced them to retreat back behind the fence.

"Your time onstage, Kitten!" Isabella said, when two paladins and a dozen guards of the Order of the Fiery Hand came out of the broken gates. "I'll hold them back as long as I can."

The knights charged as the priestess retreated into the darkness. I let the unit go past me and slipped into the village under the cover of stealth. There was a proper mess inside, with militia men hurriedly lining up, children running around and a terrified village elder issuing orders. I was only noticed by chained guard dogs, but no one paid any heed to their desperate barking now.

Frederick had marked the elder's house on the map, so I didn't have to rely on guesswork to find it. The only thing I did do was tried to keep to quiet lanes where the chances of meeting and especially alert militiaman were not so high.

I got away with it.

By the time I'd reached my destination, I'd managed to spend a little more than half of my energy, but I still had three vials held in reserve. More than enough to return. The main thing was to find the sickle.

The side door by the gates was open, so I carefully slipped into the elder's yard. Immediately, a huge guard dog on a chain burst out of the darkness! The dog's attack caught me unawares, so the only thing that I managed to do was turn around and stick my flamberge out in front of me.

This was when my Dog Slayer achievement helped. I noticed a vulnerable spot for some barely perceptible moment and gave the blade a slight turn, so the huge hound literally impaled itself on the blade.

Once I freed my bloodstained flamberge from the body of the impaled dog, I sneaked towards the house, but the backdoor turned out to be locked. Then I started to check the windows. Thankfully, my basic burglary skills were more or less enough to open one of them.

I climbed into a tiny, dusty room, which was completely empty and slipped into stealth mode again, stepping into the corridor only after that. I soundlessly padded through it and carefully looked into the lounge. The ritual sickle glinted silver on some pegs that were hammered into the wall, but something made me freeze in place.

Something was wrong with the room.

My low Perception didn't allow me to fully assess the situation, which was why I simply stood there unmoving. My hands trembled under the weight of my sword which was raised to strike, but I had no issues with my Strength level. It was just a question of concentrating. I forced myself to calm down, and the trembling stopped.

Nothing happened for some time, but then the shadows flickered and parted, as a dark figure in tight-fitting black clothing appeared. The stranger stepped very quietly, and the planks of the floor made no sound under his leather boots. One hand of this agile operator held a shortsword, while the other clutched a dagger. The blades of both weapons were blackened. None of his clothes had a single bright spot either.

A thief? What did he forget here? Had he also come for the sickle? Or was it the other way around?

The stranger stood in the middle of the

room, listening out for something. I could have easily cut into his back, but if I sliced downwards, the blade was bound to get caught on the low ceiling, while a side swing would be impeded by the wall. I had to sidestep, but I didn't want to move.

The dark figure started to turn and I had a sudden sense that made me understand that I was discovered. Or, to be more exact, I would be discovered in an instant!

A side step and a turn with my whole body! The flamberge hit in parallel with the floor and the surprised stranger had no time to do anything. The arm in the way of the strike was simply sliced in half and the undulating blade bit into his ribs.

Critical hit! Damage: 270

The problem was that my opponent stayed on his feet and even stabbed me with his sword!

Damage taken: 40 [536/576]
Poisoned weapon: Immunity

The flamberge was stuck in the stranger's

side, so I used all my strength to yank on it, slicing the blade through his body and widening the wound.

Then I immediately let through an attack on my neck.

It would have been an unpleasant surprise, but bleeding and poisoning were nothing to the dead, while half a hundred points of damage made no real difference.

I threw my opponent back off me by hitting him with the cross-guard of my blade, breaking his nose in the process.

I was about to finish him off, but he suddenly started to run away. The shadows rose and the stranger dissolved in them, but black blood immediately burst forth, running down the door and then the rogue fell out of the emptiness and fell to the floor stone dead.

Bleeding wound! Additional damage: 3
The Order of the Fiery Hand Infiltrator has been killed!
Relations with the Order of the Fiery Hand have changed. Current status: Enemy

Damn it! More problems, but to hell with

---

them!

I tore the ritual silver sickle from the wall and rushed out into the corridor. Someone had already started to shout the alarm in a far room, so I had to scram as fast as I could. Time to run!

I drank one of the Energy Restoration Potion vials and ran towards the exit, but then the infiltrator's dagger clinked under my foot. I had no time to mess around with it, so I shoved it in my inventory, came out into the corridor and rushed towards the room with the window I'd used to get inside the house.

I entered stealth mode and then jumped out into the backyard covered by the shadows and invisible.

It was just in time. Militiamen armed with axes and pitchforks were already running through the open side door.

What was worse is that two of the men had torches with them.

The darkness of the night receded, so I had to hurriedly slip towards the fence. I climbed over it, jumped into the street and stayed still in the bushes for a moment, but everything was quiet all around me.

That was it, time to go!

8.

IT WAS ALREADY DAWN when I reached the cornfield. Isabella and Frederick were waiting for me in the place we'd agreed upon, in the clearing where the crows had recently pecked at the crucified conjurer.

"Did you bring it?" the dead man and the priestess asked simultaneously.

I offered the sickle to Frederick, who carefully examined it and reverently declared, "That's the one!"

The conjurer didn't seem to have lost his strength after the magery by the village, but the priestess had quite a time of it in her battle with the paladins — her hair was singed, while her face was covered with numerous grazes. However, this didn't make the elf any less attractive.

Isabella noticed my interested look and deliberately stood in a seductive pose.

"So, Kitten. Has anything moved?"

"No," I truthfully replied.

"You impotent!" the priestess declared and strode after the conjurer, who was busy with the ties on a sack that was lying by the cross.

Frederick took a black kid goat out of the bag and raised the ritual sickle.

"Hey, is this really necessary?" Isabella asked with a frown.

What an animal lover! I was concerned about something else.

"Wait!" I shouted. "Aren't you supposed to open the portal in your village?"

"No!" the dead conjurer answered curtly as he used a single smooth movement to slash the goat kid's throat with the sickle.

The sacrificial animal dissolved into gray ashes and the weightless dust spun above the ground, went as high as the height of two men and turned into an inverted cone.

"Is that it?" Isabella snorted.

However, Frederick was not finished with the ritual yet. Quickly muttering a complex spell, the dead conjurer started to move in a circle, as the cone above his head started to widen and fill with magical power.

The Steal the Silver Sickle quest is complete! Experience: +350

Relations with the subjects of the Lord of the Tower of Decay have changed. Current status:

✟ The Dead Rogue ✟

Neutral

> *Rogue: You have gained a level!*

Neutral? I almost spat with disappointment. I had neutral relations with all of the undead anyway!

To hell with it. I increased my Dodge skill to level 3, while I put my single stat point into Agility. I started to close the stat window, but then I received a system notification.

> *Choose your specialization!*

Choose my specialization? But my rogue was only level 13! Were my 12 undead levels added to that? Then yes, it did actually come to 25 all together.

The notification kept blinking and I couldn't quite get over my insecurity and open the correct part of the game menu.

Specialization was introduced to make characters more individual and the choice of professions was different for different classes, largely dependent on the stats and skills which the hero had gained by level 25. The majority of players decided on their character development strategy at the generation stage and strictly followed the recommendations of the many guides that were around.

The most popular professions among rogues were those of Assassin, Infiltrator and Ninja, but there were more than enough narrower specializations For instance, there weren't many Pickpockets in the game, but there were many legends about the greatness of their skills.

So what would be offered to a character with high Stealth, beginner Dodge skill and 12 undead levels? What would it be, eh?

I felt ill from my bad premonitions.

The system notification kept blinking for some time, but then changed to a list of available professions by itself. It was a rather sparse list. There were only three choices: Grave Robber, Poisoner and Executioner.

This was the order in which I looked through them.

The Grave Robber turned out to be good. The dead caused it reduced damage, with the addition of resistance to death magic. The Stealth skill had quite a large bonus in dungeons and with a rise in level, there was a greater chance of remaining undetected by undead that had magical senses. However, its main feature was the Anatomist skill.

Having much experience in the dissection of corpses, you have become an expert in the formation of the human body. As it develops, this skill increases the chance of critical hits in melee combat. The multiplier for this damage increases by one. The Grave Robber isn't affected by the immunity of certain types of undead to critical hits.

Wow! If I could use my current multiplier to hit for 280 units of Health, then I would get 420 if I selected this specialization!

The problem was that the rest of the skills of the Grave Robber were of no interest to me. Death magic couldn't harm me anyway, while there was no point for me to hide from the undead. Neutrality, oh yeah. There was also a short blade specialization here, while I had stupidly included a double handed sword in my Deadman's Set. I could stop using the set of course, but...

Whatever, let's keep looking!

Things were no better with the Poisoner. With every new level, the profession received an immunity to increasingly potent poisons while acid damage resistance grew at the same time. The main weapons were poisoned daggers, poisoned throwing knives and pots of poison, while the main skill was the unique Clouds of Death.

You have been so saturated with poisons that you can hide in clouds of poisoned smoke without any damage to yourself. Your victims are unable to see you through them, while every hit will cause critical damage.

Was this any good? Not so much in the open air, but the Poisoner could do such things in enclosed spaces that they would make even high level players feel sick. However, I had an immunity to poisons anyway. There was that issue with the set again too...

What a conundrum.

Anyway, I had to think. All right, and what about the Executioner?

I didn't hold out much hope of this specialization at first and it turned out that I was right. The Executioner killed, but they killed enemies that were already immobile. In this case the critical hit multiplier increased twice over and there was a chance to kill the target with one skill, no matter their health. The chance of a mortal strike was ten percent for an opponent of the same level, while it increased by one tenth of a percent for every level under and decreased in the same way if the target was of a higher level than the Executioner.

That meant that my chance to kill a level 100 player at level 25 was only two and a half percent. I had to make them immobile first as well! A team play character that was not for me. This was a shame, because a specialization in two handed swords and axes was available.

But then I opened the description of the Incognito profession specific skill and I was completely dumbstruck.

Since the most ancient of days, executioners hid their faces behind masks. You are a master of secrecy. Whenever you want, you can hide your name and status from everyone. Only the most observant of the most observant ones can penetrate your secret and most victims will never know who made the fatal strike. But beware — the gods are all-seeing. This skill will not rid you of the mark of the murderer.

Really? You can hide your name and status?

An ideal choice for a player killer who is... undead!

Even if they won't let someone anonymous cross the threshold in many places — who cares! The main thing is that nobody I meet will try to take my head.

Profession selected: Executioner!

The system suggested that I put the available point into the development of profession specific skills and I started to look through the available options — I could either improve Incognito or Execution or I could invest in weapon skills. The icons for the swords, shields and double wielding remained inactive, but the icons for two-handed weapons and single handed short blade fighting were blinking.

I selected two-handed weapons and automatically got the Fencer status, which significantly increased my chances of parrying and also let me choose one of the special moves.

Power Strike let me make increased damage once. Constitution was added to the strength of the character which was used to calculate damage. In addition, fighters had the chance of knocking down their opponents or completely knocking them out.

Quick Strikes was an ideal skill for a dueller. The player was quickened and managed to make three strikes instead of a single full strike, even if they caused half the usual damage. The chance of success here depended on the level of Agility.

All of this would be fine, but I remembered how easily the pack of dogs tore into me and chose Sweeping Strike, which would let me hit several opponents at once. Even though the damage was lowered with each subsequent hit, the fall in the damage depended on the Armor of the targets and the Constitution of the player. It wasn't the best way to combat high level characters, but I could now easily deal with a pack of baying curs.

There were then three branches for the development of the move: Blind Strike, Controlled Strike and Circle Strike, but I didn't read their descriptions for now and opened the updated character stats.

> John Doe, Executioner
> Undead, Flesh Eater. Level 12 / Human,
Rogue. Level 13
>> Experience: [2984/3000] [3028/3600]
>> Strength: 20
>> Agility: 16
>> Constitution: 24
>> Intelligence: 5
>> Perception: 8
>>
>> Health: 600
>> Stamina: 550
>> Energy: 162
>> Damage: 80-140
>>
>> Stealth: +10
>> Dodge: +3
>> Critical damage when attacking in stealth
mode, backstabbing or attacking a paralyzed
target.
>> Professional skills: Incognito, Execution
>> Fencer: Two-Handed Weapons, Sweeping
Strike
>> Creature of the Dark: night sight, penalty for

being in sunlight, Deathgrip, Aura of Fear, Fearsome Bite.

Neutrality: undead, subjects of the Lord of the Tower of Decay

Enemies: Order of the Fiery Hand

Immunity: death magic, poisons, curses, bleeding, sickness, cures and blessings.

Achievements: Dog Slayer Grade 3

Once I'd finished with the character development, I closed all of the system windows and saw that the inverted cone had enclosed the whole clearing. The corn at the edge of the clearing went gray and dissolved, falling to the ground as weightless dust.

Isabella was looking at the portal with obvious fear. In fact, a moment later I understood that it was not fear — it was confusion.

The priestess caught my eye and declared, "It's a one way portal!"

"So what?" I shrugged. "We'll find some way to return."

"You don't understand," Isabella growled. This is a portal from the Kingdom of the Dead. We won't get there."

"What the hell?" I cursed and ran towards

Frederick.

The conjurer was walking around the edge of the clearing, and the power that followed him dried out and dissolved the stalks of corn into dust.

"Conjurer!" I shouted. "You had to open a portal into the Kingdom of the Dead, not the other way around!"

"Had to?" the conjurer laughed. "I don't owe anything to anyone!"

"But the Elder said that the villagers can hide from their enemies in the Kingdom of the Dead!"

"That's exactly what will happen!" Frederick barked in reply. "The Kingdom of the Dead is already here! It has already come, even though the mortals don't understand it!"

"The plague was your doing?" I suddenly guessed.

"Humans will only attain eternity through pain and death!"

Isabella's face twisted and her eyes burned with a malignant fire. The priestess started to transform into a fury and declared fiercely, "You are about to attain your own eternity, you piece of carrion..."

✝ The Dead Rogue ✝

However, the elf didn't have time to deal with the conjurer. A warrior with a rectangular shield and shortsword who was covered head to toe in black armor fell out of the portal. Another dead legionnaire came after him and then more and more. Judging by Isabella's worried facial expression, these were serious opponents even for her.

However, they didn't touch us because of our neutrality.

The legionnaires parted and were followed by strange creatures which looked mostly like armor that had been cut off below the belt. The flying creatures had no legs, with some sort of rags hanging down below instead.

Lost souls. I never even heard of creatures like that...

"Fly to the village!" Frederick commanded them and the flying undead swarm obediently sped away. To add to it, the status of the dead conjurer changed to the foreboding "Death Disciple".

Isabella moved backwards, as if she was about to disappear among the corn, but she noticed me and stopped.

"Bastard! What did you get me into?"

"I didn't know anything!"

"Are you seriously trying to persuade me of that, you piece of carrion?"

"There's nothing I need more than a portal to the Kingdom of the Dead!" I shouted back.

Isabella shook her head.

"I'm leaving."

However, before she could go through with her intention, the first lost souls returned. Each creature brought a villager that was scared to death. The legionnaires took the prisoners and lined them up before the conjurer. They turned undead as soon as he waved his hand.

"See the power of the Lord of the Tower of Decay!" Frederick exclaimed. "Tell everyone of the way his host arrives!"

"If anyone finds out about our part in this," Isabella whispered in my ear, "we will become pariahs." She got herself together and snorted. "But you don't have to worry about that, do you?"

"What are we going to do?" I asked in confusion.

"Let's come back to our original plan," Isabella flashed a dangerous grin. "I am going to batter you until..."

"That won't help!" I interrupted the elf. "I

could actually come back to life!"

"But you need to get into the Kingdom of the Dead to do that?"

"Exactly!"

This was the moment when the lost souls brought another party of prisoners and Isabella fell silent for a while, observing Frederick's activities.

"All right," she said after a while. "Let's try to talk to the conjurer."

The only thing was that the Death Disciple was working non-stop and it was impossible to approach him. As soon as we tried to come near, the dead legionnaires blocked our path. We may have been neutral, but they didn't consider us to be allies.

The sun already began to rise above the forest when the lost souls that had raided the village returned for the last time. They threw their prisoners down to the ground and started to circle the clearing, looking out for danger. I was sure that the army of the Order of the Fiery Hand would be here by midday with the support of Light side players. The cleverest thing that me and Isabella could do was to run away as far as we could...

That was when we heard a child shouting.

"I have seen you!" shouted a red haired child who was being dragged towards Frederick by a dead legionnaire. "I saw how you got out of the dungeon! I will tell everyone where you came from! Save me! Help me!"

Me and Isabella glanced at each other.

"The lad knows where the Death Disciple came from. Maybe he can take us there!"

"He could," I nodded back automatically.

Isabella smiled, baring her tiny and sharp teeth.

"Kitten, the boy is asking for help. Do something! Do it, or I will tear off your useless tool and feed it to Roger!"

The skull on her staff clacked its teeth and it somehow became immediately obvious that the priestess was not joking.

Damn. Out of the frying pan and into the fire.

Chapter Three

Dungeon Of The Dead

1.

CREAK, SPLASH. Creak, splash. Creak, splash.

The wooden blades of two oars descended into the water and rose back up to the regular creak of the oarlocks, spraying droplets that shone in the sunlight, before descending back into the river.

The sun hung overhead and covered everything with its blinding light, glinting off the ripples on the water, making me fidget and pull the hood tighter over my head. The infinitely white glow was everywhere, as if I was in the middle of an overexposed photo. I couldn't see anything at all.

Ah, we dead men are not suited to sunny days. At least the necromancer's clothing didn't let the sun dry me out and even though the fiery rays sometimes touched my skin, the silver amulet that I had taken off the Death Disciple immediately restored the Stamina that was burned away. I'd make it...

It was surprisingly easy to save the talkative boy from being turned undead. All I had to do was forcefully pull him from the arms of the dead legionnaire and the armored walking corpse immediately lost all interest in his prisoner. It was either my neutral status or part of the plot.

That didn't matter! The main thing was that the boy agreed to show us the dungeon that the Death Disciple came from.

"The flood had washed away the riverside there," the red and pock-marked lad reported as he evenly worked the oars. "We went fishing, so we saw how this scumbag was coming out of a hole in the riverbank. What do I mean by a hole? A big cave opened up with a ceiling the height of a man! It was getting dark and we had to come back, so we never went inside. We just found a silver sickle by the entrance. The Elder took it away afterwards. There's no way to get there on dry land, you can only use a boat..."

The boy chattered away without stopping as his scrawny arms easily rowed the oars and the boat quietly floated along the quiet river, getting further and further away from the unfortunate village. What was interesting was that our guide showed no sign of getting tired, while me and Isabella would have long run out of strength had we decided to row instead. I was sure I would have.

Sun! Light! Burning!

I pulled the cloak tighter around myself and squinted due to the unbearable brilliance of the ripples on the water. All I wanted was to go overboard and down to the bottom, into the dark and cold quietness.

Unfortunately I had no chance, if I even tried.

Even though Isabella adopted one seductive pose after another, I was completely sure that she would get me with her staff much faster than I could get into the river. What would I do on the bottom among the waterweeds anyway?

I would grin and bear it.

"So, Kitten, any movement in your pants yet?" the priestess asked, catching my eye.

"There's a child here, by the way," I reminded.

"He will be a well-behaved boy and turned away. So, then?"

"Nothing."

"Useless piece of corpseflesh," the dark elven priestess swore. Immediately, rolling thunder came from somewhere far away and there was such a bright flash from behind us that it outshone the sun for a moment.

I shivered and hunched over even more.

"We got out of there just in time," Isabella said, the dark elven woman's voice only showing relief instead of the usual irony.

Yes, it wouldn't have been too good to be the target of a strike by the Order of the Fiery Hand, considering our complex relations. They would burn us and let the ashes fly in the wind. They would do that to me several times, too.

How did we get into this situation?

I barely stopped a foreboding sigh. Being stuck in virtual reality was already bad enough, but being in the body of a dead man was beyond good and evil!

The wind blew part of the sleeve of my cloak back and even though I quickly pulled it in place, my wrist still started to hiss and smoke when revealed to the sunlight.

Damn it! This was just what I needed.

At least any feelings of pain were at a minimum. Otherwise I would have definitely gone completely mad.

However... Had my former boss hired a sniper, I would have already been taken to the morgue, but I was still moving. Once I got out of here, I wouldn't just testify, I would even invent something of my own to add. Financing Bin Laden? Oh, yes. Something like that!

"Do we still have far to go?" Isabella asked suddenly.

"Are you in a hurry?" I snorted.

"Imagine that!" the priestess gave me an angry look. "My game time limit has almost run out!"

"Aww," I shook my head. "That's a shame."

Isabella looked at the skull at the top of her staff and gave me a nasty smile.

"Roger," she asked her weapon. "Am I

wrong, or is this foul-smelling corpse making fun of me?"

I only snorted in reply. Starting a fight on a boat was a surefire way of ending up in the river. That would have been no problem for me, but dark elves are definitely not taught to breathe underwater.

"We'll get there in about fifteen minutes," the boy reported, without stopping rowing for a single moment. "We can't stop anywhere here, it's a bad place. They'll eat us."

The whiteness of the sunlight drowned all around us. All I could see was the blinding smooth surface of the river, so I trusted the word of the boy. And why not? The developers could well have surrounded the entrance to the Kingdom of the Dead with unpleasant surprises. It wasn't even a question of them being able to do this — they definitely would have done that to make sure that random wanderers couldn't get through.

It felt like we were on a boat trip — floating and floating along. Suspiciously easily. Did we really draw a blank?

I didn't share my suspicions with Isabella though. The priestess was only worried about one thing — to get to the location before she was forcibly kicked from the game when her time ran out.

I decided to use the time usefully and took out the dagger which I took from the infiltrator of the Order that I had cut down. The blade, which had seemed to be entirely black in the darkness was actually red and black. Dark and crimson tongues of flame changed their shapes under the rays of the sun.

I couldn't determine the properties of the weapon and the handle kept slipping from my fingers, no matter how comfortably I tried to grip the hilt.

"What's that you have there, Kitten?" Isabella asked with interest.

"Some loot," I replied, "I took it off an infiltrator."

"Throw it away!" Isabella advised. "None apart from the initiates can use the weapons of the Order."

"What about selling it?" I offered, sounding rather unsure.

"Have you lost your mind?" the dark elf got angry. "Want your head to get torn off?"

I snorted.

"I have "Enemy of the Order" status."

"A tiger may have many enemies, but it will first tear apart those that pull it by the whiskers!"

There was a certain reason in the priestess' words, which was why I decided against arguing with her and threw the dagger in the river. There was a quiet splash of water and the weapon sank to the bottom.

"There!" the boy suddenly shouted. "That riverbank! Look! Do you see that dark gap? That's the cave!"

I couldn't make anything out, but the elf sitting at the front turned around and took a breath of relief.

"Boy!" she asked our guide. "Get on with it!"

By the way, the boy had no name. When I looked at him, the only tag that came up was "boy". A description that was way too short for a key character in a rather important quest.

Damn it! If there was no portal to the Kingdom of the Dead in the cave, Isabella would go berserk and tear my head off. I should lean closer to the river. If all else fails, I'll go to the bottom and sit it out there. I was definitely no opponent for a fury. There was no guarantee that

✝ The Dead Rogue ✝

I would manage to hide in the shadows either. And that damn sun! Well, there was no need to talk of sad things in advance...

WHEN THE BOAT started to scrape its bottom on the gravel and its bow hit the sand, Isabella was the first to jump out and walk away from the water, but she didn't approach the dark mouth of the cave. Instead, she started to draw some sort of complex sign on the wet sand with the end of her staff. A circle, a star and some mysterious symbols...

"Let's go, Uncle John!" the boy pulled on the sleeve of my robe. "It's here!"

"Can't you wait?" I pulled my hand away and asked the priestess, "What are you doing?"

"I am building a portable altar," she explained as she took a glass bottle out of her bag and started to pour some kind of red liquid on the lines in the sand. They immediately lit up with an unpleasant crimson light.

A portable altar was something serious. Players that wanted to make a resurrection point at a place different from the last Tower of Power they visited used single use scrolls or carried raid altars, but highly ranked priests had the ability to address their supernatural patrons personally. This made their lives far easier.

"Dead one, should I include you?" Isabella asked me as she finished off the altar.

"There's no need!" I quickly replied.

The priestess considered me with an intense look and asked, "Will you be able to return to the game in ten hours?"

"I will."

"Right here?"

"Right here," I confirmed.

Isabella whistled.

"You're good at making me intrigued, Kitten! How are you going to get resurrected here, if I may ask? Using a scroll? You should keep it for the future."

"The dead have their own secrets," I chuckled and went into the shadow of the steep riverside.

The sunlight immediately died down and stopped dampening my Perception with its white overexposure. I could hear the quiet splashing of the river, the rustle of the reeds in the wind and the calls of the larks flying over head. The blue sky, the yellow sand and the green leaves.

Ah, that was way better!

"I have ten minutes left," Isabella warned as she left the magic circle. "Shall we look around?"

"Wait," I stopped the priestess. "Take a look at my status."

"What now?" Isabella frowned.

"Is it hard for you?"

Isabella rolled her eyes and read.

"John Doe, Undead."

"Is that all?"

"Level 25 Executioner," then she added. "But that comes after."

"Great!" I went into Incognito mode.

Incognito: Active
Energy: -2 [160/162]

"And now?"

"John Doe, Undead," Isabella repeated.

"Seriously?" I exclaimed and then angrily asked, "Read it again!"

"Ooh," the priestess let out. "Now you're just undead! With no name! But I know that you are you."

"What sort of shit is this!" I cursed and stepped into the deep shadows. The darkness embraced it with its soft cloak, cooling the heat of the day and making the world full of half-tones.

"Unknown!" Isabella shouted, from a distance of at least twenty paces. "How did you manage that, Kitten?"

"It's shit!" I swore as I returned to the elf. "What's the use of this skill if I can't fool a human in the light of day? It's not guaranteed to work at night either!"

The priestess laughed.

"Did I say something funny?" I asked angrily.

"How long has it been since you last looked in the mirror?" she snorted. "Go and take a look at your reflection in the river, deadface!"

"What'd you mean?" at first I didn't understand, but then put my palm to my face.

Incognito didn't create illusions — at least not at the initial level! All it did was close my status and any player that met me saw a dead man, so he would consider me undead. What a complication.

Isabella dug through her bag and gave me Venetian carnival mask covered in green and black squares.

"Try that on!" she offered.

I didn't refuse and put the mask on my face.

"How do I look?"

"Undead," Isabella read out my status. Then she told me, "Hide your hands!"

One of my deaths had put paid to my gloves, so my hands with their livid spots spoiled all of my camouflage. I closed my cloak and hid my hands underneath.

"And now?"

"Unknown!" Isabella replied. Then she stepped up close to me, took a sniff, smiled ruefully and declared "Undead!"

"Oh, whatever!"

The priestess laughed and spoke to her staff, "Roger, the Kitten is offended!"

I took off the mask, but Isabella stopped me immediately.

"Take it!" she allowed. "I can't stand to look at your bloated face anymore! I won't give you any gloves though, sorry. I have none to spare. I would advise finding some quickly, otherwise all you try will be in vain. You should also get some cologne. You still smell like a corpse."

There was no point in getting offended at the sarcastic elf, I just winced in disappointment and put the mask back on my face. It didn't confer any bonuses and it was only decorative, so it can't have been worth much.

The skill had taken ten units of Energy from me, but it was partially restored by the Silver Deadman's Amulet. I went through some math calculations and figured out that I could count on an hour and forty five minutes of anonymity. That also begged the question whether I should invest in Perception instead of Strength and Agility.

The situation could be fixed with vials of Energy Restoration Potion, but both of the unused elixirs had disappeared from my inventory during one of my most recent deaths.

"Kitten!" Isabella snapped me out of my reverie. "Let's go!"

"My name is John," I sighed in reply.

"As you say, Kitten," the dark elf carelessly dismissed me, as she deftly ran across the rocks by the entrance to the cave and looked inside. "Are you coming?"

I swore under my breath and followed Isabella.

Dark elves had night sight, while the deepest darkness seemed to be gray to me as opposed to impenetrably black, so we had no need of torches. After we took a few steps, the intricate stalactites were replaced by roughly worked stone while the tall ceiling was lost in the darkness above as echoes started to reflect from the walls of the spacious dungeon.

When the black space of a gate started to be seen up ahead, Isabella carefully approached its fallen doors and stopped, without walking on ahead.

"They look like they were broken from inside out," she supposed.

"I am sure that we know the one who did this."

The priestess retreated and said, "You know, Kitten, we should come back here tomorrow. It's time for me to leave the game."

We came out onto the riverbank, where Isabella stood in the circle of the altar and immediately disintegrated in a cloud of gray dust that fell to the ground. The lines drawn upon the ground just blinked with a red light.

The sun gradually lowered towards the horizon, but that didn't make its rays burn me any less painfully. To add to that, they kept trying to reach under my hood and poke at my

---

eyes. I returned to the cave and sat in the shadow of the sheer riverbank on one of the fallen stones.

Our guide hadn't gone anywhere and still sat in the boat, catching fish. The boy was held in place by the incomplete quest. But what was it that held me here?

My word?

Why am I waiting for the return of the elf, instead of setting off to the Kingdom of the Dead right now? Was I unsure of my own power? What about undead neutrality?

I still stopped myself from doing something in the heat of the moment. Even though I didn't entirely trust the restless priestess, but I couldn't ignore the fact that I might need her help in the future. It didn't matter if it would be in real life or in-game. Yes, the lesson with the money-hungry necromancer cost me dear, but an important quest connected me to Isabella and she had a direct interest in my rebirth. It would be stupid to lose an ally like that. Stupid and reckless.

As for that ten hour wait... Who said that I'd have to spend that time for nothing?

I didn't want to go through the bushes on the riverside on my own, which was why I pulled the flamberge out of the baldric on my back, took it by the hilt with one hand and by the ricasso with the other. The ricasso was the part of the blade between the cross-guard and sharpened waves of the blade. I tried to do a short thrust, then tried one or two slashes and then swept the blade in a semicircle while activating Sweeping Strike.

Stamina: -100 [450/550]

The hilt nearly flew out of my hands and the point dipped downwards, digging itself into the sand. Damn it!

The two-handed weapon swordfighting skill didn't make me a skilled warrior. I was far better than before, I had a feel for the flamberge, but this was not enough to be the winner in a fight with a relatively experienced opponent. I would have ideally added at least one, or a few points to this skill but I wouldn't be able to improve my profession specific skills due to my undead nature.

I sighed, took a more comfortable grip on the flamberge and repeated the swing. I did it again and again. I didn't activate the special moves anymore, I just tried to choose the correct grip. I soon started to understand how to hold the sword properly, but this intuitive understanding was similar to a feeling of deja vu and was definitely the result of game mechanics. In practice, things didn't always end up best, as weapon skills were developed painfully slowly.

Step, thrust! Stance change, swing! Position change, parry!

A dead character never felt tired, so I was happy to fill my tortuous wait up with something. Especially because I did better and better every time I tried. At least that was how I felt.

Step, feint! Dodge, block! Leap, strike!

I had to control both my hands and the position of my feet and body. The sand around me was soon pitted with the marks of my heavy boots.

Darkness gradually fell. The red-haired boy started up a small fire, put the fish he'd caught upon sticks and started to fry them on the fire.

"Uncle John," he called out to me. "Do you want to have dinner?"

"No," I replied. I made sure that the fire was out of sight of the river behind the rocks and returned to my exercises.

✝ The Dead Rogue ✝

Step, lunge! Turn, diagonal cut! Hand on ricasso, block, hilt push and an immediate short thrust!

The dusk sank into the night and countless stars lit up the black sky.

Their cold light didn't burn me with fire, but gave me strength instead. For a while I simply felt myself separate from the reality of the game and got myself into a trance as I hacked, stabbed and dodged. The sand whispered under my feet, the air whooshed as I sliced through it and my head was empty. No thoughts, only reflexes.

The darkness of the night started to clear gradually and the stars became dimmer as the edge of the sky was painted in shades of light pink. And not a hint of tiredness. The dead never tire.

A system message suddenly came up before my eyes. I flinched and the sword went aside, clinked on a stone and bounced, almost flying out of my hand.

What the hell?

You earned the Tenacious: Flamberge achievement!

I opened the description and chuckled. My exercises with the weapon hadn't gone unnoticed by the game mechanics and gave me a rather perceptible bonus in addition to being more confident with my sword.

Deadman's Bloody Flamberge: +2% to Damage and Accuracy

Any other flamberge: +1% to Damage and Accuracy

Was it only a little? Probably. But it would definitely do no harm, especially at higher levels...

I grew gloomy, took off the mask and spat on the ground.

At higher levels? Damn. I hoped I'd get out of the game before reaching those heights!

My desire for exercise disappeared. I stuck the flamberge in the sand and sat down on the cold stone. The sun became lighter faster and faster and I had to put on the necromancer's robe which I'd thrown on the ground. Here was the new day...

I shivered and slid my palm along the hilt of my flamberge.

✝ The Dead Rogue ✝

I wondered whether anyone else had ever thought of spending so much game time on pointless swinging their blade around.

Suddenly, the lines of the altar drawn by the priestess burned with a red fire and a dark figure appeared in the circle almost instantly. I drew my flamberge from the sand, but my alarm was false — it was Isabella returning to the game.

The priestess went directly to the cave and called out to me on the way, "Are you ready, Kitten?"

I glanced at the boy who was sleeping by the remains of the fire and nodded.

"I'm ready."

"Let's stop wasting time then!"

Isabella was the first to disappear into the hole. I followed her, climbing over a rock lying near the entrance, bent down to avoid the stalactites hanging off the ceiling and stood back up straight in the dungeon with the high ceiling.

"It's probably quite nice here under normal light," flashed through my head.

The fallen gates were ahead. Isabella stopped by them, waiting for me and warning, "We enter together."

"That's fine," I replied and we

simultaneously stepped into a dark corridor with roughly worked walls, an uneven stone floor and a high ceiling.

The priestess paused.

"Strange..." she said with a perplexed note in her voice.

"What's up?" I asked her with alarm.

"There are no system messages!"

"There might be something further along."

Isabella made no reply and carefully looked at the gate we'd left behind us.

"Very strange," she muttered again.

I just shrugged and set off further along, carefully peering into the cloying darkness of the dungeon. The corridor soon became wider and taller and the walls started to reflect the echo of my steps. The cave turned out to be incredibly large.

Something darted right by my face, slid along my cheek and immediately sped away.

Damage taken: 5 [595/600]

What the hell?

I started to turn around and something immediately flew at my back, cut at my neck and disappeared back into the darkness with a scratching sound that receded into the gloom.

I took my flamberge off my shoulder and slashed through empty air. I still earned two more cuts. The damage was low, but I simply couldn't see my opponent! I remembered my exercises and started to spin my blade in a figure of eight, but my invisible antagonist easily overcame my defense and slashed my back. Thankfully, my chainmail defended me from being wounded this time.

"Isabella!" I shouted. "Come here!"

The priestess emerged from the gloom and raised her staff high. A blood-red fire shone from the eyes of the skull and I managed to notice a shadow flying towards me. I cut at it with my sword, but the cluster of darkness easily avoided my blade, caught me on the shoulder and flew towards the priestess.

She had no time to dodge, but she didn't bother. Her staff bent and the jaws of the skull clacked, ending up holding tight of a huge, struggling black bat.

What made me curse was not the size of the dead creature. The light from the shining skull pushed back the darkness of the dungeon and I could see the shadows circling under the high ceiling.

Dozens of shadows. Dozens of bats.

One rapidly dived at me and whipped me with a razor sharp wing while another two or three attacked the priestess, but I had no doubt that the whole swarm would soon attack us.

"Stand still!" Isabella shouted and raised her staff again.

The skull opened its maw and the cave was filled with a bizarre and unpleasant sound, as if a hundred mosquitoes buzzed just under my ear, both piercingly and just at the edge of hearing at the same time.

The coordinated circular motions of the swarm immediately changed into a chaotic struggle, as the bats started to crash into each other, the stalactites and the walls, falling down and convulsing on the floor.

Isabella shot forwards and pushed me in the back, shouting, "Run, you idiot!"

The priestess sprinted through the dungeon while I stopped to kill one of the creatures that was struggling on the ground. Which was why I was late.

As soon as Isabella had disappeared into a

dark hole in the opposite wall, her skull immediately fell silent and the bats started to dive at me one after another yet again, slicing through my flesh with the razor-sharp edges of their wings.

I had to roll sideways and activate stealth mode. I calmly tried to move towards the hole and immediately earned about a dozen cuts! My health immediately fell by fifty points!

Damn! The bats found their way through their surroundings using ultrasound! I couldn't fool them using stealth!

I rushed towards the sanctuary of the corridor and saw a fireball fly towards me. The flame burned several of the creatures over my head, while the others quickly rose up to the ceiling of the cave.

"You're such a cretin, Kitten!" Isabella told me off angrily.

"I'm a cretin?" I argued back. "Look at yourself! A level 53 priestess running away from a bunch of bats!"

"Well, of course!" she snorted. "There's no experience from them, they're just a waste of effort! Enough! Lead the way!"

"Why me?"

"Which one of us is a rogue?"

"I haven't learned to find traps!"

"Walk ahead anyway!" Isabella demanded. "Go! I'll cover you!"

I shrugged and stopped arguing with the priestess. At the end of the day, I would regenerate sooner or later, while there was little point in a priestess with a broken leg.

She didn't know how to heal. What could you ask of a fury?

Roger had completely stopped shining by that time and we kept going in pitch darkness. We kept coming across stones and gravel, but there were no side passages or stairs along the way.

There were no traps either. No flying balls of fire, no falling ceilings crushing us and no spikes coming out of the walls to stab at us.

This was an unusually boring dungeon for a game world...

Were they trying to make us have a false sense of security?

"Hear that?" Isabella suddenly spoke to me in a quiet whisper, breaking the silence for the first time as we meandered through the darkness.

✝ The Dead Rogue ✝

I listened hard and heard something in between the splashing and rustling.

"Is that the flow of water?" I guessed.

"Sounds like it," the priestess agreed with me for once and pushed me in the back. "Get a move on!"

Soon, we saw water streaming down the walls and felt mud squelching underfoot. Large drops began to fall from the ceiling, as if a river flowed above us and then the sound of a spring intensified and we saw a hole in the floor where the excess water disappeared.

I crouched and looked downwards.

"There are steps here!"

"Go first," Isabella replied as she stood by my side.

I put my foot on a stone step which had been smoothed over by water, covered in slime and so slippery that I almost lost my balance and grabbed Isabella's outstretched hand.

One step and then another.

Muddy water started to run down my back. But that held no fear for me. I was more afraid of what awaited us below.

I let go of Isabella's hand and entered stealth mode.

2.

THE SPIRAL STAIRCASE made a few turns and then took us into a narrow room, occupied by short and ugly creatures with greenish-grey faces, large noses and big ears. They all wore leather clothing and were armed with stone hammers and black obsidian blades. Only the largest one of them was the proud owner of a steel helmet, breastplate and pickaxe.

A tag saying "Kobold Leader" lit up.

Stealth mode safely hid me from the underground creatures. I jumped over the hole where the water poured down and sidestepped, trying to occupy a position behind the backs of the ugly beings. However, the kobolds immediately seemed more alert and started to sniff at the air with their noses and move their ears. Remembering the mess with the bats, I didn't rely on the skills of my rogue and charged into the attack, activating Sweeping Strike along the way. And then another sweep, but in a different direction.

The hilt of the flamberge almost got torn from my hands when the undulating blade cut into the kobolds, easily slicing through their leather jacket and aprons, ripping open their flesh and hacking through bones.

The game log exploded with red messages about critical hits and kills. The two creatures at the edge got cut in half. The head of another came clean off and the fountain of black blood from its neck covered the floor and walls. The crossbowman that got away with only losing a hand ran to the far corner, where it fell down, finished off by the bleeding, but the leader survived. It stood in the very center and only caught the strikes when they were significantly weakened, so the flamberge hadn't managed to cut through the iron breastplate.

However, its rusty pick easily pierced my chainmail.

The kobold suddenly lunged and hacked it into my side in the blink of an eye, immediately causing one hundred and fifty points of damage. The leader immediately pulled the pick back, but I managed to catch the haft with my left hand as I smashed the hilt of my sword into its gaping maw with my right.

I was aiming for its teeth, but the leader managed to tilt his head and take the attack on its helmet. This didn't help it at all, however — Isabella came from the stairway and thrust her staff at it, with the pole piercing through the rusty iron of the armor with surprising ease. The kobold immediately turned to dust.

"What a mess you've made here, Kitten!" the elven priestess whistled, as she looked over the kobold bodies which had been hacked to death with my flamberge. "Did any escape."

"No," I replied as I opened the game stat window.

Even though the priestess had killed the kobold leader, I'd earned three hundred points of experience for killing five kobold guards and one crossbowman. This was enough to raise the level of my undead side, which made me question which stat to raise. Strength, Agility or Perception? My Constitution was great anyway and I planned to leave the development of Intelligence till last.

"Kitten!" Isabella called out to me, as she stepped up to the wide open door. "Stop standing around!"

I added a point to my current level of Perception, as I'd decided to get to at least 10 so that I could increase accuracy and the chance of critical hits as well as the level of Energy. The longer I could maintain Incognito, the better.

"Are you sure that none of them got away?" the elven priestess asked in distrust when I joined her by the door and looked out into an empty corridor.

"Is that so important?"

Isabella snorted.

"Revolutionary artificial intelligence" isn't just an advertising slogan. A guard would bring the whole tribe and we would have to waste time on a kobold genocide."

"You don't want fight our way through?"

"No, Kitten, I don't."

"My name is John," I reminded again and stepped through the door first. I sneaked along the corridor, stood at the corner and used stealth mode, but there was no one in the next dungeon, so I decided to stop wasting Energy and continued onwards in the open.

Isabella silently padded after me at a distance of a couple dozen paces. The priestess' staff kept bending slightly, so that the empty eye sockets of the skull never lost sight of me. This made me a little nervous.

One empty corridor followed another and

then a third one stretched out ahead. However, the dungeons were not uninhabited — there were more than enough smudged tracks in the dust, there was a burning smell coming from somewhere and the occasional sounds of muffled blows. We soon passed the empty opening of a well and then came across an abandoned smithy. I got the impression that the landslide on the riverside had uncovered some kind of accidental path into the outskirts of the domains of the kobolds.

Even though the victory by the stairway was easy, I kept alert and always entered stealth mode at every turn. When we started to come across crossroads, the dark elven priestess always spent a while standing still, before selecting one of the underground passages. I had no idea how she navigated, I just obeyed her orders and asked no questions.

We came across a kobold guardsman when we were about to descend to the next level of the dungeon. A short and ugly kobold stood by the stairway, lit up with the glint of torches on the walls. He held an obsidian axe and had the end of a rope going into a hole in the wall tied around his free hand.

✝ The Dead Rogue ✝

"We can't let him raise the alarm," Isabella whispered into my ear.

The priestess was saving her powers for the lower levels, so it was me who had to act. I entered stealth mode and silently crept up to the guardsman. The kobold started to worry and loudly sniffed at the air when we only had a pair of steps between us. It took me a single leap to get to its side, grab the rope and sink my teeth into its scrawny neck.

Something crunched. My mouth filled with hot blood that had an unpleasant taste.

Fearsome Bite! Critical damage! Damage: 80
Bleeding wound! Additional damage: 5
Poisoning! Additional damage: 5

The kobold started to convulse, but I held it close to me, not letting it run away or pull on the rope. The guard tried to get away, but the bleeding and poisoning finished it off and the body went limp.

The bite let me restore my Health and Stamina, but my Energy went into the yellow, which caused me some concern. It was unlikely that the dark elf would let us make camp so that

I'd have time to restore my powers. I just had to pit my hopes on the Silver Deadman's Amulet.

"You eat in such an unpleasant way, Kitten," Isabella noted when I pushed the lifeless body away from me. The priestess herself seemed to be way too clean and fresh when surrounded by the dark and grim dungeon.

I spat the blood on the floor and released the rope leading into the hole, which the guard never got to pull on.

"Come on and keep going!" the priestess demanded and I started to go down the stairs in front of her. I saw that the tunnel mouth was haphazardly blocked up once I reached the bottom, as if the kobolds wanted to barricade themselves from those that lived on the levels below them, but they didn't do it particularly well. The rocks were strewn around and there was a hole in the middle which was easily large enough for a human to squeeze through.

"What's down there?" Isabella asked me as she was covering me from behind my back.

"I can't see anything," I replied and slipped into stealth mode again. I jumped from one rock to another, slipped into the hole and crawled to the other side, quickly stepping aside to the wall to free the way for the priestess.

The dark elf didn't keep me waiting, but as soon as she joined me, there was a scratching sound and then the blockage shook and slid downwards, burying any chance we had of getting out of here the same way we'd come in.

"What the hell?" I swore with surprise.

"Be quiet!" Isabella shushed me, closed her eyes and even put her fingers to her temples. "I have two pieces of news, one good and one bad," she reported after a long pause. "The good one is that the boy was right. We are in the right place."

"What about the bad one?" I couldn't stop myself from asking.

"There are two of them," the priestess sighed, opening her eyes. "If they kill us, there is no way we can come back here. The monsters have also been generated to be our maximum level, as opposed to being in the middle. My level."

I whistled.

"What does that mean for us?"

"You will either die and drag me with you," Isabella shrugged, "or you will gain a lot of levels. If you die, I will kill you another couple of times. Got it?"

The eyes of the dark elf flashed with dark fire and I hurriedly changed the subject of the conversation.

"So why didn't I get any notifications?"

"Set up notifications to show when there is a change to the status of your active quests," Isabella advised, but then waved her hand. "No! Not now! We shouldn't waste time!"

I nodded and set off to reconnoiter. It turned out to be much drier on this level, with clouds of dust rising under our feet and I couldn't make out any tracks on the floor. Every step could activate a hidden trap, but corridor after corridor came and went and nothing happened. There was only the appearance of some scratches on the walls, as if something that was covered with spikes had been moving through these places.

Finally, we came to a pair of doors which had been torn off their hinges and broken down.

"Go!" Isabella quietly whispered behind me.

I entered stealth mode and slipped into the next dungeon as an invisible, ghostly shadow. This was when my foot caught a rope stretched over the floor.

A rope?

✟ The Dead Rogue ✟

I froze, hoping to prevent the trap from working and then carefully drew my foot back, but the rope had stuck fast to my trouser leg and dragged after me.

I immediately heard the rapid patter of claws.

My leg hadn't got stuck to a rope, but to the thread of a spider web!

A gigantic spider in a chitin carapace which was the size of a well-fed boar jumped out of the darkness and immediately charged into the attack. I thrust my flamberge out in front of me and pierced a cluster of compound eyes, but this didn't stop the horrific monster. The cave spider was by my side in a heartbeat and sank its poisoned mandibles into me!

Critical hit! Damage taken: 244 [380/624]
Right knee damaged! Movement speed reduced!

With one hit, the beast had managed to make me lose a third of my Health and almost bit off my leg below the knee!

I grabbed my flamberge by the hilt with one hand and by the ricasso with the other and raised it above my head, planning to pin the spider to the floor, but I didn't make it in time. The skull on the end of the elven priestess' staff smashed into the chitinous side of the spider with such power that it both broke through the shell and threw the monster aside. The spider hit the opposite wall and fell on its back, jerking its legs spasmodically.

"Run!" Isabella growled as she changed into her battle form. Her short armor covered her whole body apart from the head and her face showed its demonic features as her eyes lit up with predatory fire.

I swore as I hopped along on one foot. My cracked knee really got in the way, as well as the spider's filaments stretched out above the floor. I didn't always manage to jump over them, the torn ends often whipped around my ankles and slowed me down, pulling me back.

I heard a rustle in the darkness and saw compound eyes begin to light up.

"Burn in hell!" the priestess shouted, as she sent a ball of wild fire at the underground monsters.

The fireball exploded, throwing more spiders to and fro and burning away their webs, but there was no chance of destroying all of the monsters.

"To the wall!" Isabella screamed, as she cast her next spell very low, just above the floor. The fireball flew through the whole chamber, until it hit a pillar and exploded in droplets of fire that completely burned away all of the threads.

I immediately entered stealth mode, while the elven priestess sprinted towards the far door, jumped through it and shut its rusty iron bars behind her just before the spider that was chasing her.

Her pursuer fiercely clicked its mandibles and then the staff that the priestess thrust through the bars threw it back, as if it were a billiards cue sending a ball into a pocket. The spider rolled away into a far corner and went quiet, while the other cave denizens quickly crawled away in every direction of the dungeon and hid from the priestess behind the stone pillars. They didn't notice me because they couldn't find me without their web of signal lines.

Very, very slowly I moved along the wall towards the safety of the door. Sometimes, I had to stay still in one place for a long time and sometimes I had to move around the spiders or get out of their way. I was afraid of losing my balance and falling most of all, but by some miracle, I reached the iron bars of the door and whispered, "Open up."

Isabella let me in.

"You utterly useless piece of carrion!" she declared, just as I expected.

"Are you serious?" I chuckled, as I sat down on the floor. "Everything here is especially made to be against rogues! Bats that see through stealth! Kobolds that can smell and hear stealthy types! Spiders that catch stealthy characters in their webs!"

The priestess glanced at me from head to toe and sneered.

"The balance developer tried hard. Otherwise a noob rogue like you could have gone through the whole dungeon on his own."

I let out a string of curses.

"Did you get hit hard?" Isabella asked.

"I'll be as good as new in an hour or two," I replied, mentally weighing up my regeneration speed. "My knee will probably be all right before that."

The elf gave me an angry glance and cut me off.

✝ The Dead Rogue ✝

"We can't lose that much time!"

I sighed, rose to my feet with some difficulty and limped off down the corridor. Thankfully, the domain of the spiders didn't go beyond the barred entranceway and there were no webs or scratches left by their spikes on the walls. The passage soon started to angle downwards and we came across empty and rusty torch sconces. I slowed down my pace and started to pay a lot more attention to what was under my feet.

There was little hope of noticing a trap in advance with my level of perception, but I didn't want to give this up to chance. I turned out to be right. A stone cube that was slightly crooked compared to its neighbors soon came before my eyes and as soon as I looked at it intently, the silhouette of a discovered trap appeared.

"Be careful!" I warned the priestess. "Follow right after me!"

There was no guarantee that I would make out all of the traps and there could never be only one, but following each other step by step allowed us to reduce the risk of activating the defensive mechanisms of the dungeon to a minimum.

"All right," Isabella replied curtly. She

deliberately fell behind again and followed me at around ten to fifteen paces away.

I couldn't blame her for that, as I'd have happily let someone else walk on ahead of me. This way, I had to stand still for a moment after every step, expecting the creak of some rusty mechanism underfoot with every movement.

Nothing happened though. We managed to make it to the descent of the next level without any adventures.

The railings around the stairway leading down was made out of human bones, with the eye sockets of the skulls built into the walls burning with a blue fire. They didn't provide much light, but were great at creating a depressing atmosphere.

I started to feel uncomfortable, and you need to try hard to scare a dead man.

There was no better place for traps, but I took my first step on one of the wide marble steps without hesitation. I didn't even hold my breath.

I didn't breathe anyhow.

First step, second step, third step and then the stairs ended unusually quickly and I found myself in the middle of a spacious dungeon with a high ceiling that was decorated by glowing crystals. The uneven walls were covered with cobwebs, but these were normal webs, without the huge lines and sticky ropes of the monsters of the level above.

I stepped away from the staircase and stopped, waiting for Isabella. Suddenly, the wall moved! The cobwebs slid away and the skull of a skeleton that had been immured in the wall came before my eyes. It clacked its lower jaw and suddenly demanded, "Kill me!"

That was exactly what Isabella did. She just cracked the skull with her staff and gray pieces poured down onto the floor. The skeleton shuddered and fell apart into separate bones. I picked up a femur and found that it had been chewed upon by powerful teeth.

"Have you fallen asleep, Kitten?" the elven priestess asked me.

I ignored her and wiped the dust off the neighboring skeleton. It turned out to have been chewed on just as much as the previous one.

"Kitten?"

"There's a layer of ghouls or some other carrion eaters somewhere around here," I told the priestess.

Isabella rubbed at her chin thoughtfully.

"So these aren't just decorations?" she asked.

"I doubt it," I chuckled as I pointed to a mound of bones piled in the corner. They were cracked into pieces and the marrow had been sucked out.

"Well," the priestess sighed, "now we know what awaits us ahead. How's your knee?"

My health hadn't fully recovered yet, but my leg could already bend and the shards of my meniscus no longer crunched with every step. I could move normally.

That's what I told Isabella.

"Onwards!" was what she commanded in reply.

I looked around and moved towards the dark doorway that I could see far ahead. As I passed a stone pillar, the skeleton which was chained to it awakened and asked, "Kill me!"

Isabella immediately fulfilled this request and crushed its time-worn yellow skull.

"What a pest!" she said indignantly.

I got distracted and nearly missed a stone slab which was askew. I took a closer look and saw that it was definitely a trap.

"Walk around it!" I warned the priestess,

while I carefully stepped up to the door and had a look at the next dungeon. It turned out to be a catacomb full of disturbed graves.

The graves were built into the walls and followed one after another in several stacks which rose to the very ceiling. The narrow passages were littered with shards of bone, shreds of shrouds and pieces of stone slabs. It actually smelled of something far nastier than dead flesh here...

I activated stealth mode, took a few strides and then stepped over a trap that I discovered. The scratches on the slabs of the disturbed graves were shocking because of their depth — it was as if someone had deliberately chiseled into the stone.

I got distracted from looking at the floor for only a moment, but that was enough. Something crunched underfoot and I jumped forward, but I still didn't manage to fully avoid the attack. A huge weight fell upon me, something hit me on my head and I got thrown to the floor.

Damn! I somehow got up from the floor and discovered that my head had twisted to the side. This sort of wound would have definitely killed any living character, while I just couldn't move my neck.

"Are you all right?" Isabella asked as she stood still by the slab that had fallen from the ceiling.

"Partially," I gurgled and grabbed my head to turn my face forward, accompanied by the crunch of broken vertebrae. I let go and understood that my neck didn't twist by itself anymore.

Horrible.

I took a step and I suddenly got strongly drawn to the side, as if the wound had also affected my vestibular system. I swayed as I walked a little further and was relieved to find that I could still keep my balance.

"Useless piece of carrion," I seemed to hear from the darkness, but it could have been an illusion. I'm not sure at all that Isabella said it out loud.

However, there is no need to say certain things out loud as they are that obvious. A level 26 rogue, who was actually level 13 was not at all the best companion for walking around dungeons which were generated for characters at level 50!

After taking a few more steps I decided that I had finally gotten used to my ramrod straight and immobile neck, but when I wanted to look under my feet, I bent over too much and almost fell forwards. I swayed, waved my hands and suddenly saw movement in the next passage out of the corner of my eye. I turned sharply, raising my arm to block and almost took the attack of a scavenger on my shoulder!

The rat-faced creature with powerful front paws was no bigger than a child, but smashed into me like a cannonball and easily threw me to the wall.

I backed into the unevenly laid stonework and pushed the scavenger with its open maw away from me.

The long claws that it sank into me tore apart my already bedraggled cloak but powerfully slid off the steel links of my chainmail. The carrion eater that I threw off made an agile turn in the air, landed on its paws and immediately rushed back towards me. I met it with a flamberge attack, but the creature somehow managed to avoid the blade and slash at my face with its clawed forepaw.

My cheek was sliced down to the bone and the game log flashed red — the hit caused double damage. I was enraged, so I used Sweeping Strike and the beast didn't manage to avoid it this time as the blade caught it as it jumped and threw it back down to the floor. I slashed down at it with the flamberge and took its front paw clean off.

"Step back!" Isabella shouted, but I didn't listen to the priestess and slashed the creature's ugly head in half with my next sword strike.

Got it!

Another creature immediately darted towards me from the dark passageway. Diving under my arm, the ratling thrust its clawed paw into the hole left in my chainmail by the kobold's pick and the world went red.

Claws of Darkness. Double damage!
Damage taken: 148 [252/ 624]
Stun: Save Failed! 00:29... 00:28... 00:27...

Stunned? I froze as if I was a statue, unable to move hand or foot!

A ball of lightning hit the scavenger on the back and tore it into pieces, but it made no difference. A squall of ratlike beings burst out of the darkness and they buried me underneath and tore me apart in an instant.

An especially horrible death...

✠ The Dead Rogue ✠

3.

DARKNESS. HEWN STONE. Pieces of bone.

I was resurrected inside one of the side niches and immediately put the skull that I had in my hand back in my inventory. I no longer had my chainmail hauberk. It was either left on my corpse or it had fallen to pieces, having lost the last of its durability. Thankfully, my other items were intact.

I fell off the stone shelf onto the floor and someone whistled in surprise nearby.

"Oh, Kitten, you are so full of surprises!" Isabella drawled. "How did you manage to return to the dungeon? Just don't tell me that you have a portable altar! It's useless down here. I checked!"

I didn't answer the uncomfortable question posed by the priestess and asked one of my own instead.

"Was I gone for long?"

"For around a quarter of an hour," Isabella replied. She had been roughed up rather badly in her battle with the scavengers. "Try to hold out for a little longer next time, all right?"

"I think I'll try."

The dark elf snorted and turned her face away from me, as it was covered with cuts from the slicing of claws. There was a small glowing cloud above her head and a used Scroll of Regeneration lay at her feet.

Isabella suddenly smirked and licked her smashed lips with the tip of her tongue.

"If you are able to get resurrected right here, we can use you for scouting... A bit more actively."

"When I listen to you, it sounds like I didn't do anything!" I replied indignantly.

"You did," Isabella admitted and then started to hurry. "Let's go, we need to burn out the rat nest."

"Are you sure?"

"They have had a taste of you, Kitten," Isabella replied. She winced, adding, "They had a taste of me too. If we don't exterminate them, they'll come at us from behind."

I left the dead end together with the priestess and saw that the narrow passage was covered with scavenger bodies. With body parts and burnt guts, to be more exact.

Isabella spat with annoyance and started to

look for something among the bloody mess. She soon chose a scavenger that was not burnt as badly as the others, took one of the long pins out of her hair and stuck it in the scruff of the dead creature's neck.

The scavenger shuddered, got back up on all fours and started to crawl along the blood-stained floor of the dungeon, its paws moving slowly but surely.

"So you're a necromancer as well?" I asked with surprise.

"I am the servant of the Mistress of the Crimson Moon, Goddess of Birth and Death," Isabella replied and then ordered, "Get moving!"

"Me again?"

"Who else? I'm no tank, Kitten, you need to cover me!"

I couldn't argue with that so I followed the zombie scavenger. We passed the dungeon with the graves and started to see more immured and chained skeletons along the walls.

"Kill me!" one of them asked in the usual way, but I passed it by. I heard a crunching sound behind me and the voice immediately fell silent.

The dead ratling, as my companion decided

to call them, kept crawling along, but it wasn't particularly fast. I easily fell in step with its unhurried movements, following behind and looking around tensely, ready to enter stealth mode at the first sign of danger.

Nothing happened, however. We managed to pass several empty halls unchallenged, but when we reached a fork in the passageways, there was a sudden thud and our guide was hacked to pieces by blades which came out of the wall.

"Damn!" Isabella spat out.

We didn't really need the sluggish zombie anymore anyway. I noticed a hall behind one of the pillars which looked like the scavengers had dug their lair right into the body of the rock.

"What're you waiting for?" the priestess hurried me along.

I got down on all fours and started to make my careful and unhurried way towards the hole. If it was even a little narrower, there would be quite a risk of getting stuck and there was no way to use a flamberge normally here, unless I only used it for thrusting.

The hole gradually narrowed and I would have begun to sweat with fear, but the dead do not sweat. There are many things the dead never do...

Thankfully, the rathole was not too long and we soon came out onto a small stone platform on the wall of a spacious and dark cave. A side staircase led downwards with narrow and uneven steps, but Isabella didn't want to descend.

"Cover me!" she demanded, as she started to do some sort of sorcery. The energy which poured from the hands of the priestess hung in the air in glowing lines, which then came together to form the outline of some sort of complex figure and carried themselves somewhere under the vaulted stone ceiling of the cave. A ghostly cloud started to form there and gradually turn an intimidating shade of crimson. The brighter it glowed, the louder were the sounds of squeaks, scratches and creaks.

"Hold them back!" Isabella growled, her gray face filling with blood and darkening from extreme concentration. Fat droplets of sweat rolled down the cheeks and forehead of the priestess, as her cheeks drew in and her eyes sank deep and started to burn with a dark fire. The same fire burned in the eye sockets of the skull on the staff that she had slung on her back.

I didn't get distracted by Roger or the glow intensifying under the ceiling. I changed my grip on the flamberge and got ready to fight back against the attack. Thankfully, all I needed to do was to knock scavengers off the narrow stairway. Nevertheless, the first scavenger caught me unawares. It took a low jump from the stairs onto the platform and skillfully dodged under the blade of the flamberge, but then got caught by a kick from my boot and flew off downwards.

I heard the echo of a muffled thud and another scavenger appeared. My flamberge took its clawed paw and the retreating creature fell off the platform without outside assistance. The next creature chose an absolutely ideal moment to jump and attacked me when I was only about to raise my sword. The scavenger had quite a good chance to push me off the platform, but I was saved by my Dodge skill. The creature missed and flew into the darkness, almost clawing at Isabella on the way.

"Watch out, you idiot!" the priestess cried out angrily.

A complex pattern could be seen in the glowing cloud more and more clearly. It was like a heater filament that was burning and heating up the vaulted stone ceiling of the cave, but what the elven priestess was planning remained a mystery to me.

I kicked another scavenger off the staircase, but the agile creature managed to rip open my shin. The one that came after literally impaled itself on my blade and started to convulse in agony, pulling my weapon along with it. The hell it would!

Fearsome Bite!

My teeth easily tore the throat out of the disgusting little beast and then stepped on its dead body with my boot to push it off my flamberge as well as throwing some more scavengers off the stairs. The caustic blood made my mouth burn like fire, but I managed to replenish my health and heal the leg that had been clawed down to the bone.

"Let's go!" Isabella suddenly shouted and jumped into the hole first, without waiting for me.

I retreated from the stairway and cast a quick glance at the cave ceiling. I almost went blind from the shining brightness of the cloud of magical energy. The stone had become red hot and the stalactites were cracking, breaking off and flying downwards one after another.

As soon as I could, I slipped into the hole, but a grasping paw caught me by one of my boots and tried to pull me back. I had to turn upon my back and try and fight back with my sword. It was pointless! It was extremely uncomfortable to use a flamberge in a narrow rathole and I started being pulled out of it. Isabella came to the rescue. The strong hands of the priestess took me under the arms and pulled me back sharply. Pulled me back so hard that another of the sharp-toothed scavengers was dragged back inside with us!

The scavenger opened its mouth and I drove the point of the blade into the roof of its mouth with full force so that the bloody steel protruded from the back of its head.

"Let's go!" Isabella shouted into my ear. "Get a move on!"

We really did need to hurry — a natural firestorm had started in the cave. The ghostly cloud exploded in crimson flame and melted granite poured downwards. The long tongue of flame that entered the hole set my torn cloak on fire, but didn't cause any damage, burning away all of the oxygen instead. While the undead are completely fine without air, Isabella was racked with coughs when she fell out of the rathole. As soon as I emerged after her, there was a dull boom behind my back and the collapsed hole breathed out acrid smoke and intolerable heat. One of the scavengers that was trying to catch us ended up crushed by the collapse and let out deafeningly shrill squeaks as it convulsed and bled.

I got up on my feet, raised my sword and slashed downwards right through its scrawny neck.

Execution! The Grizzled Scavenger has been killed!

Experience: +140 [3 619/4 320]; +140 [3 663/4 320]

Undead: You have gained a level! Rogue: You have gained a level!

Excellent! I'd increased my Perception and Agility and then invested my skill point into Dodge. However, it wasn't as easy with the profession specific skills, I had to dig deep into their descriptions. I spent a long time dithering, thinking whether it was better to improve Incognito, but in the end I decided against it. I also decided against learning the moves that became available after Sweeping Strike, choosing Power Strike instead. It would be good to sometimes be able to hit an opponent with the full power of my inhuman Strength.

I distracted myself from my character stats to take a look at Isabella, but she was completely outside the game world. She had probably also earned a level raise after burning the scavenger nest and was now thinking about how to distribute the points she received.

I put my flamberge on my shoulder and walked to the fork in the underground passages, but I didn't spend much time there and returned as I didn't want to leave the priestess on her own.

Isabella soon came to and got on her feet. Her level did actually rise to 54.

"That wasn't too much of a powerful spell that you used, was it?" I asked, as if in passing.

"It is powerful, but very slow," the priestess shook her head. Her face had been cleared of scratches and grazes in some magical way. "In a normal situation, the opponent will attack or run away long before a portal to the infernal plane opens and the rain of fire comes."

"I see."

"Are you ready?"

I gave her a reluctant nod and stepped into the corridor. A skeleton on the wall twitched and barked, "Kill me!" right into my ear.

"I'm fed up!" I swore from the unexpected interruption and knocked the skull to the ground with my elbow and then kicked it as hard as I could with my boot. "What's this all about, anyway?"

"Look under your feet," Isabella demanded, but then relented and decided to explain. "This is probably the spirit of the dungeon. Someone was imprisoned here so they would watch over the groundwater and prevent collapses."

"Oh," I replied in surprise and started to look for traps. However, the ones we came across on the way had all been set off already. From time to time there were the decayed remains of scavengers lying nearby.

We didn't come across any more side passages and then the corridor inclined again, taking us lower and lower. Whenever another skeleton asked for death from the wall I silently strode past and the dark elven priestess would knock off its skull with her staff.

She definitely got annoyed at those skulls.

A ghostly glow soon appeared up ahead and I slowed down my pace and then even entered stealth mode. Isabella fell behind, giving me a chance to scout ahead, but it turned out that there was no need for this precaution. We found the descent to a lower level in a small and round chamber. That was where the pale deathly bluish light was coming from.

"Everything is a bit too straightforward," I grumbled, stopping a step away from the stairway.

"Do you also think that there is a trap up ahead?" Isabella asked.

I shook my head.

"That's not it. It's just a bit... boring or something?"

The dark elven priestess laughed quietly.

"Believe me, there are more than enough locations in this game that are far more complex as well as really exciting quests. The most interesting thing isn't the setting, but the interactions with other players. Battles, alliances, intrigues. Everything is like real life, but without moral limitations. Well, almost without."

I wrinkled my nose.

"I noticed."

"Are you unhappy with something, Kitten?" Isabella narrowed her eyes, thinking that my grimace was related to her.

"Don't worry about it," I said dismissively. "I have no problem with you. This just has nothing..."

"Have you already managed to have a problem with someone?"

"Well, yes," I frowned, as I had no doubt that Garth Deathblade wouldn't even think of leaving me alone. I was sure that the stubborn necromancer would show himself yet. Even though I had an immunity to death magic, there were many other ways to reduce the undead to their component parts.

"You have such an exciting undeath, Kitten!" the priestess laughed and pointed at the staircase. "Come on, get going!"

I entered stealth mode and started to carefully descend to the next level, flamberge at the ready. The staircase led to a gallery that ringed a cavernous chamber with a tall, dome-shaped ceiling. The magical crystals fixed to the walls filled everything with a bluish glow, while the shattered bones of the skeletons from the walls were strewn all around the floor. The scavengers had been here as well.

I bent down to come up to the railing and look downwards. The tall gates on the opposite side of the chamber were blocked by a rockfall, but there was a manhole in the center which was covered with a massive metallic lid. Eight dark figures stood frozen around it. They were completely still, but they were not statues. The remains of scavengers that had risked coming too close to the guardians of the dungeon could be seen well from up above.

I concentrated my eyes and managed to make out enough to see a system message saying "Bone Golem" above the nearest of the figures.

I couldn't see anything else that was dangerous, which was why I turned off stealth mode and returned to the staircase.

"Isabella!" I called the priestess over and she hurried to join me.

"What do you have there?" the dark elf asked, without calling me "Kitten" for once.

"Bone golems," I reported. "Eight of the things."

Isabella placed her back flat against one of

the pillars, looked down and cursed.

"Damn. They are wearing black mithril! I'd have no problem crushing two or three of them, but eight is too much! Can you sneak past them?"

"What's the point? As soon as I start to lift the manhole cover, they'll notice me!"

"True, that," Isabella agreed and then smiled suddenly. "Kitten, we are unbelievably lucky!"

"What do you mean?"

"Neutrality! We have neutrality from the subjects of the Tower of Decay!"

I checked their status and it was true — it turned out that the bone golems were not hostile to us.

"So what are we waiting for?" I replied happily and started towards the closest side stairway, but the priestess stopped me.

"Stop!" she hissed angrily. "Who knows what is coming next? We are at the very end of the way!"

"So, what do you propose?"

The priestess rolled her eyes and raised her hands to place a blessing. The air around her flickered, but nothing happened to me at all.

Blessings didn't work on the undead.

Immunity!

"Piece of carrion!" Isabella grumbled and changed into her battle form. Her armor fully enclosed her body, only leaving the head unprotected. The skull on her staff grew sharp spikes and its empty eye sockets burned with crimson fire.

This didn't seem enough for the priestess, so she appealed to her goddess.

"Mistress of the Crimson Moon, I appeal to thee! Imbue me with thy sacred wrath!"

Nothing happened for a moment, but then a special glow started to come from Isabella and the facial features of the priestess altered to become sharp and predatory.

"Let's go!" the priestess commanded with an unfamiliar voice, as she created a large floating sphere of flame that she then clutched with her hands to create a much smaller but brighter fireball."

It started to become... unpleasant to be by Isabella's side, but I didn't wait around. I put the flamberge upon my shoulder and descended from the gallery first. The golems made no move when I appeared.

✝ The Dead Rogue ✝

They looked far more imposing up close than they did from above. Their ungainly figures were the height of a man and a half and turned out to be assembled from bones, but unlike the skeletons I had seen in the game they were not made mobile by magic but by black metallic wires that played the part of their sinews. The breastplates that protected their chests, their helms with their closed visors and the leaf-shaped points of their spears were made of the same metal. I could see that the golems were composed of different sets of bones which didn't always match, but that made these dark creations look even more brutal.

"There's so much black mithril!" Isabella whistled with surprise.

"Is it expensive?"

"You can't even imagine!" the priestess nodded and hurried me up again. "On you go!"

She was prudent enough not to be in a hurry to approach the golems herself.

The bone golems stood in an even circle. I stepped inside that ominous ring very slowly and carefully. The slits in their visors immediately started to burn with an orange fire and I heard creaking and rasping sounds, but the golems didn't react to my invasion in any other way.

Status? Neutral!

I let out a string of curses in relief. I was spared!

"Go!" Isabella hurried me along.

"Should I open it?" I asked as I turned around when I reached the manhole cover in the floor.

"Go for it!" the priestess waved at me and hurried to my side, passing the circle without any problems.

I returned the flamberge to my baldric, gripped the handle and pulled on the massive manhole cover. That was when everything turned into complete chaos!

The neutrality of the dungeon guardians disappeared as if it was never there and the bone golems readied their spears. There was an immediate deafening explosion and shards of bone and mithril flew everywhere!

Isabella started the tally, but I didn't get any successes to boast of. Once I'd let go of the cover, I activated stealth mode, but the closest monster blindly thrust out its spear before I could make a move and the leaf-shaped point pierced through me to emerge between my shoulder blades.

I immediately lost half of my Health and the serrated blade also held me in place like a fish pierced by a harpoon. There was no getting away!

I understood that I was about to get finished off by one of the other golems, so I grabbed the haft of the spear with both hands and pulled on it with all my strength, drawing my body even further onto it. No one alive would have been able to pull off this trick, but the undead do not feel pain, so I managed to get close enough to the golem to strike at it with my sword, even though that made my health go far into the red.

I pulled my flamberge out from behind my back and swung, using my newly acquired Power Strike ability and activating Sweeping Strike at the last moment as I knew that I would never have the time for a second attack.

My heavy blade swung forward like a blurred line, smashing into the joint of the shoulder guard and slicing diagonally into the black cuirass. The wavy blade reached the middle the golem's chest and the slits in the enclosed visor immediately went dark as a flame started to burn inside the split breastplate and sparks flew out of the breach.

Scythe of Death combo!
Stamina: -300 (316/616)
Structural damage! The Bone Golem Guardian has been destroyed!

I simply had no time to tear the spear that pierced me from the golem's bony hands. Something hit the back of my head and my consciousness dove into impenetrable darkness.

4.

DARKNESS. COLD STONE. Shards of bone.

I was resurrected in the same stone niche as before, but Isabella was nowhere nearby this time. I doubted that she was still in the dungeon quite a lot...

After turning my neck from side to side, I jumped down onto the floor and followed a familiar path to the hall with the bone golems.

"Kill me!" demanded one of the skeletons and I didn't hesitate to crush the talkative skull with the hilt of my flamberge. I was in a foul mood.

I reached the gallery in stealth mode and immediately crouched by the railings, but the surviving golems seemed careless about what was going on up above. Four of the guardians remained. They were all rather badly burned and the mithril sinews of one showed signs of melting, so it stood skewed to its right side.

I cursed. I could never expect to get down to the lowest level without Isabella's support and judging by the drying pool of blood and the hairpins that she must have lost she hadn't run away but went straight to the resurrection point. Even if the priestess had already been resurrected up above, the blockage would stop her from getting back here!

And I... I was stuck in the dungeon! Most probably forever! I would get reborn over and over in a narrow stone niche on the shards of the bones of others.

This thought burned me hotter than fire. I punched the wall with all my strength and then immediately forced myself to calm down and open up the stat window. Unfortunately, even though I received a thousand experience points for killing the bone golem, it was not enough to reach the next level.

So what if I would have done so? There's no way I could beat four golems!

I had to pin my hopes on stealth mode.

I quietly descended from the gallery and warily stood still on the last step, but my invisibility held and hid me from the golems so they didn't notice anything. I approached the spot of dried blood and picked up the pins dropped by the priestess, trying to move slowly and without sudden movements. The guardians remained immobile. However, as soon as I laid a hand on one of the spears they had dropped, with its serrated point, the helms turned towards me in unison. They turned blindly for now, but just a little more and...

I stood stock still and then carefully unclenched my fingers and moved aside. The mechanical guards kept looking at the spear I left behind.

I got away with it...

I sneaked towards the manhole cover, crouched and put both of my palms on the metal handle. If I hesitated, I'd be torn to pieces immediately. My only chance of survival was to pull on the cover as hard as I could and throw myself down the hole before the golems could intervene.

That was exactly what I did. Tore at the cover, jumped and then flew aside with a spear protruding from my side!

"They throw them, too!" was the last thought that flashed through my head a moment before another, more powerful hit sent me to be resurrected.

I TRIED. I tried again and again. At the end of the day, it didn't matter how many times I'd be killed before I managed to slip downwards, but after my fourth attempt it became obvious that I simply had no chance of success. The dungeon guardians were simply too fast.

Could I kill the golems one by one? I tried that too. A Scythe of Death combo from stealth mode should have split one of my opponents in half, but the difference in levels showed itself. These mechanical monsters always managed to parry my flamberge with a spear or bracer or just dodged out of the way with a grace which was unbelievable for such huge creatures. The most I managed to achieve is to scratch their black armors

A complete waste of time...

DARKNESS. STONE. Grave dust.

I got out of the niche and trudged back to the hall of golems like a man condemned. I can't even remember which time around it was. "The game never puts you in hopeless situations", "The game never puts you in hopeless situations", "the game..." spun around inside my head like a mantra.

That much was true. It never did. Never put players in them.

I was not quite a player. And I was definitely not an NPC. Something in the middle.

The usual rules didn't apply to me.

Damn it!

Suddenly, there was a clang under my foot and a spike that jutted out of the wall nearly pierced me right through. My body twisted at the last possible moment, letting the point go past and the steel sting powerlessly rang out against the stones.

I stopped, made myself calm down and continued along, paying way more attention to what was underfoot, but then a skeleton started to twist and turn on the wall.

"Kill me!" it demanded, clacking its lower jaw.

"It's a pleasure!" I replied with fury and raised my sword.

"Not here!" the skull suddenly said. "I'll help!"

I froze with my flamberge upraised.

"What did you say?" I asked, unfazed by the fact that I was talking to a skeleton. "You will help? Help me?"

The skeleton clacked its jaw.

"I'll help you. And then you will kill me."

"Why were you silent before?"

"Little strength. Not enough... Help..."

"Tell me!" I offered.

The skeleton rattled its bones and got to the heart of the matter.

"I will tell you how to go down below and you will kill me. Do you agree?"

Do you want to accept the Kill the Keeper of the Dungeon quest?
[Yes/No]

There was nothing else I could do. I agreed.

"Count the pillars on the right side of the gallery until you reach the seventh one. That's where you will find a burrow dug by the scavengers to the lowest level. You will come out by a sarcophagus that has a secret compartment inside. You will take the bone hook inside and kill the man that is immured in the wall there. You will kill me! But beware the captain of the guard..."

The fires in the eye sockets of the skull started to fade and I hurriedly shook the skeleton.

"Stop! Where's the portal to the Kingdom of the Dead?"

"It's not here..." the skeleton replied and fell apart into a pile of bones. I was left holding a collarbone.

No portal into the Kingdom of the Dead? Isabella would tear me into pieces!

If I ever managed to get out alive, of course...

THE BURROW LEADING DOWN was exactly where the keeper of the dungeon said it was. The burrow was so narrow, that an armored man would hardly have been able to squeeze inside, considering that I found it difficult even though I wasn't wearing chainmail.

It was surprisingly cold at the bottom. The two rows of sarcophagi were covered in hoarfrost, a thin layer of ice lined the walls and pillars inside the crypt and spread all over the floor. The bluish light of the magical crystals provided no heat whatsoever and the glowing rocks were covered by gnarls of ice themselves.

I broke one of them out of a niche in the wall, cleaned the ice off it and discovered that the cold glow didn't come from a magical crystal but from a skull that had been skillfully hewn from a single piece of crystal. It was identical to the artifact that I used to resurrect the Death Disciple.

After a little hesitation, I put the skull into my inventory and switched my attention to the sarcophagi. All apart from one had been disturbed and their stone covers were broken, with chewed bones strewn all around. However, one thing that was interesting was that a crystal skull glowed by each sarcophagus apart from the only one that had escaped undisturbed. A wall niche next to it was empty.

I had a funny feeling that was where the

Death Disciple had come from. He must have taken the magic artifact with him.

I tried to push the lid of the undisturbed sarcophagus aside but it was way too heavy. Just as I used the hilt of the flamberge to crack the layer of ice upon it, I heard the thud of heavy steps. A shadow flashed past. The dark figure of a bone golem appeared in the doorway. The captain of the guard held a curved sword in each hand, with a five-pointed crown upon his head, each point looking like a deadly dagger.

The golem walked between the tombs. I hurried to crouch behind the sarcophagus. When the terrifying monster returned to its guard post, I started to break off the ice much quieter and more carefully than before. After that, I put my back into moving the stone slab, but only managed to move it a little, wary of any traps that might be installed inside.

No, all was clear.

I couldn't see the contents of the sarcophagus through the narrow gap, so there was nothing left to do but to move the stone slab aside a little and steel myself before putting my arm inside. I didn't manage to find a bone hook, but I managed to pull out some sort of complex

✝ The Dead Rogue ✝

golden amulet.

Considering the clinking sounds, there were still many similar things still inside and I could spend an hour taking them out one by one. I was forced to risk attracting the attention of the guard and move the slab completely sideways.

There were no human remains inside the sarcophagus, but it had been filled with all sorts of different amulets. My character's Intelligence was insufficient to work out their properties, so I just put all of my loot in my inventory. The last thing I picked up was a double-edged bone hook which was covered with intricate carvings.

Several system notifications immediately popped up.

Deadman's Set: Altered
Deadman's Set: Saved

What in the name of...? I opened the stats of the predatory looking hook and swore because of the feelings that overcame me.

Soulkiller Bone Hook (Deadman's Set: 4 out of 13)
Damage: 2-4

Special feature: When a wound is opened wider, damage increases exponentially and becomes the same as damage from soul magic.
Status: Unique

Increases exponentially? Damn! This hook would never pierce any kind of normal armor! What was the point of this kind of progression? What would I need this trinket in my set for? Who would I gut with it?

Saying that, the handle of the curious weapon lay in my hand very comfortably both with a standard and reverse grip. It was unpleasantly warm to the touch, however. It was as if the hook was alive, so I hurriedly put it behind my belt. What I mean is that I put it into the second weapon slot. It's not like I would throw it away. I still needed to complete the quest. The damned set also just got saved, too...

I re-armed myself with the flamberge and saw that even though the rust on the blade never went away, some perfectly visible runes had been added to it, while the hilt became decorated with black engravings. Its stats improved yet again.

I guessed that by the time that I'd collected the full Deadman's Set, the flamberge would become a deadly weapon, able to take away four hundred points of Health with one strike.

Not bad. As long as the other parts of the set didn't end up being as useless as the bone hook.

This was definitely not the time to worry about that, so I sneaked towards the entrance to the next chamber. A trail of tracks was left behind me in the rime, but this didn't matter anymore — I could see my target. A man was frozen into the opposite wall, his open eyes looking right at me, as if they could see me through the fog of invisibility.

Perhaps they really could?

A shadow moved by the stairs, as the captain of the guard looked like he was worried by something and looked around the room through burning eye slits. I have no idea why, but I quickly stepped behind a pillar.

That was when I saw Her. Him. It.

A cluster of pure light glittered on a short pedestal and when I saw it, my heart fluttered. Fluttered and started to beat!

I couldn't believe what happened, so I put my hand to my chest, but no, my heart wasn't beating. Something was just trembling and beating in turn with the pulse of the light.

A soul?

Ghostly strands reached from the pedestal to the dead man on the wall, as if the cluster of light was feeding power to the keeper of the dungeon and I couldn't hold myself back. I sheathed my flamberge behind my back, gripped the hook in my hand and ran headlong towards the pedestal.

The golem immediately rushed to intercept me, but I managed to overtake him and grab the shining light which scalded me with its coldness. As soon as I threw myself towards the dead man frozen into the wall, a curved black sword hit me in the back, giving me additional impetus. I ran two more steps and then my legs gave way so I only managed to pierce the chest of the keeper of the dungeon with the point of Soulkiller as I fell. My hand dragged the hook down with me and it ripped open the frozen flesh and ribs with uncanny ease, like a knife through butter.

The burning eyes of the dead man immediately went out and then I saw the second curved sword rise above my head, but the blade never found me. The walls cracked and the ceiling collapsed.

† The Dead Rogue †

This time I was crushed. To a pulp.

SAND. SAND. SAND.

The harder I tried to climb out of the grave, the more sand poured in from above and I risked being buried alive forever, but then someone started to dig me out. The help was very welcome, as it was extremely difficult to get out even like that.

I crawled away from a hole with eroding edges and discovered that I it was the boy guide who helped me get out. Incredibly, the red-haired lad had waited for me and Isabella, even though he hadn't a thing to do here after the collapse of the dungeon whatsoever.

Anyway, was our task even complete?

I called up the latest system notifications and scratched the back of my head in confusion.

The Kill the Keeper of the Dungeon quest is complete.
Experience: +1000
Undead: You've gained a level! Rogue: You've gained a level!

You have received a new quest: Sphere of Souls

And that was it. What the hell?

A kick in my side distracted me from my thoughts. The sharp point of a boot got me right under my ribs and made me flinch and turn towards Isabella, who had silently come up behind me.

"What's going on with the portal to the Kingdom of the Dead?" she demanded.

"Take it easy!" I countered as I jumped back up to my feet and took out a pair of the hairpins that she'd lost in the dungeon. "You lost these."

Isabella took the pins and started to fix her hair. However, she didn't let me distract her.

"What happened with the Kingdom of the Dead?" the priestess repeated.

She wouldn't stop, would she?

I didn't want Roger to have a meeting with my head, so I stepped back from the priestess just in case, pretending that I was looking for a darker shadow.

"Didn't you see the change in quest status?" I asked her with feigned surprise.

"There were no notifications!" the elven priestess assured me. She opened the menu and swore. "What the hell? The Kingdom of the Dead quest is inactive! It's not complete, but it's inactive!"

"What about the new one?"

"I don't have any new quests!" Isabella furiously replied.

I considered whether I really needed the help of this volatile elf, but then decided that I wasn't ready to interact with other players yet and sent Isabella an invitation to join the Sphere of Souls quest.

"Catch!"

The priestess stood still for a moment and then said, "I can't accept! I need to have some sort of shard!"

I hesitated for a moment, but then got the cluster of shining light out of my inventory. Its light was not as intense as it had looked in the darkness of the dungeon, but it was still perfectly visible. Hoarfrost ran along my fingers, freezing my wrist and crawling further on. I have no idea how it would have ended if Isabella hadn't grabbed the artifact out of my hand.

"Kitten, have you lost your mind?" the priestess exclaimed. "You can't take such things without the proper protection!"

I had no idea what it was that had fallen

into my hands, so I had to ask.

"Do you have it?"

Isabella glanced back at me with complete condescension.

"Kitten, I am protected by the patronage of the Mistress!"

"Yeah, yeah," I replied with a frown. "What about the quest?"

"I have already joined you," Isabella replied, "but I still don't understand what it has to do with the Kingdom of..." She suddenly cut herself short and said with great surprise, "It's like that, is it?"

"What?"

"Don't interrupt!" the priestess waved me away as she sat down on the sand.

Considering her distracted appearance, Isabella was busy looking through the game forums or chatting to someone, so I decided not to bother her and worked on my level advances.

As always, it was easier to distribute the points for my undead side. I just increased my Agility by one and everything else changed by itself. My very being changed too. In the same way as before, at levels divisible by five, my undead nature changed and the emotional game mechanics changed me into a Grave Desecrator.

The swelling subsided without a trace and I became rangy, if not to say deathly thin. My eyes sunk even further, while my nails went black and sharp so they looked like the claws of a scavenger. The livid spots didn't disappear completely, but turned into something akin to tattoos and covered my body with dark and thin lines.

To add to all that, I now had a new ability — Claws of Darkness. The very ability that the ratling had used to attack me in the dungeon. Every claw that scratched the victim dealt a base damage of one and also had a chance of paralyzing and stunning an opponent.

Well, now I'd never ever be unarmed!

I started to develop my rogue by increasing Strength and Dodge, but then spent a long time deciding on the profession specific skills as I didn't know which branch I should develop to the detriment of the others. I even decided to raise Incognito, but this skill could only be raised at level 35. After hesitating a little, I chose one of the moves that learning Power Strike had opened up.

Knockout Artist, Crusher and Wallbreaker

allowed a character to knock an opponent off their feet, disarm them and break shields and armor, but I preferred Power Lunge to all of those as it was aimed at making penetrating hits.

If I was to stick my flamberge into someone's belly, there would be lots of critical damage as the blade was double-edged and the blade had waves on both sides!

John Doe, Executioner
Undead, Grave Desecrator. Level 15 / Human, Rogue. Level 15
Experience: [4 619/ 5 184] [4 663/ 5 184]
Strength: 21
Agility: 18
Constitution: 24
Intelligence: 5
Perception: 10

Health: 720
Stamina: 675
Energy: 225
Damage: 119-176

Stealth: +10
Dodge: +5

✝ The Dead Rogue ✝

Critical damage when attacking in stealth mode, backstabbing or attacking a paralyzed target.

Professional skills: Incognito, Execution

Fencer: Two-Handed Weapons, Sweeping Strike, Power Strike, Power Lunge

Creature of the Dark: night sight, penalty for being in sunlight, Deathgrip, Aura of Fear, Fearsome Bite, Claws of Darkness

Neutrality: undead, subjects of the Lord of the Tower of Decay

Enemies: Order of the Fiery Hand

Immunity: death magic, poisons, curses, bleeding, sickness, cures and blessings.

Achievements: Dog Slayer Grade 3, Tenacious

After figuring out my level raises, I felt much more sure of myself. It was level thirty, if it was considered as a whole! The sun also blinded me a little less. So I would keep fighting on...

Isabella was taking a really long time figuring out the new task for some reason!

What if it had nothing to do with the Kingdom of the Dead?

I pushed away this treasonous thought and

stepped towards the dark elf, but as soon as I left the shade of the riverbank and stepped into the sun, the world suddenly turned into a fiery desert. My skin started to hiss and smoke and my Stamina started to rapidly burn away.

Unfortunately I'd left my cloak as well as my chainmail hauberk back in the dungeon, while the mask that Isabella had given me only protected my face from the burning rays.

I had to jump back into the shadows.

"Hey!" I called out to our guide. "Boy!"

The red-haired boy looked up from his fishing rod and turned to me.

"Yes, Uncle John?"

"There were some rags on the boat. Throw them over here!"

"All right!"

The clothes that the boy brought turned out to be a torn fisherman's cape that a scarecrow would be ashamed to wear, but beggars can't be choosers. I put it on and pulled the hood over my head.

That was better. At least I could get out under the sun now.

Isabella suddenly came to and rose in a smooth motion.

"Kitten," the dark elf shook her head, "you're full of surprises!"

"What do you mean?" I asked, as I adjusted my flamberge in its baldric.

"Relax!" Isabella giggled. "Things aren't that bad!"

The skull on her staff clacked its bottom jaw, confirming the words of its mistress, but I didn't let my guard down.

"What have you found out?"

"Our dungeon was not unique, there are many caves like that. No wonder it seemed to be too simple to you. According to legend, the Lord of the Dead hid his disciples everywhere so that they'd awaken from their lethargy at the right moment and gather an army of the dead."

"And what about the Sphere of Souls?"

"Spheres of Souls are the focusing lenses of the Tower of Decay. One shard was placed in each hideaway and if the sphere is completely assembled then it's possible to open a passage to the Kingdom of the Dead. They're already offering ten thousand or more for a small piece at auction. The prices keep growing. The first to assemble a Sphere will organize a raid. The leaders of the top clans can't wait."

"Isn't owning just one shard enough to interrupt this?"

"The shards aren't unique. You just need to gather a certain number of them," Isabella explained and flashed a strange smile. "There's a proper power struggle going on. Just the time to catch some fish in troubled water!"

I thought I would have a stroke.

"You're not planning on selling the shard, are you?"

"What nonsense," the dark elf snorted. "This is a pass to the Kingdom of the Dead! We're going to look at the balance of power and offer it to the one who needs it the most!"

I nodded in agreement and asked, "How do you imagine that happening?"

Isabella drew a line in the sand with the point of her staff and declared, "I will open a portal to the Tower of Darkness."

The red-haired boy almost jumped for joy.

"We're going to the capital of the dark side? Hurrah!"

"We?"

I exchanged glances with Isabella whose eyes displayed just as much surprise as mine, but she immediately composed herself and started to draw a complex design with her staff.

"Kitten, the boy has grown attached to you!" the priestess said as she started to fill the portal she was preparing with power. "Now it's your load to bear."

"Why the hell?"

"The dungeon quest has not closed completely and the boy is part of it. There's nothing else we can do. We are responsible for our pets."

I cursed.

"Kitten, stop swearing in front of children!"

I swore again, but kept it to myself this time. The quest probably hadn't closed properly because the game considered me to be an NPC, which meant that it would probably remain frozen until I came back to life. Did this mean the boy would follow us around the whole time? They won't even kill him! Child characters had complete immunity to all types of damage in this game.

Just my luck.

My heart began to weigh heavy and it became somehow uncomfortable to be on the riverbank. The sun was reaching its zenith and the shadows were turning into a thin strip, so I wanted to get to the Tower of Darkness as soon as I could. It was the capital of the dark side of this world.

I had no idea how much a player using Incognito would be accepted, but I doubted that it would be worse than the playpen, where a powerless undead was being killed by hyperactive newbies time and time again.

"It's ready!" Isabella declared, when the complicated diagram on the sand started to burn with black fire. "Kitten, don't fall behind!"

The priestess was the first to disappear into the black flame and the boy dropped his fishing rod and ran towards me, bouncing as he went. I didn't wait for him and stepped towards the portal.

A moment later, I was knocked off my feet and rolling along the sand!

Shackled soul attack!
Death Magic: Immunity

I rose on one knee in confusion, noticed a shimmer in the air and rolled aside. The spirit missed me, but then another joined it, flying in from the river and tearing a path through the reeds in its way.

I entered stealth mode and rolled along the sand again.

Shackled soul attack!
Death Magic: Immunity
Stealth mode: Off

Damn it! Spirits couldn't harm me in any way, but they were great at knocking me out of stealth mode! They could see the invisible!

I bounded back up to my feet, but I wasn't fast enough. A fireball flew out of the reeds and exploded, leaving a deep crater of melted sand.

The explosion immediately took off a quarter of my Health. The raincoat started to burn, so I had to roll along the ground to extinguish the flame. Without stopping, I made a forward roll towards the portal, but a shackled soul was waiting for me and hit me in the chest throwing me back. Whenever I tried to move towards the river, its companion would smash into my side!

I leapt in another direction, entered stealth mode and tried to run... Who cares where! Another hit on my back sent me sprawling into the sand. The spirit pushed me down to the ground and a new fireball found its mark. I was engulfed in flames and it wasn't easy to put a magical fire out.

In the end, I ended up burnt from head to toe and only one hundred points of Health separated me from death. This was bad, incredibly bad...

"So, we meet again!" Garth Deathblade shouted from the reeds. He'd managed to get himself up to level 35 and get the Soulcatcher profession. The white-haired necromancer held a staff covered with complex engravings with a shining crystal at the top in his hands. "I had to spend quite a lot on my preparations, you scum, but trust me, it was worth it!"

It was worth it? No wonder! Garth intended to sell my skull to Kogan's goons and the banker under investigation would definitely be happy to pay the money to shut the mouth of a key witness for the prosecution.

Lost. I was lost!

Garth opened his mouth again, but I didn't listen to him and immediately took off and went straight into stealth mode as I went. The shackled souls went to cut me off to stop me reaching their master, while zombies rose from the sand around him, but I had no intention of carrying out a suicidal attack. I managed to dodge a soul that tried to attack my legs at the last moment, grab the enchanted skull from my inventory and send it flying into the middle of the river. Far away. Where it was deepest.

The second shackled soul immediately knocked me off my feet and a burning flame immediately exploded towards me. Before I went to be resurrected, I heard how Garth scream, "Noooo!" as he was cheated of his prey yet again.

Yes!

Chapter Four

In The Circle Of Death

1.

THEY SAY THE DEAD never get tired. Like hell they don't!

They get incredibly tired.

As I ran, my Stamina continued sinking into the red. The narrow road twisted between the steep hillsides but I couldn't climb them — by the time I'd reached the top, my pursuers would have had a hundred opportunities to pepper me with arrows.

The barking behind my back got closer and

closer. Those were no village curs, those were infernal hunting dogs.

I was being hunted.

And everything had actually started rather well...

STICKY RIVER SILT, waterweeds and the ripples on the river above my head.

I was underwater.

I already had had experiences with resurrection in puddles, but I'd never ever come back to the game at such depth. Yet I still kept lying still in the river silt without moving and gathering my thoughts. I was waiting.

Water drained power from immaterial beings so the shackled souls could never get me from the bottom, but I had no doubt that the stubborn necromancer would find some way to get the artifact he needed so much out of the water.

My skull.

When a long shadow cut through the body of the water and the small fishes scattered, I never made a move. I could remember very well how I'd drowned a rogue and wanted to repeat that dishonorable trick again. War is war.

The bottom of the boat approached. A rope with a rock tied to the end went to the bottom. The boat was carried a little downriver by the current, but then the rope went taut and held it in place. That was when a man dove over the side.

Garth spent some time swimming over the river bottom and looking for my skull and then surfaced, paddling with all his might to try and overcome the strong current. He soon reached the boat and climbed back on board, but then dove again and went deeper. This time, the necromancer chose the right direction and saw the whiteness of the skull among the waterweeds, but decided not to risk it and surfaced again, to my great disappointment. It was only after getting his breath back that he went for his coveted prize, paddling fiercely and kicking with his legs.

I burst out of the sticky embrace of the silt like an underwater monster. Garth tried to avoid me, but he moved too late so I grabbed him around the waist and dragged him to the bottom. The necromancer thrashed around desperately at first but then he must have recognized how pointless it was and tried to stab me with his dagger. This didn't help him either — movements were slower in the water, so he couldn't make a hard thrust. The blade just left a shallow scratch.

While I held onto the necromancer with one hand I spread out my fingers on the other and stabbed at him with my black claws which easily cut through his flesh.

Claws of Darkness! Damage: 110
Stun! 00:06... 00:05...

The necromancer immediately stopped twitching and went limp, a thin line of bubbles escaping his mouth towards the surface of the water. I didn't wait for my opponent to stop being paralyzed, I pulled him under me and sunk my teeth into his skinny neck.

Fearsome Bite!

I ripped out a huge chunk of flesh with my jaws and the water was colored with the carmine taint of blood. Even though his wound was serious, the necromancer started to come back to his senses, so I had to grab him with both arms again and use all my strength to press on his chest and squeeze the last of the air from his lungs.

It helped, as Garth twitched, opened his mouth and drowned.

Player Garth Deathblade has been killed!
Experience: +1500 [6119/6220]; +1500 [6163/6220]
Undead: You have gained a level! Rogue: You have gained a level!

A pathetic three thousand experience points for a level 35 necromancer?

Some sort of penalty must have been applied because I sent the same player to be resurrected in a very short time period.

I would have spat with disappointment, but my mouth was full of water.

To hell with it!

I started to search the lifeless body of my enemy and swore again. My only prize was his money pouch. Anything was better than nothing.

I put my enchanted skull into my inventory and pushed myself off the bottom with my feet to try and get to the surface, but to no avail. I had to crawl towards the anchor and climb up to the boat using the rope. As soon as I got out of the

water and climbed over the side of the boat, I
heard a splash behind me. It made me jump and
grab my flamberge, but it was a false alarm — the
red-haired boy was swimming towards the boat.

"Uncle John," he shouted as he gripped the
side. "The portal has closed!"

"I see," I sighed hopelessly, put the sword
aside and opened the game menu.

Over the time since the portal's closure
Isabella had literally smothered me with personal
messages and the longer time went on, the
angrier they'd become. I should have replied and
calmed her down, but I only had read-only access
to personal messages, the same as all game
chatrooms.

"What're we going to do?" the boy asked as
he climbed into the boat.

"We're going to go to the Tower of Darkness
by river," I replied without hesitation, as the
shard of the Sphere of Souls was in the hands of
the priestess.

"How cool!" the boy happily sat behind the
oars. "It'll take us about four days! What an
adventure!"

I wasn't too good at the geography of the
world of Towers of Power, but as far as I could

remember, the capital of the dark side was located on a bunch of islands in the delta of the Azure River. We might well have been traveling along one of its many tributaries right now.

The boy worked the oars, while I went deep into the game stats. I invested the points I got when I raised my levels into increasing Strength, Agility and Dodge, but it wasn't as easy with my profession specific skills. Every top level combat move provided access to a whole branch of other moves which could then be combined, so I was overcome by the number of variations in which my character could be developed.

Suddenly, a red flash came from the sandbank where we'd made camp, which was now rather far away. I couldn't know for sure, but I didn't have many doubts that this was Garth returning to the game. It seems that he'd decided to have some additional insurance and fixed his resurrection point in advance.

Damn.

I was sure that the necromancer would have no difficulty in tracking me and then no river would save me. It would be foolish to underestimate my opponent and think that I'm cleverer than everyone else. That would be the path to ruin.

I swore again. Then I looked at the red-haired boy. Neither Garth nor his shackled souls could harm him as he was saved by the immunity given to him by the developers. I didn't know whether that also applied to theft, but who'd think of pickpocketing a little urchin?

"Hmm..." I cleared my throat. "Young one, I wanted to ask you something..."

"Yes, Uncle John?"

"Can I ask you to store something for me?"

"Yes, of course, leave it with me," the boy replied without a care in the world.

We were talking about my life and death, so this sort of carelessness cut me a little, but after a little thought I still called up the quest generation menu.

Store the skull until I take it back. Get to the Tower of Darkness. Find Isabella Ash-Rizt.

At the end, I made the reward for the task one gold piece and saved the conditions.

"I'll get it all done, Uncle John!" the red-haired kid promised, his face lighting up with a dimpled grin.

I really didn't want to part with the skull so much that I wanted to grind my teeth, but I overcame myself and gave it to the boy. I immediately came to and checked that I hadn't made a mistake and that the crystal skull was still in my inventory. I hadn't thrown it away as I'd intended to sell it once I'd reached civilization.

"Row us to the shore," I asked the boy and jumped out of the boat into the shallows. I parted the reeds with my hands as I walked directly to the sandy bank.

"Uncle John! Where are you going?" the boy asked in distress.

"Keep rowing!" I demanded. "I'll find you later!"

The boy became gloomy and frowned, but at least I didn't have to ask him twice as he started to work the oars again. The boat floated away.

I had a heavy heart, but I got myself together and continued onwards. The reeds were soon behind me, but tall sedge started to cover the flood meadow so I could pick up my pace a bit.

I needed to get away from here as fast and as far as I could.

✠ The Dead Rogue ✠

Immediately!

Garth couldn't stay in-game for twenty four hours. If I held out until the time that the necromancer would have to stop his chase, I'd win a day or maybe two for the boy, who was taking my enchanted skull with him. It would no longer matter whether the necromancer would be successful in his search or lose track of me. Even if he caught up with me and killed me, death would immediately throw me many miles away. A win-win situation!

The further the boy could manage to row away, the harder it would be for Garth to find us next time, which was why I really needed to win at least some sort of head start from fate...

THE PURSUERS FELL BEHIND. I looked back from time to time, but saw no sign of pursuit and continued running at an even pace. When my Stamina went into the red I slowed down to a walk, but I never stopped even for a moment.

I ran and walked. Walked and ran. And got further and further away from the river.

The meadows changed to fields of fruit orchards. I jogged along a road which was rutted with cart tracks, ready to hide in the tall grass at the first sign of danger, but my surroundings were empty of people. Here and there, I could see clouds of black smoke rise up to the sky — they were from the burning villages and homesteads.

I tried to avoid battlegrounds, but I didn't always manage to do so. I came across hanging bodies on the roadside trees and the remains of bonfires full of human bones. Dead horses and armored knights lay strewn across a trampled field of wheat. Fattened crows circled in the air overhead. The standard of the Order of the Fiery Hand lay in the mud at the crossroads between two country roads. A little further along a body lay in pieces in a ditch, then another one and more. Some of the severed limbs continued to move.

The Lord of the Tower of Decay was trying to impose his rule upon new lands, but when steep forested mountain slopes started to appear up ahead it became clear that the army of the dead was not doing particularly well.

The air was full of smoke that floated along the ground, fountains of fire occasionally flew up to the sky and something exploded and made loud noises beyond the trees. Screams and the clang of steel rang in the air. There were more and more roadblocks on the roads. Apart from the orange banners of the Order of the Fiery hand, with their black trim there were the occasional black and white banners of the Night League. The paladins of light summoned fire elementals for assistance, while the followers of darkness summoned infernal beasts from other planes of being, ones that didn't care whether the victims they tore to pieces were dead or alive. The tall and hunched figures of demons that strode among the tall wheat inspired fear with their very appearance. They were surrounded by a palpable aura of fear.

Do the dead know no fear? I wasn't so sure...

There were very few of the walking dead around. They either crawled out of their lairs at night or the army of light had managed to achieve overwhelming supremacy here. The rare Death Disciples paid no attention to me, due to my neutrality. I had way more issues with the reconnaissance groups of light side players and sometimes I only avoided discovery at the last moment by diving into the bushes or the tall grass.

When darkness fell, I finally had to leave

the roads and go straight through the fields. Fires burned at every crossroads which was even remotely important and the risk of coming across an especially observant watchman overcame all logical limits. Conjurers knew how to see the invisible, so stealth mode might not even help.

Should I use Incognito? With a heavy sigh I looked at my hands with their long black claws. I had to find some gloves first.

When the trampled and burnt fields and the rotting corpses that littered them were behind me, I went deep into the forest, looked for an animal track that snaked among the trees and started to run again. The chance of a random encounter in the thick of the forest at night was not too great and even if I came across someone, I would be sure to have the time to hide in the bushes. It was too dark in the shadows of the trees for normal people.

From time to time, I saw animals that I disturbed among the trees, but I didn't distract myself with them, continuing my even paced jog. The first time I stopped was when I heard screams up ahead and the path took me to a forest clearing with the gaping hole of an abandoned mine in the middle. Two groups of players were enthusiastically fighting each other. They were letting attacks through and dying but then coming back to the game almost immediately by the raid altars that were installed nearby and simply charged back into the fray. The resurrection points were protected with such powerful enchantments that there were few who were brave enough to attack the enemy camp.

There was no way that a battle could have started in such a strange place at random. The strange mineshaft was probably the reason for the fight. It was even possible that this was another Death Disciple lair with another shard of the Sphere of Souls.

I wanted to sneak inside the dungeon, but then I saw a fireball fly from the clearing and hit the pine tree beside me, making the huge tree light up like a match. I retreated and ran away.

And again, I ran and ran and ran. All night through.

The dead have no need for sleep, but when it was getting close to dawn I couldn't even think clearly anymore. I was just mechanically moving my feet and looking from side to side thoughtlessly.

Twenty-four hours on my feet — anyone

would have lost their minds!

The path had also taken me to the foothills, so I had no need to choose directions anymore. You run and run along the side of the mountain waiting until you find a crossing. I had no map of my surroundings, so I had to take things as they went.

My tiredness had lowered my level of attention, so I didn't notice the rope stretched across the path with the grass twined around it and just felt its taut resistance, the creak of a tree and the rustle of leaves. My leveled up Dodge skill saved me. My body moved aside by itself and bent down so that the log that flew out of the darkness missed me and swung on the ropes.

My apathy disappeared as if it was never there and I slipped into the bushes, activating stealth mode.

I was just in time!

The bearded man with an axe that jumped out onto the path looked to and fro in confusion but didn't notice me. I didn't spend time working out whether this was a bandit or a simple hunter, I stepped up behind him and swung my flamberge, hacking through his chest from his left collarbone to his solar plexus. The ruffian fell to the ground, drowning everything around in his blood.

The inertia of the strike made me turn around.

I found myself face to face with two vagabonds that were coming at me from behind. One bore a short hunting spear while the other was swinging around a club with metal spikes.

I only needed a little experience to reach the next level, so I didn't run away, getting a better grip on my two-handed sword, I prepared to down my opponents using Sweeping Strike. I'd already stepped up to them but then suddenly became wary.

The bandits weren't shouting or gnashing their teeth, their eyes were empty. And dead.

They were undead!

So what happened to neutrality?

I felt the touch of cold on my back, spun around and caught the shadow flying from the bushes with a strike of my flamberge. My wavy blade was right on target, but caused no damage at all. More than that — it was spun around and torn out of my hands!

Shackled Soul: Immunity to damage!

The angry spirit attacked again. I struck back with my clawed hand and it went straight through the ghost, while I was thrown onto my back.

I fell onto the path by the bandits and immediately knocked the legs from under the bearded man with a spear. I had to roll away from the other thug before he could use his club. My roll finished in the spiky bushes, where I was attacked by yet another shackled soul while trying to push my way out of the thorns. My hand fell on my bone hook, so I pulled it out from behind my belt and blindly fought back against the spirit.

The shackled soul simply dissolved into thin air!

Soulkiller's runes shone with ghostly fire and the handle became noticeably warmer, as if the weapon had imbibed the power of another.

I broke out of the bushes and looked around, searching for the second spirit, but it managed to hit me from behind and knocked me over into the grass. I didn't manage to get back to my feet this time — Garth appeared as if from nowhere and stabbed the ashen stake he held in his hands straight through me, pinning me to the ground with the sharpened piece of wood.

The ash pierced my lungs and cracked my ribs and my body still became paralyzed even though my spine was intact.

I could move neither hand nor foot!

What the hell?

Natural rejection of unlife: Save failed!

Garth Deathblade fearlessly crouched by my side and stretched his hand out to pinch me on the cheek, but thought the better of it and adjusted his dusty mantle. He didn't move away though.

Why would he anyway? The piece of wood that was imbued with druidic magic had immediately sucked away all of my Stamina and taken root, with buds and leaves starting to grow upon it. Its outgrowths started to pierce my lungs and suck the liquid out of me. They weren't even killing me, but honestly and shamelessly using me.

"There are many ways to kill one of the walking dead and I chose one of the most unpleasant for the victim," the necromancer told me in a confiding manner. "I had to spend some gold as the druids charge huge amounts for their services, but I would only save the best for you. This is only the beginning. When I set up your new log-in location then you'll fully appreciate my fine taste, I assure you!"

Garth bared his dagger and opened up my rib cage, but he was unable to cut out my heart because it was already entwined by roots.

"Are you sure you want to say that you threw the skull somewhere along the road and that you will be reborn somewhere else? No! You ran away as fast as you could! Anyway, there is no way you can hide from me. You are like an open book to me and I can see right through your thoughts. Don't even hope for the skull to go down the mouth of a volcano! You'll not get away that easily. I'll make sure that you are kept in a comfortable dungeon. Your friends won't be shy about paying for my services and I'll provide them with online streaming services instead. They'll have something to watch."

I could have told him that I felt no pain, but I couldn't.

Paralysis, damn it.

TO BE HONEST THOUGH, it made no difference.

✟ The Dead Rogue ✟

Garth managed to scare me. I knew that his talk wasn't cheap. That is what he would do.

Or what he would do if he could, to be more precise. But not this time.

The roots of the ash stake that pierced me reached my head, my eyes went dark and then I went to be resurrected again, how many times, I don't know.

Before the world finally went dark, I received a system notification.

Vendetta: Garth Deathblade

I guess we killed each other too many times so it can't have gone unnoticed by the game mechanics...

2.

MUD. REED ROOTS. Muddy water.

I got out of the swamp onto a relatively dry patch and powerlessly collapsed onto the sedge.

It was morning and the sun had already risen about the horizon, but it wasn't too high yet. I was protected from its fiery rays by the bushes on the riverbank. I also still had my cloak and mask. At least something decent had happened, apart from the fact that I'd managed to outfox the insane necromancer yet again. If I could only work out where I was...

"Uncle John?" I heard from somewhere nearby. "Have you already come back?"

"Yeah, I've come back," I confirmed, rising on my elbow and then asked the boy, "Do you have my skull? You haven't lost it, have you?"

"How could I?" the boy replied resentfully. "It's here! Do you want it back?"

"No, keep it with you." I saw down on the cold earth and discovered that I was covered with clay from the swamp from head to toe. "Where are we?"

"Near Stone Harbor. It's a town on the Twisted Lake."

I thought of the map of the world and worked out that the Twisted Lake was a large body of water with many islands that was two days from the Tower of Darkness. The Azure River led into it from one side and left on the other, taking its waters to the ocean.

The town of Stone Harbor was on a river island connected to the mainland by two bridges.

I didn't want to waste time on visiting it, so I asked, "What happened to the boat?"

"The bottom got breached upon the rocks," the boy sniffed. "We can't sail any further anymore, anyway. The Twisted Lake is so stormy now that even the barges don't dare sail on it."

I could barely hold myself back from cursing and just muttered, "I see..."

Did I see? Not really, I had no idea what to do next. We couldn't stay in one place and we needed to move, otherwise the insane necromancer would catch up with us. However, going around the Twisted Lake on foot would be incredibly stupid. Garth could teleport himself to any town on my way and ambush us on the road.

Teleport himself?

I snapped my fingers. That's right! Teleport!

There should definitely be a Tower of Power in Stone Harbor, which meant that it was possible to use a teleportation portal. It would be rather expensive to teleport to the capital, but if I sold the amulets, I should have enough money. Probably...

"Let's go!" I called the boy. "How do we get into the city?"

The red-haired boy cast a wistful look at

the reed shelter and the fish on sticks over the fire but then immediately forgot about them and strode off along the shore.

"We'll have to walk until we reach the bridge," he said to me as we walked along. "There is a guard detail there and they don't like vagabonds, but if we have some sort of business, they will let us through..."

"A guard detail?" I asked warily.

"Yes, because the army of the dead is somewhere nearby."

That was the last thing I needed! The proximity of the army of the Lord of the Tower of Decay didn't worry me at all, but how would I go around the bridge? I couldn't even think about walking across the river as its bed became noticeably narrower here and the wild stream of its water jumped and foamed over the rocks. If I even tried to go there, I'd immediately be carried into the lake. The bank on the other side was practically vertical. It would be impossible to get to the top without mountain climbing skills.

That meant that I'd have to rely on Incognito...

I looked at my black claws doubtfully, sighed and looked for my money pouch. I took out a large silver coin, gave it to the boy and asked, "Go to the shop, buy a pair of gloves and come back. I will be waiting for you here."

The quest generation menu opened automatically and I just needed to confirm the quest for the boy to start off on a bouncy run along the path that followed the shore.

I stood there for a little while, thinking about the situation that I found myself in and then followed the boy. I climbed up onto a small hill overgrown with hazelnut trees, where there was a view of the bridge. It turned out to be made of solid stone, with two guard towers on the other side. There were no gates in between them, but judging by the tight chains I saw, the guard could raise the last part of the bridge on that side. The pennants hanging on the spires fluttered in the piercing wind that came from the side of the lake. I couldn't see the guards as they must have gone inside to hide from the bad weather. It was no wonder, as the clouds hung low and there was an unpleasant drizzle.

It didn't make my fisherman's cape any drier, which was why I descended from the hill, adjusted the flamberge on my back and walked back towards the reed shelter. I escaped the rain, sat down on the bedding and cracked my knuckles.

I felt uncomfortable. I was annoyed at the delay.

I was way more than annoyed.

To occupy myself with something, I opened my character stat window and thoughtfully stared at the profession specific skill point that I hadn't assigned yet.

What could I do with it?

I suddenly remembered how well the bone hook had destroyed the incorporeal spirit, so I started to study the one-handed swordfighting section. The set of skills in it turned out to be the same as the moves for two-handed weapons, but there were some small differences. For instance, there were two new moves in the list: "Accurate Strike" and "Sudden Strike".

The first of these moves would allow me to strike right at the precise point I needed with my blade and increased the chance of crippling the target. The second could be useful for player killers. If an Executioner used it to initiate combat, they would deal a critical hit even without being in stealth mode. However, the increased damage didn't always apply — it all depended on the comparative Agility of the warrior and the Perception of their victim.

I invested the point I had into one-handed swordfighting which made the moves I studied for two-handed weapons unblocked in this section as well, to my great surprise. I added "Sudden Strike" to them.

Was I a rogue, or what?

It was a shame that it wasn't possible to use this trick with two-handed weapons...

THE RAIN WHISPERED softly on the roof of the shelter but it didn't pour inside, so my cloak started to gradually dry out. The swamp mud didn't go anywhere, though. I looked like some sort of vagrant. A proper scarecrow!

I got out of the shelter, went down to the water and started to wash my clothing. I never managed to clean it entirely, but the fisherman's cape still started to look relatively acceptable. At the end of the day, the weather was terrible and a traveler couldn't stay clean no matter how much they wanted.

After I washed my hands, I stood back up and went back to the shelter, but a tall elf suddenly came out from behind it, dressed in green britches and a brown jacket, with a longbow behind his back. The bowman was as surprised at the unexpected meeting as I was and was dumbstruck with surprise for a moment.

Ranger, Level 27 was all I glimpsed from the tag that appeared in the corner of my eye before I dashed off, but being in a hurry didn't do me any good. I should have gone into stealth mode and only attacked my opponent afterwards, while this way I had jumped up close to the bowman when his companions appeared — a level 23 priest and a level 28 duelist warrior.

"I've put my foot in it," flashed through my head. The only thing that could save me in this situation would be running away, as jumping into the river would see me smashed to pieces against the sharp rocks.

So I didn't jump into the river. I sent the elf there instead. I just grabbed him and threw him forcefully into the wild stream of the river. My superiority in Strength and Constitution showed itself, as the thin ranger flew from my arms as if he was a missile flying from a catapult. All he could do was scream.

The priest raised a staff with a shining crystal above his head, but I felled him with a powerful kick under the chest and drew the flamberge from behind my back. I immediately hacked its wavy blade into the duelist and growled with disappointment. The warrior had managed to arm himself with dual wielded sabers and crossed them to parry the attack.

I stepped back but then attacked again, using Sweeping Strike. The flamberge whooshed through the air, but the warrior parried the blade with his saber and used a quick pirouette to step aside while cutting at me with the weapon in his other hand.

The damage was not great, so I charged my opponent, wanting to cut him in half with a powerful strike before the priest could get out of the mud. The duelist demonstrated a level of swordfighting unimaginable to me again. Somehow, he got out of the way of my blade and then his twin sabers turned into propeller blades.

One! Two! Three! The rapid cuts took off almost a third of my health. The attacks hit my back so they didn't inflict any crippling wounds, but my movements still became slower, with my long and heavy blade shaking in my hands.

Damn it! A rogue should never get into a fight with a warrior! Swordfighting is a great skill!

I jumped back and entered stealth mode. This was when the one-sided specialization of the warrior showed itself — he didn't have enough perception to see me. The duelist retreated, slashing empty air with his sabers.

Catch!

I leapt over to his side and brought my flamberge down on his collarbone.

The duelist managed to raise his shoulder at the last moment, so that my blade got caught on his shoulder guard instead. The hit was made lighter and didn't completely destroy my opponent, it only took away half of his life.

The sabers rose, one cutting the neck and the other almost slashing open my head. My Dodge skill saved me, but I still went blind in my left eye. I had to jump back, preparing to go into stealth mode yet again.

The duelist also wasted no time, as he took a flask and drank a healing potion.

"Light!" he shouted at the top of his voice.

What was that all about?

I went into stealth mode again and raised my flamberge when I heard a bright flash behind my back. All of the shadows disappeared and it made me turn into a shadow. An ugly and twisted shadow, but one that was perfectly visible with the naked eye.

The duelist charged me, easily dodged my flamberge and swung his sabers. I had to take the left blade on the cross-guard while the rest cut into my hip down to the bone.

I had no chance to oppose a skilled warrior in an honest fight, so I turned around and rushed towards the priest whose shining staff was covering everything with unbearable light.

Sharpened steel cut into my back, immediately throwing my health into the red, but the duelist never expected such speed from me and only chased me after an unforgivably long break for an experienced warrior. I managed to get away.

The priest stared at me, his eyes wide with horror as he obviously rarely had had to meet an enemy face to face. I took the flamberge by the ricasso and hilt, holding the sword in front of myself like a spear and this was when an arrow flew out of the reeds to pierce my neck.

The ranger had joined in the fight, damn him!

I only had to run three strides and the arrows going into my body didn't manage to kill

me.

"Run!" the duelist shouted to the shocked priest, but it was too late.

I put all of my strength into my last attempt and activated Power Strike. The blade of my flamberge easily went through the cassock of the priest and came out of his back. Blood sprayed out of his mouth and then it was joined by gobbets of brains that flew out of my skull that was split in half by the strike of a saber...

Not the best of all trades...

3.

TURF. Stone. Rain.

Stones were not so bad if you didn't have to dig a deep grave in stony soil yourself. It was easier to dig yourself out.

After I tore through the turf, I climbed out and immediately started to roll down a steep slope, but I very quickly hit a rock and lay spread-eagled across a narrow mountain path.

The red-haired boy looked at me from above with surprise.

"Uncle John! I was just bringing a pair of

gloves for you!"

"Give them here," I demanded. "No, leave the change for yourself."

There were several new holes in the fisherman's cape and it had lost half of its Durability, but it could easily hide my undead nature from curious eyes together with the mask and gloves. No one would see that I was undead in Incognito mode. Well, I hoped so, anyway...

I put on the gloves, adjusted my mask and got to my feet. There was noticeably less money in my wallet and some of the amulets I'd looted had vanished, but my latest death didn't cause any other problems. It was actually the other way round — I wouldn't have to mess with the heads of the guardsmen on the bridge.

And another thing about my death....

I opened the game log and started to look through the messages that had appeared after my death. It turned out that I hadn't managed to kill the priest with one hit, but blood loss had finished him off. I received eight hundred points for both classes from this, taking me to level 34.

The duelist's mastery of swordfighting left a lasting impression on me, which was why I raised my two-handed weapon skill to level two.

Unfortunately I didn't get any new moves to learn.

I immediately started to have doubts. Maybe I was wrong to do things so hastily? An Executioner is no opponent for a Duelist in an open fight, so maybe I should have learned special moves even more? I took that priest apart really well...

Ah, to hell with it! I shook my head and asked the boy, "Is it far to the city?"

"We'll get there in ten minutes," he reported.

"Are there many people around?" I asked, as I didn't know whether I had to activate Incognito then and there.

"Nope!" the boy waved his hand dismissively. "There's no one."

"And why's that?" I asked with surprise.

"They ran away!"

"Who from?"

"They are waiting for the army of the dead to come any day now," the boy started his introduction of local affairs, "so they ran away. But that's not all. The second bridge has been washed away by the flood and there's a storm over the lake. Whoever didn't leave immediately is trying to organize the defense. But there are only a quarter of the citizens left. And the outsiders can be counted on the fingers of one hand."

The boy obviously meant players when he spoke of outsiders and this news made me much happier. Less players — less problems. The storm on the lake was no problem — I'd be traveling to the capital using the portal anyway.

We went up to the hill and stopped, looking at our surroundings. It turned out that there was a proper road leading here as well as a mountain path and it was just that the boy had chosen the shortest way through the hills. Fires burned by the guard towers and there was a military camp, but there were few defenders by the crossing. I also thought that they were probably all NPCs.

The drawbridge mitigated any advantage the army of the dead would have. Would it even get here anyway?

The shaggy clouds flew low over our heads, almost touching the tops of the trees and a sharp gust of wind almost blew us from the path. I lowered my head and adjusted the hood of my cloak. A farm was on the slope of the next hill, but the windows of the low house which faced us were boarded up, the cattle pen was empty and the barn stood with its gates wide open.

The city itself wasn't that big and it was right by the lake, which stretched to the horizon with its gray, unquiet and endless waters. Huge waves rolled over the breakwater, splashing over it and scattering as white foam. From time to time, the water flooded over the Stone Harbor, touching the walls of the houses and flowing over the stone-flagged streets.

The majority of the buildings had two floors, so the two towers in the city stood out among them. A dark black edifice stood tall in the central square and a lighthouse faced the wild waters upon the headland. Its fire wasn't lit and only some sort of silvery winged figure stood upon its spire.

No matter how much I looked at the streets of Stone Harbor, I didn't notice any of the locals. Smoke only came from around a dozen chimneys.

There was a feeling of abandonment and hopelessness.

That didn't matter though! I had no intention of spending too much time in this backwater town. I would walk to the Tower of Power and immediately use the portal and that's all they would see of me.

✝ The Dead Rogue ✝

Expensive? Yes, but it would be quick, and money was worth its weight in gold right now.

How long would they keep my body on life support in the hospital? Would it be until my medical insurance ran out or longer? Even if the state took over paying for my bills, the longer I'd spend in a coma, the harder it would be to come back to normal life.

Time is money? Hell, no! Time is life!

The red-haired boy started to go down the hill and I followed him. The wind howled among the stones and nearly swept us off our feet, but calmed in the middle of the hillside so my cloak stopped streaming in the wind.

I soon saw another abandoned farm and the path started to twist through the clumps of hazelnut trees, so I had to use the Incognito Executioner skill. Even though my Energy started to decrease, but they definitely wouldn't be happy to see one of the undead here and any meeting with the locals or other players was bound to end in battle.

The twisting path soon led us to hill bottom of the hills and turned towards the road. Orchards soon appeared by the roadside and then huts with straw roofs were in front of our eyes.

Time is money? Hell, no! Time is life!

Very quickly, the winding trail descended from the hills and turned to the road. On it I went further. Soon fruit groves stretched behind the roadside, then the roofed huts of the huts began to come to their eyes. Some time later, the stone houses appeared, but on the outskirts they all stood alone, as one, with boarded-up windows and doors.

Somehow it's quite sad...

The narrow streets of Stone Harbor were unusually confusing, and although the bulk of the tower of Power constantly loomed somewhere above the roofs, I had to wander along a bunch of wet alleys before finally reaching the city square through the dark arch.

And immediately jumped system message:

Received the task: "Defend or Die"!

Surprised, I lost my footsteps and turned my head, but the square was empty, only the shadows were rolling at the foot of the tower, much darker and denser than one would have expected even from the most cloudy day.

✟ The Dead Rogue ✟

I stopped and opened the window with the terms of the job. They were very laconic: the players were ordered to assist the citizens in the defense of the Stone Harbor from the army of the dead. Participation brought the achievement of "Defender Stone Harbor", the flight threatened with the brand "Deserter", but I didn't even understand the possible bonuses and penalties and went straight to the tower of power.

From afar it seemed black, but the closer I approached it, the clearer the reddish glow became. It was as if the building had been white before, and then it poured with darkness, through which the former coloring could be glimpsed, outliving the darkness in a sinister purple.

Soon, between the stones of the stone pavement, dark veins began to spread, they cut through the square like a network of blood vessels, or the anthracite cobweb of a giant spider. The sky had darkened, the tower had grown filling everything around with its bulk. The shadows swirling around it dissipated into separate tufts of darkness which floated towards me.

"Off!" a ghostly exclamation cut through

the silence of the square. "Get out! Fight or die!"

The shadows were condensed and turned into disembodied puppets, ministers of the local lord. Awe-inspiring they were, their limbs bending at strange angles, their powers impressive.

"I need a portal!" I shouted, but to no avail.

"Begone!" the answer thundered. "Fight or die!"

The phantom puppets approached, and I hurried back to the arch. The shadows followed. "Fight or die!" They sang in a thousand otherworldly voices. "Fight or die!"

I couldn't stand it anymore. I turned around and hurried away. The creatures followed me as if I had honey on my backside.

They seemed to want to make sure that I didn't run away.

How could I? The portal is unavailable, one bridge is destroyed, and the other...

I clicked my fingers. Exactly!

The drawbridge hadn't yet been raised, and the guards probably wouldn't hold anyone on the island. I could have easily crossed to the other side and gone to a nearby town along the shore of the lake. Unlike ordinary players, I didn't face any problems with the dead subjects of the lord of the tower of Decay.

The red-haired boy was waiting for me in the archway. Toward the tower he didn't dare approach.

"What were you standing there for?" I asked, when the boy skipped alongside.

"We can't get any closer, Uncle John!" the boy replied. "Our Lord doesn't want to see anyone!"

I swore, went out of the arch and immediately stopped dead. The street was blocked by a small group of players. A blond witch in shining clothes was accompanied by four fighters in armor, which seemed to be bathed in a white glaze.

My eyes shed tears from the bright light. No matter how I strained my sight, I couldn't make out the status of those I met. But the sorceress didn't manage to cope with my Incognito.

"What kind of creature are you?" She asked with unconcealed contempt.

Familiar intonations something awakened in my memory, but before I could deal with my own memories, the shadows that followed me escaped from the arch.

"Get out!" they hissed. "You don't belong here! Begone!"

Frost spread over the cobblestones and the walls of the houses around the white witch. It grew noticeably cold. The radiance of the slender figure became unbearable, but the servants of the local lord didn't think to retreat. On the contrary, the ghostly puppets began to pour out of the gateways and boarded up windows, merge into one sinister figure that seemed to say in a thousand voices:

"Begone! Begone! Begone!"

The local ruler of the battles between the players categorically disapproved, and the white witch had to back down. Bodyguards covered her with shields and began to retreat, and when they disappeared around the corner, I turned and hurried in the opposite direction. The shadows didn't pay any attention to me and crawled along the damp dark courtyards.

4.

I DIDN'T GIVE UP on my desire to run away from Stone Harbor so I went to the crossing. It was a

---

waste of time. The drawbridge was already raised and the guards stood on the watchtowers in full battle gear, occasionally loosing off arrows at the other shore. I couldn't work out who they were shooting at, but there was no doubt that the siege would take a long time.

Damn it! How could I have got stuck in this God-forgotten city?

The second bridge had also survived. Still, after I questioned the boy I came to the unfortunate conclusion that going there would be a waste of time. The river had started to flood its surroundings because of the bad weather and the banks had turned into an impassable swamp.

My energy had started to run out as well. I couldn't maintain Incognito for a long time, so I had to find shelter in one of the abandoned farms or run to the city and rent a room in a inn.

The cold and rain didn't worry me at all, but I felt uncomfortable when I thought about the white sorceress. I decided not to risk it and avoid getting into trouble yet another time.

Any player stuck in Stone Harbor would try to find something to do and I never wanted to be the main attraction in a game of "Kill the Undead". Who knew who might decide to check the abandoned farms? They would definitely not dare to break into someone else's hotel room though. I didn't feel that the local Lord was a weakling that tolerated lawlessness in the city.

THE FIRST TWO INNS along my way turned out to be closed. It was no wonder, as the streets were empty of both local residents and players. It was as if everyone in the town had died out.

When I was closer to the city square, I glimpsed a sign that depicted a strange winged creature. The place was called Silver Phoenix Inn. I could see the gleam of candles in its barred windows as smoke streamed up from the chimneys on the roof.

A huge man in armor stood by the inn porch, wearing a soaked cloak. The warrior had no helmet on his head. His long hair had stuck together and hung down, matted and disheveled.

"Level 30 warrior," I said automatically.

My arrival seemed to have cheered the man up. He put his hand upon the hilt of his claymore. "Hey, you! Who are you?" he demanded.

That was rich!

My Energy was running out so I really had

no time for arguments and mutual insults. I slipped into stealth mode. The big man swung in place with his sword drawn, waiting for an attack.

Was that stupid? Not really, because the most important thing in a one-on-one battle with a rogue is to survive their first attack and parry the next one without allowing the invisible assassin to get away and slip into the shadows. Almost all of the rogue professions were balanced for the use of daggers and shortswords, so that their hits were painful but unable to immediately kill a high level player.

My flamberge was something else entirely. One strike with it was well enough to smoke the most powerful opponent.

I didn't attack the warrior. I only sneaked behind his back and shouted in his ear, "Boo!"

The warrior jumped, leapt away and turned with his sword upraised, but stopped without actually hitting me. Striking first in a situation like this was the same as losing. Even if you won, you'd definitely get the PK mark, while your enemy would remain clean if they were successful. That didn't matter out in the sticks somewhere, but here they made sure to maintain order, as I later found out. A PK mark was no joke. Anyone could attack a pariah like that without fearing any punishment.

"Scumbag!" the warrior shouted, still not ready to attack. "Stupid idiot!"

Ignoring the insults, I calmly stepped up on the porch. After a moment's hesitation, I got hold of myself and pushed the door open. I simply had no other choice — Incognito was consuming the last remnants of Energy that I had.

The spacious dining hall was dimly lit. The candles only burned on one of the tables, plus there was a fire burning in a great fireplace.

A dark spot on the far wall immediately caught my eye. It gave me the impression that there used to be some kind of mural there before.

Whatever must have been painted there once didn't attract my attention for long. I was far more interested in the players that were staying in the inn. There turned out to be five of them, all levels 30 to 40. An archer, two warriors, a female rogue and a druid.

Thankfully, the three that I'd fought on the shore weren't there. Neither was the sorceress nor her terrible bodyguards.

When the players turned to the sound of

✝ The Dead Rogue ✝

the door shutting behind me, I decided to play it bold and casually waved my hand to everyone as I headed for the bar. An elderly orc with a face covered in ritual scars stood there. Incognito seemed to be working fine as no one had grabbed their weapon upon my arrival.

"What a scarecrow!" I heard.

A red-haired warrior whistled in surprise at the sight of me, but remained sitting at his table. His druid friend didn't move from his place, either. So far, everything was within limits. Hiding your identity was no crime.

Pretending I hadn't noticed his insulting exclamation, I bent over the bar. "I need a room."

The orc scratched his greenish cheek with his claws and pointed at the boy behind my back. "Is he with you?"

"Yes."

"One gold piece a day."

I had no time to haggle, so I put a heavy gold coin on the bar while the orc took a sizeable key with the number "7" hammered into it.

"Second floor," he said.

I took the key and moved towards the stairs. The red-haired warrior whispered something to his druid friend, but I wasn't

---

thinking of them now.

Up the stairs, quick, quick...

I shut the door behind me, pulled the bolt shut and lay down on the bed. As soon as I closed my eyes, I received a system notification.

"Do you want to make this rented accommodation your new login location?"

Unfortunately, my happiness didn't last long — both the accept and cancel buttons were inactive. I had to close the window.

To hell with it all. I had no intention of staying there for long.

Absolutely not.

MY PLAN OF ACTION was simple. I would leave Stone Harbor, get to the capital and find Isabella there. I hoped that she'd already used the shard of the Sphere of Souls and if she hadn't, we could do it all between the two of us. I had to get to the Kingdom of the Dead and I would get there. It might only be the first step towards freedom from virtual reality, but it was the first step that counted. I'd get it done.

There was nothing else that I could do.

✟ The Dead Rogue ✟

"Tick-tock," the time slipped through my fingers. "Tickety-tock."

After Incognito had stopped working, the Silver Deadman's Amulet started to quickly restore my Energy. Finally I was able to relax with my hands behind my head, staring at the ceiling.

Still, "relax" was different. I didn't feel tired nor did I need rest. My mind was gradually getting used to controlling a piece of dead flesh, which scared me the most.

Trying not to distract me, the red-haired boy quietly watched the pouring rain beyond the window.

I sat on the bed and started to look at all the potential combos. I'd only be able to judge their effectiveness in battle. The only thing I'd managed to glean was that the combos burned far more Stamina than the actual blows they contained would have on their own. This situation put very peculiar limitations on my abilities. One or two combos and I'd be done.

Not good.

The room turned out to be cramped. I couldn't train with a two-handed sword in it at all. I started studying the updated skills of my undead side instead of swordfighting.

Deathgrip still only sucked the Stamina and Health out of my victims, but Aura of Fear now had the option of fine-tuning the terror inspired in those around me. That was nothing to sniff at!

The ability to scare off animals or complicate a caster's task to curse or enchant me was great, of course. Ditto for the ability to immobilize an enemy warrior in combat. Still, sometimes it was much more useful to be able to manipulate opponents without being noticed. Who knew when I might have to seem a bit stronger and more fearsome than I was in reality?

When my Energy was completely restored, I got up off the bed.

"Are you hungry?" I asked the boy.

He sprang from the windowsill and laughed. "You bet, Uncle John! Of course I am!"

"Come on, then."

We went out into the corridor. When we reached the second floor gallery, I held the boy back by the shoulder. "Wait!"

There was a noticeably greater number of players in the dining hall. They'd gathered around the central table where a huge broad-shouldered barbarian was using beer and breadcrumbs to draw some sort of diagram. It looked clumsy but no one joked about it. The huge man who only wore a loincloth was a level 47 Berserker; he was a member of the Black Trackers clan, with two other clan members sheltering from the rain in the inn even though their levels weren't as high as his.

"This is a tributary of the Azure River," the berserker declared, drawing a curved line on the table with his finger. "It's the border between those that serve Light and Dark. The Dark shore is flooded, so even if there are undead there, they can't maneuver."

"We shouldn't expect any help from there either," sneered a half-elf with a shaved head covered in an intricate tattoo.

"Exactly!" the barbarian snapped his fingers. "This damned storm won't let us send reinforcements by water!"

"What about using the portal through the Tower of Power?" the question on the tip of my tongue got asked by a petite female rogue dressed in black velvet.

"The Death Disciples are blocking the city tower with their magic," the orcish inn keeper reported as if the girl's words had activated some script inside him. "No one can leave through the portal or get into the city."

Seriously? At least there was one piece of good news for today. Even if Garth would track me down, he wouldn't be able to get into Stone Harbor no matter how much he wanted to. The crossing was blocked and the portal wasn't working.

The inn keeper's words were no surprise for many of those gathered there.

"If you get killed, you won't return to the game in Stone Harbor, but to the previous Tower of Power," said the only conjurer in the inn, a short man of around level 25 in azure robes. "If you don't want to battle the undead, just cut your own throat and you'll be fine!"

"You don't have to bother! I'll rip the heads off the deserters myself!"

Ripper, the red-haired warrior who'd called me a scarecrow, stubbornly stuck his jaw out. "Hey, Grakh! Why are you ordering everyone around here? Who made you leader, eh?"

The barbarian looked down at him from his impressive height and bared his teeth in a way which was just as unfriendly. "Is there something that doesn't satisfy you, o clever one?"

The warrior looked around, but none of the other players offered their support. He couldn't win this argument even with his druid friend's support. Both the Ripper and the Thorn Master were only level 35, so the berserker could make quick work out of both in his rage. Which was probably why the warrior shrugged his massive shoulders and stayed silent.

"There you go!" the barbarian chuckled and then raised his head to address me. "Do you want to come down here?"

I shook my head. "I can see better from up here. Continue."

Grakh pinned me down with his intense stare but didn't insist. He drew another curve one the table. "The followers of Light have blocked all of the mountain crossings and they're pushing the army of the dead to the lake," he threw a piece of bread on the table to mark the position of Stone Harbor. "The Fiery Hand and Night League aren't interested in politics. All they care about is who will cut up more deadmen, but they definitely won't manage to kill them all in time. The city will be stormed very soon. The units of the undead have already reached the crossing."

The conjurer who'd previously talked of the advantages of suicide tapped the diagram with his fingers. "We're here and they are there. We'll just waste our game time. The army of Light will strike at the rear of the undead and throw them into the river."

The barbarian shook his head. "If the Light side wanted to do that, they would have attacked long ago."

The archer with the tattooed head laughed unhappily. "The Light side has deliberately herded the dead over here! They just want to win Stone Harbor back!"

As it turned out, the light color of the Tower of Power that could be seen through the layer of darkness was no illusion of mine. They'd introduced the opportunity to capture enemy cities in the previous update which provoked numerous border conflicts. While the Dark side led in the undeclared war, they'd managed to win four towers and only lose one of their own. The Stone Wasteland had been previously controlled by the Lady of White Silence. The Shadow Puppeteer had replaced her now — a second degree entity of the pantheon of the Dark.

None of the players had initially started the

game on the Light or Dark side. To establish you position, you had to join a clan or accept the patronage of one of the gods of the game world. Everyone gathered in the inn was either a subject of the Dark side or they were still undecided. None of the Light side players were to be seen in the city — the local ruler simply couldn't force them to take part in the defense.

"Guys, we're doomed!" the conjurer in the azure robes whistled. He seemed to be a right little pessimist. "If the zombies don't kill us, the Light side will finish us off!"

"Shut up!" Grakh growled at him as he started to assign roles. That made the discussion go into an argument which even the berserker couldn't stop. It became truly serious, which was why I descended to the first floor, threw a silver piece to the inn keeper and pointed at the boy. "Feed him."

"Hey, Scarecrow!" Ripper shouted. "Do you take him with you everywhere like a pet?"

"Quest," I replied monosyllabically as I activated my Aura of Fear. A miasma of insecurity and worry started to spread all around me, so Ripper stopped bothering me and went to join his druidic friend.

Both seemed rather strange and shifty to say the least. But even if they spent their time attacking other players, their PK marks must have already gone. Even Incognito couldn't hide a label like that.

The boy got a bowl of broth from the inn keeper and took it into a corner. The orc started to count the change but I stopped him.

"Just keep feeding him," I pointed at my companion. "Is that a deal?"

The inn keeper nodded.

"Have you had this terrible weather here for long?" I asked curiously as I listened to the howling of the wind. Sheets of driving rain rattled the windows. The brutal storm seemed to shake the buildings from the foundations to the second floor.

The orc thoughtfully scratched his scarred cheek and shrugged. "There's been a storm since the lighthouse went out."

The small conjurer in the azure robes walked over to us and added with a glum expression, "Stop your chatter, green one! Better pour me a beer!"

When the inn keeper turned towards the beer barrel, the permanently pessimistic conjurer chuckled. "The lighthouse went out! Why wouldn't it? It was the storm that blew it out!"

"*Karl Lightning, Level 25 Thunderbringer,*" I read.

Big deal. I turned away with a condescending chuckle.

The conjurer took a mug of light beer from the inn keeper and walked off. He was either uncomfortable because of my Aura of Fear or he just had no desire to socialize.

The huge berserker decided to exchange words with me instead.

"Want to open your profile?" he asked, obviously at a loss because of my equipment. A two-handed sword, a ripped cape and the complete lack of armor weren't that common in the game.

I calmly shook my head in reply. "No, I don't."

Grakh didn't insist. "How good are you with the sword?"

"Better than the undead," I answered as honestly as I could.

The barbarian turned around, raised his hand and snapped his fingers. "Victor! Mia! Come over here!"

The rogue girl and the half-elf with the tattooed head came over. She had disproportionally large eyes, pale skin and sharp ears which suggested she came from some sort of night people.

Victor turned out to be armed with a longbow and had black-fletched arrows peeking out of the quiver upon his back. Mia carried a miniature crossbow.

A Ranger and an Invisible, levels 33 and 35 respectively.

The berserker turned back to me. "What's your name?"

"John," I replied.

"Well then, John Scarecrow, you're going to cover these guys and be responsible for them with your head, got it?"

"I'll cover them," I promised as I carefully examined my subordinates.

The half-elf turned out to be tall and wiry, with forgettable facial features. The complex red and blue tattoo that matched the color of his clothing completely covered his shaved head and also went under his hunting jacket.

The rogue girl was petite and very lovely. She obviously loved black velvet, and it even suited her.

However, the girl didn't have the best of manners.

Mia loudly drew in the air and screwed up her face. "Ugh... You really smell, Scarecrow."

I felt like I was completely mortified, but then immediately gathered my wits and snorted. "After ten zombies you won't smell of roses either, darling."

"Have you already been fighting the undead?" Victor asked with interest. The eyes of the half-elf turned out to be strange, with a violet iris.

"Yes. While I was getting to the city, I got into a fight with them," I replied, then turned back to the inn keeper. I wanted to finish this conversation as soon as I could. "Have you climbed up into the lighthouse? Shouldn't it get fixed?"

The orc shrugged. "It's not alight."

The green-skinned bastard wasn't too talkative, was he? Still, I got what I wanted: the long-range fighters left me alone and went to sit at one of the tables. I now was on my own at the bar.

New players came down to the dining hall

---

from time to time, some burning with the desire to fight back against the attacks of the undead, while others were swearing at the developers that had locked us in this backwater place. However, no one was in a hurry to follow the advice of the whiny conjurer and commit suicide. The mark of the deserter could make the game a lot more difficult in the future, spoiling relations with the subjects of the Dark side, not even mentioning the lost XP.

The inn filled with noise as there were constant arguments at the tables, but the barbarian turned out to have a great organizational talent. He completely ignored the others' grumpiness, forming the players into groups and distributing duties among them, marking the required positions on the map. The fearsome image and bad reputation of berserkers made everyone else obediently dance to his tune as no one dared to confront him. Even the aggressive Ripper and his little druid friend didn't try to do anything.

Incognito was slowly sapping my Energy so I decided to go up to the room. But as soon as I stepped away from the bar, I heard a bell tolling outside. It just wouldn't stop pealing.

5.

NO ONE WANTED to stay behind in the inn. Every single person rushed to repel the attack of the undead. There was even a jam in the doorway.

I ran up to the red-haired boy. "Go to the hills where we met and wait for me there. Run!"

I hurried after the players. The street met me with darkness, stormy wind and rain, with torches flaming in the night in a long row along the road to the bridge. There wasn't that much confusion though — the berserker had quite masterfully split the unit into groups of three or four people. I noticed Victor and Mia sticking together, caught up with them and ran after them, not forgetting to watch my falling Stamina and Energy.

The road snaked through the hills. The rainwater came down the stony slopes forming deep puddles and wild streams with makeshift bridges built slapdashedly over them. The direct path was much shorter but even for me with my night sight it would have been a challenge, let alone the players who risked to break their necks and legs despite their torches.

We'd be in time, anyway.

We *were* in time.

When our motley company ran out to the crossing, there were scorpion teams busy at the top platforms of the towers. Archers were taking on bundles of arrows while the city guards lined up with their halberds under the cover of the raised drawbridge.

As I remembered the fast current and the precipitous cliffs, I didn't believe in a successful storming of the city at all, although Grakh immediately started to shout at the players, posting them to their pre-arranged positions. We, or Victor and Mia to be more exact, had to occupy a hill to the left of the road. Another three archers and the conjurer that had been attached to reinforce them went to the neighboring hill. The rest of the players turned out to be armed with melee weapons and stood behind the halberdiers in case the undead forced their way through.

"Just a waste of time getting wet in the rain," I grumbled as I sat down on one of the rocks.

The rogue girl snorted. "You can definitely do with a wash."

I kept quiet, picked a stalk of wormwood

and started to rub the flowers between my hands, trying to get rid of the stench. Damn the fine sense of smell of the non-humans.

The most surprising thing was that I definitely liked Mia. If things had been different, I wouldn't have said no to getting to know her better. Still, I had to keep my distance for now. What sort of fun could I have in the game now?

This wasn't a game at all, anyway.

I heard the snap of the scorpions and saw spears that flew to the other side, glowing orange. It was followed by a loud thudding noise. The earth shook beneath our feet. The Death Disciples had sent a dark cloud to attack the defenders of the city in return, but the towers had turned out to be defended by something darker, and the darkness inside their walls easily absorbed the attack spell.

The mountain then started to shake, as if echoing the steps of an invisible giant. More spears launched by the scorpions flew to the opposite shore.

Then we heard an inhuman howling. The players below laughed and started to exchange jokes, even though I could see something the size of a two-story house approaching the crossing from the hill.

Had the Death Disciples managed to build a siege tower?

This was no tower, however. A huge mountain troll entered the bridge, dead and bloated from decomposition.

The archers rained a hail of arrows from the towers down on the beast, turning it into a giant pin cushion. This didn't even make it miss a step, however.

Boom! The earth shook underfoot. *Boom!*

"Conjurer!" Grakh shouted at the top of his voice. "Do something!"

What could a humble level 25 Thunderbringer do though? Nothing. We simply had no other battlemages in our group anyway.

The troll crossed the bridge and stepped into the gap. It didn't fall down into it though. Instead, it grabbed the opposite edge with its swollen fingers, replacing the drawbridge with its own body.

The dead immediately moved towards the new crossing. Nimble skeletons jumped out from behind the cover of wooden shields and rushed across. A poisonous green glow burned in their empty skulls stronger and stronger. Even though the archers took them out with one hit, a few of the quick creatures managed to reach the troll and used it to bound towards the raised section of the bridge.

I heard a crashing noise. The thick logs flew apart into sharp shards; this deadly shrapnel cut down almost the entire first row of halberdiers. The second row was immediately crushed by the dead as they rushed through the gates. They may have been slow and bloated from decay, but they were still there.

"Attack!" Grakh barked.

The company of players cut into the crowd of zombies, shouting and catcalling. Raised swords and two-handed poleaxes fell upon the undead.

Victor and Mia started to shoot at the enemy, with the archers on the neighboring hill being just as fast. Even the conjurer occasionally threw spiky balls of lightning down below.

It was slaughter, but it was but a prelude to an even greater massacre.

"Damn it!" I rushed down the hill, forgetting about the berserker's orders. "Get back! Retreat!"

No one heard me.

Then the chaotic crowd of the undead suddenly bristled with the points of long pikes. The dead legionnaires stopped hiding behind the bodies of yesterday's peasants and stepped forward, immediately impaling almost half of the careless players.

With a heart-wrenching howl, two dozen lost souls flew over the river. The flying undead started to pepper the archers in the towers with arrows, but the latter confidently paid them back. The archers in their turn had quickly switched to these new aerial targets because the rusty armor of the spirits couldn't protect them against the players' arrows.

The surviving defenders of the crossing fell back from the square. The dead legionnaires immediately got rid of the clumsy zombies, made an even front and formed a wall of rectangular shields. The pikes became a deadly fence as the undead creatures moved to the attack in equal lines.

Grakh couldn't do anything in this situation. A Berserker Rage and Stoneskin were quite a lot of help in battle, but the barbarian couldn't get through their monolithic formation. He would simply be skewered with spears.

✝ The Dead Rogue ✝

"Wait!" I growled as I ran into the square and went into stealth mode. I immediately got myself in front of the enemy formation and attacked them with a series of well-practiced combos. I didn't aim for the legionnaires who were protected by a wall of closed shields but for the poles of their black pikes.

The Scythe of Death burned away more than half of my Stamina, but it was worth it — the wild swings of my flamberge left a significant hole in the fence of spears, easily cutting off their points.

Once again did I raise my undulating blade, bringing it down on my nearest opponent. The sword shattered a shield and threw the legionnaire back. A breach appeared in the formation. And I — I ran away!

My Dodge skill helped me avoid a pike aimed at my side. A fiercely roaring Grakh jumped up to the legionnaires in several rapid bounds and burst into their ranks. His huge double-headed axe slashed in a semicircle, cutting through armor, crippling and knocking down the dead, with the newly encouraged players rushing after the berserker.

The formation of legionnaires scattered.

The individual superiority of living warriors immediately made itself felt. The enemy warriors in their solid black armor were pushed towards the gates and getting killed one by one. The druid turned out to be quite a good healer and cast one healing spell after another. The green gleam of his magic kept flashing here and there.

I didn't take part in the general carnage and returned to the foot of the hill. A couple of the undead that had spread out around the area tried to take out my subordinates. I cut down one from behind and slashed open the head of another. I received almost no experience for them.

Everything was going quite well for us in the square. Led by the huge barbarian, the players were pushing the dead legionnaires onto the bridge while the archers had destroyed all of the flying spirits and launched their arrows in a curve, shooting at the reinforcements that were coming to help the dead. The huge numbers of undead kept falling from the bridge into the river.

"Charge them!" Grakh shouted as he swept a legionnaire off his feet and swung his terrible axe. However, he didn't attack the stunned warrior but the fingers of the mountain troll holding the bridge together.

He hit it once, twice, then three times. He struck at it while completely ignoring the blows of the shortswords coming from all directions. The druid kept healing the berserker.

The ravaged hand of the dead troll slipped off the bridge. Now it was hanging on one arm. The legionnaires lost their balance and dropped into the water while the barbarian used several powerful blows to cut through the monster's other wrist.

Its giant body let go of the bridge and fell downwards.

The undead fighters retreated and were replaced by skeleton crossbowmen, but the archers at the tops of the towers quickly chased the undead away.

The status quo had been restored.

Problem was, we'd already lost half our fighters and the gates even before any of the Death Disciples had joined the battle.

WE RETURNED to the inn unhurriedly. We were tired and drenched, but we were satisfied. Mostly satisfied. The wounds that some had were so serious that the druid's magic couldn't quite deal with them: they needed divine healing or treatment from a surgeon. However, even the wounded forgot about their injuries when they looked at the game statistics. They were primarily interested in the progress of the Defend or Die quest.

It was amazing that my green bar filled over half the scale, even though the undead I'd killed weren't particularly strong. The best result was shown by one of the bowmen and another couple of fighters that had done well in the fight by the bridge. There was Grakh as well, of course. He'd managed to gather three quarters of the experience needed to complete the task in one battle.

The red-haired boy joined me when I was already by the outskirts of the city, but I immediately sent him to sleep. I too wanted to go upstairs to my room, but Grakh clapped his hands several times to attract the attention of the players.

"Everyone must come back by the evening!" he declared. "They won't storm the city during the day, so don't waste your game time! We won't fight back so easily tomorrow!"

"Too damn easy," one of the wounded said

as the tired players started to go to their rooms.

The only people that remained in the dining hall now were me and Victor.

"Why are you still here?" the barbarian stared at us, his skin covered with welts from his latest scars.

The half-elf smoothed his tattooed head and explained, "My capsule has been rented, and the time hasn't yet run out."

"Same with me," I lied.

The berserker nodded and shouted to the inn keeper, "Hey, boss! Bring us some beer! It's my round!"

"You shouldn't," I tried to refuse but the barbarian didn't listen. He looked down at me from his great height and slapped me on the shoulder. "You really helped us, John! I heard that warriors with two-handed swords used to break open spear formations by cutting through the poles of their weapons!"

Victor sat down at our table and chuckled. "The only thing is that the legionnaires didn't have spears,"

"I am talking of another time!" the berserker dismissively waved his hand, grabbed one of the mugs brought by the inn keeper and saluted us. "To victory!"

The half-elf sipped his beer. I didn't follow his example.

"I'll drink it in my room," I said.

"You won't take off your mask?" Grakh narrowed his eyes.

"I won't," I confirmed.

The barbarian just shrugged and kept sipping his beer. After a while he wiped his mouth with the back of his hand and shook his head. "I don't understand you, John. You walk around with a two-handed sword, but you have no armor..."

I sat on a chair and sighed. "I used to have armor. It's left somewhere in the fields."

"Why don't you buy a new set?" the barbarian asked with surprise.

"Where? It's like the city has died out!"

Victor finished his beer and made a suggestion. "There's a weapon shop by the pier. I bought some arrows there."

"There you go!" Grakh pointed his finger at me. "Go get something for yourself. Otherwise they'll do you in with a couple of hits, even though guys like you will still be useful to us. By the way, would you two like to join a clan at all?

✝ The Dead Rogue ✝

You seem to be rather decent guys!"

Me and Victor looked at each other in confusion. Clans were a good thing. However, choosing a clan would force the selection of the Light or Dark side and I'd never heard of the Black Trackers before.

Damn it. What clan? I was a walking corpse! We were sitting and talking to each other nicely right now, but if they discovered the truth, my drinking buddies would immediately go for their weapons.

This wasn't good in any way. I wasn't an undercover policeman that was infiltrating a gang or a secret agent in a terrorist lair. I was a corpse. It wasn't romantic at all.

Victor and Grakh exchanged contact details while I just promised to think about the barbarian's proposal.

"Do you think we'll manage to hold fast?" I asked.

The berserker suddenly gave me an honest answer. "Nope. If we don't get reinforcements, we're toast," he looked at the empty hall. "Just keep this between us, all right?" he warned.

I chuckled. "Silent as the grave!"

Victor frowned. "Why won't we manage? We

defended well enough today!"

"There were no Death Disciples around today," the barbarian frowned. "Magic would completely crush us. We just have a barely trained conjurer and a druid in our team and they won't make much of a difference."

I nodded. "Yes, I already noticed that mages are nowhere to be seen. Quite strange."

"It *is* strange," Grakh agreed. "But we did have some! Then they disappeared somewhere."

"Mages and priests know how to build portals," Victor suggested.

"So where will they go next with the deserter's mark?" the berserker snickered. "However, who knows what mages are thinking? They could bribe everyone. Money can buy everything here. Provided you have enough."

"Yes. By the way," I remembered. "Did you see the white sorceress? I couldn't get a good look at her but her level must be rather high. She had four warriors as her bodyguards. Probably mercenary NPCs."

"No, I never saw her," Grakh answered after thinking for a short time and then looked at the archer. "What about you, Victor?"

The half-elf silently shook his head. Silence

fell.

I asked a question to fill the uncomfortable pause. "What about the Lord of the local Tower — the Shadow Puppeteer or whatever? Won't he help us?"

"He'll help us in the city," Grakh said. "But there are too few of us to fight in the street. We won't hold the city."

"I'm sick of these undead now!" Victor swore. "Damn it, couldn't the developers think of something better? Some sort of demon? Succubi?"

The barbarian shrugged his powerful shoulders. "At least there's some movement. The Light and Dark used to kill each other before, but now there's a new force."

The archer didn't agree with this statement. "A new force?" he snorted with disgust. "What sort of force is that? Cannon fodder! How can players join the side of the dead? Feel like a walking corpse! Level 5 zombie, heh. They're a piece of piss to crush."

"Look deeper," Grakh advised. "All of the Towers of Power are controlled by Light and Dark gods right now, who are in fact AIs and moderators. What about the Tower of Decay?

When the kingdom of the dead falls, who will get it?"

Victor frowned, deep in thought, then waved it away. "They'll just give it to the next tramp that comes along!"

"Not necessarily," the barbarian shook his head. "Some clan could take it for itself."

"What's the point in that? The Spawn of Darkness and Sons of Light are the projects of the developers. It's a well known fact!"

"There are other clans," Grakh said meaningfully.

Victor and I could only laugh. The Sons of Light and the Spawn of Darkness were fighting for supremacy in the game from day one while the Blades of Chaos who were third in the rankings had had no chance to fight them for the leadership.

Victor got up from behind the table. "Time for me to go."

I also decided to leave the dining hall and went to my rented room. I felt vile about myself.

A game world was a new world. People didn't just level up their characters and smoked monsters but also interacted with each other, found new friends and even fell in love.

✝ The Dead Rogue ✝

And me? All I did was survive. I did my best. I lay in hiding.

Just like in real life.

What the hell...

6.

ONCE I'D GOTTEN to my room, I'd sent the boy to bed — I really had to come up with a name for him, dammit! — and perched on the windowsill staring into the night. The storm kept raging, dashing water against the window panes.

I didn't give a damn. Let the living suffer from their joint pains.

I disabled Incognito. My internal energy levels began to creep out of the red. But even that didn't make me happy. Stone Harbor wasn't such a big city, after all. I could always go back to the hotel and restore. But what was I going to do in the capital? Was I supposed to lurk in some dark corner waiting for my internal energy to pick up? That was a problem.

I still had to get there, anyway.

I shrugged, driving the gloomy thoughts away. I really had to use the opportunity to level up Incognito once I reached level 35. It just might require less energy.

Would be good, wouldn't it?

IN THE MORNING, I paid the orc for the following night and left. The sun had already risen above the rooftops but the sky was covered with a thick layer of clouds. Some may call it miserable, but at least the bright light didn't offend my dead eyes. It was drizzling; the wind was driving the rain from one side of the street to the other. My cape got soaked immediately.

The door slammed behind my back. I turned round and saw Mia who'd left the inn after me.

"You're an early riser?" I smiled.

"You'd better get washed up, Scarecrow!" the thief girl walked past me, demonstratively pinching her nose. When she was about to turn a corner, she swung round and shouted to me, "And once you get clean, come to the bridge! It's gonna be fun!"

I very nearly followed her but reconsidered just in time. I shook my head and made for the pier.

The wretched stench of decay! It deprived

the walking dead like myself of any kind of social life.

Last night I hadn't gotten the chance to see the city which was why I now got lost very quickly and ended up by the Tower of Power, of all places. Or rather, by the houses that surrounded the town square. You could only get inside through one of the four arches. There was no other way of access. There were no windows in the walls, either. It was a veritable fortress.

I continued on my way until I came to a small market. There, I came across the first townspeople. They looked, how can I put it, rather scared.

I'd also stumbled into the inseparable Ripper and Thorn Master. I wanted to ignore them but the warrior noticed me and shouted,

"Hey, Scarecrow! Are you coming to the bridge?"

"Later!" I said before turning off into a side street. I didn't mind the druid but his friend was driving me up the wall. Or was I afraid of him? I just didn't know what to expect from him.

Even if the two had followed me, they must have fallen away quickly. I spent some more time meandering around the crooked side lanes until I came to a straight street from where I could see the gray waters of the Twisted Lake.

That was exactly what I needed.

As I approached the lake, the wind became fiercer. Now it wasn't playing with you anymore but blew in powerful gusts over the waves which roared, crashing over the pier and covering the cobblestones in white foam.

The water was rising. The bottoms of the house doors were boarded up. I walked out into the open and was very nearly blown over by the wind. The bay was empty, free from both boats and locals. The expired lighthouse towered on a cliff nearby. Now in the light of day it gave me the impression of being shrouded in a bleak gray haze. It wasn't darkness nor shadows but something completely different.

Although it could have been my imagination, of course.

I looked around and saw the shop sign of an armorer swinging in the wind. I hurried over to it. The door wasn't locked. A dwarf with a braided gray beard stood behind the counter. A curved dagger was stuck in his belt. A hatchet lay on the counter next to his hand.

He didn't seem thrilled by my visit.

✝ The Dead Rogue ✝

"I don't think I can help you today, stranger," he said, preempting my questions. "The city guards have confiscated all my stock. And I can't order anything new because of this wretched storm!"

"Yeah, it's a real humdinger," I agreed. Still, I wasn't in a hurry to leave. I studied the empty shelves. There were virtually no weapons or armor left on display but there were plenty of arrows and batches of crossbow bolts in drums near the counter.

"Come some other time," he suggested.

"You think you might have a set of armor for me?" I asked.

"Hm," he said pensively. "I have this thing that doesn't fit anyone.'

He reached under the counter and produced the finest chainmail shirt I'd ever seen. "This is double Elven weave!"

I whistled but immediately lost interest. The item had an "Only for the warrior of Light" restriction on it. I wouldn't be gaining anything by acquiring it.

"Well, as you wish," the dwarf shrugged. "I did tell you my stock is limited."

"I wanted to buy a present for a necro I

know," I said. "You don't happen to have something from the Deadman's set, do you?"

Predictably, he shook his head. "I would have sent you to a couple of places where you could have asked about it," he said, "but they're all shut now. Wretched storm!"

I heaved a sigh. "And what's with your lighthouse?"

"The wretched lighthouse! The moment it went out, the storm started."

I nodded and left. I hadn't even tried to offer him my trophy amulets. If Isabella managed to ID them, I wouldn't have to fork out to have it done by a professional sorcerer. Also, the prices in the capital were probably better. They might fetch me more.

The wind was still raging. It blew, it howled, it ripped, throwing bucketfuls of rain in your face. The rain would ease up only to return in force, pelting you with volleys of different caliber.

So what was I supposed to do till the evening? The enforced boredom was driving me mad. The only thing that made me feel slightly better was that my "sworn friend" Garth couldn't get into the city no matter how hard he tried. And the moment the siege was lifted, I'd make a beeline for the capital.

And what if it ended in defeat? Never mind. Even if the dead took the city, I wasn't afraid of that. The subjects of the Lord of the Tower of Decay couldn't hurt me. But still, I didn't want to prolong it much further.

I looked at the lighthouse. Should I go and see it, maybe, while Incognito hadn't yet syphoned me dry of internal energy?

I found it strange that the locals kept mentioning it whenever they spoke to me Could it have been a prompt of some kind?

I was just about to do so when I heard a far-off rumble in the air.

What the hell? That was one hell of an explosion! And it sounded as if it had come from the bridge!

I cussed and dashed toward the bridge across the entire city. It was actually good I hadn't bought that chainmail. My cape didn't hinder my movement and used virtually no stamina. That wouldn't have been the case had I had to run in full armor.

I noticed the smoke from afar. The wind was whipping up billows of black smoke; but even now as they dispersed, they continued to glow green. There must have been some powerful sorcery involved, and not of the nicest kind.

Death magic.

When I'd run around the last hill and rushed out onto the square in front of the bridge, there was only one tower left standing. The other one lay in heaps of smoking masonry and had partially collapsed into the river.

The bridge's meager garrison were rushing around like headless chickens, preparing to meet the army of the dead. Five players were awaiting the assault next to them. But two archers and three warriors could do precious little to change the course of the battle.

Mia wasn't there. Had she been smart enough to go back to the city?

Bows snapped on top of the surviving tower as the bridge defenders began to fire at the dead. The latter had brought some fat pine trunks with them and mounted them onto the bridge, intending to repair it. The defenders had killed them all but more and more zombies kept pouring out from behind the mound, replacing those who'd dropped into the river. They continued dragging the pine trunks along to the damaged section of the bridge. The defenders engaged incendiary missiles. Despite the rain, the tree trunks caught fire straight away, forcing the dead to retreat.

The players cheered. From the other bank, catapults fired wooden barrels across the river. I ducked behind a boulder, expecting them to go off, but the missiles hit the ground and fell apart, sending bits of wood and human bone everywhere. There was nothing magical inside them.

Having said that...

The human bones hit the ground and began to join up, forming human figures.

Bone golems.

Shit!

A new volley from the catapults had hurled more barrels onto our bank. I hurried to help the players. They'd split: two shielded warriors had advanced and began to slaughter the undead. A scout lancer was stabbing the zombies with his lance from behind while the archers climbed the hill from where they kept loosing off arrow after arrow with little success.

I stealthed up and ran into the enemy's rear where I hacked at them with my flamberge.

To my surprise, its undulating blade had sliced through their backbones with remarkable ease. The golems collapsed to the ground in heaps of bones.

The players had finished the two remaining skeletons and hurried to frisk them, looking for any loot. I stared in disappointment at the XP I'd just received for the killing.

This was a far cry from the dungeon's guards in their black armor.

More barrels smashed into the ground. More bones stirred. The players perked up and hurried to smoke the skeletons one after another while I shouted to the archers leaping from rock to rock,

"Have you seen Mia?"

"The thief girl?" an Elf replied, sweeping his braided silvery hair aside. "She's just been here somewhere!"

"Where did she go to?"

"I didn't notice!"

The third volley of barrels overshot the square and burst open on the slope overhead.

Magic flames flared up amid the stones. The archers scampered to safety, away from the skeletons. This time I saw some Death Disciples among them. The warriors with the raised shields started up the slope while I ran around it, aiming to climb the hill from the opposite side and attack the undead from the rear.

As I left the square, I came across Ripper and Thorn Master and shouted to them as I ran,

"Did you see Mia?"

"Follow us!" the warrior signaled. "She's over there!"

We darted along the road, then turned off onto a trail hidden by the bushes. Soon it had taken us to a rocky plateau where it wound its way along the bed of a precipitous canyon.

Suddenly I realized I was running alone. The players had lagged behind.

What the hell?

I turned a bend and very nearly bumped into a Death Disciple immobilized by the long branches of a thorn bush. The thorns had sunk deeply into his dead flesh even though they couldn't deal him any serious damage, just kept him in place.

The crystal skull that topped his staff began to glow, emitting a blue light. Instinctively I shrank back. Too late: the magic thorn bush had already blocked my retreat, growing bigger by the second.

That was the druid's work! The two bastards!

Death magic: immunity!

The spell cast by the dead sorcerer went right through me and burned a hole in the thorn bush. Still, new shoots just kept growing in place of the ones scorched by the spell.

The druid and his buddy hadn't been running away from the battle. They'd lured me into a trap. An ordinary player had no chance against a Death Disciple.

A bit further on, I saw a shred of black velvet. Then I knew that I didn't have to look for Mia anymore.

Bastards! They drove other players into a trap, then looted their bodies!

Scumbags.

How I wished I could hack them both to bits!

Instead of fighting with the ever-growing bush, I drew my Soulkiller and unhurriedly headed for the Disciple. He cast a couple more combat spells on me. I buried the hook under his collarbone and leaned with my whole weight on it, widening the cut. The hook sliced through the dead flesh and the bones. I released it, then sliced through the monster's larynx and broke his backbone.

His head dropped onto his chest. He let go of his staff which I caught just in time. It crumbled in my hands. I was dying to add another crystal skull to my collection but it too disintegrated into dust.

I didn't care.

I slid the hook in my belt, drew the flamberge from its scabbard and ran down the path. By then, the thorn shoots had already shriveled up. One whack with my sword was enough to disperse it.

I stealthed up and returned to the road. The two bastards were nowhere to be seen. Shame. I'd seriously intended to rip them to shreds. I didn't give a damn about receiving the PK mark. I just didn't care.

Still, the two lowlifes had already legged it. My fury began to subside. I returned to the square and froze, open-mouthed.

The powerful wind ravaged the square. Dustdevils played havoc with the bodies and bones, eventually merging into one gigantic tornado. It then fell apart, releasing a bone dragon into the sky.

The archers on the surviving tower tried to bring him down. The undead creature saw their efforts. With one powerful wingbeat, it collapsed the firing platform on which they stood into the river.

The bridge had fallen. The approaches to the city were now open to the army of the dead.

7.

THE DEAD HAD neither attacked during the day nor at sunset. It was only at twilight that their troops marched into the ravine between the hills. By then, most of the surviving players had already returned to the inn. The moderators had deliberately given the city defenders enough time to regain their strength. But even so, our decimated ranks hadn't the slightest chance of repelling the invasion.

But even though Stone Harbor wasn't ringed by walls, Grakh hadn't even thought about ordering a retreat.

✝ The Dead Rogue ✝

"They're just a bunch of brain-dead zombies!" he announced out loud over the clamor of voices. "They can barely move! We'll wipe them out provided we don't panic!"

Somehow I doubted his fiery speech could inspire anyone. At least no one laughed at him. After all, one's participation in an unwinnable battle was a requirement for the Defender of Stone Harbor achievement. All you lost in case of death was your XP. For all of them, this was just a game.

WE'D DECIDED to face the dead at the roadblock by the entrance to the city. Our warriors took cover behind the high barricade. The archers climbed onto the nearby roofs.

Grakh left me in reserve. As the preparations for the battle unfolded, I kept looking for Ripper and Thorn Master but they were nowhere to be seen.

What a shame.

However, very soon we had more important things to take care of. The first wave of the dead fell upon us. The barricade became the scene of a massacre. The players had no problem killing zombies who were stupid, clumsy and unarmed.

But they were only a cover for the arriving legionnaires, followed by lost souls. Our archers on the roofs were forced to switch their attention to the enemy archers, leaving our warriors without support.

Volleys of arrows showered the ground beyond the barricade. Someone screamed with pain. An arrowhead ricocheted from another warrior's sturdy armor. Luckily, my Evasion protected me from the deadly downpour as I seemed to know where exactly they would land and dodged mechanically without even thinking.

And then we discovered that the army of the dead wasn't going to play ball. While the legionnaires engaged our main forces, the dead had spread into nearby streets and attacked the few city defenders on the flanks. The latter weren't able to offer much resistance, retreating in panic toward the Power of Tower.

"John!" Grakh shouted. "Bring more men here! Don't let them surround us!"

Bring more men? We were literally down to a few: the lancer scout covered in blood, a warrior whose left arm was hanging uselessly, and a knight, powerful but too cumbersome in his armor studded with arrows and crossbow bolts.

✝ The Dead Rogue ✝

Plus me.

Still, we had nothing to do, so I turned to my handicapped platoon, "Follow me!"

We hurried along the street, turned a corner and bumped right into a crowd of zombies. Just our luck. Still, their rusty swords and battleaxes hadn't prevented us from overpowering them and then heading for the crossroads. From there, a straight road led directly to the main square.

We were not the only ones attracted to this strategically important position. A pale glow spread in the night air.

"Retreat!" I shouted.

Too late. The ball of ghostly light hit the scout who staggered and turned to us, raising his lance. His eyes lit up with an ominous pale-blue flame. Still, the newly-baked zombie didn't get the chance to attack us as the knight who was running behind him smashed his brains out with his gauntleted fist.

Blood and gore flew everywhere.

I rushed forward, taking the next strike onto myself. My immunity to magic hadn't let me down. A new attack spell seared me with a wave of cold but dispelled without actually harming me.

The pallid-faced sorcerer, as tall as a beanpole, raised his staff again. I hurried to stealth up. I took a swing with my flamberge and gave him an almighty whack, adding my Constitution bonus to the damage. At the very last moment, he'd managed to detect my attack. The crit failed but the undulating blade of my sword cleft him in two, from his left collarbone to his right thigh. I'd literally split him in half.

Next one!

Experience: +300 [7 694/8 950]; +300 [7 738/8 950]

Undead, the level is raised! Rogue, the level is increased!

Achievement received: "Man of Habit"!

My success gave me wings. I pressed on. I beheaded a skeleton brandishing a halberd, then turned to a zombie crossbowman and lowered my sword onto his swollen head in a rusty second-world-war helmet.

The towering bulk of a dead mountain troll appeared from around the corner, his head reaching the third-floor windows, his burly shoulders blocking the daylight from the street.

He raised his clawed hand. I dove under his swollen mitt and drew my flamberge across his exposed knee. The sword went into the rotting flesh with remarkable ease but failed to reach the bone. I had to dodge his new attack and retreat.

Still, now I knew I could do it.

The dead troll was enormous and strong but terribly slow. He just couldn't react to my lunges in time. Any other rogue would have had their work cut out for them trying to pierce his hide with their miserable daggers. Not me, though.

I had my flamberge.

Dammit! Inspired by my example, the knight raised his two-handed sword and fearlessly joined in the fray. The troll's mitt grabbed him by the waist and hurled him head first at the wall, then squeezed him and discarded his corpse like a used tube of toothpaste, coloring everything red.

I slashed my flamberge across his swollen hand, chopping off his pinkie. The wound oozed puss. Clumsily the troll began to turn round, offering me a perfect opportunity to attack his legs again. This time I used the "Powerful Blow".

The sword sliced through the flesh, hitting his kneecap. The sword very nearly flew out of my hand but he'd received a "Crippling Blow".

His enormous bulk listed to one side. I barely had time to duck out of the way. The troll clattered onto the pavement. He reached up and grabbed at a second-floor window trying to scramble back to his feet but failed. He was stuck.

I jumped at my chance. I darted back toward him and buried the tip of my flamberge into his bulging eye. The sword met no resistance as it pierced the monster's brain.

The troll opened his jaws exposing his rotting teeth. He shuddered and died, for good this time.

Execution! The Dead Mountain Troll has been killed!

I let out a howl of triumph and pulled the soiled sword out of his eye socket. Mechanically I glanced at the XP bar.

Big mistake. The troll's body shuddered in one last spasm. His hand convulsed, still grabbing at the window. The stonework gave way

---

and collapsed right on top of me.

TURF. Stones. Drizzle.

I'd come back into the game on a hilltop at dawn.

"Good morning, Uncle John!" the boy greeted me. He was sitting on a mossy boulder next to a bush.

My head was still smarting from the impact of the falling masonry but I forced a smile. "Hi kiddo. Why don't you start a fire?"

"There's a dragon nearby."

There was only one kind of dragon that could be here: the Bone Dragon.

I walked over to the edge of the bluff. "Where is he?"

"I can't see him anymore," the boy said. "Usually he prefers to circle the tower. But he does fly over to the river now and again."

The top of the hill offered an excellent view of Stone Harbor. Much to my surprise, the battle was still raging in the city.

Houses were burning. Flashes of combat spells raked the air. The army of Light was trying to cross the river right on the enemy's heels. Still, the dead stood their ground and fought literally to death.

The air quivered with all the loose magic, spreading a ghostly glow which trailed along the ground, then rose into the sky.

It looked as if the subjects of the Tower of Decay had won this round. Sooner or later, they were going to polish off the few city defenders. The army of Light had its work cut out for it trying to break through their defenses.

"Don't the dead come here?" I asked the boy as I'd noticed about twenty grim prisoners, all city dwellers, being escorted somewhere by a Death Disciple and half a dozen zombie crossbowmen.

"No, they don't," the boy replied. "They don't dare to. Only the dragon flies around."

I sat on a boulder next to him and stretched my legs.

"Uncle John, d'you want your skull back?" the boy asked. "It's sort of weird. Sometimes it gets real cold from inside."

"I'd like you to keep it for a while," I asked as I opened the stats window. I had to distribute the points I'd received. Also, what was that achievement with a funny name, "Man of Habit"?

I opened its description. Oh wow.

☥ The Dead Rogue ☥

25 levels with one weapon!
Bloody Flamberge (Deadman's Set)
+3% to Damage and Accuracy

Did I just say wow? This was off the scale!

With the previous achievement, I now had 5% to both Damage and Accuracy. That was nothing to sniff at!

And if I managed to keep it for 50 levels, what kind of reward would they give me then?

I stopped and knocked on the nearby tree, not wanting to jinx it.

Oh no, sir.

A player's initial advance through a game is usually rapid. But once you reached level 50, you had to fight for every little bonus. Even investing real money wouldn't help you much. It was just that my case was so special. It might take me a while to reach my ceiling. Still, sooner or later that would happen.

I added one point to Agility. After some hesitation, I invested the other one into perception which directly affected internal energy. It was vital for me to keep Incognito up and running.

I selected Evasion from my list of skills.

Instead of improving combat skills, I chose to level up Incognito seeing as now I had this opportunity.

And that's where bitter disappointment lay. I'd naively thought that now my skill would spend less internal energy. In fact, it turned out to be quite the opposite.

Incognito II

By now, you're so used to hiding from unwanted stares, you can actually sense them.

A perception bonus: a "Watchful Stare" ability allowing you to sense when somebody's eyes are upon you.

+10% to Stealth

Was that it? So much for my great expectations! I should have learned a new combat or fencing technique instead. What a predicament!

Still, I couldn't undo what I'd just done.

Never mind. I'd survive.

"There's the dragon coming," the boy suddenly said, wrapping his wet shirt tighter around his shivering frame.

I awoke from my musings. "Where do you

see him?"

Then I saw him myself, his gray shadow flitting over the landscape.

The bone dragon flew toward the city. He was gliding really low, tracing every curve of the hills below like a rocket with magic wings. Some kind of haze enveloped him which concealed his outlines, turning him into a shapeless blob of matter. Grass withered in his wake; the trees crumbled to weightless dust which covered the scorched earth.

Even from this distance, I sensed the weak traces of death magic he exuded, alluring and repulsive at the same time. I'd already experienced that with the fragment of the Sphere of Souls.

The dragon sped towards the city. Having reached its outskirts, he soared upwards, banked into a steep turn, then dove onto the Tower of Power under the cover of the smoke that filled the air.

The shadows closed up but the creature broke through their barrier with remarkable ease and hurried on. It took me some time to realize that only momentum was now keeping it aloft. The creature crumbled to bone dust which then rained down on the nearby roofs.

The Shadow Puppeteer had destroyed its very soul.

I'd never seen anything like it!

Oh. Would the dead manage to take the city before the powers of Light defeated them? Or should we expect Dark reinforcements?

Doubtful. The weather was getting worse. The sky had darkened; gusts of piercing wind had brought more rain.

The wind was ripping the hood from my head. I clung on to it, wondering what I should do next. Was it worth it trying to get to the Tower of Power and then die a hero like all the other players? What good would I be to them? Probably none.

Still, sitting here on this wind-lashed hilltop wasn't an option, either.

How about the lighthouse? I peered at its far-off tower, its spire assaulted by lightning. After some hesitation, I decided to check it out. It had been mentioned too many times in too many conversations to be an empty word.

And even if it were, what did I lose? Time? It wasn't as if I was in a hurry to get somewhere.

"Come on, now," I said to the soaked boy.

✝ The Dead Rogue ✝

We followed a narrow trail down the hill only to start going up the next one.

The courtyard of the farm was strewn with dead zombies. I activated Incognito. I really didn't want to waste any internal energy but I had to, otherwise they'd never let me anywhere near the portal. No amount of trinkets like that "Defender of Stone Harbor" achievement would help me then.

Actually, the achievement bar was still only 75% full. Should I go and smoke a few deadmen?

Hardly. The subjects of the Tower of Decay gave the hills a wide berth. And trying to attack them in the city or by the bridge would have been way too risky.

It was settled, then. I had to go to the lighthouse.

I FOLLOWED A MAZE of trails meandering over steep hill slopes, gradually closing in on my goal. The sky overhead darkened ominously. Lightning kept hitting the silvery figure on the lighthouse's roof. The black thunderclouds swirled into twisters while the gusts of wind very nearly blew us off the path.

The rain didn't help, either. I was soaked to

the skin.

I kept casting glances at the boy but he didn't seem to mind. He waded barefoot into the puddles without complaining about the cold or the wind.

Shit. I seemed to have gotten used to considering him human. And he was no more than a bunch of pixels. Did they even have pixels here? It didn't matter, anyway. He was only part of a program code, admittedly useful but no more than that. Program code don't get cold.

Neither did I, come to think about it.

A wet, miserable Executioner is a sorry sight, let me tell you.

The wind was growing fiercer. The sky had grown dark. Now the lightning started hitting the trees around the lighthouse. I felt uncomfortable thinking that the hilt of the flamberge behind my back would act as a lightning conductor. I wasn't looking forward to receiving a mega-million-volt strike which would roast me alive. Not a good idea.

I wound my head back into my shoulders and quickened my pace. The trail led uphill. The lighthouse tower loomed before me reaching for the sky, its spire piercing the low clouds.

✝ The Dead Rogue ✝

My ears rang with the constant thunder. The countless flashes of lightning flickered in my eyes. I ducked into the wide opened door without even checking it for any potential traps.

I didn't give a damn about them. Lightning was a much bigger threat.

The floor inside the lighthouse was covered with footprints. It looked as if a whole squad of warriors had taken refuge here. The sensation of being watched sent shivers down my spine. I turned to look but saw no one, so I stepped up onto a spiral staircase which encircled the inner wall of the tower. It went down as well but I had no business to be there.

"Wait here," I said to the boy, then began my ascent.

The lighthouse proved to be quite tall. Very tall. From the outside, it hadn't appeared half as big as it actually was. I kept walking along the narrow staircase which had no railings at all. From time to time, I came across narrow slits in the thick wall. At first I could see the roofs below, the hills and the raging lake. Then the view was concealed by the wisps of low clouds and the flashes of lightning which hit the spire.

The thunder grew ever louder. The air filled

with the tang of ozone. My hair stood on end with the static. I really didn't feel like going on — but coming back from halfway there seemed rather stupid. I'd wasted so much time I might just as well persevere.

By the time I'd reached the upper level, I was almost crawling on all fours. The wind hit me in the face, threatening to blow me into the bottomless stairwell. I was scared witless.

A game? I beg to differ!

How long had I been here already? A month? This place just felt too real for me. Scary real.

I reached the doorway and took a peek.

The crystal resting on its pedestal was the size of a mountain troll's head. It was gray and listless. Dead, I'd say. Its force still pulsated within it but its magic had ceased to glow: rather, it seemed to infect everything around it with its strange disease. It seemed to poison the world, turning it bleak and unwelcoming.

It hadn't touched me, though. I was already dead, anyway. Dead as a doornail.

Still, even a deadman like myself would feel uneasy next to this loathsome object.

I began backing off. For a while, I

scampered down the steps backwards on all fours. Then I scrambled to my feet and hurried down.

It would have probably been quicker to just jump down. I ignored the provocative thought and quickened my step, counting the stairs.

One, two... In the end, I lost count and stopped doing it. Pointless. And once I'd finally descended, I stared at the dark mouth of the basement with suspicion.

The place must have already been stripped of every bit of loot by the countless players before me. Going down there was a waste of time. Then again, why not?

This wasn't the real world, after all. What if the game had a surprise in store for me there?

Gingerly I stepped onto the muddy step.

"Uncle John!" the boy called me. "Can I come with you? This place is so scary when you're alone."

The atmosphere inside the lighthouse was indeed remarkably oppressive. The wind whistled through the window frames. The powerful walls shuddered every time the building got hit by a lightning. I felt sorry for him.

"Come on," I said, then remembered.

"Won't it be too dark for you there? I've got no lamp."

The boy pulled a torch out of its wall mounting and relit it with a practiced hand, using a tinderbox.

"All done!" he grinned a toothy smile.

We started down the steps. In the uneven torchlight, I noticed traces of fire on the stone ceiling. We came across a thick door ripped off its hinges. A bit further on, the passage must have once been blocked by some rusty bars which had now been forced open. A picked lock lay on the stairs nearby.

We continued our descent. The spiral staircase seemed to be leading deep into the mountain. The stairs were littered with clumps of earth flattened by the boots of earlier passersby, human and not. I cast wary glances at the ceiling but the masonry seemed to be stable.

But the provenance of the earth remained a mystery.

Finally, the stairs brought us to a horizontal corridor. I made the boy stop and listened. The silence was perfect. You couldn't even make out the sounds of the thunderstorm.

I paused, listening, then continued our

wary advance. I looked intently underfoot but saw no signs of any traps. The tunnel was lined with half-burned torches mounted on the walls; every time we passed them, the boy relit them. Soon an entire string of lights glowed in our wake.

In front of us though there was nothing but darkness.

For some reason, the fact seemed to unnerve me somewhat. Scared me even.

That wasn't normal. A deadman wasn't supposed to be afraid of the dark.

Having said that, there was no knowing who might have found refuge in this dry, dark basement.

Or should I say, a *crypt*? This wasn't just any old basement. This was a tomb.

Here, the walls were lined with empty burial vaults. After some time, we started coming across some that must have been closed and sealed. The slabs of stone which covered them bore all kinds of names and other symbols, the most common of which was that of a phoenix.

The further we went, the more masterful the carvings were, as if the later burials had been performed already at the time of the city's decay.

"Uncle John, is this where they buried the lighthouse men?" the boy asked.

I shrugged. It definitely looked that way.

For a while, I was afraid of grave robbers but it didn't appear as if any of the graves had been desecrated. I couldn't see any bits of skulls or chewed bones lying around. Only footprints in the dirt.

Then the corridor opened into a large underground hall with a vaulted ceiling. The boy walked along the wall, lighting the torches. I didn't need light, so I made my way to the center and stopped by a deep hole in the floor.

Here, the intricate marble tiles had been broken. The floor was strewn with fragments of stone and clumps of dirt.

"What is it, Uncle John?" the boy asked after he'd finished his rounds.

I looked into the jagged hole. It appeared to be five or six foot deep.

I shrugged. "A grave?"

Indeed, it was a grave. Very recently robbed, too. The footprints on the dirty floor were very fresh. The robbers must have been here less than a week ago. Judging by the grave's luscious engravings, this was the resting place of someone really important. Having said that, why on earth would robbers, after having taken all the jewelry, weapons and precious armor, also pilfer the coffin?

Or had there even been a coffin?

Coffin or no coffin, they must have had a deadman there, that's for sure.

I already turned to go when a ghostly groan echoed behind my back.

I drew my flamberge — but my opponent turned out to be a spirit. Just a shimmering white cloud.

Great. Where was my Soulkiller?

"Help me!" the ghost wailed. "Help!"

"Stay away," I warned him, backing toward the door.

"Are you all right, Uncle John?" the boy asked, concerned. "What happened? Who are you talking to?"

I cast a quick glance at him. The ghost noticed it.

"He can't see me," he explained in a normal voice. "Only those in possession of sorcerous skills can talk to the world of spirits."

I chuckled. Sorcerer, of all things, I was not. "You don't mean it!"

"Deadmen too. But they're not interested in talking."

This had struck a sore point, so I hurried to change the subject. "What do you want?"

"I want you to return my body to my grave!" the ghost demanded.

Immediately, a new system message appeared, offering me a "Stolen Remains" quest.

Still, I wasn't in a hurry to accept it. "What's in it for me?" I asked instead.

"I am the first lighthouse keeper and the Grand Master of the Order of the Silver Phoenix!" he announced.

If he'd wanted to impress me, he'd failed miserably. "You *were* the first lighthouse keeper," I grinned. "Now you're only a pile of bones. Literally."

His aura began to blink and ripple. Still, the ghost had restrained his anger and turned my attention to rewards.

"If you bring my remains back, I'll share with you some of the Order's sacred knowledge."

I snorted.

My skepticism hadn't gone unnoticed. The ghost raised the stakes. "A lot of things have been revealed to the world of spirits. I know about your interest in the Deadman's set. If you help me, I'll get one of its items for you."

"Which one?" I demanded.

"The one you need most."

The promise was vague to say the least but something in it had piqued my curiosity. I'll tell you more: this guy knew how to hook me.

"Agreed!" I said, accepting the quest. "Where are your bones now?"

"They're in the hills to the east of here," the spirit told me. "Not very far. Less than a mile, I think. They're in some sort of dungeon. But the exact location I don't know."

The glow faded as the spirit had left the tomb. I didn't fancy staying there, either.

"Uncle John!" the boy demanded, bursting with curiosity. "Who were you talking to just now?"

He cut himself short and gasped, "Uncle John!"

"Watchful Stare"!

My new ability pierced my heart like an icy needle. I swung round. A black shadow slid through the corridor against the backdrop of the string of torches.

The stranger must have realized he'd been discovered. He stepped calmly into the tomb. It was Karl Lightning, the sorcerer from the inn.

He grinned and said without further ado, "Listen up, Scarecrow! I just happened to overhear your conversation. D'you mind if I join you? It would be easier together."

Lanky and scrawny, he didn't strike me as an experienced player. But if there was one class of players you should never judge by their appearances, it was the sorcerer.

I hesitated, then offered him my conditions, "The Deadman's set item is mine. The sacred knowledge is yours to do what you want with it. All right?"

"Sure," he accepted my terms and offered me his hand, apparently in a hurry to shake on it. "You can send me the invitation."

Something glinted in the sorcerer's hand. My deadman's nature kicked in at once. Instead of shrinking back and asking him questions, I attacked him first.

My assault was swift and powerful.

"Sudden Strike"! *"Powerful Blow"*! *"Claws of*

Darkness"!

I invested my all into a shove to his stomach. My hand dug deep into his belly, my fingers closing around something supple and slimy. I retrieved my hand, pulling out a bunch of bluish guts.

The sorcerer froze, his mouth open in silent agony. An amulet dropped from his slackened hand onto the floor.

Stun: 00:24... 00:23...

Twenty seconds was plenty.

I drew my flamberge from behind my back, took a broad swing and pointed it parallel to the ground, aiming at his skinny neck. I whipped his head off with one blow like a seasoned executioner. A fountain of blood spurted up to the ceiling. The sorcerer's beheaded body stood a moment, then collapsed convulsing to the floor.

"Critical hit"! Player Karl Lightning has been killed!
Experience: +1 094 [9 678/ 10 750]; +1 094 [9 722/ 10 750]

✝ An NPC's Path: Book One ✝

Undead, the level is raised! Rogue, the level is increased!

PK mark: 06:00:00... 05:59:59...

The relationship with the Swords of Chaos Clan has been changed. Current status: enemy.

What the hell? The PK mark I could understand. After all, I'd attacked him first. But that was no reason to make me the clan's enemy! Even though the sorcerer was apparently a clan member, blacklisting me was a bit too rich!

Shit!

I cussed and kicked the headless body. Then I forced myself to cool off and picked up the amulet. I didn't have enough Intellect to read the intricate black symbols that covered its silvery surface. Also, it made my fingers go numb, so I hurried to put it away into my inventory.

I could still swear he'd been about to kill me. I just hadn't given him the opportunity.

In any case, it was too late now.

I heaved a sigh and frisked his body. On top of the amulet and some money, I also became the proud owner of a magicless leather jacket with no stats. I didn't even try to put it on. In fact, I was about to discard it when I looked at the boy standing by the wall.

I hurled the trophy clothing to him. "Come on, try it on!"

He promptly obeyed. Even though the jacket reached down to his knees, he was grateful.

"Thank you, Uncle John!"

The sight of the beheaded body didn't seem to faze him in the slightest.

It certainly didn't faze me, either. I was much more concerned about my enemy status with the third most powerful clan in the local rankings. Ditto for the PK mark which my Incognito couldn't conceal.

In any case, it wasn't as if I would come across any players in the hills. So off we go in search of the ghost's pilfered remains, then! But first, I had my stats to take care of.

8.

I DIDN'T THINK long about which stats to improve. I increased Strength, Agility and Evasion. As for professional skills, I once again chose fencing with two-handed weapons, bringing it thus to the third level. This didn't make me a killing machine yet, but at least I wasn't some shabby newb anymore, either. Also, the skill was passive which meant it was operable all the time and not only when needed. Plus it didn't require any Stamina. It was all pros and no cons.

Also! The icon of the "Accurate Strike" had now appeared in the two-handed weapon section. I could select it the next time. But first, I needed to read its description.

As for the quest received from the spirit, it had turned out not as easy as I'd first thought. I studied the map but saw no new markers, only a circular patch which now surrounded the lighthouse, with about a half a mile radius. You could spend any amount of time combing through the nearby hills in search of the desecrated remains of the first lighthouse keeper. Also, the storm outside was gaining strength.

I spent some more time walking around the tomb looking for something — anything — that could give me any ideas but found nothing, so I went outside. It was bucketing down. The looters' tracks had long been washed away by the rain.

Just my luck.

I pulled my hood down over my face and

stepped out the door. I was soaked instantly. I was even a bit jealous of the boy's new leather jacket. I could use some kind of raincoat, preferably waterproof.

However, water from the sky was no threat to a deadman. It wasn't holy, after all.

I decided against using Incognito, unwilling to waste internal energy. It wouldn't conceal the PK mark, anyway. If I came across other players, a fight was inevitable. Even if somehow I doubted I would.

The downpour had extinguished the fires that had raged around the city but the gleaming of combat magic continued to flash on the streets of Stone Harbor. The dead hadn't yet managed to take over the Tower of Power. All players must still be there.

I came to a fork in the road and turned off onto the trail that led to the hills. It meandered for a while until it brought me to the road leading to the crossing.

Immediately a Death Disciple and two dead legionnaires appeared from around the bend. They set their sights on the boy. But the moment I took him by the hand, those servants of the Tower of Decay immediately lost all interest in him and continued on their way to the city.

We walked so for a while. When we'd reached the abandoned farm, I told the kid to climb into the attic of an empty shed and continued on my own.

At first the mud in the road was covered in a multitude of fresh footprints. But as I turned a bend, every trace of them vanished. That set my alarm bells ringing. Still, I carried on for a while until my doubts got the better of me. I turned round and went back.

The footprints disappeared in a big puddle of rainwater by the roadside. A narrow trail led into the thick bushes next to it. Not a trail even but rather a gap between two precipitous cliffs. That's where I headed. Very soon I found myself standing at the edge of a canyon which ended with a gloomy gaping entrance to a mine.

Another dungeon? How very original.

The tunnel's wooden supports were crumbling and rotten. Still, I entered it without hesitation. Even if it collapsed on me, I wouldn't respawn here but at the abandoned farm where the boy was waiting for me now, keeping my skull safe.

Darkness enveloped me. My night vision

didn't allow me to see any details, so I very nearly fell down an open hatch. I sensed an emptiness underfoot and froze. I groped around for a ladder and used it to come down, only to discover that the access to lower levels had been blocked by a pitfall from a side tunnel that appeared to have been freshly dug. A light glowed at its far end, too bright and level to be a torch or oil lamp.

Electricity?

Electricity my ass! That was magic!

Indeed, the light was emitted by veins of crystal permeating the ore. As I walked, the sorcerous light grew brighter and more sinister.

Two bone golems in mithril armor froze by the entrance to an underground hall. I approached them warily but they didn't even budge. I stepped into the cavernous hall and shielded my eyes with my hand from the piercing light. It made everything appear clear and bright but at the same time strangely distorted.

Grotesque figures cast sharp shadows across the floor. All I could see was a Death Disciple, a few zombie crossbowmen and a bathful of blood made from a whole crystal.

A death sorcerer stood behind it, his skin taut over his skull. His nose was missing, his lips bloodless.

A Lich
The lighthouse keeper, transformed

For a moment I was taken aback. This must have been the lighthouse keeper which had gone missing a few days ago. And what about the remains of the first keeper? Where were they?

I discovered them in the crystal bath. The moment I saw them, a new system message appeared,

Defend or Die!
New objective: to abort the ritual

Piece of cake, yeah right! And what about my neutrality with the subjects of the Tower of Decay?

The moment I attacked them, I'd become their mortal enemy. And if I used Incognito, the bone golems would make mincemeat out of me just as I entered because they wouldn't be able to see my Neutrality status.

But why should I fight them if I could just die?

I'd simply steal his remains. The moment I did so, the ritual would get aborted automatically. And even if it didn't, at least one quest would be completed.

But I failed to bring this promising idea to fruition. I simply couldn't stealth up. The sorcerous light that filled the grotto didn't allow me to do it.

Damn this game balance! What's the point leveling up rogue if the game developers try to hinder your progress at your every turn?

So what was I supposed to do now?

I couldn't afford to lose my Neutrality with the subjects of the Tower of Decay. After all, my objective was to procure a Scroll of Rebirth, not some ancient relics. And defending Stone Harbor, even less so. Having said that, all these additional quests weren't only a source of XP but also offered new possibilities. If I could only manage it all!

Eureka! I clicked my fingers and hurried off.

00:00:03... 00:00:02... 00:00:01...

I began to act the moment my PK mark was

gone. By then, the army of the dead had already captured most of Stone Harbor. In some places in the city there were still skirmishes going on, but the attackers simply avoided them, in a hurry to attack the Tower of Power.

The main entrance to the Silver Phoenix Inn was barricaded so I had to use the back door. I activated the Incognito, stole over to the door and knocked softly. There was a clanging of armor inside as someone came to the door.

"It's John!" I said. "John the Scarecrow!"

Strangely enough, they opened straight away. Just my luck that the guard posted by the door was someone I knew.

"John?" Victor's eyes widened as he let me in. "They said you'd been buried in the collapsed house!"

"I dug myself out," I replied, sliding the bolt across. "Are there many of us in the game?"

"About a dozen. Why?"

"Need to talk. Let's go."

The atmosphere in the dining room was bleak. The few lucky survivors of yesterday's battle peered sadly through the cracks in the boarded-up windows, occasionally checking on the progress of the Defend or Die quest. Grakh wasn't among them. Most of the survivors had been the archers on the roofs.

"Graph's been killed by the legionnaires," Victor said, rubbing his tattooed head. "We're in a power vacuum now."

That complicated everything. I decided not to convince them to join me. Instead, I just sent them invitations to join the quest I'd just received in the crystal grotto.

"A new objective!" I announced out loud. "Everyone who joins is guaranteed to receive the Defender achievement!"

They hurried to study its requirements.

"But that means leaving the city," one of them said disappointedly.

Luckily, Victor agreed with me. "Our main forces are now storming the Tower of Power," he said pointedly. "We can do it. Sign me up."

A few archers and a couple of gladiators immediately followed his example. They hadn't logged in for a few days and had thus missed all the fun. Which was why they had now jumped at the opportunity to receive the coveted achievement.

I didn't feel the slightest pangs of conscience for my little white lie.

For them it was only a game. Whereas for me, this was a question of life and death.

This may sound like a typical excuse of every scoundrel throughout history but I decided not to beat myself up about it. I looked at the remaining players. "And you? You gonna hang here bored out of your heads?"

A dark-skinned bounty hunter in composite laminate armor nodded his agreement. "Okay, you've talked me into it. Let's have some fun!"

After that, it was all plain sailing. No one wanted to stay behind in the inn. In the end, our kamikaze group counted all of eleven people: too few to battle through to the Tower of Power but well enough for a lightning raid behind enemy lines.

"I'm gonna stealth up and go first," I said once everyone had gathered by the back door. "If I notice any deadmen, I'll let you know. Don't attack anyone before I do that!"

"We know, we know," Victor cut me short, laying an arrow across his longbow. "Come on now! I need to log out soon!"

I flung the door open and stepped outside.

✝ The Dead Rogue ✝

STRANGELY ENOUGH, we didn't have problems getting out of the city. The battle was still raging in the center of town, leaving the outskirts deserted. We hadn't met anybody on our way, either dead or alive.

With one exception: as we'd already reached the hills, a Death Disciple appeared out of nowhere accompanied by two dead legionnaires. We made quick work of them. In one lightning lunge, the bounty hunter flew at the sorcerer and cleft his head with a scimitar while the archers peppered the legionnaires with arrows.

"There're two golems guarding the entrance to the grotto," I warned the others as we'd approached the tunnel. "Watch out."

They nodded a nonchalant agreement. But the moment we'd reached the lower level, the gladiators launched themselves onto the golems, blocking the archers' field of fire. A gladiator's net immobilized one of the golems, allowing the other players to easily chop him to bits with their swords. Unfortunately, they immediately paid for their indiscretion. A spell rocketed out of the cave, showering everyone with cascades of gray sparks, and cremated them on the spot.

✝ An NPC's Path: Book One ✝

The surviving golem headed for us. Bowstrings began to twang. The golem staggered but remained standing, virtually unharmed. The bounty hunter stepped forward, parried the golem's spear and gave him a God-awful whack on his helmet with his scimitar. I slid past the mechanical monster and darted into the grotto.

The Death Disciple stepped in my way. His hands oozed a ghostly glow which pushed me in the chest but failed to do me any harm. The low ceiling prevented me from taking a good swing with my two-handed sword, so I thrust my flamberge into him at full tilt, transpiercing him. I forced him onto his back, yanked the sword out and slashed him across the head several times.

Damage received: 48! 67! 42! 55! 63!

A group of five zombies loosed off their crossbows into me. No amount of Evasion could help me dodge the bolts at such short range. I staggered but regained my balance and leapt aside.

Not a moment too soon. A second group did the same, their bolts striking sparks off the wall.

A black-flighted arrow flew past me, hitting

the empty eye socket of the nearest zombie and sending him to the ground. Ignoring the zombies already reloading their crossbows, I went for the lich.

"Scythe of death"!

The undulating blade struck the undead lighthouse keeper and rebounded, very nearly flying out of my sprained grip. Was he immune to conventional weapons?

The next moment, the sorcerer grabbed my hand and squeezed it tight, breaking my fingers like dry twigs.

"Touch of death!"
"Paralysis": defense intact!

The lich had almost immobilized me. And since conventional weapons couldn't hurt him, I had to use the "Soulkiller". The blow dealt by my left hand had been inaccurate so the bone hook had barely grazed the dead man but he recoiled like a devil from an exorcist.

Damage dealt!

With my next swing I ripped his thigh open,

then hit him in the neck but missed and severed his collarbone instead. A crossbow bolt hit me in the back, stripping me of another 50 pt. health, but that didn't force me to retreat.

I kept lunging at him in an amuck-like state. Kill the bastard! Slice him up! Take him apart!

Even when the dead lighthouse keeper collapsed, I kept thrusting the hook into his unyielding flesh. Take that! And again!

The Lich has been killed! The task "Abort the ritual" is completed!

Experience: +2 000 [11 978/ 12 900]; +2 000 [12 022/ 12 900]

Undead, the level is raised! Rogue, the level is increased!

I turned away from the shredded body. By then, the others had already smoked all the crossbowmen. By the same token, only four of our archers had survived.

I slid the hook behind my belt and tried to pick up the flamberge lying on the floor. My broken fingers wouldn't function. Dammit!

As if echoing my thoughts, a voice said

behind my back,

"What the hell? The task is still at ninety-nine percent!"

I looked back at the anxious Victor. "Wait a bit. I'm gonna sort it all out now."

I turned to the archers. "Vacate the room!"

They ignored my words as they continued to loot the bodies. I cussed, flung my flamberge on my shoulder and left the grotto first.

Victor ran after me. "John? You sure it's gonna work?" he asked me anxiously as he caught up with me in the tunnel.

"Don't even doubt it."

We climbed out of the tunnel back into the open. The half-elf stopped in his tracks and whistled in surprise. "The storm is over!"

Indeed, the downpour had stopped. The clouds had disappeared. The trees above the canyon's edge were no longer bending in the wind.

"It worked!" Victor exclaimed as he began climbing the crude steps cut into the rock.

I couldn't follow him so easily with my broken hand which was why I let all the other players follow him first and only then scrambled up to them. The view from the top of the cliff was

---

quite encouraging. The wind had died down. The long silhouettes of barges crossed the lake's calm waters. Had it not been for the sun blazing down from the sky, it would have been perfect. Honestly, being a deadman, I much preferred the gloom of the stormy twilight. The sunlight was just too much for my eyes.

"Look!" one of the players shouted. "The reinforcements are coming!"

Indeed, the moment the first ship entered the harbor, a new system message popped up,

The task "Defend or Die" is completed!

Achievement received: "Defender of Stone Harbor" Grade 1.

Experience: +2 500 [14 478/ 15 350]; +2 500 [14 522/ 15 350]

Undead, the level is raised! Rogue, the level is increased!

Awesome. Two more levels earned. Had I not been afraid of falling to my death into the canyon, I would have danced. The others, however, showed no such restraint. My ears rang with their whistling and cheerful cajoling.

"Let's go smoke some zombies!" someone

shouted the moment the first flashes of combat spells exploded by the pier.

"And some Lighties!" Victor agreed.

Everybody hurried down the hill. He lingered next to me. "John? Aren't you coming?"

"No. I need to log out soon," I lied.

But was it a lie? Now that the siege of Stone Harbor was over, nothing prevented Garth from coming here. I needed to make myself scarce.

"I see," he nodded his understanding. "And where are you going afterwards?"

I saw no point in making a secret of my plans, so I replied in all honesty, "To the Tower of Darkness."

"What, to the capital? See you there, then. I might be there in a week's time. Grakh asked me if I'd join the clan."

I just laughed. "I don't think there's much chance of us meeting up in the capital!"

"Why not? We've completed a quest together, haven't we? Now we'll always know each other's location. Well, I'll see you around!"

He hurried to rejoin the rest. I froze open-mouthed.

What had he just said about knowing each

other's locations?

That didn't make sense.

I opened my settings and began looking through them. He was indeed right. You could go back to any of the quests you'd completed and locate any of the players that had participated in them.

Dammit!

So that's how Garth had always managed to find me! He'd taken the skull out of the playpen, hadn't he?

And just think of all the lies he'd told me! I was like an open book to him, yeah right! Telling me it was pointless to hide from him! Saying he'd always find me...

And the answer was simple.

I found the right quest and launched a map search for my pursuer. Much to my disappointment, Garth turned out to be very close to where I was. His marker was just near the bridge which was currently contested by the deadmen and the army of Light. Luckily, Garth was still on the far bank.

I had to get away from here.

Still, I suppressed my first impulse. I removed the tick from the box which had allowed him to track me. Only then did I scramble down the slope, slowly and gingerly. Very slowly and very gingerly.

A stupid death could upset all my plans. Wasting several hours resurrecting was the last thing I needed.

9.

BACK IN THE CRYSTAL grotto, I fished out the stolen remains from the bath of blood, quickly wiped my hands and was already heading to the exit when I noticed the bone golem's pauldron — a crumpled piece of black mithril — which must have flown off into the wall. I didn't want to leave it lying around. I placed it in my inventory and hurried off to the lighthouse. I popped in on the abandoned farm on my way and called the boy who'd been hiding in the attic.

Somewhere on the very edge of my vision a new message kept flashing: an offer to raise my character level. Still, I had more important things to do than stat crunching. That could wait. Everything could wait. Except escaping.

I wondered whether returning the remains

was worth the time, or whether I should hurry over to the unblocked tower. The battle was still seething in the city with no sign of letting up. The players who'd arrived on the barges had joined the fray unhesitantly, eager to get their share of fame and XP. And the deadmen had nowhere to retreat to.

"Uncle John!" the boy shouted. "The lighthouse is burning!"

Indeed, the top story of the tower was now enveloped in a uniform glow, visible even in the sunlight.

The boy followed me down into the basement. I hadn't told him to clear off. I didn't care anymore. Time was an issue and I really didn't want to waste it on pointless arguments.

The darkness of the tomb welcomed me as if I belonged there. So much so that I wanted to sit down on the bottom step and close my eyes burned by the bright outdoor light just for a moment. Still, I overcame myself, hobbled over to the crypt and flung the bag of bones into the robbed-out grave.

"Well?" I shouted because no system messages had appeared.

"Bury it!" a ghostly voice rustled.

✝ The Dead Rogue ✝

My broken right arm still didn't move, so the boy volunteered to help with shoveling. When clumps of earth began to fall onto the bag of bones, a silvery glow rose under the vaulted ceiling.

"I am the Grand Master of the Order of the Silver Phoenix!" the ghost announced solemnly. "I am inseparably connected to the lighthouse, the last surviving sanctuary of the order. The renegade tried to cast a curse in the city with the help of my mortal remains. He summoned storms and high winds. You two have stopped him and deserve a decent reward."

"Us two?" I frowned in confusion, but then one of the stone slabs collapsed, revealing a hiding place within the wall. Inside was a long chainmail shirt fashioned of some silvery metal.

Deadman Set: Changed.
Deadman Set: Saved.

Excellent.
The spirit hadn't lied to me in promising me an item from the kit.

Silver Scale (Set of the Dead Man: 5 of 13).

15 Armor.
Stealth: +5.

I donned it straight away. Even though it reached my knees, it didn't hinder my movements due to the deep side cuts on the hips. The sleeves surprised me a little: the right one only reached the elbow while the left one was nowhere to be seen. Strange.

"That's not all," the spirit announced solemnly. "You have the great honor of reviving the former greatness of the Order! Please accept the sacred knowledge of the Silver Phoenix!"

There was a flash of silver. A sharp pain pierced my head.

Damn it! I couldn't remember the last time I'd sensed something like that!

Attention! Your race, profession or religion does not allow you to join the Order of the Silver Phoenix.

The task "Stolen remains" is completed!

Experience: +3 000 [17 478/ 18 100]; +3 000 [17 522/ 18 100]

Undead, the level is raised! Rogue, the level is increased!

✟ The Dead Rogue ✟

I read the system message and laughed out loud. Somehow I doubted they refused to accept humans — or executioners, for that matter. Most likely, they had a sign on their front door, "Only for living beings". If that wasn't segregation!

But then I looked at the red-haired boy, and I immediately began to laugh.

The kid was enveloped in a bright silvery glow.

Bang! The word "boy" disappeared from his description, replaced by the following,

Neophyte of the Order of the Silver Phoenix. Level: 1.

What the devil?! Spirit, you bastard, what have you done?! Change it all back now!

But the ghost had already left us, and the only thing that remained for me to do was dig up his skeleton, shatter his joints and suck out his bone marrow.

I didn't. I should have, but I didn't.

"Hey, boy," I said wearily. "What's your name... Neophyte... Neo! Give me my skull back!"

"Of course, Uncle John!" the lad said as he walked over to me and complied.

✝ An NPC's Path: Book One ✝

As if mocking me, the game system had added a new line with his name to his description. *Neo.* Now the boy was called Neo.

You bastards! You should all be blown to kingdom come!

Children enjoyed full immunity in the Towers of Power. No one could harm them. But only children. And the boy had just had his category changed. From now on, he was a Neophyte of the Order of the Silver Phoenix and therefore, any scumbag could kill him and take my skull.

That bastard lighthouse keeper had really done the dirty on me. How I wish I could resurrect him only to kill him again!

I struggled to pull myself together, grinding my teeth in impotent fury, and headed for the exit.

"Come on, Neo!" I called the kid who skipped along behind me.

Oh Jesus. Now I had him to take care of.

If he got killed, would he return to the game? I doubted it very much.

I got goose bumps down my spine. True, Neo was only part of the program code, but I'd spent too much time in the game just to unflinchingly write him off. That didn't sit well with me.

When we came out of the basement and went out into the street, I was seething inside. I just didn't know what to do. I had no idea. And I still had to lug the skull around with me!

The cliff offered a view of most of the city. I shaded my eyes with my hand and squinted, but couldn't see much in the dazzling sunlight.

"Neo!" I called. "Have they already taken the city?"

The boy stood beside me. "Yes, the dead were forced out into the hills."

"Excellent!" I chuckled as I stepped onto the path. "Come on, then!"

We had to get out of Stone Harbor while we still had a chance. Leveling up could wait. We needed to escape.

Escape!

Neo trotted along beside me. "Uncle John, where are we going?"

I'd already forgotten what normal communications were so I answered without hesitation:

"First to the Tower of Power, and onto the capital by portal."

The boy froze in his tracks. "I can't."

"What do you mean?" I asked. "Why? Didn't you want to see the capital?"

Neo sniveled and shook his head. "I can't go there, Uncle John! I have a quest!"

"What the hell are you talking about?"

A message window opened obligingly,

Would you like to join the "Restore the Temple of the Silver Phoenix" quest?

[Yes / no]

I cussed under my breath, then answered in the affirmative, hoping to be able to decide on the quest's deadline, but nothing changed. Neo was still in charge.

As we came down from the hill, he kept talking about the temple. There was no way I could change his mind.

Let the boy go alone? And how long would a level-1 character last outside of the playpen? Five minutes? Ten?

But I couldn't afford to waste time on some stupid quests! The ruins of the wretched temple were located in the floodlands a day's travel away. By the time we got there and come back...

no.

Also, I had no idea how long it would take us to restore the temple. To hell with it! To hell with the phoenix!

The path led us to the road. I decided to tell a little white lie.

"Let's do it like this," I offered the boy. "We're going to go to the Tower of Power and-"

"Watchful Stare"!

I didn't turn around and let on that I'd sensed danger. I simply gasped, "Run!" as I held the grip of my flamberge. Thankfully, my right hand had already begun to knit and I could move my fingers.

Neo darted off down the road. A whizzing sound sliced through the air. My Evasion forced me to duck. An arrow flashed overhead and sank into a tree, its white flights quivering.

I stepped to the side, then dove as another arrow disappeared into the foliage. I hurried to stealth up. My chainmail changed its color to a strange dull gray and clung to my body like a knitted jumpsuit, turning into steel scales.

I swung round. But before I could dart off,

two chained spirits went for me. My high Evasion had now paid for itself a hundredfold as I effortlessly dodged the malicious specters' attacks. They turned round but lost their impetus. I raised my bone hook, cleaving one of them in two and wounding the other.

Both dead!

The brief combat had thrown me out of stealth. I bucked sideways but failed to outsmart the archers. Both hit me. A barbed arrowhead hit my chest but bounced off my chainmail. The other hit my unprotected left shoulder and pierced it through.

Although it didn't hurt, the complex pattern of magic runes covering the arrow's shaft began to glow with a scarlet flame, activating the spell which blocked my stealth mode.

I didn't panic nor did I lose my footing. I dashed for the bushes, then immediately changed direction missing the next two enchanted arrows. Without stopping, I raised my arm and easily bit through the shaft with my sharp teeth.

The wood snapped. I was free, lurking in the shadows.

I was invisible again. And it might take the necromancer some time to resummon his chained spirits.

But my joy was short lived.

"Set the hell hounds on him!" Garth Deathblade shouted. "Move it! I need the skull!"

With a popping sound, the hell's gates opened somewhere nearby. I rushed off. A bone-chilling howling echoed behind my back.

Chapter Five

The Cursed Temple

1.

I WAS RUNNING. The hell hounds howled behind me, closing in. So I had to run.

I'd been lucky in one thing: the demonologist had failed to bring the infernal creatures under his control straight away. By the time they'd started chasing after me, I'd already put a considerable distance between them and myself. Still, I wasn't even trying to confuse my tracks but simply scarpered along the road as fast as I could.

✝ The Dead Rogue ✝

The river. It was my only chance. No amount of hell hounds could get me once I'd gotten to the bottom.

Yes, but how about amphibian mercenaries? Dammit! I just hoped Garth hadn't had the intelligence to hire some divers. Or had he?

The uncertainty of my situation hadn't forced me to lose my step. I sprinted like mad, trying not to even look at my rapidly dwindling Stamina bar.

I just had to lose them, that's all.

It didn't work though. And I didn't get to the river either.

The hell hounds were much faster than myself. Their forked serpent tongues quivered with excitement; their eyes glowed with scarlet fire; the venomous saliva frothed and hissed on the cobblestones. Those sinewy long-legged monsters with sharp claws and broad jaws chock full of sharp teeth bore only a remote resemblance to real dogs. No idea what had prompted the game makers to class them as canines. They couldn't see me, but their otherworldly instincts allowed them to follow me everywhere. You could neither escape nor hide from them.

Reluctant to waste my last precious stamina points, I grabbed at a bush growing on the slope and climbed onto a high boulder. Leaping from one rock to the next, I began climbing up the steep hill. But the moment I'd reached the trail I could see from the road, the first of the demonic mutts leapt gracefully after me.

The archers, the necromancer and the demonologist had fallen far behind. I drew my flamberge and turned to face my pursuer. The hell hound opened his terrible jaws, howled and lunged at me, swift and fearless.

Too fearless and not swift enough.

The curved blade of my sword met the infernal creature halfway, chopping his front leg off at the joint. The smell of sulfur rose in the air. Drops of black demonic blood fell onto the grass, setting it on fire.

"Crippling blow"!

Yes! Who would have thought that the Dog Slayer achievement would have come in handy again?

✝ The Dead Rogue ✝

I stepped back, looking for another vulnerable spot, but the crippled creature had lost its balance on the steep slope and tumbled back onto the road to its impatiently howling buddy.

Without wasting my time, I hurried along the path hoping to cross the summit and hide from my pursuers on the other side of the hill. Almost immediately, the first arrow hit the rocky soil. The impact reverberated through the air. I had to hide in the shadows. The moment I'd done so, I heard Garth Deathblade yell,

"The skull! I'm only paying for the skull! Whoever brings me the skull will be rewarded!"

The archers froze with their bows drawn as they peered into the shadows trying to detect the slightest stir in the undergrowth which covered the hillside. The demonologist kept the crippled hound and sent the other one away on some sort of mission. And if that wasn't enough, I saw three black gladiators climb after me with their nets and tridents.

"That's it, you wretched creature!" Garth shouted. "Now you're finished! I'll destroy you!"

I was dying to come down and make mincemeat out of him. Still, I didn't turn back.

The gladiators kept climbing up the slope, fast and agile, gradually closing in. I could tell this wasn't the first time they'd had to chase invisible prey.

Lots of things can betray a stealthed-up player: the echo of their own footsteps, the quivering of a tree branch, or even their own smell.

Twang! A long arrow pierced the ground less than a foot away from my head. The archers with their maxed-out perception could be a big problem too.

"The skull!" Garth raged below. "Don't let him hide the skull!"

I cussed and kept going, trying to get to the hilltop as soon as I could. My haste had almost become my undoing as I lost my footing and very nearly tumbled down the slope.

The moment I regained my balance, I heard the victorious howling of a hell hound overhead. The blasted creature had reached the hilltop before me.

The beast had successfully blocked my retreat route. The gladiators were close on my heels. The archers were ready to stud me with arrows like a porcupine.

✝ The Dead Rogue ✝

What could I do in this situation?

Nothing. Die as a hero, I suppose.

Alternatively, I could hide the enchanted skull so that my pursuers couldn't find it. But what could I do with it? Where could I hide it?

Funnily enough, Garth gave me an idea.

"A double reward to someone who'll bring me the stone skull!" he kept screaming, encouraging the gladiators.

The stone skull?

Really?

I reached into my inventory for the skull. Not my own, you understand. The crystal one. The one I'd rescued from the Death Disciples dungeon. There was no way you could tell them apart from a distance, especially if you'd never seen either of them before.

I took an almighty swing. The crystal glistened in the sunlight. And just as I did so, another arrow pecked the skull, knocking it out of my hand. The artifact rolled down the hillside, bouncing off rocks. Forgetting all about me, the mercenaries rushed after it, trying to catch the useless chunk of crystal.

I continued my climb. The hell hound overhead was hissing and spitting venom — but the necromancer who'd summoned him was now too busy rummaging through the grass in search of his artifact. The pooch tried to claw me; instead, I sort of clawed him myself with the "Soulkiller". The bone hook sank deep into the creature's flesh. I jerked hard, throwing the monster off the hilltop.

The infernal creature tumbled down, leaving scraps of his hide on the boulders. Its impatient howling had died away, replaced by plaintive whimpering. I set one foot on a cracked boulder and pulled myself up to the top.

Immediately I heard screaming coming from the foothill,

"It's the wrong skull!"

My heart missed a beat. The advantage I'd thought I'd gained with my clever maneuver had turned out to be too short-lived.

Having said that... it looked like I'd underestimated the power of human greed.

"Pay us now!" one of the mercenaries demanded.

"But that's not the right skull! That's not the one I need!"

"We don't care! Close the task now, noob!"

I didn't wait for their discussion to end but

began climbing down the opposite slope. Luckily, it wasn't as steep.

Somewhere in the distance, I heard the clanging of metal and the sound of an explosion as someone had activated a combat spell.

I didn't give a damn. I didn't even look back.

I had to hurry.

2.

TRAVELING with NPCs has its advantages: while I was legging it trying to escape the mercenaries, Neo had already managed to procure a boat.

Procure? Hmm... I knew the boy didn't have any money. Which meant he must have stolen it.

Still, I wasn't too interested in the moral side of it at the moment. Straining the last of my powers, I finally reached the destroyed bridge.

"Uncle John!" the boy waved his hand to me. "I'm here!"

Before that, I hadn't bothered to track Neo's position on the map too closely. Which was why the presence of the boat turned out to be a pleasant surprise.

I collapsed into it. "Let's go!"

Neo kicked the boat away from the river bank and took up the oars.

"Everything all right, Uncle John?" he asked, steering the boat away from the collapsed bridge pillar.

I raised myself on one elbow, looked around the deserted shore and grinned. "Yeah, for the time being."

I just hoped that the mercenaries and necromancer had failed to find common ground and consequently smoked each other. Or had at least sent Garth back to his resurrection point. And if the guild of mercenaries blacklisted him, as well... that would be excellent. On his own, he was an absolute nobody. Also, he wouldn't be able to track my location on the map. There was no way he'd be able to find me.

I so wanted to believe this. I really did.

But I couldn't.

Once you got yourself a mortal enemy looking for a chance — any chance — to destroy you and trample you into the ground, you shouldn't relax. One single mistake, and you're done. In a game, it's way too easy to end up on someone's black list: one word leads to another until one of you slams his club on the tavern table in anger and then all hell breaks loose. There're no shades of right or wrong left here, as all moral principles seem to be left behind IRL. No one's afraid of retribution.

I wouldn't have minded it so much but the problem was, for me this wasn't a game anymore.

WE'D REACHED the middle of the river when the two crippled hell hounds appeared on the bank. Their howling echoed over the water. Still, they hadn't dared swim after us. They just stood there howling.

I didn't give a damn, honestly.

As the boat continued on its way, I began to realize what must have prevented them from using it to send in reinforcements. The river had flooded the valley, turning it into an impassable quagmire. Tree tops peeked above the water; I could even make out a few rooftops, chimneys and lopsided fences where the water level happened to be lower.

There was no way you could take an army through here. The warriors would sink in the quagmire while a tow boat would run aground in no time.

Now our little boat, she was different.

Neo kept rowing, trying to stay away from the trees while steering the boat into deep ravines and bits of lowland. Occasionally the boy had to fight the current, but the unhurried muddy waters didn't hinder our advance.

At first, I kept squinting my eyes, shielding them from the river's surface glistening in the sun, as I looked for our pursuers. Then I began to pay more attention to my surroundings, especially the bushes peeking above the water.

These were uncharted lands, after all. You never knew who might be lurking in an ambush.

Still, the place seemed perfectly calm. I put my flamberge aside and decided to look into my stats. I had a few points to distribute. I should also work out a leveling strategy. My leveling rate was about to slow down, so I had to start thinking about the future.

After some quality brain-racking, I decided not to overcomplicate things and focused on Strength, Agility and Perception. I wasn't really interested in either pickpocketing or lock picking. My Stealth had considerably grown too thanks to my chainmail, which allowed me to fully concentrate on Evasion.

As always, I had the biggest problems with professional skills. The thing was, you could mix and match combat techniques to create all sorts of combinations — and each new blow you learned gave you access to a great many more combos.

I was really spoiled for choice.

So I decided to choose useful over everything else. The first thing I studied was "Accurate Strike". Even though damage was on the low side, it offered a decent chance of striking the seams of an opponent's armor or thrusting your sword into their visor slit.

This choice had opened me access to new combat techniques, so I invested my new point into "Crippling Blow". I'd done so for a reason. Today, I'd been lucky to chop the hell hound's leg off. I hadn't at all expected my "Dog Slayer" to kick in. Had I missed, I wasn't so sure I'd have been able to escape the mercenaries so easily. I also had a funny feeling I still had some escaping to do. In this situation, the ability to cripple the fastest or most observant pursuer was worth a lot.

Even though this passive skill didn't

guarantee a 100% chance of chopping off an enemy hand or foot, it worked with "Accurate Blow" and didn't put an extra toll on internal energy. Which was a nice little bonus for a beginner bandit.

AFTER THAT, I opened the "Sweeping Strike" and invested my last point into a level-2 "Blind Strike". Its use, in turn, significantly increased accuracy in case of loss of vision or in total darkness and also could be applied to the attacks on invisible creatures.

Why did I need that, might you ask?

But what about the ability to feel someone's gaze?

It was true that no stealthed-up rogue could catch me off guard. But expecting an attack was one thing and being able to deliver a preemptive strike, quite another. A dagger against my flamberge? I was pretty sure I could surprise any cunning bastard!

I saved the changes and spent some time admiring my new characteristics.

John Doe, Executioner, Hangman
Undead. A Night Hunter. Level: 22 /

✝ The Dead Rogue ✝

Human, Rogue. Level: 22

Experience: [17 478/18 100]; [17 522/18 100]

Strength: 26.

Agility: 25.

Build: 24.

Intelligence: 5.

Perception: 12.

Life: 1056.

Endurance: 1100.

Internal energy: 374.

Damage: 192-288.

Covert movement: +10.

Evasion: +11.

Critical damage when attacking in stealth mode, backstabbing or attacking a paralyzed target.

Professional skills: "Incognito", "Execution", "Hangman".

Fencer: two-handed weapons (3), weapons in one hand, "Sweeping Strike", "Powerful blow", "Power lunge", "Sudden blow", "Accurate Blow", "Crippling blow" and "Blind Strike".

Creature of the Dark: night sight, penalty for being in sunlight, Deathgrip, Aura of Fear, Fearsome Bite, "Claws of Darkness", "Sprint".

Neutrality: subjects of the Lord of the Tower of Decay

Enemies: Order of the Fiery Hand, the Swords of Chaos clan.

Immunity: death magic, poisons, curses, bleeding, sickness, cures and blessings.

Achievements: "Dog Slayer" Grade 3, "Tenacious", "Man of Habit", "Defender of Stone Harbor" Grade 1.

Wow, what a change! Now I was a Night Hunter and a Hangman to boot!

"Uncle John!" Neo called. "You seem to have grown taller! Your arms are longer, too."

I got up from the bench. Indeed, my whole body felt taller and lighter. I seemed to have become faster, too.

I sat back down and removed the mask. "Scared, aren't you?"

Neo just shrugged. He caught his breath and returned to the oars. "It's no worse than it was. Only you're quite thin now."

That I'd also noticed. My swollen flesh had shriveled somewhat, my pallid skin clinging to the bones. The death spots were gone now, too, replaced by an intricate network of fine black lines that covered my body all over like pagan tattoos.

Never mind. I'd never been a pretty face. What I found much more interesting, was what kind of surprises my Night Hunter had in store for me in the murder department?

And the Night Hunter hadn't disappointed. The properties it came with! It offered +25% to speed in the dark and in dungeons devoid of sunlight. In combination with "Sprint", that made me almost supernaturally fast. The only problem was, this amazing little skill didn't perform so well in daylight.

Still, it wasn't bad at all. Now, what's with the Hangman?

Hangman
Unlike an Executioner who can either kill his victim quickly and painlessly or prolong their death throes for days and even weeks, Hangmen aren't known for their finesse or self-control. They're steeped in blood up to their elbows. Hangmen kill without hesitation and in the most cruel way possible.

No idea what bonuses Executioners

received for their finesse in dishing out punishments, but a Hangman had extra chances of dealing a "Crippling Blow" as well as the minor possibility of rendering their victim comatose with pain.

I was swift and lethal.

How cool was that?

While I was thus busy, twilight had come. The sky above Stone Harbor kept flashing gold and crimson. It looked like the battle was still in full swing. Either the army of the dead had dug their heels in, or it was the powers of Light and Dark contesting the city.

"Uncle John!" Neo called. "I'm tired! And I'm hungry."

My jaw dropped.

He was *what*? *Tired?*

Could it have been the fact that he'd entered a new stage in his development? Naturally, human players needed to eat and drink. But apparently, that applied to NPCs as well.

I had nothing else to do but replace him and get rowing. As for food... that was something we didn't have.

"How about you catch some fish?" I

suggested.

"We don't have a fishing rod, do we?"

Dammit! I had to swim to the nearest bushes, cut a long straight branch and sharpen one of its ends. I handed the makeshift harpoon to the boy who immediately started looking for fish in the murky waters. He missed twice but quickly got the hang of it. Soon half a dozen large fish wriggled on the boat's floor.

With a sigh, I started looking for a place to moor. Me, I could have easily rowed through the night as the Deadman's amulet restored my stamina in no time. But by then, the going had gotten tough. The deep water had by now given place to flooded fields. From time to time, shallow waves rocked the boat. I dreaded to even think what kind of monsters circulated in the murky depths.

We'd chosen a flooded farm to stop for the night. The master's house stood on a hill surrounded by the flooded river. It was dry inside. We even managed to start the fire.

Neo got busy cleaning the fish while I checked the rooms and sat on the porch, the flamberge in my lap, listening to the chirruping of the crickets. Gazillions of bright stars appeared in the night sky.

Did I feel good? I sure did.

Still, rather than admire these digital views, I'd much rather have woken up in my virtual capsule, had my rehabilitation, then testify in court. At some point, I might even want to go back to the world of the Towers of Power but it wasn't going to be any time soon. Oh, no.

I saw the darkness — which an ordinary person must have found impenetrable — as a multitude of shades of gray. My Night Hunter's refined ear could discern the slightest noises, so we didn't have to worry about any sudden attacks. I leaned back against the wall and began studying the changes introduced to my Deadman kit. Just like before, the addition of a new item had improved the properties of all the others.

Having finished with that, I decided to check on Garth, just out of sheer curiosity. Still, the sly necromancer had followed my example and blocked me. The thought that he might be anywhere now sent uncomfortable shivers down my spine. I tried not to think about it.

I didn't give a damn. The important thing was, they couldn't track *me* down now.

Or could they? I froze open-mouthed.

What an idiot I was! Hadn't I taken part in that Defend or Die thing? Garth could ask any of them to give him a hand.

I hurried to check on the task. Much to my relief, I discovered that all the tracking permission boxes were unchecked.

But of course! I'd already been Incognito when I'd accepted the task. And I hadn't shown my profile to anyone after that. Now Garth would never be able to find me.

I looked at the unchecked box next to the half-elf's name. Victor and I seemed to have gotten along pretty well. Still, the risk of Garth using him to get to me was too great. I could always find him myself later. If push came to shove.

"Uncle John!" Neo called. "Dinner's ready!"

"I'm not hungry," I replied. "Eat and get some shut-eye. Tomorrow's gonna be a long day."

3.

I SHOOK THE desperately yawning boy awake at dawn and sent him to get washed while I walked toward the beached boat and dragged it back to the river's edge. None had attempted to break in during the night but I discovered plenty of signs of nocturnal visitors in the mud. This backwater was home to giant crocs — provided they were crocs, of course.

This time I took up the oars straight away and began rowing steadily. The boat crossed the flood plain and entered a quiet creek. All around us lay expanses of quagmire studded with waterlogged bushes and strewn with swamp grass. A careless step to the side could see you sucked into the quagmire and drowned without a trace.

I rowed unhurriedly, casting an occasional glance at the map. I found it strange that the marker which denoted the position of the old temple was approaching too slowly. If it was approaching at all.

Should I just forget the whole thing and go back to Stone Harbor?

To tell you the truth, I'd been toying with the idea. The only thing that stopped me from returning to the city was fear. I didn't doubt that Garth wouldn't stop at anything to find me. He'd probably wait for me by the Tower of Power for at least a few days.

✝ The Dead Rogue ✝

How about Incognito?

What Incognito were we even talking about if I was still walking around wearing this tatty cape? Changing into something else might help for a start.

So in the end, I didn't go to the city. I headed for the temple.

Neo kept nodding off without distracting me. I could hear the splashing of water and the birds singing. The bright sunlight began to bear down on me, stripping me of my strength. I only felt better whenever the boat entered the long shady passages under the waterlogged tree tops. The semidarkness of their thick foliage had a pleasant cooling effect.

The farther we moved away from the Broken Creek, the fewer flooded houses and cleared fields we saw. By noon they'd disappeared completely. Only once had we passed a cliff where somebody had drawn a huge, lopsided letter M with a piece of coal.

I looked around warily but didn't activate the Incognito mode. The risk of meeting other players in this backwater wasn't too high.

Soon the swamps began to recede, the land became drier, and the trees higher. Their dense crowns merged overhead into a dense dark canopy. In places where some of the trees had been blown over, pillars of light shone through the gaps.

The creek had narrowed into a fast-moving stream. Now I struggled to row against the current. The ground here was covered with a thick layer of wet fallen leaves which prevented us from telling whether we'd already left the marshland behind. We were also worried about rustling sounds in the bushes. We really didn't have the time to fight any forest inhabitants. What if some of them were venomous? For me, that wasn't a problem, but Neo didn't have much health to begin with.

Gradually the creek had become shallow and rocky. There was no way we could continue. There was nothing else we could do other than pull the boat ashore.

"Stick with me!" I warned Neo, then walked ahead along the forest path. The air under the trees was hot and wet. The putrid smell of decay was unpleasant. Really, this wasn't the right time for my olfactory senses to kick in.

The path followed the stream for a while, then turned off. Soon fragments of red granite began to peek out from under the rotting foliage.

For a while, Neo kept sniffing unhappily behind my back, then complained, "I've got blisters on my feet."

That was the last straw. We had to stop for a break and make him a pair of sandals out of the strips of leather left from the jacket. As a result, I received the "Shoemaker" achievement which unfortunately didn't give me any special privileges. A shoemaker is a shoemaker, big deal.

"Do they fit you well?" I asked the kid.

Neo laced the sandals up and took a couple of steps to try them out. "Fine," he said with a happy smile.

Good. Time to get going.

HERE, THE FOREST was more tropical. The air was close and humid. Exotic flowers abounded amid the creeping vines. Occasionally, we came across some local beastie which would scamper away at the first sight of people. Every time it happened, the forest echoed with the sounds of the disturbed undergrowth.

Gradually the path went uphill, giving us hope that soon the moisture and stuffiness of the lowland would be left behind. But the stench of decay only intensified. We started coming across withered trees with moldy trunks covered in moss. Everywhere we turned, we saw dry boughs and bare branches protruding everywhere.

"This is a bad place," Neo suddenly said.

I stopped. "What makes you think so?"

"I don't know. It's just bad."

"Well, you brought us here," I chuckled. 'Never mind. Keep your eyes peeled."

You couldn't scare a deadman with a macabre atmosphere. Personally, I didn't sense any real threat, but drew my flamberge just in case and rested it on my shoulder. Just for my own peace of mind.

But when about five minutes later the dead black grass began crunching underfoot, I started to feel it too. I stopped and listened, sniffing the air, then looked around.

Nothing aroused any fears, but some kind of gut feeling didn't allow me to move on, whispering softly in my ear, "Run! Run! Run!"

I didn't budge. Instead, I continued to carefully examine the gnarly trunks of the dead trees.

Death! Yes, I could feel death here.

I gently tugged at the sleeve of Neo's cloak.

✟ The Dead Rogue ✟

"Uncle John!" he whispered. "Look!"

I glanced in the direction where he was pointing. Only then did I notice an orcish totem pole among the dry tree trunks. Its carved demonic faces scowled in every direction.

"That isn't right!" Neo said suddenly. "It shouldn't be here! We need to cut it down!"

"What, and wake up half of the forest?" I snorted.

The boy didn't listen to me. He fearlessly stepped off the path and prepared to kick it.

"Don't break any of your own bones," I chuckled.

Immediately I sensed a glare boring through my back.

This was no gut feeling. This was my Executioner skill at work.

A group of squat forest orcs emerged from the thicket with arrows at the ready on their short curved bows. They weren't aiming at me at all. I rushed to Neo and covered him with my back. Instead of piercing the boy's body, the bone arrowheads were deflected by my chainmail.

I swung round to see that the archers were already drawing new arrows from their quivers. Their shaman had now joined them, his unkempt hair braided with dirty red ribbons. A cluster of wispy gray fog swirled in between his outstretched palms.

"Sprint"!

The Night Hunter's skill pushed me forward, squeezing me through the thickened air, then threw me onto the ground within a few feet from the green-skinned caster. The continued momentum of my falling arm brought the flamberge onto the shaman's head, knocking him off his feet. The force of the blow had very nearly wrenched the weapon out of my hand, but I'd already had some experience handing a two-handed sword. I took advantage of the spin to turn around to face the archers and wipe them out with a "Sweeping Strike".

Green blood splattered everywhere. The orcs lay writhing on the ground. I staggered as the cooldown overcame me. My knees buckled. My flamberge stuck in the ground was the only thing that saved me from collapsing onto the rotting mulch.

"Uncle John!" Neo rushed over to me.

"It's all right," I said. "I'm okay."

✝ The Dead Rogue ✝

"You've got an arrow sticking out of you!"

I pushed the arrow's shaft through my wounded ankle, then walked around, checking on the orcs lying on the ground. One of the archers was still alive but I didn't have to finish him off as he soon croaked from blood loss.

"What are we going to do with the idol?" Neo asked when I began inspecting the bodies.

"What do you want with it?"

"We need to destroy it!"

I looked back at the withered tree trunk covered with demonic faces, shrugged and handed the boy an orcish hatchet. "You want it, you go and cut it."

Neo grabbed the hatchet with both hands and resolutely went toward the idol. I continued collecting the loot. Soon I'd become the proud owner of several gold nuggets and a precious stone — apparently a ruby — which I'd picked out of the shaman's staff with my bone hook.

The hatchet began hitting the dry tree; I joined Neo and watched his efforts for a while as he continued destroying the idol. Then I shrugged, went back onto the path and carefully looked around.

I didn't feel like helping the stubborn kid.

You never knew what he might come up with the next time. It wasn't in my job description to cater to his whims.

About five minutes later I heard a crashing sound as the idol collapsed into the adjacent trees, caught up on their dense branches, then slowly slid to the ground.

A happy Neo came running, hatchet and all.

"Throw it away," I demanded.

"This is my weapon!" the boy said stubbornly.

"Later we'll find you something more suitable," I promised. "Come on, let's get going! The sun is setting!"

With a wistful sigh, Neo dropped the hatchet onto the grass and ran after me.

Gradually, the path widened. As we walked, we started coming across skulls — some of animals, others of orcs and even humans — which seemed to be lining the way.

They seemed to be saying, *"You are not welcome here! Turn back!"*

We didn't. The abandoned temple was located somewhere very close to here. We only had another hour or two. With a little luck, we'd find it before dark.

But luck was what we didn't have.

4.

AFTER WE'D LEFT the glade with the idol, the path had meandered around the forest for a while, then took another sharp turn and arrived at the foot of steep cliffs.

"Orcs!" Neo cried out, alarmed.

I grabbed his hand and dragged him back into the bushes.

A precipitous gorge gaped between the cliffs. The passage was blocked by a rickety stockade. Two watchtowers loomed nearby, followed by the roofs of orcish huts covered with reeds.

Orcs were there too, what do you think?

A squat lancer stood guard by the half-opened gate. Two archers hovered on the towers, bored out of their minds. A thin stream of smoke rose to the sky from behind the fence.

"What are we going to do, Uncle John?" Neo whispered. "We're not turning back, are we? Tell me we aren't! I have to get to the temple!"

"No, we're not turning back," I reassured him. I wasn't going to change *my* plans because of three scruffy forest orcs. The Temple of the Silver Phoenix intrigued me, and the longer I thought about it, the more I wanted to give its storerooms a good check.

But... what about the orcs?

Had I been alone, I would have quietly stolen past the sentries under the cover of night. But with Neo, this trick wasn't going to work.

Should we battle our way through? And what if the orcs called for reinforcements? This wasn't the actual settlement: this was only an outpost. The moment the guards sounded the alarm by banging their battle drums or whatever orcs had, the entire horde would come running, and I wasn't that great a warrior to confront a whole tribe on my own.

Neo tugged at my sleeve again. "So what do we do?"

"We wait," I replied curtly.

I had the inklings of a plan. And even though it offered little chance of success, I could always revert to manslaughter if it failed.

WHEN THE SUN had sunk behind the rocks and

the surrounding area had submerged into the twilight gloom, we headed for the outpost. Now that the bright light had stopped assaulting my eyes, my movements had become remarkably smooth and noticeably more precise and quick. I'd chosen against stealthing up and walked toward the outpost in the open, after telling Neo to stay behind me and keep his head down.

The guards had noticed me halfway. Alarmed, they hurried to lock the gate. Still, they didn't shoot: they must have believed themselves to be perfectly safe

I walked over to the stockade, removed my mask and said, "I'm going to enter whether you open the gate or not."

The invisible "Aura of Fear" enshrouded us and penetrated the fence, making the orcs freeze and shrink back, immobilized with terror.

How I understood them. I too would have frozen in terror on seeing such a monster.

They might think that humans made a tasty snack and easy dinner. But creatures like me wouldn't say no to a nice crunchy bit of a careless orc.

A series of rustling sounds came from behind the stockade. A disheveled head covered in shamanic tattoos appeared above the edge. The old shaman began chanting exorcism spells but the moment I gave him my sinister Cheshire-cat grin, he lost the plot and stopped.

A grin? More like a scowl, really.

"Open the gate," I offered him the deal, "and I won't touch any of you. Or I can go in by myself, in which case I'll kill everyone."

"What do you want?" the shaman asked, overcoming his fear.

"I want to go through."

"Where to?"

"That's none of your business!" I growled. "I need to go to the mountains!"

A maxed-out "Aura of Fear" syphoned off the internal energy surprisingly quickly. It wasn't in my interests to drag the negotiations out. "Well?"

The bolt creaked. The doors parted slightly. I pushed the gate open and glared at the shaman who shrank back to a reed hut.

"I have your word!" he reminded me.

I put the mask back on and kept walking along the trail. Neo ran after me.

The old orc noticed the boy and shouted after him, "Leave him to us!"

✝ The Dead Rogue ✝

"He's *my* food!" I growled, then snapped at the bewildered kid: "Come on, chop chop!"

Neo dashed after me as fast as he could.

"You were only joking, Uncle John, weren't you?" he asked as he caught up with me.

I just snorted.

THE GORGE was damp, dark and narrow. Its moss-covered walls rose up steeply, as if the rocks had been cleft by the blow of a giant sword. There was nowhere to turn off here, nowhere to hide. We had to hurry.

When we'd cleared the gorge, Neo drew me toward some wide steps cut into the cliff. "It's over here, Uncle John!"

"Come on, go up," I said. "I'll catch up with you in a moment."

I stood next to the gorge mouth and studied the orcs settlement. I could see low huts peeking from behind the trees in a small valley below. There were at least a couple dozen of them.

If all of the tribe's warriors came out to face us, we'd never come out of this alive.

Suddenly I heard the sound of bare feet on the rock. I stealthed up and took cover in the shadows. A young orc archer from the outpost came running after me. He squeaked briefly when he stumbled upon my fist, flew across the gorge and collapsed onto the rocks.

I fell upon him and squeezed his scrawny neck with my clawed fingers. Orc even stopped breathing.

"So what kind of game is this?" I hissed into his face.

The archer made some unintelligible sound. I loosened my grip and demanded, "Either you forget you've ever seen me or I'll kill you all and use your bones to make flutes. Do you understand?"

The orc nodded warily. I let go of his neck, took his bow, broke it in two, then handed it to the guard. "Get out of here!"

The archer darted back toward the outpost as if the devil himself was after him. I wasn't. I just stood there. I just hoped that my little lesson would work and that those green-skinned idiots wouldn't trouble us anymore.

I shook off the stupor and hurried up the stone steps. Soon I caught up with the panting boy. I slowed down and walked behind him, studying the view which opened from this height.

✝ The Dead Rogue ✝

The orc houses down in the valley were even more numerous than it had seemed at first. Directly below us, a perfectly round lake glistened its dark, deep waters.

"Uncle John?" Neo called to me.

"Coming!" I replied and hurried on.

The boy leapt up onto the next step like a gymnast. The stone slab gave and tilted to one side, sending him down into the abyss. Neo threw his hands in the air and began to fall from the cliff. I grabbed the boy by the wrist and jerked him up towards me.

Had this happened in the real world, we would both have dropped into the lake. As it was, the momentum swung me round as the boy had landed on the step next to mine.

"Thank you, Uncle John!"

I cussed. "I'll walk first now."

Had I been alive, my heart would have jumped out of my chest. But as it was, I hadn't even broken into a cold sweat.

All this was just part of a program code. Just part of the code, nothing else.

But every time I repeated the mantra, it seemed to work less. I shrugged off my irritation and continued to climb.

Program code my ass!

BY THE TIME we'd reached the top of the rocky ridge, we'd come across three more traps. Every time that I sensed the stone slab growing loose underfoot, I stopped without actually stepping upon it. Then I'd check the next step, stepped onto it and helped the boy to cross the dangerous spot.

Much to my relief, Neo had stopped complaining of hunger and fatigue. He just ran after me without lagging behind. He was one hardy kid.

That was good news. Still, I was very pleased when I finally saw the stone dome of the temple loom in the night sky. It was shaped like an astronomy observatory, with no windows in its blank walls. The tall fence around it had for the most part survived. Only one of the side towers had collapsed, as had the bridge built across a deep crevice with a rapid stream raging along its bed.

We had to cross the crevice along a pine tree trunk that lay across it. Somehow I doubted the tree had fallen so successfully by itself; someone must have dragged it to the top of the cliff and laid it to rest against the stone pillars of the bridge.

"Wait here," I said as I warily stepped onto the tree trunk.

It hadn't even budged under my weight. I spread my hands to my sides and crossed to the other side. Those weren't the most pleasant seconds of my life, I tell you. I didn't fear the height that much but the roaring of the rapids below sounded a bit too ominous for comfort.

"Can I?" Neo shouted.

"Come on, then," I shouted back.

The boy deftly ran across without losing his balance once.

I was the first to approach the demolished gate. Warily I looked over the place. There were neither humans nor orcs behind the fence. A huge round temple towered on the opposite side of a small square. A little further on rose the darkened ruins of a watchtower. The fence was lined with collapsed outhouses.

"Let's go, then," I called Neo and headed for the tower. I thought I'd noticed an unintelligible inscription on its wall. I walked over to it and read it.

Not good.

Beware, someone had written in a dark brown ink.

Or could it be blood?

Whoever had been here before us remained a mystery, but it was also clear that only players could have left such a warning. Which meant that all the storerooms had long been emptied. I could forget loot. What a shame.

"Wait here," I muttered, then cautiously walked through the doorway. I studied the empty chests, even checked under the bench and walked back outside with a doomed sigh.

"We must go to the temple!" Neo demanded excitedly.

I tousled his hair. "I can see in the dark but you?"

"Not really," the boy confessed.

"So what do we need to get first?"

"A torch?"

"Right!"

I could have gone on my own, but Neo was the one with the quest. Some key details may have been available only to him. Which was why we had to check out the long single-story barracks first.

Inside, everything was turned upside down

---

just as it had been in the watchtower. Ditto for the basement which must have housed the storerooms once. Now the spilt contents of the crates heaped up on the ground. The players who'd looted this place hadn't been interested in monastic robes. I picked up a white cassock and shoved it over to Neo.

"Get changed!"

I got some clothes for myself too, completely filling one of my inventory slots. I could use a change from that unpresentable fisherman's cape.

I hadn't found any torches in the basement. I was already on my way to the exit when something clanked underfoot.

I felt under the robes strewn on the floor. My fingers closed over a round piece of metal. I couldn't work out the engravings in the dark so I just climbed back upstairs, pensively playing with its long chain.

Somehow I doubted the looters hadn't seen the amulet. They'd probably thought it wasn't worth the trouble. Never mind. Waste not, want not.

I finally located some torches in the ruins of a corner watchtower. All other outbuildings had been either looted or burned. This one hadn't been touched — apparently because the looters had been too afraid of falling to their deaths into the abyss.

"Now we can go to the temple," I announced when Neo had lit one of the torches. "No, wait!"

I took out the amulet I'd just found. The picture of a phoenix glinted on its silvery surface. This just had to be some sort of magic artifact but I couldn't figure out its purpose.

"May I?" Neo held out his hand.

I placed the amulet into his outstretched palm.

"This is the Silver Phoenix amulet!" he boy announced without hesitation. Then his voice dropped as he added, "It's only good for the temple disciples."

Aha. That's why no one had taken it. "Can you use it?" I asked.

Neo nodded.

"Take it, then."

"No way? For real?" the boy's face dissolved into a happy smile. He hurried to put the amulet around his neck. "Thank you, Uncle John!"

"You're very welcome."

✝ The Dead Rogue ✝

I approached the open doors of the temple and looked cautiously inside. The floor was strewn with broken fragments of bones and the deformed armor of the order's guards, all of which sported the image of a phoenix chiseled into the metal. No weapons anywhere though.

Neo followed me. The torchlight cast an uneven glow on the stone walls of a narrow corridor that encircled the main hall. There were no doors to the internal premises, so we set off in search of a passage, moving clockwise.

Here and there we came across the evidence of a fierce battle that had once raged here. Still, the only bodies we'd seen belonged to the temple's defenders. We still had no idea who'd managed to defeat them — apparently without suffering any losses.

We were already a quarter of the way through when the black mouth of a passage gaped open before us. That must have been the entrance into the main hall. Or so I'd thought at first, but as it turned out, the door led to the next corridor, which encircled the temple just like the first one did.

The builders had faced the inner wall with sheets of polished metal. The torchlight reflected from them, flooding all around with an uneven light.

Something crunched underfoot. I bent down and picked up a skull with an unusually massive jaw. Judging by its flat forehead and long fangs, it used to belong to an orc. There were plenty of other bones lying on the floor, but unlike the previous corridor, there was not one piece of deformed armor which used to belong to the temple defenders.

Was it suspicious? Very.

The light trembled.

"Don't play with the torch," I snapped at the boy.

"I'm not."

He was right. There was nothing wrong with the torchlight. It was its reflection from the polished walls that was quivering and blinking as it was separating into a blinding light and the deep black shadow.

Then one of the shadows flowed away from the wall and lunged at me.

I barely managed to cover myself with my hand, but even so the left half of my body had turned numb and lost all sensitivity. The ghost began spiraling up my forearm, snaking its way toward my neck...

A *ghost?*

I shook myself out of my stupor and drew the "Soulkiller" from behind my belt. With a single swing I sliced through the shadow that had entangled my arm. It disappeared in a flash of silver flame as more whiffs of darkness generated by the reflection of our torch, were already leaving the walls and hurrying toward us.

"Put it out!" I shouted as I began to lunge at the shadows.

Still, there were too many of them. The ghosts wrapped themselves around me, syphoning my life.

The fact that I was already dead didn't seem to baffle them in the slightest.

A few shadows clung to Neo. The boy dropped the torch on the floor and began stomping on it, extinguishing the flames. The fire flared up momentarily, then went out.

Immediately the cold had receded, dispelling my stupor.

The shadows had faded into darkness. They were gone.

Dammit! Bastard things!

I cussed, grabbed Neo by the shoulder and

dragged him to the door. "Keep quiet! Follow me!"

We walked out into the outer corridor and hurried to the exit. I pushed the boy outside, then stepped out after him and swung around to face the gate.

Still, the shadows couldn't exist without light. Having extinguished the torch, Neo had killed them all at once.

"What are we going to do, Uncle John?" the boy asked. Large tears of disappointment welled in the corners of his eyes.

"We're gonna go to sleep," I said. "We'll come back here in the morning."

"As if that's gonna change something!" Neo said in a surprisingly wise voice.

"We'll figure it out," I shrugged. "Hungry?"

"I've still got some baked fish."

I looked up at the temple dome and thoughtfully scratched my cheek with my claws. "Okay, you can have your dinner but don't go to bed before I come back. I want you to keep an eye on the gate."

"Do you think the orcs might come?"

I shrugged. "Everything's possible."

With that, I walked back to the temple.

A Night Hunter has no need of a torch.

✝ The Dead Rogue ✝

WITHOUT THE LIGHT, the inside of the temple was extremely dark. Still, my night vision allowed me to at least navigate the corridors, threading my way past the empty suits of armor that used to belong to the warriors of the Order of the Silver Phoenix lying around here and there.

I entered the second corridor with a certain apprehension, but the darkness had already dissolved and absorbed all the shadows, so the ghosts didn't attack me.

The bones of the hapless adventure seekers had ceased crunching underfoot long before I'd reached the passage to the inner hall. It was huge and completely empty. A dark pedestal — an altar? — rose at its center. Massive stone columns supported the ceiling.

For several long minutes I didn't move. Then I took a couple of cautious steps, listening warily to the rustling sound of my own feet. The place seemed safe. The stone tiles didn't sag under my weight. No traps were creaking into action. My anxiety had eased a little.

But not completely, not at all. There was something wrong about the place. The spine-chilling, hair-raising kind of wrong.

Did I tell you that the dead were insensitive

to the feelings of depression and spookiness? Well, I was wrong.

Overcoming myself, I headed for the pedestal at the center of the hall and very nearly stumbled over a shriveled skeleton. The dead man lay on the floor, straight as a die; his white robes stood out against the background of the dark stone.

A priest.

I wanted to walk around the remains but some premonition had held me back. I looked down. A dark line was drawn on the floor right at my feet. Another one joined it at a sharp angle, but the darkness prevented me from seeing their design in every detail.

Deciding not to take any risks, I walked around it and very soon came across a second body. I stopped next to it and looked down at the floor. I wasn't even surprised when I'd discovered another sharp angle right next to the corpse.

It was a pentagram. Or rather, a pentacle. Its circle had faded to the point of being almost invisible.

Someone must have held a ritual here with human sacrifices. The temple had been desecrated.

✟ The Dead Rogue ✟

Approaching the pentacle, I strained my eyes, looking at the pedestal at the center of the hall. After some time, I'd managed to work out a tree stump mounted on it. The face of a demon was carved into it, grinning at me. Was it my imagination or was it glowing in the dark?

And then I felt someone's unkind gaze on my back.

Someone was staring at me.

I swung round. The hall was empty. There was nobody there except me.

Having said that... A giant silhouette of a sprawling leaping figure had been slapdashedly painted on the dome with some sort of light-colored paint. The figure was undoubtedly demonic.

Clawed paws and a gaping mouth enveloped in flames.

A phoenix it was not, that's for sure.

Anything but a phoenix.

The feeling of me being watched had grown stronger, sharper. Threading my way around the pentacle, I hurried toward the exit. I slid out into the corridor and darted away.

Had I forgotten my own immortality? If not, why was I scared like a little boy?

So what if I was? I'd spent enough time in virtual reality to still believe all this to be a game.

5.

WHEN I WALKED back outside, Neo was sitting on the steps of the watchtower yawning his head off but keeping a watchful eye on the gates.

"There's been no one, Uncle John!" he reported, then hurried to ask, "What's in there?"

I told him.

The boy's face darkened. He fell silent for a long time.

"It isn't right!" he finally said, frowning. "There must be a magic crystal, the same as the one in the lighthouse! We need to bring it back to its place!"

I didn't ask him how he knew. Instead, I just said, "So where do you suggest we should look for this magical crystal?"

"At the orcs'," Neo said, nonplussed. "They desecrated the temple and replaced the crystal with their pagan idol! We must convince them to return the relic!"

Convince them? Yeah right. As if they'd

listen to us! And fighting a forest hunter tribe was a pretty hopeless undertaking. Although if you couldn't negotiate, intimidate or take what you needed by force, why not just steal it?

I was a thief, after all. And that's what thieves do for a living; they take other people's property without their permission.

A magic crystal should be of considerable value. I was pretty sure that if I searched the dwelling of the tribe leader or their chief shaman, I was bound to find the relic there.

"Uncle John!" Neo called to me. "You think you could help?"

"Go to sleep," I said. "I'll try to find out something about your crystal."

"I'll go with you!"

"Sleep now!" I barked. Reluctantly the boy went back into the tower.

I rotated my head a few times listening to the soft crunching of my vertebrae, then went to the temple gates. I froze there for a while, listening to the rustling sounds of the night and the distant splashing of water, then stepped onto the pine tree trunk and confidently crossed to the other side.

From the height of the cliff, the orcs'

settlement lay clearly before me. I spent a few minutes studying the layout and trying to determine which one was the leader's dwelling, then moved down the steps, checking each one to make sure it didn't collapse underfoot. Because of this safety precaution, it took me some time to descend — but at least I didn't risk falling to my death into the abyss.

I didn't want to die. And a stupid death like that definitely wasn't in my plans.

WHEN I'D REACHED the middle of my descent, I heard a loud, wheezy snorting. I clung to the rock and froze, fading into the shadows.

An orc with a crossbow appeared from around the bend. He didn't notice me and continued his ascent. He was followed by three more dark figures: the tribe's shaman and two burly warriors.

The wrinkled caster didn't lag behind the young fighters with virtually no help from his gnarly staff. A white fang necklace glowed on his chest. His gray hair was braided with an array of motley ribbons.

The warriors were armed to the teeth. Each of them had a massive scimitar. Curved daggers and throwing knives were stuck behind their belts. Both were clad in bronze breastplates and helmets.

The warriors snorted noisily, heavily flaring the nostrils of their flat noses. Both were dangerous opponents. Yet I started with the shaman.

I poked him in the neck with my index finger. The claw punctured his larynx with surprising ease. The caster threw his hands in the air and dropped from the cliff, silently opening and closing his mouth.

The warrior who followed him grabbed at the scimitar, but I kicked him hard in the breastplate, sending him flying onto the one in the rear. Both warriors tumbled down the steps without actually falling down, which was a great shame.

The echo of a dull blow came from the foot of the cliff. I received a message awarding me with XP for the killing of the shaman, then another one about me receiving a new level.

I didn't give a damn. I had more important things to take care of.

I turned to the orc crossbowman a couple of steps higher. He raised his scimitar, but my bone hook slithered forward, snake-like, and slashed across his torso just below his breastplate, leaving a deep cut from one hip to the other. Blood gushed from under his short kilt. The orc froze, his eyes bulging in agony, as the wound stunned him.

To miss such an opportunity would be unforgivable. I leaped toward the enemy and tore the crossbow off his back, then sent him after his shaman master.

From below, the two warriors already hurried toward me, furious about their comrades' deaths. I raised the crossbow and fired at the one closest to me. The bolt easily pierced the breastplate. No idea what kind of magic had been cast on it but the green-skinned warrior immediately turned into a withered mummy.

I hurled the unloaded weapon at the remaining warrior. He parried it with his scimitar — and avoided my attack entirely. I lunged upon him, burying the Soulkiller bone hook deep into his burly shoulder. I then pulled the hook back to myself, ripping through his arm from shoulder to the wrist.

The warrior howled and dropped the scimitar. Still, he didn't give up. With his left hand, he tried to draw his dagger from his belt. I closed my clawed hand around his bicep and started hitting his unprotected neck with the hook.

The warrior shuddered. He stumbled and fell to one knee, then collapsed face down on the rocks. Life was quickly draining out of him, along with the green blood that escaped his terrible wounds.

Who's next?

I was the Night Hunter, swift and lethal, just as I liked it.

I laughed quietly but immediately stopped short and froze, listening to the quiet of the night.

Nothing. The brief fight hadn't alarmed their guards. They probably hadn't even heard it. Excellent!

I frisked the dead orcs but didn't take anything. They didn't have anything of value with them, and their bulky weapons didn't interest me.

A message kept flashing, informing me of new levels gained by my both alter-egos. I skimmed through it, invested one point into Agility, then froze, unable to choose between Constitution and Perception.

Or should I invest into Strength?

It all depended on what my playing style was going to be. For rogues, well-developed perception was almost as important as for casters and shooters. It affected accuracy, observation, and internal energy, while health and stamina depended on constitution. And what was wrong with the ability not to buckle under blows?

Why would a rogue need strength, might you ask? Well, firstly, my flamberge's damage directly depended on it. That was just the weird kind of thief I was. A thief with a two-handed sword.

In any case, I stood no chance in protracted combat with a high-level fighter. So I decided to bring the Perception to fifteen points, and then invest only in Agility and Strength.

This time I chose stealth over dodge, and since the third level of the Incognito mode was now available, I didn't hesitate to bring that up too.

The description that came up caused me to give my head a puzzled scratch.

Incognito III.
You've become a real master of disguise.

✦ The Dead Rogue ✦

People around you simply don't notice you anymore. When you are among other people, an outside observer can't recognize your use of the Incognito skill until you attract his attention.
Stealth: +15%

Hm. They hadn't made it very clear, had they? But at least no one was going to stop me just because of my private profile settings. For a city, it might actually be a very good idea.

6.

I HADN'T GONE to the orc village. Seeing as they'd sent assassins to the temple, they must have thought of hiding the magic crystal from me too. The forest was huge. There was no way you could find anything there.

Instead, I'd turned to the outpost. The guard on the tower was almost asleep. He can't have noticed the shadow that slid in the night past him. I got to the first hut without a problem. It was occupied by sleeping orc archers. I decided against waking them up. Instead, I slid into the shaman's hut.

I lay one hand over his mouth while half-strangling him with the other.

"If you make a noise, you're a dead man," I said softly, feeling the old man's muscles tighten. "Then I'll have to kill the guards and go to the village. To kill everyone else I see."

I relaxed my grip on the shaman's mouth.

"What do you want, you wretched monster?" he croaked.

"There's a temple on the mountain. You took something from there. A magic crystal. Where is it?"

"No!" the orc wheezed. "You aren't getting it!"

I chuckled. "Of course I am. Where are you hiding it?"

"Hiding it?" the shaman rose from the mat in amazement. "That wretched thing has summoned a demon into our world! We paid in blood but we did get rid of the crystal! No one can bring it back!"

I wasn't too enthusiastic about his answer so I closed my clawed fist tighter on the orc's neck. "Where's the crystal?"

"At the bottom of the lake!" the shaman replied with spiteful joy in his voice.

✝ The Dead Rogue ✝

I closed my fingers ever tighter. The old orc croaked, but managed, "The guard of the Equinox will stop any-"

Then he fell silent. Dead. You don't live long with a crushed larynx, a broken spine and torn veins.

I wiped my bloodied hand on the mat and quietly slipped back into the night.

It was just a computer-generated char. A toon. I'd warned them, anyway.

Hadn't I?

Still, I felt like shit. What was I now, some stupid conscientious objector?

It had been an orc, dammit! Just an orc!

And I was just a dead man. All of us had to play the roles we'd been chosen for.

I DIDN'T WANT to meet the mysterious guard of the Equinox, so I didn't go to the lake shore. Instead I picked up a heavy boulder among those lying at the foot of the staircase, lifted it onto my shoulder and began walking up the steps. I'd spent a quarter of my endurance on the climb but reached the ledge overhanging the lake, then stepped down from it.

A moment of free fall ended in me hitting

the dark water's surface. Surrounded by air bubbles, I began to sink to the bottom — swiftly first, then slower.

The guard would stop me? That remained to be seen.

I saw a magic crystal from afar. It lay on the rocky bottom. The water around it sparkled with a silvery sheen. I let go of the boulder and reached the glowing rock in a few decisive strokes.

It was the size of an adult man's head. I wrapped my hands around it and began to climb to the surface.

It wasn't easy. The lake was deep and shaped as a funnel. I would have gladly placed the precious item into my inventory and begun paddling with both hands, but for some reason it didn't fit in the slot. There must have been some restriction regarding its size or volume.

When I was already halfway to the surface, I came across the crossbowman I'd thrown down the stairs. He stared at me with reproach.

Nonsense. The fish had already eaten his eyes. He had nothing to stare at me with.

I paused, took a few crossbow bolts from him, then continued my ascent. Finally, I got out of the water and collapsed onto the pebble shore.

You can't imagine how exhausted I was.

I heard a creaking noise. I looked up and didn't believe my own eyes.

A knight was approaching me.

A real knight in black armor and a helmet with a closed visor. The visor's eye slit glowed an evil purple. The handle of a two-handed sword protruded from behind his right shoulder.

An orc knight?! Jesus...

This really was an orc. His silhouette was too unmistakably squat and powerful.

Guardian of the Equinox

I shook off my stupor and rose to my feet. The orc raised his gauntleted hand and lay it on the hilt of the sword. I still had the chance to stealth up and disappear into the shadows, but what the hell?!

I was the Night Hunter, swift and lethal! I shouldn't be afraid of them. They should be afraid of me.

In a lightning move, I darted toward him, forced my way through the thickening air and found myself next to his sinister figure. There was no way he could have reacted in time to my assault and still he'd somehow managed to draw his two-handed sword and point it at me.

I basically impaled myself on his black double-edged sword — all the way to its cross-guard.

Damage received: 528 [576/ 1104]

The sword's point had pierced my chainmail and came out between my shoulder blades. My flamberge went flying from my hands and skidded across the pebbled beach while I froze in place like a pinned beetle.

The orc tensed and began to raise his sword.

The blade ripped through my insides, causing additional damage, until my legs lost contact with the ground. Now I hung in the air, pierced by his sword.

The black knight threw back his head and fixed his glowing purple gaze on my face, enjoying the sufferings of his victim.

Well, he should have.

"Accurate Strike"! "Claws of Darkness"!

✝ The Dead Rogue ✝

I threw my hands in front of me and thrust my thumbs into the narrow eye slit of the visor. My claws hit something soft. The purple glow faded as the orc roared and jerked his sword free, dropping me to the ground.

The sky flashed before my eyes. Black steel rose and fell. I rolled aside in an incredible somersault which saved me from the lethal weapon that had very nearly cleft me in two.

The orc raised his two-handed sword once more. He spun on the spot, brandishing it randomly around himself.

One glance at the logs gave me hope. The damage caused by my claws hadn't been much. But my specialization had.

I'd blinded the orc. I'd managed to poke his fiery eyes out.

The black knight turned to me again. This time I slid silently aside, grabbed my flamberge and approached my enemy from behind. The combination of two blows — one Accurate, the other Powerful — had very nearly broken every sinew and ligament in my body. The blade whooshed through the air as it dropped onto the orc's knee. It sliced through the steel knee joint of his armor and crushed the bone. The orc collapsed in a heap but I deftly rolled away. He swung his sword through the air in a sweeping motion, trying to cut my legs.

I jumped over the black blade and lowered my flamberge onto the helmet of my now defeated enemy. The blow hadn't been too accurate. The blade had only brushed the armor. Also, at that very moment I'd glimpsed some torchlight amid the trees.

I had to grab the crystal and get the hell out of there. Still, I lingered.

I dodged another blind swing, changed my position and raised my flamberge over the Orc Knight's head. Straining my every muscle, I lowered it, hitting him between his neck and his pauldron.

I heard a clank and a crunching noise, then he stopped moving and lay motionless on the ground. But he wasn't dead yet. I had to climb on top of him and drive the sharp bone hook into the slot in his armor.

I'd rather have used a Misericorde stiletto to finish him off. Still, I'd had to do without one.

The orc drew his last breath. I picked up the terrible black sword that had fallen from his hand.

✝ The Dead Rogue ✝

That was the extent of the loot he'd dropped. The killing of the guard had garnered me his fearsome sword and two thousand XP. Plus some serious trouble.

Guttural voices shouted something behind the trees; the torchlight flickered ever closer. An arrow whizzed overhead and splashed into the lake.

I decided against confronting the orcs. I slung both of my two-handed swords — my own as well as my freshly-acquired trophy — behind my back, picked up the magic crystal and stealthed up.

Becoming target practice for orc archers wasn't part of my plans.

STAGGERING, I reached the gates of the temple by dawn on my last 100 pt. Endurance. The rock climb had cost me too dearly. The orcs had been close behind me; I'd also had to carry the crossbow I'd picked up on the steps. As far as I could see, the blow from the scimitar hadn't done it much damage.

"Uncle John!" Neo rushed toward me. "You've found it!"

I lay the spherical crystal on the ground

and rolled it toward the boy. Then I discarded my swords and began to string the crossbow. It didn't have a pulley. I had to place my foot in the stirrup and pull hard at the bow string.

Something seemed to have snapped inside my back but I managed.

The drowned orc had had only five bolts on him, one of which I now loaded. The bolt was absolutely covered in runic carvings. I just hoped it wouldn't hinder its accuracy.

I set the crossbow aside and inspected my chainmail. Luckily, the hole in my chest had already closed. I picked up the Orc Knight's sword. Its blade was long and as black as darkness itself. All my attempts to equip it failed, though. My fingers kept sliding off the handle.

Longsword of the Autumnal Equinox
Restriction: can only be used by those in whose veins flows orc blood.

The remaining characteristics of the weapon remained hidden. In any case, I had more important things to do. My pursuers had just appeared on the top of the cliff.

A quick scout ran along the pine trunk,

then promptly retreated the moment I raised my Flamberge. I hadn't shot at him. I needed to save the few bolts I had for more advantageous targets.

God was I right.

When a dozen fanged bandits rushed to the attack, assaulting the area with their blood-curdling war cries, I waited until two of them had climbed the trunk, then buried a bolt in the first one. He collapsed, knocking his comrade into the precipitous abyss with him. The others retreated and took cover behind the rocks.

I reloaded the crossbow and called the boy who was hiding in the guard tower,

"Neo!"

"Yes, Uncle John?"

"Run to the temple and check the locks. I need to know if they're still okay."

The massive doors stood intact. If we managed to barricade ourselves inside, the orcs would have their work cut out for them trying to get to us.

At that moment, the shaman jumped out into the open space, whirling in a ritual dance. A dustdevil rose next to him. I had to spend another bolt on him. Even though I failed to hit him, he promptly made himself scarce. The tornado fell apart.

Archers started firing at me non-stop. Their arrows thudded against the stone wall, ricocheting off it in every direction.

"Uncle John!" Neo shouted from a distance. "The locks are okay!"

I picked up the crossbow, stealthed up and hurried to the temple. I leaned against one door half and forced it shut, then grabbed at the other one's handle and pulled it toward myself. At first I couldn't even move it until finally I could step back as the gate halves closed with a soft thud.

The glow from the magic crystal flooded everything around. I reached into my inventory for the monastic robes I'd saved for a rainy day and threw them to the boy. "I want you to wrap this around it."

"Why?"

"The shadows, remember?"

Neo began wrapping the cloth around the crystal. I barred the gate and picked up the crossbow I'd left on the floor.

"Follow me! Don't stray away," I ordered when the shine of the artifact had expired, concealed by the thick fabric.

✟ The Dead Rogue ✟

The temple plunged into darkness. Neo grabbed at the sleeve of my cape and followed me, staggering under the weight of the magic ball.

"I can't see anything," he complained.

"You don't need to," I muttered.

When we entered the inner hall, I lay the crossbow by a column and took the wrapped crystal from him. "This thing needs to be returned to the pedestal, right? Does it matter who does it?"

"No. Anyone can return the relic," Neo replied confidently.

"Wait for me here," I said as I headed toward the pedestal. I absolutely hated having to step over the pentacle painted on the floor but nothing had happened. If indeed there'd once been a demon living inside it, he must have returned to his underworld a long time ago.

I elbowed the orc idol from the pedestal, then watched as the elaborately carved tree stump rolled over to the wall.

"Well..." I gasped. "Let's do it!"

I ripped the robes from the crystal and set it onto the pedestal.

The crystal lit up, flooding the temple with

---

its soft glow and illuminating the dead bodies on the floor and the brown-red of the pentacle. The columns cast a great multitude of shadows — but none of them turned into an attacking ghost.

Strangely enough, the return of the crystal to its original place hadn't closed the quest. Frankly, I didn't know what to think.

"So, what now?" I asked the boy who stared open-mouthed at the picture of a demon painted on a stone dome. "Neo? Hello!"

He didn't seem to hear me. "This shouldn't be here," he said.

"So what do you suggest?" I suddenly got angry. "Should we give it a lick of paint?"

"No," Neo said, pointing up. "Look, Uncle John!"

I raised my head and saw what must have been a hole at the center of the dome and which was now closed with a diaphragm shutter.

"We need to let the light inside!" Neo announced. "There must be a switch somewhere to open that thing!"

He had a point. It was his quest, after all.

I started looking around in search of an opening mechanism. Still, the boy was first to see a huge brass helm the kind they use on sailing boats. With a scream of joy, he ran toward it and set all his meager weight against it.

A series of deafening screeching sounds came from above as slowly the diaphragm began to open.

We saw that the hole in the dome was covered with a crystal lens which now focused the rays of the sun rising above the horizon.

A pillar of blinding light hit the altar, filling the magic crystal.

The artifact began emitting a light much more powerful than before until it flooded the entire temple. The withered bodies on the floor crumbled to ashes. In a silver flash, the figure painted on the dome started to flesh out, gaining depth and size until it floated in the air like a weightless hologram. Moments later, the materialized demon crashed to the ground.

He was huge, horrible and enveloped by black infernal flames.

The walls shuddered from the impact. Bits of stone and marble flew everywhere from under the creature's claws. The demon fell on all four legs and immediately jumped to his feet. He was the height of two humans, his back and shoulders covered in tall spikes, his slimy skin oozing black fire, his broad wide jaws lined with two rows of sharp fangs. Darkness swirled in his gaze.

Then his glare alighted on me, so small and defenseless.

Nest Hunter, his name flashed in my view.

Then he went for me.

I parried his attack with my trusty Flamberge.

Ugh! My sword's curved blade bounced off without causing any harm to the infernal creature. A blow from his clawed paw sent me flying through the entire hall until my back hit one of the columns.

Damage received: 437 [457/ 1104]

The demon's claws had slid off my chainmail, but even so his powerful blow had stripped me of half of the remaining health. Devil!

No, this wasn't a devil. This was a Nest Hunter.

With a powerful roar, the infernal abomination went for me again. This time I thought better of it and just rolled out of his reach. My Dodge skill was just a tad too low for him: the demon's long claw ripped my ankle open.

You bastard!

I stealthed up, or rather, I tried. The glow of the magic crystal illuminated me, not allowing me to hide in the shadows. The demon himself didn't seem to mind the bright light. On the contrary, he seemed to bathe in it, becoming stronger with every passing moment.

The Nest Hunter threw himself at me again. I dashed aside. He resumed his attack.

This game of cat and mouse couldn't last long. Still, I didn't intend to compete with the monster. Instead I ducked behind a column and stepped into the shadow cast by it. Gone!

The demon dashed after me but I'd already stepped into the next shadow, not letting him find me.

Then the Nest Hunter saw the boy.

"Oh, a neophyte!" the creature whispered. "Fresh meat!"

Damn it! If I escaped now, I'd leave Neo behind to a certain death. And if I joined the uneven fight, my participation would forever bind me to the temple, to be killed by the demon every time I respawned.

What could I do?

I hesitated only a moment, then hurried to the exit. I grabbed the crossbow I'd left there and buried the enchanted bolt in the demon's back.

The infernal monster hadn't even flinched. The stone floor crumbled under his claws while the boy stood frozen in place, not even thinking of fleeing.

"He's only part of the program code," I said to myself, pulling the bone hook from behind my belt. "Just a piece of code..."

Neo crossed his arms on his chest. His figure flashed with an unbearable silver light which spread rapidly through the temple and threw the demon away. I stood further away but I too felt its effects. A wall of fierce heat came over me and threw me against the wall, knocking me down.

Exile: Immunity.

Immunity was good, but the left side of my body which had taken the brunt of the attack was now smoldering. My left cheek had in fact burned partially away, exposing the smoking cheekbone. A movie-perfect cyborg, if you disregarded my still-intact eye.

I struggled to my feet and tore off my burning cape. My health had plummeted deep into the red. Endurance wasn't much better.

A piece of fried dead meat, that's what I was.

But the demon was in a much worse way. The light wave had dragged him across the stone floor, broken off his thorns and ripped his skin to shreds, then hurled him against the wall and fused him into the masonry. The Nest Hunter's black flames had expired in a most unnatural way, condensing into thick slime and sizzling to the ground, eating through everything in its path.

Neo stood with his eyes closed. The radiance he'd emitted had faded and didn't assault my eyes anymore, as if the strength of the young neophyte had come to an end. He wasn't strong enough to exorcise the demon and send him back to the netherworld. Sooner or later the creature was going to come round, struggle himself free and rip our heads off for us.

Should we escape? And how far would we be able to get before the Destroyer broke free and chased after us?

Neo's knees gave under him. He dropped to

the floor in a heap. The demon startled, then emitted a weak whimpering sound. Limping on my burned left leg, I hobbled toward him and grabbed at one of his thorns to keep my unstable balance.

Then I swung round and buried the Soulkiller bone hook into his powerful neck. Its sharp point easily pierced the demon's scorched skin causing him some petty damage. The demon's health bar hadn't even stirred.

I didn't give a damn. I kept hitting him with the hook, slicing through his chest and shredding his neck.

The demon stirred. The masonry creaked. Then his black eyes snapped open, and the creature tried to grab hold of me with his free paw.

I easily evaded the clumsy swing and continued to wield the hook, faster and faster. The Nest Hunter roared and struggled, forcing dust to cascade from the ceiling.

His stone trap couldn't keep him there for much longer. And his Health bar was still at 80%! The hook was doing a great job piercing the demon's skin but it couldn't cut or shred it.

And yet I didn't give up. The theory of

probability was on my side. I could only hope that luck would not turn away from me.

The demon finally managed to grab at my shoulder but his terrible claws kept sliding from the steel weave of the chainmail. A few drops of his venomous slime did fall on my skin though, hissing and eating through my dead flesh.

Enraged, the demon jerked and very nearly broke loose. The stonework around him covered with a net of cracks.

Despair gave me strength. My next blow drove the Soulkiller unexpectedly deep into his flesh. The blade sliced through his heart, turning the demon to stone.

His terrible figure broke and fell apart.

"Execution"! Nest Hunter is killed!
The Temple of the Silver Phoenix is restored!
Experience: +5 000 [24 178/ 24 600]; +5 000 [24 222/ 24 600]
Obtained achievement "Demon Slayer of the 4th Circle", "Crusher".
Undead, the level is raised! Rogue, the level is increased!

Yes! It worked!

The demon had been fused into the wall and therefore was considered an immobilized target to which my "Execution" skill applied. And even though I'd had to deal him over twenty blows, in the end I'd smoked the monster! I'd sent him back to hell!

"Soulkiller", I just loved it! "Execution", nothing could be better!

I turned to Neo who suddenly shot up into the air. Electric discharges began to course his body.

At first I recoiled in fright but then realized that I'd only received half the XP. He'd gotten the other half, all 10,000 of it, allowing him to jump from the first to the nineteenth level.

How cool was that?

But I shouldn't complain, really: not only had I earned another level, I had very little left until level 50. And I was dying to find out what my next undead title would be. Honestly, I couldn't wait.

Neo was still hovering in mid-air so I turned to my characteristics. I improved my strength, agility and evasion, then selected the "Rapid Strike" from the Executioner's skills. The ability to befuddle the enemy with a hail of swift swings might come in handy one day, you never know.

At that point, Neo stopped hanging in the air and lowered himself back to the floor. His status had changed from a Neophyte to a Disciple.

"Uncle John, I'm so sorry!" the boy pleaded. "I didn't mean to burn you!"

I touched my scorched cheek. "What was it exactly?"

"That was the Silver Blessing of the Phoenix."

"Some blessing..." I snorted. "It's all right. I would have never smoked him on my own."

Something clattered underfoot. I reached down and fished out a dagger with a silvery blade from the stone remains of the demon.

I handed it to the boy. "This should go well with your amulet."

The moment Neo took the dagger, the flame engraved on the blade came alive and began to flicker.

"And what now, Neo?" I asked after I'd rummaged through the debris and become the owner of several star sapphires, a couple of hundred gold coins and a large piece of demon's bone, black and still hot.

The question seemed to have baffled him. "What about now, Uncle John?"

"The temple has been restored. Would you like to stay here?"

Neo shook his head. "Oh no! Please don't leave me! I'd like to go with you! To the city!"

Oh Jesus. I hadn't been hired to babysit him!

Angry, I kicked one of the rocks. How strange. Its shape was too regular for a broken-off fragment.

Could it be the demon's heart?

But no, it turned out to be an egg. The small egg of a phoenix.

"It's not your birthday today, by any chance?" — I laughed, intending to give it to the boy. Strangely enough, I couldn't do it.

Sorry! This artifact is non-transferrable

In any case, Neo showed no interest in the egg. He was much more interested in the dagger, which in his hands appeared almost as big as a real sword.

Neo had long forgotten about his fight with

the demon. He must have had a very adaptable mind.

Not many human beings could boast that.

I heaved a sigh and began studying the egg. It turned out to be a pet but not a proper one. Just a temporary companion, irretrievably disappearing after the player's logout. Something between a sorcerer's familiar and a sample product used in advertising.

Never mind. It wasn't as if I was going to log out any time soon.

Chuckling, I picked up the white monastic robe from the floor, draped it over myself and turned to Neo, "Are you ready?"

"What did you say? Oh! Yes, Uncle John! Yes, I'm ready!" the boy shoved the dagger behind his belt and headed for the exit.

I stopped him. "Your magic. Do you control it?"

Neo hesitated, then admitted, embarrassed, "Not really."

"What other spells do you know?"

"I know "Blessing", "Network", "Spear" and "Shroud"," Neo began to recount.

I didn't have enough health left to take another demonstration of priestly skills, so I just asked, "Leave the orcs to me."

But the orcs weren't outside. Their axes and scimitars had left some deep notches in the gates. I carefully examined the square in front of the temple and stepped cautiously out.

No one. Really, not a soul in sight.

"Doesn't the church require supervision?" I asked Neo when the boy had joined me.

He shrugged. The gates behind us slammed shut on their own accord even though no one had touched them.

"I think the Silver Phoenix will take care of itself," Neo decided.

It was my turn to shrug.

The church didn't need a guardian? Excellent.

Time to get out of here!

7.

STRANGELY ENOUGH, we'd got back to Stone Harbor without any further ado. That was unusual for a world entirely devoted to the entertainment of players. The orcs were nowhere to be seen. They'd abandoned the outpost leaving it unguarded. All forest beasties fled from our path. We'd even managed to spend the night in the already familiar flooded farm.

By noon the next day, our boat had landed not far from the magic-fire lighthouse. We set off for the city. I chose the narrowest of trails just in case until I reached the city limits and took cover in the bushes.

"Do you remember the guys we ran away from?" I asked Neo. "Go take a look if you can see any of them near the Tower of Power."

The boy nodded and ran off.

The Darks had retained the city. With my status of "Defender", I should be quite a welcome guest here. Still, it's difficult to defend one's right if everyone around is eager to crucify you. If Garth somehow managed to uncover my true nature — and there had to be some undead-detecting spells in the arsenal of necromancers — no one would care about my past achievements. I might run into some very big problems.

I didn't want to risk it. Rightly so.

Finally Neo came back, panting and out of breath. "There's one of those catchers with the net by the tower!"

A catcher with the net? Ah! A gladiator!

✝ An NPC's Path: Book One ✝

What a shame. And I'd been hoping that they would break up with the necromancer after their last fiasco! These guys had had all the time in the world to remember me; no amount of Incognito or monastic robes could fool them.

They'd recognize me, that's for sure.

"There's no one on the pier," Neo added.

I stared at the boy in bewilderment. The pier? What would we need the pier for?

He flashed me a toothy smile. "It takes a barge two days to get to the capital! It'll be cheaper, too!"

A barge? I hadn't even thought about it. In a game, time costs a lot of money. It had never occurred to me that one could waste it so foolishly.

But if you think about it, an ordinary player spends less than eight hours a day in a virtual capsule. So what difference does it make to him what happens to the character for the rest of the time?

And not everyone needed to travel such a long distance, either. Most players moved from one little town to the next, unhurriedly discovering their new world.

That was it, then. I lifted the hood and

concealed my face behind a mask.

"Let's go to the pier!"

THE GOLD I'd amassed in the course of the game proved to be more than enough to pay for two tickets to the Tower of Darkness. I paid some more for a separate cabin and meals. We had to wait another half an hour for our departure. After that, the river orc crew raised the sail and punted with their poles, driving the barge away from the shore.

None of the few passengers had lingered on the upper deck. Even Neo had gone back into our cabin as soon as the city and the lighthouse had disappeared into the haze. I'd stayed, though. The fanged sailors paid no attention to the eccentric anonymous passenger. And I still had plenty of internal energy left. This was better that the cramped confines of our cabin.

The low waves caressed the boat's sides. The mast creaked. A friendly wind kissed my face. A new stage in my virtual life had just begun. But how virtual was it, really?

I scratched the handrail. It didn't look like part of computer animation at all. In fact, it felt quite real.

I cussed. My brain frantically searched for a way out of this situation but failed to find it and therefore tried to lull itself into a false sense of security.

Did I really want to live my life here? Hell no!

It wasn't even the fact that here, I was a deadman. The problem was, sooner or later they'd unhook me from life support. Then I'd become dead for real. If I died there, I'd die here as well. I'd be dead everywhere, once and for all. For ever and ever.

And I didn't really want to die, come to think of it.

Shit! I was quite prepared to get ten Scrolls of Rebirth if that could get me my life back! A hundred, if necessary! With or without Isabella's help, I had to do it!

Overtaken by fury, I was close to losing it. I had to take my mind off it. I took out the phoenix egg, cradled it in my hands and shook it. In order to bind the pet, I had to sprinkle the artifact with blood. I sliced my wrist with my own sharp claw and pressed the egg to the fresh wound.

THE SHELL began to glow from within: a gentle

silvery glow, soft and undisturbed. Immediately it faded, replaced by a pitch-black darkness.

The artifact cracked open. A black head poked out, its dead eyes white and nebulous.

The disgusting creature spread its wings and rose into the air, emitting loud crowing noises. It made several circles over the barge, then landed on the mast, gripping it with its terrible claws.

The thing didn't resemble the temple phoenix pictures in the slightest. It looked rather like a raven with a disproportionately powerful beak, bare legs and bristling black feathers.

Still, that was a phoenix. Or should I say, my dead black phoenix. A perfect companion for me, courtesy of the game.

The creature opened its beak wide and emitted an ear-splitting *Craaah!* as the barge carried me off to my new adventures.

All the way to the Tower of Darkness.

End of Book One

Want to be the first to know about our latest
LitRPG, sci fi and fantasy titles from your favorite
authors?

Subscribe to our **New Releases** newsletter:
http://eepurl.com/b7niIL

Thank you for reading *The Dead Rogue!*
If you like what you've read, check out other LitRPG
novels published by Magic Dome Books.

Reality Benders LitRPG series by Michael Atamanov:

Countdown
External Threat
Game Changer
Web of Worlds
A Jump into the Unknown
Aces High
Cause for War

**The Dark Herbalist LitRPG series
by Michael Atamanov:**
Video Game Plotline Tester
Stay on the Wing
A Trap for the Potentate
Finding a Body

Perimeter Defense LitRPG series by Michael Atamanov:
Sector Eight
Beyond Death
New Contract
A Game with No Rules

**League of Losers LitRPG Series
by Michael Atamanov:**
A Cat and his Human
In Service of the Pharaoh

**The Way of the Shaman LitRPG series
by Vasily Mahanenko:**
Survival Quest
The Kartoss Gambit
The Secret of the Dark Forest
The Phantom Castle
The Karmadont Chess Set
The Hour of Pain (a bonus short story)
Shaman's Revenge
Clans War

More books and series are coming out soon!

In order to have new books of the series translated faster, we need your help and support! Please consider leaving a review or spread the word by recommending *The Dead Rogue* to your friends and posting the link on social media. The more people buy the book, the sooner we'll be able to make new translations available.

Thank you!

Till next time!

www.ingramcontent.com/pod-product-compliance
Lightning Source LLC
Chambersburg PA
CBHW052348020726
47503CB00001B/151